FLESH & WIRES

FLESH
& WIRES

JACKIE HATTON

Aqueduct Press

Aqueduct Press, PO Box 95787
Seattle, WA 98145-2787
www.aqueductpress.com

ISBN: 978-1-61976-085-1

Library of Congress Control Number: 2015908765

10 9 8 7 6 5 4 3 2 1

Cover illustrations: "Cable in human hand. Power and connection"
© Can Stock Photo Inc./SergeyNivens
Cover design: Jackie Hatton and Kathryn Wilham

Printed in the USA by Thomson-Shore, Inc.

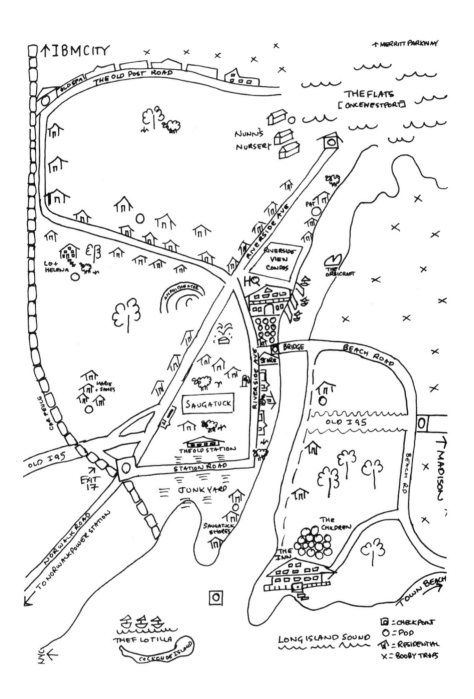

1

Lo was deep in the vegetable patch picking tomatoes when the alarm sounded. Great hawking wails cut into the thick summer air. The sound was coming from the loudspeakers at HQ, a mile down the hill on the banks of the Saugatuck River.

Whoop, whoop, whoop.

Red alert: full safety protocol.

Lo didn't just hear the alarm; she felt it as a fizzy heat that exploded in her brain and radiated through her body. In a fraction of a second her wires had twitched her muscles into gear. Fingers tingling, she reached for her weapons glove—but she wasn't wearing her holster today. It was sitting on the dining room dresser. Close enough, she'd thought when she set it down there this morning. Not close enough now.

Swiveling on her bare feet, Lo turned and made for the house without regard for the strawberries. Toes bleeding red pulp, she vaulted over the animal fence and sprinted down thick green lawn toward the back of their patched white cottage. Her worn denim cutoffs and old one-piece swimsuit moved with her like skin. The rose-gold waves of her hair, cut above her shoulders for the season, bounced up and down behind her, cooling her neck. Although her feet made little noise, her electrified body broke the air with a crackle. Hens and sheep scattered, unnerved by the disturbance. Only the cow stayed put, lazily chewing away at the grass.

"Move," Lo screamed.

The cow didn't move. It didn't know fear, which was why it would ultimately become meat. Lo leaped with ease over the stubborn animal. Bounding onto the worn deck, she flicked away the grape vines hanging from their DIY pergola. The back door was now within arm's reach, but the sight of the smoking barbecue stopped her dead in her tracks. Helena. Lo's heart lurched as she remembered firing up the rusty old Weber half an hour earlier, ready to start cooking the minute her wife walked through the door back from delivering food and supplies to the power plant in Norwalk Harbor. Naturals didn't usually work the convoys—they were just a liability—but one of the engineers had needed medical attention. Lo felt like screaming. Instead, she closed her eyes, opened the comms channel wired into her frontal lobe, and tried to exchange a message with the convoy. Total silence. That suggested they were still beyond comms range.

Torn between racing out to the Saugatuck/Norwalk Road to look for the convoy and heading straight down to HQ to deal with the emergency, Lo squeezed her fists so hard that sparks flew out on either side. Safety protocol demanded that she hide and await further instruction. The only problem was that she was supposed to be the one giving the instructions. She should never have agreed to take a day off. Animals and ferals and other scary things lurking in the wilderness didn't take days off. But her crew had insisted. It had been over a month. She'd been kind of tetchy lately. It was *summer*. Lo should listen to the people who cared about her. She'd listened.

She should never have listened. Frustration coursed through every wire in her body. She needed to do something before she burst, but it needed to be the right something...

"Whaaaaaat?" she roared as she swiveled to face the sound of the sirens.

No reply. Lo deployed all her senses, straining as she grasped in the ether for the nature of the emergency. Silence prickled at every hair on her body. Usually if the sirens went off Lo was overwhelmed with messages, women cramming her head full with their fears: creatures inside the perimeter, unknown boats out in the Sound, evidence of tampering at the fence. Even when the sirens weren't wailing away she was constantly barraged: meetings here, disputes there, permission needed. Hell, sometimes she couldn't think straight for all the friendly hellos and how-are-yous? This wasn't normal, this hollow silence, this echo chamber in her skull. Where was everyone?

Lo looked up into the fading blue of the early evening sky. Pat and Marie were scheduled to fly the pods today, but there was no sign of them in the air. She checked to make sure no one was coming through the dense vegetation surrounding the property. Not even a squirrel. She listened for company in or near the house. Nobody. She reached out for other minds. Nothing. As far as she could tell, she was completely alone. It was the strangest of feelings. Nine hundred survivors were living together in close proximity in this modest New England village: eight hundred were women, seven hundred were telepathic to some degree. Lo hadn't been truly alone in some thirty years.

Head down, thumbnails pressed into her forehead, Lo tried to isolate Yaz in the comms room. First she zapped her with static, a practice they all hated because it reminded them of the occupation. Then she beamed her a message: *what—where?*

Lo's eyes blinked and shoulders tensed as she expelled each word from her mind. As always it rankled that she couldn't transmit more than three short words at a time: *thump—thump—thump.* Her personal communications weakness wasn't the problem here though. The problem was a complete comms breakdown. Lo feared a serious problem at HQ. Responding to the sirens had to be her first priority. However, before Lo could even begin to move, the alarm changed.

Whaap, whaap, pause.

Orange alert: heightened vigilance.

Lo felt reason return as her system switched down. It was only a minor alert after all, probably relating to the comms glitch. She still needed to get to HQ, but she now had a few seconds to think properly. First things first, that barbecue. Lo looked across at the collection of rain-water-filled buckets they kept on the edge of the old deck. Focusing her gaze on the nearest one, she narrowed her eyes into a hard stare. As the energy surged out through her pupils, she raised the bucket into the air, rolling her head as she controlled its upward arc. Eyes, mind, and wires as one, she tilted the faded green plastic tub and doused the fire in one great hiss. On a whim she flung the empty bucket high over the abandoned house filled with medical supplies next door—aiming for the perimeter fence half a mile away. She had her strengths. Then she turned toward the back door.

She wasn't going anywhere without her weapons glove.

The first time Lo had killed anyone with a glove was thirty years ago, right when the occupation was coming to an end. Three years before that a fleet of spheres had turned Earth's cities into sink holes in a cacophony of sonic booms. When they were done obliterating the cities, the attackers landed, in millions of beautiful flying glass pods. Out of those pods came an army of small fragile creatures with pinched faces and delicate silver-coated skulls—*Ruurdaans*. They looked so benign until they began their cull: crushing, incinerating, and composting. The Ruurdaans liked to obliterate their victims. They only used the glove if time was of the essence—even though they must have known the glove was by far the best way to go. Zap, sizzle, body on the ground. After a while people even got to begging to die that way. Lo would have had to be able to speak to beg. She did nothing, just let it all happen to her. Silence equaled survival. Helena still counseled a number of women who had never regained their voice.

When the Ruurdaan cull was done, nothing but a handful of young women in a state of near-vegetative fear remained. That was when the bantam aliens began a program to wire them for labor. Telepathic conduits made complete Ruurdaan control possible, and biotech enhancements made the women better workers. For three years Lo operated a pod—moving debris (often bodies) and overseeing a small team of outdoor laborers. Who knew if the Ruurdaans had a better long-term plan for them? They never said—and now nobody would ever really know—because the Ruurdaans all died of some kind of plague three years after they arrived. They left a world bereft of any kind of organized civilization, sparsely populated with strangely altered women, littered with great mounds of eight-foot round glass pods. They also left millions of gloves.

When the Ruurdaans first began dying of their plague, Lo grabbed the nearest free pod and flew away from her work camp in Fairfield, just ten miles up the road from Saugatuck. Looking down upon the repurposed university campus that had been her home for the last three years, Lo saw hundreds of debilitated Ruurdaans crawling out of their mobile glass habitats, gulping as if seeking uncontaminated air. At first she just gave a small cheer. Then, realizing that even as they died the creatures were still trying to connect with the minds of their slaves, Lo flew back down, grabbed a glove, and began finishing the little fuckers off. That was thirty years ago. That was the first time.

The last time Lo had killed someone with a glove was a year ago...

Believe it or not—life is stranger than fiction—three years earlier *another* group of aliens had shown up fifty miles north in Madison, Connecticut. When discussing the unlikely event, Lo often liked to invoke the analogy of the native Americans, also periodically assaulted by a wave of new weird, scary people. "I don't care that they didn't have enough information. Those guys shouldn't have even been a tiny bit welcoming." Of course, the women up in Madison just went and repeated the mistakes of history.

To be fair, it would have been a challenge to repel the incoming aliens, *Orbiters* as they were called. Apparently, 2000 of them just floated down from the sky in heavy metal crates. Lo's crew of forty fliers would have struggled to cope with an invasion of that scale. Madison—a town without any strong-wired women—had no hope. They didn't even try to fight. They didn't even call for help. They made *peaceful contact.* Idiots. Soon after the event, Lo received a report from the mayor, Gail Benson, describing the aliens as mostly tall, well-mannered, humanoid males with advanced technological skills. Whatever. Lo wanted nothing to do with any kind of alien. A small and vocal minority of Saugatuck's women, however, were curious about the new arrivals. What if these Orbiters knew something about Ruurdaan wiring? Maybe they could tell them why they weren't aging, or if they would age? Maybe they could even restore their fertility? It was impossible to deny the importance of those questions. After considerable debate, the council persuaded Lo to organize a diplomatic visit. A date was set.

Then came the bad news, filtering through in the usual patchy reports. Some of the Orbiters had turned out to be exiled criminals. Others were damaged ex-junkies. Even the good ones were religious whackos, members of a strange missionary group who neurotically scrubbed and bleached. Saugatuck postponed the date indefinitely. Not long after they sent their regrets, Gail reported that she had expelled five hundred of the Orbiters. She didn't say why or how; she just said, *please be aware.* Soon after that, rumors started circulating that the exiled aliens were attacking vulnerable settlements in the area. Lo beefed up the perimeter fence, increased security measures, and hoped the Orbiters weren't stupid enough to try attacking Saugatuck.

Try they did. Last summer an armed group had attempted to steal food and supplies (including five kilos of marijuana) en-route to Norwalk. Dina and Leslie were doing the run that day— two strong and experienced women with excellent wire-skills. The road was booby-trapped on all sides, had been for years. It should have been an easy delivery. However, all of a sudden, halfway down the road, seven tall hairy men emerged from the dense undergrowth and fired a couple of rifle shots into the lead jeep, striking both its front left tire and the driver, Dina. The jeep came to an abrupt halt. Leslie, trapped behind in the second jeep, ducked under the dash and beamed for help. By the time Lo and her crew reached the scene, Dina was already dead from a bullet wound to her aorta. Leslie lay frozen in a coil of terror on the floor of her jeep while the men loaded supplies from the rear storage compartment into their backpacks.

Lo and her crew disarmed the men before they had a chance to shoot again, burning the weapons right out of their hands. The men began shouting their excuses: Dina had been struck by a ricocheting bullet, they'd never intended to hurt anyone, look, they hadn't even touched the other woman. Lo didn't care about intentions. She lashed out with a furious, grief-stricken passion. Most of the others followed her lead, their bodies literally pulsating and glinting with anger. When they were done they threw three dead bodies to the wild dogs and told the surviving four Orbiters to run for their lives. As far as Lo knew those hairy wildebeests were still out there somewhere—three of them hobbling around on poorly healed fractures, one of them blind. It was an extreme measure but it seemed to work as a deterrent—because that had been the last time...

✄

Just as she opened the back door to fetch her glove, the phone on the far wall started ringing. In a single move, Lo sailed across the kitchen and pulled it from its beige plastic cradle, jerking the ancient hand-piece to the limits of its cord.

"Helena?"

"No. Sorry. But thank God I caught you in time..."

It was Janine, one of the "younger" women, twenty-two when her biological clock stopped ticking thanks to the Ruurdaans and their wires. At fifty-five she was still a bubbly little blonde with a seemingly endless supply of blue mascara and a penchant for short low-cut dresses. Janine ran everything social in Saugatuck, organized all those events and committees that Lo considered a waste of time and energy. She used to be a flight attendant, economy class. Now she could fly like a top gun, first class. It was a contradiction that had long ceased to interest Lo. All that mattered was that the woman did her job without too much argument. Lately there had been way too much argument.

"What's the problem?"

Janine replied, "There's no problem per se, just an unusual situation. A small spaceship has landed at the dock and two men have come out of it."

"What the fuck? You let them land? Where are you?"

"I'm calling from your office. Don't worry, I can see them fine from here. And I didn't *let* them do anything. They couldn't be stopped. But they've got their hands up and they're clearly unarmed. I talked to them before I lowered the alert. They're friendlies."

Lo almost hung up and ran for HQ, but it would take too long.

Her voice was tight. "Are you crazy? Men in spaceships are by definition invaders. There are probably two thousand more coming up behind them, like in Madison. Reinstate the red alert, Janine. Shoot them medium-hard in the hands and legs, then get the pods to remove them to Cockenoe Island. If they try anything funny, go ahead and stun them. I'll deal with them when they come back around."

"You're not hearing me, Lo. We *can't* remove them to Cockenoe. All the pods are, like, frozen in the sky. Our comms systems are down. The only thing working are the landlines. And anyway I'm not shooting them. They're *friendlies*, Lo."

"Let me talk to Ruby." Lo remembered assigning her to this slot with Janine. Ruby had been one of the women at the Norwalk convoy with her last summer.

"Sorry, she's not here. Leslie's with me. She swapped her bar assignment with Ruby tonight so we could work a shift together."

Nobody had run that past Lo.

"You can explain later. Now get back downstairs and start shooting. Leslie too, if she's capable. I'm not saying kill this bunch of guys — just remove their alien asses."

"No, not this time, Lo. You need to get down here, but you need to come down easy. These men are displaying an American flag and a peace sign on their clothes. One of them says he grew up here in Saugatuck, over on the other side of the river where you lived. He says his name is Will Warren. Warren, Lo! He says that you…"

"I said shoot them and remove them, Janine, *and that's an order.*"

Lo sucked in sharply as she slammed the phone back onto its cradle. No way. Absolutely no way. Her father, Will Warren II, was buried in the garden of their old place over the river, and her brother, Will Warren III, was most likely interred in the cement pancake of what was once Cape Canaveral. He had been a psychiatrist to the astronauts. Lo used to fantasize that he got away. But to where? The moon? Mars? Nobody could survive out there in the barrenness of space, and the Ruurdaans definitely wouldn't have allowed anyone to return. No. These so-called friendlies were messing with them. She didn't know who or why, but she smelled the shit-bag of a Trojan horse.

Lo grabbed her glove-holster off the dining-room dresser and began wrapping the clear stretchy band around her hips as she raced through the house to the front door. She gave the porch steps a miss and flung herself through the air toward the big glass pod parked on their overgrown driveway. As her feet touched gravel, she suddenly swiveled and headed down the front lawn toward the remains of their old street. The pod might be the safest choice, but according to Janine the pods weren't working. Besides, running was faster across short distances, and a ground approach offered the benefit of stealth.

Hitting the weedy broken surface of the road running, Lo slipped her hand into the holster on her hip, passed it through the stretchy holding-band of the glove, and slid her first two fingers into the beam conduits. The rubbery Ruurdaan substance molded itself around her hand, contouring itself to her flesh, feeling for her pulse, her energy source. As she gathered speed, internal dampeners scrambled all pain signals, allowing her to override her natural limits. Her feet barely touched the ground. It took two minutes to get to the bottom of the crumbling road, two more to sprint past the community park on her right. She crossed Riverside Avenue, ran straight across the front terrace, and along the side of the big faux colonial building that used to be the Saugatuck Boat House. She stopped short when she reached the back corner of the gray wooden structure. She peered around at the grassy back lawn leading to the river and the dock.

What she saw jarred her senses. Usually at this time the dock would be alive: women coming in from a day of fishing, gathering to share their catch, helping pack up. Now the dock was virtually empty. A number of boats appeared to be pressed up against each other in the water, pushed aside to make way for a strange craft—a blocky pyramid, like an inverted yacht made of dark-red metallic Legos—bobbing half-submerged at an unnatural angle in the river. A chain-link row of thin gold metallic slabs connected the opening in the craft to the dock. Two very tall men in skin-thin unitards stood, arms loosely raised, at the lawn end of the dock. Twenty feet away on the grass Janine was just standing there, chatting in a sequined pink tube dress. Long, skinny Leslie looked frozen stiff standing next to her, her distinctive cascade of shiny brown hair lying perfectly still on her bright floral slip. The get-ups reminded Lo that it was Friday. TGIF. That meant probably upwards of a hundred women were hiding in the vicinity, nervously awaiting instruction or the all-clear. Lo sensed their presence, but none of them were communicating. In spite of the siren blaring intermittently, an eerie silence prevailed.

The men were disconcerting too. One was a pale-faced twenty-something with stringy brown hair, scrawny beard, and droopy moustache. Built like a beanpole, he was tall, at least six feet, but nothing like the Orbiters that Lo had fought last summer. He was wearing a pewter-colored unitard with a glowing yellow peace-sign on the chest. He was also grinning and nodding at her crew. Next to him stood a towering blond. This guy had to be almost seven feet, closer to forty than thirty, skin the color of watery oatmeal, a growing-out buzz cut and very well built. His unitard was dark blue and featured the stars and stripes glowing brightly on the front. Once upon a time the peace sign and the flag might have reassured her. Now they were both a joke.

Lo looked up and saw two glassy orbs hanging low in a sky just beginning to hint at sunset. Neither were moving. In one of the pods she recognized Pat's distinctive bulk and bushy helmet of hair. Using her glove to deflect what was left of the sun up onto the pod, creating a flash of light, Lo managed to catch Pat's attention. Pat threw her hands up in frustration. In the other pod, Marie began making similar gestures. Something was clearly rendering their pods little more than sky decor. Lo indicated that the fliers should stay in position. There might be more intruders in the air, and if necessary the fliers could try crashing their pods into the uninvited spacecraft. Lo hoped it wouldn't come to that, but she knew the two women up there would do it if she asked.

Lo began running down the lawn, glove hand raised. The two men looked up but made no move to withdraw, arrogant in their nonchalance. Without breaking stride, Lo pointed her trigger fingers and shot the long-haired grinning guy in the right foot. He cried out as he dropped to the ground, grabbed his injured extremity, and rolled into fetal position.

Janine shouted out in protest. "No. There's no danger."

There was always danger. Lo saw that Leslie had begun to shake like a wet dog. Someone needed to end this bullshit and get that woman some medical assistance.

As she willed the energy back into her right hand, simultaneously stirring the air to create a barrier with her left, Lo took a long hard look at the piercing blue eyes of the massive blonde with the striking knife-edged nose. They weren't right. He wasn't right. He should be begging for her consideration at this point.

The guy just shrugged and winked.

She fired at his knee.

"That's for not calling home in thirty years," she said.

2

Lo remained in position, legs apart, right hand ready to fire again, left hand waving back and forth. The air around her rippled violently, causing the three chestnut oaks standing between the dock and the neighboring condos to shake like a congregation of God-fearers. Janine and Leslie were now both frozen in shock as bright green leaves fell over their hair and clothing. Lo noticed that another one of her strong-wired deputies—Adrianna—had run out in front of the useless pair. Adrianna was also dressed for the party—clean and shiny brown curls falling in a cascade over that black silk jumpsuit she always wore—but she was scowling like Medusa, and her right hand was gloved and pointed by her side, ready to fight. She nodded at Lo, awaiting instruction.

The pods continued to hang surreal and silent above their heads. The hairy guy stayed huddled in a ball. The big blonde remained standing. If he had even flinched when she shot him, Lo had missed it. His pale and unnaturally smooth face gave little away, although there was a weary tilt to his head and a slight questioning crease around his eyes. Lo was tempted to shoot him again, this time with more power in her beam, but she knew it would be a pointless gesture. He was protected somehow. She lowered her left arm. The storm abated; the trees fell still. She imagined she could hear the anxious rustling of the others just out of sight. Keeping her weapons glove pointed at the bizarre digital flag on the blonde's chest, she waved her finger back and forth.

"Have you got invisible protection?"

"If that's what you want to call it. My bodcoz is armored—advanced technology like that glove on your right hand—and our orbicraft is also deploying a fifty-meter wide defensive field. It's a good thing, too. You tried to shoot me, Sis."

Lo shrugged. "Just testing. I figured you were protected."

The blonde raised his straight, fair eyebrows. Lo raised her eyebrows back and pointed at the guy on the ground. The blonde smiled and kicked his buddy, who immediately stopped moaning and started unfurling. Leslie released a startled little cry. Janine sighed with relief. Adrianna spat on the ground and gave him the finger. The guy sat up into a cross-legged position, smiled with pressed and apologetic lips, and held two fingers up in a peace sign.

Adrianna fired off an angry beam. A streak of silvered air skirted a small curved line around what now was clearly a force-field. As the energy skipped away, Lo raised her left hand.

"Careful, Adrianna. We don't want beams flying every which way."

Adrianna nodded and lowered her hand.

The blonde said, "Before anyone gets hurt, will you please listen to me. I'm sorry about landing on you like this. I wish I could have sent warning. You must have thought I was dead. Now suddenly here I am, looking different, stepping out of an unfamiliar spaceship. I understand your hesitation. But come on, it's me, Will."

Lo said, "Name our one and only pet."

"Percival the parrot."

"First girl you ever had sex with?"

"Hmmm, I think you know I always preferred boys, but there was that fling with your friend Meredith Lambert at the Lilith Festival."

"Not my friend anymore after that."

"It's me, Lo."

Lo shrugged and waved her weapons hand up and down his huge body.

"How'd you get so tall?"

"Nutritional supplements," he replied. "They helped me reach my full height potential. Six ten. This is it, though, and where I come from this is shorter than average."

"And where exactly do you come from?"

"The Hrhnvrngh Orbitals—a small galaxy with eight inhabited planets about six months from here. I live on the main government orbital. It's called Crn."

"Cern or Corn?"

"Orbitaal is difficult to pronounce. Let's just say I'm from the Orbitals."

Lo screwed up her face. "We already know about the Orbitals. It's where Orbiters come from, right? We met some of those guys last summer. Hairy fucking beasts."

The big shiny plastic version of her brother looked surprised, which was exactly like the old Will, thinking she knew nothing. He said, "There are many different kinds of Orbiters. Some of them are hairy, yes, that's a genus."

"The ugly, criminal genus. How exactly did you end up with people like that?"

"Oh, it's no big story. I was on the official NASA space shuttle that launched from Cape Canaveral. The Orbiters detected our mayday and came and picked us up."

Lo wasn't sure. She pointed at the other skinny guy.

"What about him? You expect me to believe he's a NASA astronaut?"

The skinny guy laughed and said, "No way, Jose. I don't even know what NASA stands for. I wasn't on your brother's shuttle. I was on an unofficial shuttle that launched from Alaska. My dad ran a secret program up there. I was interning on a food longevity study when, you know. I'm a biologist."

"That's really interesting," piped up Janine, "We're trying to grow cof…"

Lo threw her a filthy look and she shut up.

Will said, "I can vouch for his keen interest in plants. Bob spent the whole trip out trying to cultivate space fungi. We hardly saw him, he was so busy with his shrooms."

"You make that sound wrong, dude," said Bob.

"So what *are* you doing here together then?" Lo asked.

Will answered for both of them. "Coming home."

Lo ignored a twinge of emotion. "Are you alone?"

He replied, "Totally alone. There's a somewhat bigger ship in orbit, but it's eight hours away, and nobody's there right now, anyway. This is not another invasion, if that's what's worrying you. This is a homecoming, and a miraculous one at that."

"I don't believe in miracles. I don't believe in brothers who stretch."

In lieu of a reply, Will bent over and ran his fingers up the back of his left calf. His suit peeled open like a splitting tomato, revealing a pale hairless leg. Clearly visible was a jagged green lightening tattoo, bigger than Lo remembered and very faded now. It looked like it had been crafted in a prison cell using a Stanley knife and old ink cartridges. Will and his friends had done them together back when they were about fourteen. The tattoo had impressed Lo at the time, although not her parents. Will had gotten blood on his tennis shorts, and Mom had made a fuss. Dad had asked if they were honoring Flash Gordon, and Will had angrily informed him that the tattoo represented a piece of jagged glass, a symbol of their blood oath. After that Dad called all Will's tattooed friends Flash. One of those old buddies was James Nunn, a local loser that Will had left behind without a backward glance when he finished high school. James Nunn was now one of the few male survivors living in Saugatuck.

"You and James Nunn were friends for life after those tattoos."

Her brother scoffed. "Nice try. Come on, Lo. You know it's me."

Lo waved her hand up and down in the general area of the invisible force-field.

"So come out from behind that shield and give me a hug, Flash."

Will said, "I'd love to Lo, but you have to promise not to attack us again. You know, I thought I had a deal with Janine until you showed up and started shooting."

Lo shook her head. "Janine doesn't make the deals around here, but maybe we can work something out. For starters, you're going to have to lose the unitards. I'm seeing alien technology. We'll get you something else to wear."

Will balked at the suggestion. "Forget it. I'm willing to lower the force-field and turn off the blocking technology, but we have to retain our *bodcoz*. The technology in them doesn't just protect us—it performs critical biological functions. I'm older than I look, Sis. I have medical needs."

Lo hesitated, but it really was Will.

"Oh alright then, you can keep your *bodcoz*, but you have to release the force-field and stop blocking our systems. And I promise, if you make one false move I'll throw every beam I've got at you and believe me I've got plenty."

Will smiled. "Why don't we call that a deal then?"

Lo just nodded. Will muttered something into a roughly triangular brooch lying flattish on the breast of his bodcoz. Lo heard a strange little ticking, sucking sound. The Lego gangway began rolling itself up piece by golden piece and slotting back into place on the ship. The moment the outer door clicked shut, Lo was blasted by noise coming down the airwaves, terrified women all transmitting messages at her like crazy. She could barely hear the questions for the screeching of her wires. What was going on? Where were they supposed to be? Was it safe to come out now? Did she need security backup? The only beam she really cared about was the simplest one: *Helena—safe.*

Lo sent out a universal message to the wired—*friendlies—all—clear*—then allowed all the other messages to subside into background noise. If it was critical, they'd find a way through to her. Then she turned back towards HQ and looked up to the third floor observation room from which Yaz ran comms. She made a gesture with the side of her hand across her neck. A second later the sirens stopped. Finally, Lo looked up to the pods and twirled her hand in a downward spiral. Pat and Marie began to descend. Then she flung her arms out wide, beckoning and shouting to anyone within listening distance.

"All clear, people. Lower your weapons. Come out when you're ready. All clear."

A visceral sense of relief coursed through the area as thousands of tensed wires relaxed. The air filled with the chatter of brightly dressed women who now appeared from everywhere: behind the side-hedges, inside boats at the dock, under picnic benches and tables. A couple of women rushed to put their arms around Leslie. Lo smelled the distinctive aroma of marijuana as they lit her a joint—the only medicine they had left for damaged nerves. She also watched as Janine rushed over to Bob as if he were the guest of honor and she the host. They would be discussing her failure to comply with orders later. For now though it couldn't hurt to have one of her crew glued to that particular visitor's side. That wasn't going to be enough, though...

Lo beamed across to Adrianna: *initiate—covert—security.* Brother or no brother, Lo wasn't taking any chances. Adrianna shook her head in acknowledgment and turned her hard brown body towards HQ. Lo beamed Yaz up in the control room. Not that she actually needed telling, but Yaz should communicate with any naturals who were not within shouting distance. Everything was fine but they should stay at home for now.

Finally, Lo looked over to where Will was clearly waiting on her. He struck a pose, the fake photo kind that had always made her smile. Lo felt her face crinkle into an involuntary smile now. Will didn't hesitate. He took three long strides in her direction, picked her up in a great bear-hug, and swung her around, her feet flailing wildly in the air.

"I'm so happy to see you, you psychopath," he laughed.

"You too, you plastic freak," she said, laughing as she whirled around like a rag doll. He had whirled her like this many times before; he was always that kind of brother, expressive when the moment suited him, and especially so in the presence of others. Will the shining star, Will the magic maker...

As Lo spun around she saw the first streaks of sunset lighting up the rippling waters of the Saugatuck. Caught in its glow, the Orbiter spacecraft was transformed into a fiery modern art installation. The air hummed with the sound of insects in the reeds that lined the shore. As more and more women rushed onto the grounds of HQ, curious about the newcomers, uncertain about the situation, furiously communicating in words, beams, and gestures — literally buzzing — Lo felt herself flush with an unfamiliar elation. It had been years since she had experienced even a fraction of this joy. Perhaps back when Helena gave birth to Reid and they shared that happiness, that hopefulness.

Lo put her feet on the ground. It took a moment to regain her balance. She wobbled and staggered and waved her arms about. A number of her crew rushed to her side. She shooed them off and looked around to make sure everything was all right. A small crowd had gathered around Bob. The women were vying for his attention, most out of curiosity, but some almost flirtatiously, pushing their chests forward, showing their glittery legs. Although most of these women were in long-term relationships, Lo sensed a certain frisson between some of them and the newcomer. They were excited by his novelty. Well, Lo sure hoped that was all it was.

"Let's take this inside," she shouted to them all. "Someone must have known these guys were coming because the entertainment committee prepared a party!"

Everyone laughed and began moving towards HQ. Lo bit her lip as she walked. Happy as she was to see her brother, in her brain, the sirens just wouldn't stop wailing.

3

Outside, the sun set on the Saugatuck River. Inside, its reddish glow gave the crowded room a bacchanalian cast. The large space looked a bit like the vestibule of a grand hotel: overstuffed velvet couches and silk reading chairs, massive oak bookshelves, gold-framed paintings and mirrors, even a large anthropologist's vitrine filled with ornaments. In the middle of the room stood an O-shaped mahogany bar, matching stools all the way round, polished nice and smooth over the years by a bunch of old, dead-lawyer asses. Fifteen years ago a salvage crew had found the bar in a restaurant in New Canaan and brought it back here to Saugatuck, piece by precious piece. Now it was simply known as the O. To one side of it lay clusters of seating. On the other side the space was crammed with twelve large dining tables, each one a masterpiece in its own right, known collectively as the mess. Tonight the tables of the mess were richly dressed, as were the hundred plus women now gathered inside, all of them desperate to know what was happening. While they waited they talked loudly over the eclectic sounds of the TGIF playlist, currently playing an old Amy Winehouse tune. Some things endured.

Lo sat up at the bar with Will—her head bursting with questions, her heart leaping with emotion—and tried to keep her priorities straight. Her people had to come first. Swiveling on her stool, she evaluated the situation. The women were all keeping a respectful distance, avoiding her side of the O. They were mostly the usual TGIF suspects, but the curious had begun dribbling in too. Lo didn't expect a crush tonight, in spite of events. Most people would wait on a detailed statement before they came back out.

Various members of the security crew were spread strategically throughout the room. To the unacquainted they were indistinguishable from the other women. Adrianna lurked twenty feet away in a chatty group. Ruby was tending bar. Pat was even closer; Lo's second-in-command had perched her ample ass a few wooden stools down and was making a poor job of pretending to study the very limited drinks menu. The ex-parking officer's bulk and proximity was always reassuring. Just beyond Pat, on the top curve of the O, Lo saw that Janine and friends had encircled Bob. Janine could still expect an earful about disobeying orders, but not tonight. Tonight, she was doing a great job of distracting Bob while their techies evaluated the spaceship in the river.

Lo swung back around and slugged on her beer. Will was thirstily draining his second pint-glass of nut-brown ale. "Careful, bro," she said, "that stuff is eight percent."

"I need something strong," he replied. "It's unnerving here in electric lady-land."

Lo followed the sweep of his head around the room and suddenly saw her world through his eyes. Light sparkled off thousands of silver wire endings—a glittering sea of cyber-women. What a shame most of them weren't as powerful as they looked. Seven hundred hot-wired female power-houses and only forty of them strong-willed enough to fly. It was a thirty-year-old source of disappointment. They ran workshops, they offered therapy, they had done everything in their power to turn the weak into the strong. Most of the women had learned to send as well as receive messages, about half of them had gotten quite good at minor telekinesis. It wasn't anywhere near enough...

"Behave yourself and you'll be alright. So what do you think of the old place?"

"Amazing, transformed."

"Yeah, we've been working on it for years, repurposing, extending. Capacity is currently six hundred at a squeeze. Two hundred upstairs, same downstairs, and more again in the hole. We rarely use all the space at once though, only when there's bad weather... or intruders."

Will didn't bite. "Nice, but it's the décor that amazes me. I remember when this was an ugly rec room with plastic tables and chairs and flags on the walls. Everyone looked sallow under the fluorescents, it echoed like crazy, and the atmosphere was all school gym. Now it's like the Plaza meets ABC Carpet and Home—with a New England twist."

"You say that like it's a good thing," said Lo, "like home décor still matters."

Will winked at her for no good reason. Then he picked up his empty glass, shook it at Ruby, and winked at her too. Oh, oh. Lo waited for it, but the red-headed punk said nothing, just poured another beer. Then she raised the glass to her mouth and slowly ran her pierced tongue around the rim before handing it over. She winked as she did so. Once with each eye. Tiny jets of lightning leaped out in Will's direction. He ducked and roared with genuine laughter. They all roared with laughter. Will then picked up the glass and took a big wet slug.

"Sorry, ladies," he said. "Two beers and I'm already sloppy. What can I say? I'm not used to alcohol. I'm in a state of shock. The whole situation is totally surreal. I mean, I'm pretty sure that's an original Edward Hopper hanging on the wall over there."

Ruby answered, "It is. We found it in one of the deserted McMansions."

"That's not stealing then, that's liberating..."

"You don't approve?" Ruby placed her hands on her hips.

"Are you crazy? I totally approve. This place is lush. I feel like Jay Gatsby."

"Yeah, well you look like his wax effigy," said Ruby.

They all laughed again. You didn't have to look hard to see the Gatsby in Will.

Will asked, "So who did all this? Is there a designer among your group?"

"*A* designer. Are you kidding? A team of twenty-three did this—including five architects. They had a field day emptying out all the most expensive houses. Remember the kind of women who lived in this town thirty years ago, all thwarted talent and domestic neurosis? Well in spite of everything, some of them are still a bit that way. I love this place, I really do, but the obsessive crafting and decorating drives me crazy. I mean who cares about Baccarat crystal when what we need is shampoo and gas and paper? What good is a new bay window with stained-glass relief when what we need are defense walls and supply bunkers?"

"I get your point, but this place is a beautiful testament to survival," said Will.

Lo paused to bite her lip, then replied, "Don't go all psychoanalytic on me, Will. This place is not a symbol. It's a functioning military installation, it's the local bar and restaurant, it's the town hall, administrative offices, police station, you name it."

Will smiled. "Whorehouse, Church, Hospital?"

"Forget about whores. No demand. Fuck church. There's obviously no God. And as for hospitals, well we do fine with the old Hoffman and Weingartner surgery—not that we have much call for medical care these days. I mean, look at us. We don't seem to be getting any older."

Lo waved her hand over her face. Her skin was the same lightly speckled eggshell of her youth, smooth and tight over sharp bones. She had only the finest of wrinkles, and the single hard worry line that slashed her brow in two by the end of every day seemed to dissipate every night. She looked like Mia Farrow in her thirties, only with a silvery web of wires sparkling under the skin at her hairline, a halo of metallic freckles.

"You certainly have aged well, Sis."

"I was sixty-five on my last birthday, Will."

Will nodded. "I know, but you look twenty-seven."

"Flatterer. I look thirty-two—the same age they put the wires in every vein, nerve, and muscle in my body. But hey, you're looking good too. Sixty-seven going on forty."

"Forty! I don't think I look at day over thirty. But I don't want you getting the wrong idea. Nobody did this to me, Lo. I paid to get it done. Enhancement is a cultural norm for Orbiters. I did what was necessary to assimilate into my new crowd."

"So you've become an Orbiter then?"

"Not really, although I'm happy to have been accepted by them. They've done a lot for me, starting with saving my life. I was incredibly lucky they were in the Milky Way when trouble hit. After Ruurda blew up, a couple of Orbiter explorer vessels were sent to investigate reports of a massive fleet. But maybe you know about that already?"

Lo nodded. "Some. The Ruurdaans didn't tell us much, and tell is not really the word, because they didn't speak—they transmitted—but we worked a few things out. I know they created irreparable fissures in their own planet with all their sonic prayer crap. They should have questioned their religion at that point, but instead the Ruurdaans decided to come here and have another go at divinity, transcendence, whatever..." Lo trailed off. She figured Will didn't need to be a shrink to know how she felt about that shit.

"The Ruurdaans were the architects of their own destruction. I know it's no consolation to anyone on Earth, but all the known cultures agree. The Orbiters did send what little help they could at the time. Of course, it wasn't enough."

Lo snorted. "That's an understatement. I remember looking at the specs for your shuttle when I visited you in Cape Canaveral that Easter. Eight people, right? Maybe you squeezed a couple more in? Ten? Twelve? How many of you did the Orbiters save?"

"I was the sole survivor of an eight-person crew. The Orbiters were a long time coming, and supplies were limited. I was the leanest, my body the most resilient. It was a similar story with the Russians and the Chinese. Bob's group was the luckiest—four of them survived. In total the Orbiters rescued nine of us space drifters."

Lo chose not to comment on the loss of all Will's companions; she had experienced that kind of loss too. "So what happened to everyone that survived?"

"We were given new lives on the Orbitals. Bob chose to live in anonymity, forget about the past entirely. He retrained in Orbital biology and went to live on a burb planet."

"And you? Don't tell me you retrained as an alien psychiatrist?"

Will laughed and said, "Don't think that wasn't my original fantasy..."

He paused, turned to Ruby with hang-dog eyes, and raised his hands like paws. She smiled broadly, revealing her old tongue-piercings, and began pulling on the pump.

"...but psychiatry is more like pharmacology in the Orbitals. Too scientific for my tastes. So I looked around and began accepting other opportunities—guest appearances in the media, advisory boards, promotional work. That's still pretty much what I do, attach my name to worthy projects, offer unique Earthan insight to the public."

Lo laughed. "Oh my God, you're a celebrity survivor." She shrugged at Will's tight-lipped smile. What, he thought he'd had it tough? Nothing funny about what happened to him? Yeah, well try being her, watching the world you knew die and everyone you loved die with it. Finding nothing but evil within those beautiful, terrible pods. Armies of cone-headed killer children who never once blinked as they inserted those hair-thin wires using finger-beams and eyes. The root canal from hell, deep surgical acupuncture. And then the messages in your head. Lift this. Bring that. Move this. Fly there. Jump here. Hit this. Hit that. Most of the women couldn't remember everything. Lo remembered it all. Lo had fought every minute of every day to retain control of her mind.

"Maybe you're right, maybe I have made compromises..."

Lo cut him off. "I'm sure we've all done things..."

"It was always about getting home one day."

"Does that mean that you're home for good."

Will coughed. "Well no, not this time. This time it's just a visit. I have an obligation to the Orbiters, responsibilities back home, a job, a house, friends…"

Lo snorted. "I don't want to hear about any obligations to the Orbiters, Will. The ones we met were straight out of a *Mad Max* film. They killed my friend."

Will shook his head. "I'm sorry to hear it, but those can't have been Orbiters. Orbiters aren't violent. Physical aggression is against their nature and against their laws."

Lo spat beer into the air in derision, but Will kept going.

"Listen to me. I think you met up with some *Unans*—there *were* a few of those in the group that went to Madison. Unans are exiled Orbiters who live on the planet Una because they won't live by Orbiter rules. They are *nothing* like regular Orbiters."

"Semantics. They are still Orbiters, same way killer dogs are still dogs. And if there's something wrong with them, then what the fuck are you doing sending them here? Do we look like Australia to you?"

Will's eyes widened. "No, no. Nothing like that. The Unans do sometimes act out, but they're definitely not criminals. They're political idealists. I don't know why they—"

"Act out! Your so-called political idealists machine-gunned two women to death in Weston this winter—all for a shitty farm-house with some skinny animals and a veggie patch. There are six of your Orbiter friends living there now. I wanted to flatten the place—but my bleeding-heart council decided we didn't have enough proof to act unilaterally. Now I don't sleep nights, worrying if they're going to try and raid us…"

Will leaned in for another long sip of beer. If he didn't slow down he was going to be pretty drunk, pretty damned soon. Lo looked across at the Tiffany clock by the door to the office suites: 7:56. The women were starting to serve dinner. She'd been so caught up with Will she'd almost forgotten about the others—but they were waiting on her. She looked over at Pat and flashed her right hand open and closed twice.

Lo looked back at Will and said, "Enough with the small talk. What are you really doing here? You didn't really come looking for me. You must have thought I was dead."

Will shrugged and threw his hands open. "Of course I thought you were dead—but I came looking anyway. So what if I'm helping the Orbiters while I'm here? From what I'm hearing you could all use a helping hand."

His tone was defensive, the exact same tone he used to take whenever they talked about Jake—his smart and funny speechwriter boyfriend who rocked pastel scarves and shimmied like Beyoncé at Cousin Emma's wedding. Jake was Lo's idea of perfect back then, but Will kept cheating on him with young Air Force cadets. Or so Jake said. Will said Jake was imagining things because he had abandonment issues. Whatever.

"What kind of helping hand, Will? And none of your bullshit. Be specific."

"Okay, okay. I am *specifically* hoping to help resolve the problems up in Madison. I know the woman who was assigned to that settlement—Retske—she was one of the Russian survivors. She's always seemed quite capable to me, adaptable. However, pretty soon after she got here she sent a message saying she had lost control of the Unans. The realities of distance mean it's taken us this long to receive that message and respond—and the situation seems to have deteriorated in the meantime..."

Lo said, "If you're supposed to be in Madison, then what are you doing here?"

"That's a good question. I was going to come here last, after I was done in Madison, but I couldn't help myself. I diverted here first. I had to see home. See if anything, anyone..."

Lo responded in a near-whisper. "Why didn't you come sooner?"

Will shook his head. "It's not so easy to get here. First there's the cost, then there's the nightmare trip. I've been rattling along in a big tin space lizard called an explorer for over six months now. Imagine eighteen large adults crammed together like sardines. Imagine sharing an eight-feet-square bunkroom with that fool Bob and fat, flatulent Captain Syd. The only thing keeping us all sane has been our virtual lives, linked to stim sims fourteen hours..."

Lo cut him off. "Yeah and I'm sure the food was horrible too. You know I nearly lost my mind going over and over the survivor lists that IBM City compiled..."

"IBM computers?"

"No. IBM *City*. It's a big settlement out at the old corporate headquarters in Armonk. Almost twenty-thousand people. I'm surprised you don't know about it. I mean it's no big secret. They're constantly broadcasting, trying to reach anyone left out there. Currently they're the center-point of a loose regional alliance, but they have longer-term plans for a new government. They've also been trying to create records of the survivors. The women doing the analysis estimate that there are about three hundred thousand of us left here in the US."

"Yeah—one percent—and ninety-five percent of them women—those are our estimates too. Does that mean that everyone else..." Will leaned across the counter and took her sinewy hands into his own rubbery grasp. His breath was thick and yeasty. The home brew was finally starting to pummel the big guy, filling him with cheap emotion.

Lo pulled away from his hands, which were sweating like waxed fruit. "Yes, it *means*. They're all dead and they mostly died badly. Do you want the gory details?"

"If I can help by listening."

"I certainly don't need you to, but if it will help assuage your survivor's guilt..."

Will had the decency to look down as he nodded. They both knew it was true. He'd escaped and left them to their fate. She filled him in on what he'd missed...

On Day One of the attacks, Mom had been flattened along with everyone else in Bridgeport Hospital. On Day Two, a whole lot of other people they knew died when the main town of Westport was reduced to a low-lying plain of rubble over which the old river quickly began to flow. On Day Three Dad was killed in the cull of Saugatuck. That was the worst. She and Dad had been hiding out together for two days when the pod landed on the lawn. They were dragged out from their boxes under the porch — pulled straight through the trellis like it wasn't there. While they both lay there stunned on the ground, a Ruurdaan crushed Dad's head using just a hand gesture, exploding it like a tomato. Then the creature began the process of turning Dad's body into a liquid pulp that could be pressed easily into the ground. Bone meal. Lo lay there watching the whole time, eyes frozen open, too scared to turn away. When it was done the Ruurdaans scooped her up into a net and flew away. Brown splatters remained on her clothes for days, until she was stripped naked and sprayed into the sheer chemical sheath...

Will listened in silence, concern in his eyes, fear on his frozen lips. It was not her stories that scared him, though — it was her, the pure unadulterated horror of her.

She called over to Ruby, "Get him another beer will you, before he passes out."

Will tried to pull himself together. "Lo, I'm sorry. It's a lot to process."

"Don't worry about it. It's too much even for a psychiatrist. I get it. It's too much for us too. But stop looking so fucking terrified. I'm not the monster in the cupboard."

Will said, "You're right. I'm sorry. I'm struggling with everything I'm seeing, hearing. I don't know what to say to you, how to respond..."

"I don't need your pity," she said. "All I ask is that you don't let me down again."

"I'll definitely try not to," said Will.

"I'll take that as a blood oath, Flash," said Lo, leaping to her feet and turning her attention to those who really knew about blood oaths.

4

Lo jumped onto the nearest coffee table and began conducting the air. The wall of French doors leading to the great porch, open to let the breeze in, banged back and forth in thrall to her arms. The women stopped talking but the White Stripes kept going. Lo beamed the stereo system, and the music cut out. She gestured to Ruby, who began pulling the special-occasion-only bottles of Grey Goose and Ketel One off the shelf and throwing them out into the waiting crowd. The cheering began.

"Ladies, ladies, and more ladies," Lo shouted over the crowd Everyone hooted and hollered.

She raised her hands for silence. "Thanks for your patience. I imagine you've all been wondering about the two freaky-looking tall guys in the onesies..."

Half the crowd cheered. The other half made a variety of noises: grunting, groaning, murmuring, whistling. It wasn't quite clear how this would go.

"...all jokes aside, I'm happy to report that the two men in question are my brother Will Warren and his traveling companion, Bob—fellow survivors."

Bob stepped forward, hands pressed together and said, "Namaste."

Never one to be upstaged, Will stepped out, curtsied and said, "Enchanté."

Cheering and whistling broke out again. However, patches of deep mistrustful silence lingered. Lo ignored them for now. If she said this was her brother back from the dead, then this was her brother back from the dead.

"Right now I'm still catching up with Will's story, and I'm afraid I haven't had time to get to know Bob—although I'm sure Janine already has the scoop."

Everyone laughed. Janine was popular.

Lo continued. "What I do know is that my brother and Bob both escaped Earth in NASA shuttles and were rescued in the Milky Way by the Orbiters."

A wave of concern traveled through the crowd; Lo both heard and felt it.

She shook her head, gestured for everyone to settle down. "I understand your concern, but it's okay. There are only two of them, and they're definitely not Orbiters. In fact they've been sent here to deal with those beasts up in Madison."

A few women cheered again, but the mood remained nervous.

Then Marie shouted out. "That's what they say, but why should we believe them? I don't know, Lo. No offense, but your brother doesn't even look human to me."

Lo wasn't quite sure what to say. From birth until the age of eighteen she had lived opposite Marie. Marie was an indispensable member of the crew. But Marie had issues, arguably bigger than her own.

A male voice yelled, "Yeah, that freak looks like a big wax statue." It had to be James Nunn, Marie's pathetic excuse for a husband, but she couldn't see him anywhere.

"Oh come on, you guys," she said, looking pointedly at her deputy. "You know how cautious I am on your behalf—to a fault is what the council keep telling me. So you have to trust me on this one. I know my own brother. Didn't I test him hard enough when he landed? What more do you want me to do? Perform an autopsy?"

"It's what you'd usually do," said Marie.

"It's her *brother*. And we've got 'em pretty well surrounded," said Pat.

"I'm not scared of them," yelled Janine. "They're just normal men."

"Yeah, dumb, ugly freeloaders." That was Adrianna.

A few of the women laughed, but others continued to shake their heads and mutter. A couple of older men were in attendance, although none of them spoke. The younger more vocal guys were all still on lockdown at the youth rec center. Safety precautions for all naturals. Heads down until strictly instructed otherwise. Lo could have overridden the protocol but had opted to leave it in place. Two strange visitors, one alien spaceship, and a building filled with over one hundred demanding women was enough for her to deal with tonight. Even under her control the situation remained awkward.

A lean woman with a black crew cut stood up from one of the velvet couches and said, "Look, I feel safe enough, but perhaps those who don't should raise their hands."

Lo nodded and said, "Good idea. If you're feeling nervous, raise your hand."

About twenty hands shot into the air. Ten more hesitated. No crew except Marie.

Lo said, "O—K. So what I suggest is that those thirty of you who feel unsafe go elsewhere. You can take your drinks down into the hole, or you can go home."

"It's not us who should have to leave," shouted someone.

"Enough," Lo shouted back. "We've had the show of hands, I've proposed a solution, and I shouldn't have to tell you that I have it under control. I'm not up for a long discussion before I've had time to really assess the situation. However I do totally understand your concerns and questions. What I suggest is we set up a meeting schedule for tomorrow. Anyone who'd like to talk to our visitors in person can go upstairs and sign up with Yaz right now. I'm also calling a general town meeting for the day after tomorrow. We should be able to have a more informed discussion at that time. Until then though, I suggest we *celebrate* our newest survivors. Seriously, ladies, we shouldn't be treating these guys like the enemy; we should be raising our glasses to them."

"I agree. To surviving," shouted Ruby from behind the bar.

Pat echoed her cheer. "To surviving."

Adrianna chanted like a football fan, "Sur-viv-ors."

The mood caught and spread. A small table of women raised their silverware into the air—some with their hands, some with their minds—and begin clanging it together in a cacophony of metal. *Survivors, survivors.*

Lo looked over to the corner where the ancient iPod sat docked in the O-shaped speaker in the corner. Spinning her finger through the air, she quickly changed the music. *Groove is in the Heart.* The song dated from before most of them were born, but everyone knew it because Lo insisted on playing it whenever she was in a good mood. It was something of a village joke. Lo couldn't think of a better time to play it than now. *Dum, da da, dum, da da da.* Heads began to nod as the crowd picked up the beat. Adrianna's spirals bobbed distinctively. Catching Lo's eye, the ex-dancer raised her hands to shoulder height and pumped her breasts back and forth, left-right, left-right, to the music. *Deep in the rhythm.* Too erotic. *My succotash wish.* Too public. Lo tried to disguise her embarrassment in a smile, then turned and stepped toward Will, waiting patiently, slightly unsteady on his feet now.

She said, "I went out on a limb for you there, bro."

"I appreciate your support. What can I do to help build trust?"

"Oh, I don't know, show us a few alien dance moves."

Will laughed and waved his hands in the air.

"*So de-lovely, and de-licious.* Oh, man, I used to love this song."

It was skinny Bob, sidling up like this was some cheesy nightclub. No sooner had he spoken than Janine grabbed his hand and pulled him toward the dance-floor.

"I think he's in her clutches for the duration," laughed Lo.

"Do you see him complaining?" Will replied.

"No. Not gay then?"

Will leant in closer and whispered, "Orbiters don't distinguish, but I know he's coupled. Female partner and three kids in a two-bed unit on one of the lesser suburban orbitals. You can tell your girl if you like—although I doubt anything would stop her."

The booze really was loosening his lips.

"Don't call her girl. But do tell me more."

Will hesitated. Lo gestured with her hands. *Gimme.*

"Oh, what the hell. He's not my friend or my responsibility. He's here on community service. Got caught trying to cultivate magic mushrooms in his greenhouse. Highly illegal *and* stupid. There are plenty of legal drugs available on all the Orbitals, but I guess none of them are psychedelic enough for Bob. Anyway, he was sentenced to a long stretch on Una but someone intervened and had him sent him to Earth instead. He's supposed to spend at least two years in Madison helping the Orbiters integrate. In a couple of years another ship passing through will collect him. I can't see how much use he's going to be to Madison though, given that his only interests are getting high and watching porn. Oh yes, and he knows a lot about Alaska."

Lo hadn't seen this side of Will since well before he became Mr. Career-Psychiatrist. Perhaps the amusement showed in her face, because Will suddenly said, "You're right. I'm talking like an asshole. The alcohol has gone to my head. I need to eat. Do you mind? That buffet looks amazing and I haven't had a steak in thirty years."

Lo started. The word steak had triggered a chain of thoughts. Barbecue, Helena. Lo had thought about her occasionally in the last couple of hours, but had always shoved the thought aside. Helena was safe—she would turn up eventually. Now, moving toward the buffet, Lo searched the room, checking all the corners where a shy observer might lurk. Bingo. Perched on a window-ledge near the toilets in the far corner was a willowy older woman: gray-streaked, brown hair gracefully pinned up into a bun, gray t-shirt dress hugging thin bones.

Lo beckoned with her hand. Helena shook her head. Usually Lo would try coaxing her, but not tonight, no time or patience. Spreading her hand into a big fan, then curling it in the air as if around Helena's slender waist, Lo dragged her wife across the room, maneuvering her around people and tables with great precision. She smiled like it was something cute. By the time she reached them Helena's face was blotched pink with resistance, her eyes blazing with quiet resignation.

"I've asked you not to do things like that," she said.

Lo ignored her. "Hey, I'm not sure if you heard the speech I just gave, but this is my brother Will. Will, I'd like to you to meet Helena. Helena is my..."

"Wife." Helena filled in the blank.

Will didn't miss a beat. "Then I'm doubly delighted to meet you," he said, reaching out both his hands to clasp Helena's delicately extended right.

Helena added her left to the mix and smiled. "It is so great to meet you too, Will. Beyond great—miraculous. I look forward to getting to know you better when you have more time."

She turned to Lo. "I assume I should make up the spare bed?"

Lo looked at Will, who said, "That sounds wonderful."

Helena said, "Great, wonderful, miraculous—our supply of words is so inadequate for describing feelings and experiences of this magnitude, isn't it?"

Will started to answer, but Helena had already turned and slipped away.

As they walked towards the buffet, Lo said, "Just when you least expect it, she'll be pinning you down for a deep and meaningful discussion."

"Yes, I definitely get that feeling. How long have you been together?"

"Twenty-five years. We hooked up a few months after she walked into town with sixteen unwired survivors who'd been living in a small eco-disaster shelter outside Milford. She knew about it because she was a doctor. Yale. Pediatric oncology."

"Impressive" he replied as they began filling their plates.

Indeed, but why was she trying to impress him? When they had both loaded their plates high with meat and fresh salads, they sat at a table that had been cleared for them and began eating fast, both of them clearly starving. Will murmured over the food to the point that Lo had to say, "Stop having sex with it, will you."

The minute her plate was empty, Lo said, "So I've been thinking about how you're technically en-route to Madison. If you're still planning to go, I'd like to go with you. I know the woman who runs that town—Gail. I'd like to talk to her about what's happening with the Orbiters, if they're going to be contained within that area. It should be safe if I travel with you. You have the force field."

Will threw up his hands, cutlery and all. "Whoa. Sis. Can't this wait until tomorrow? How about that one night of unqualified celebration and happiness you mentioned? I'm enjoying getting drunk and disorderly. I don't want to plan. I want to dance and fall down on my ass."

He said *ath*. Surely, she was safe with her own drunk brother.

She looked away from him a moment and began flicking around with her finger, looking for a tune on the iPod. *I see you baby, shaking that ass.* Memories flooded to the fore. New York City, back when she was still young and vaguely fun. Her long-term boyfriend Ben was away in Japan on one of his many field trips. Will's long-term boyfriend Jake was visiting a sick friend in some remote state. Time to party. Things got blurry over the course of the evening: dinner at the Gramercy Tavern, drinking in leather bars on the West Side, playing pool in some dive near NYU, dancing in her funky little flea-pit on the edge of Alphabet City. She had ended up sleeping with one of Will's gay friends. He was smoking clove cigarettes in her bed when she woke up. They'd sworn each other to secrecy, but Lo was pretty sure Will knew. He'd never said anything, though, not like her, not like all the times she'd said stuff to him about Jake.

"Oh, whatever. Show us those all those alien moves you promised."

Will took her literally. He flung his cutlery down and leapt up from his chair, dragging Lo as he went. They joined the crowd of women dancing in the spaces between tables. Will loomed even larger over the group than Bob, dwarfing them all. Laughing, he pressed the metallic diamond-shaped button on his bodcoz. In a spreading pattern of disco-diamonds the rubbery-metal fabric gradually turned white. The women all roared and clapped. Will then did some strange thing with his both his arms, bent them at unnatural degrees and began to move his torso from side to side. If MC Hammer was a big plastic white guy with some Bollywood moves…

Pat shouted, "Hooah," and the crowd went wild.

5

She woke to a vicious ray of sunshine poking her in the eye, accusatory and dizzying. Her internal organs felt as if they were poaching in their own juices, and every part of her cried out for ice cold water. The wired women of Saugatuck might not seem to age, but they weren't entirely invulnerable. If they jumped off a bridge, they died. If they guzzled too much home-brew before dinner, *then* merrily chugged down a bottle of filthy corked red wine, *and* topped off their binge with a third of a bottle of Grey Goose, well, they got a hangover. Sure the recovery time would be shorter, but still...

Lo looked over at the chipped and peeling window-frame and raised her eyebrows to open it. The window creaked up about an inch. It had been sticking for the last twenty odd years, but nobody ever got around to fixing it. Concentrating harder, Lo began flicking her head in short sharp bursts, like a psychotic remote-control. The window ricocheted from side to side in painfully small increments, rising slowly upward until it stuck at an awkward angle. It would have been quicker and easier to walk over and lift it. Tossing aside the thin worn comforter, Lo stretched, arched her back, and raised herself into a crab. Post-apocalyptic Pilates. Groaning, she flipped sideways in a twisting motion from the bed toward the floor, pulling the glass on the bedside table through the air toward her hand as she landed. Unfortunately she faltered on both the twist and the landing *and* failed to catch the glass—which wobbled along in tandem with her then fell with a crash to the floor. Shit, fuck, shit.

Lo supposed it served her right. She listened for Helena and heard the familiar sounds of clattering kitchen utensils and the pure throaty vibrato of Dusty Springfield. Helena and her old-fashioned heartache. The music used to make Lo smile, but now it just felt old, like Helena. Although at the age of sixty-five Lo was actually seven years older than Helena, she still looked, thought, and acted thirty-three years younger. It must be down to her wiring. What else could explain why she recently let her son's friend, Ned, pin her down in a quiet sandy cove and ram her like cattle? Afterwards she told him that if she caught him out of bounds again she'd permanently ban him from training for the security crew. He told her she was the eighth woman he'd been with since he turned seventeen in the new year. All wired, all fifty going on twenty. Lo was by far the oldest, but also maybe the hottest. Lo felt so sick as they flew home in the pod that the wires in her throat vibrated. She'd felt the same thing same three months earlier when she found herself riding atop the pungently obese president of the Norwalk Power Cooperative on the couch in his office. He had four wives, but he'd still been asking her for years, always with the same joke, that something electric surged between them.

The real electricity though, the real problem, that was Adrianna. There had always been a pleasant tension between her and the anarchic Latina. They had a powerful working relationship, albeit one that sometimes boiled over into conflict. Recently the tension between them had changed shape. Last Tuesday after work, Adrianna had talked her into spinning mid-air cartwheels in the summer night sky, arms outstretched, bodies entwined, legs pressed together at the groin like interlinked scissors. It was a cute new trick, and the crew standing around drinking with them after a long, hot shift had cheered at their prowess. As soon as she'd bounded back down to the ground, however, Lo raced straight home, her face and groin burning with a heat that she feared everyone present had sensed. She also feared that it was only a matter of time before the spark between her and Adrianna ignited.

Lo wasn't sure which of the liaisons her community would find worse—the boy, the gross married man, or the other woman—but all of them demeaned Helena and diminished her. What was it with her these days? Truth be told, she'd even felt a frisson in the presence of those savage, bestial Orbiters—the heat steaming off their ripe bodies, their breath moist with fear and exertion—just before she'd killed two of them.

Lo wandered over and stood in front of the mirror, pulling her hair back tight to expose her taut forehead with its mottled ring of silver freckles. Was it her wires? A midlife crisis? Yaz said Lo had been at war with the world for too long. She needed to do something more constructive, let others do the fighting. Yaz was just echoing Helena. Helena Theresa, as Lo now called her. What the hell had happened to the woman who fought by her side all those years before the fence was complete? Back then, Helena was fierce and strong and the undisputed political leader of their community. Lo had loved and respected that woman beyond words. The new Helena retired from politics three years ago, saying her work developing their infrastructure was done and she wanted to devote herself to those suffering long-term psychological trauma. She would continue her medical work, but she no longer wished to play a leadership role. Then if that hadn't been bad enough, along came her newfound spirituality, which manifested itself in meditation and soft mannerisms, walking slowly and talking in calm, quiet tones. Like some kind of mendicant or guru. Lo hated herself for feeling this way about Helena, but she hadn't promised to love, honor, and become a Buddhist.

Even on this morning, more exciting than other mornings, more joyous than other days, Lo felt dogged by her personal problems. Will's return had changed everything—and nothing. Her home life was still a mess. Dusty still sang the blues. Helena still awaited her downstairs in the kitchen. Lo tried to disperse some of that negative energy. She clenched her fists and tensed her body with a tremulous fury. The mirror began to fracture in a slowly developing series of starbursts. Her face contorted in a silent scream. The glass continued to pop and splinter. Only when the mirror-scape became so bubbled and jagged that she could barely see her face did Lo relax, forcing all her muscles to release and her body to become still. The reflective glass scratched and ground to a halt in its own time, bound by the laws of physics. There was one last percussive pop. A bursting bubble or a cracking shard. Before her, Lo saw an imploded mess of reflective glass. Her own shattered image. She heard Helena call from downstairs.

"What's that noise, Lo, is everything okay?"

"Fine, fine, dropped a glass, cleaning it up now, coming in a minute," she yelled.

Fashioning her arms and body into an old yoga pose, Lo took a moment to calm herself. Then she set about repairing the fissures in the reflective glass, moving her fingers carefully over each small crack and rupture and smoothing the glass back together. Her work was imperfect—the mirror ended up bubbled like antique glass—but the sheer pleasure of being able to repair it with her bare hands bucked her spirits. Her wires gave her strength. That strength had gotten them through everything—the Ruurdaans, the vicious attacks, the starving winters, the unbearable choices— and it would get them through this too. Pulling a tight gray vest over her muscular chest and drawing the string of her favorite loose pants, Lo braced herself for a challenging day. Family. Strangers. Men. Friends of the Orbiters. Not to mention a spacecraft bobbing in the river. She would need all her leadership skills today. Nine hundred Saugatuckers, nine hundred different perspectives, never as aligned as Lo would like. Somebody had to guide them through this situation. That somebody used to be Helena. Now it was her.

She instinctively reached down and grabbed her glove holster from the floor where she had drunkenly abandoned it last night. Although she hoped she didn't have to use it again today, there was some truth in Helena's observation that she thrilled to the pulse of her glove, that she found relief in unleashing her powers in battle. Perhaps Ruurdaan evil lurked in her wires. Pushing that old bad thought away, Lo walked out across the landing and leaped from the top of the stairs to the bottom in one bound.

When she got downstairs she saw that the back door was open. Will stood outside on the soft green lawn, sipping at a mug of something, probably herbal tea. It was certainly not coffee; they had run out of coffee years ago, and all attempts to grow it in the cold northern climate had failed. In spite of having to drink herbal piss, Will was clearly enjoying his first summer morning back in New England. His head was thrown back to capture the light, and he was wearing what looked like a sarong, slung low around his bony hips. He was the color of glass noodles. Clearly visible on his chest was a striking tattoo of sorts, an accumulation of piercings that formed a clear cross—except that where you might expect an intersection there was a kind of orb. The tattoo, if that was the right word, stretched from nipple to nipple, clavicle to solar plexus—and appeared to be encrusted in precious gems. Lo wanted to step straight outside and ask him about it, but there was a more pressing matter at hand.

Helena was leaning against the door jamb, waiting for her. Lo didn't waste her breath on good morning. "I'm sorry about last night, pulling you like that," she said.

"Good morning," said Helena, stepping forward to greet her, wrapping both arms around her and kissing her softly on the cheek. Lo tensed and pulled back. In the beginning, Helena had been one of the very few people she would allow to touch her. These days it was a case of anyone but Helena. It was totally fucked up, Lo knew that, but she couldn't help herself. Don't blame the long, hard years. Blame her mysterious body. No, blame her. Lo reached out for Helena's hands. They were bony and dry, like the rest of her. Her eyes were still the same, though, deep brown pools of wisdom and pain. Helena spoke gently, hands squeezing, eyes locked tight. She was a hard woman to avoid.

"What was all that crashing and banging? Is something bothering you? It would be normal to have conflicting emotions about your brother's strange return, you know."

Lo resented Helena's clichéd insight. She pulled her hands free, lowered her gaze to the top of Helena's thin, brown shoulder and said, "Oh, please—I dropped a glass."

Helena said, "You don't have to pretend with me. It's great that Will's back, but I know he let you down badly in the past. He may not have meant..."

"Leave it Helena, that's old stuff. I was over it years ago."

"Yes, but now he's back, and..."

"No buts—it's all good," said Lo, walking over to the stovetop and poking around in their old black skillet. "Great—hash browns—I'm starving. Should I serve myself?" She went to grab a plate from the drying rack.

Helena was emphatic. "No. We've been waiting to eat together. Will says you always sat down to a cooked breakfast together as kids. Your Dad liked a hearty breakfast, and he liked to spend time with his family, too. He was a big burly man, wasn't he? You and Will look more like the photos of your mother. Racehorses. You both have her sharp nose too. I'm assuming that's natural. Does he look very altered to you?"

"Not so much more than me, I guess. Just in different ways. He looks like he's been taking formaldehyde, and I look like I've been stung by a thousand alien bees."

"You're both beautiful," said Helena.

"I'm not really though," said Lo, "not inside. You know it. I know it."

"You're struggling at a crossroad," said Helena, "that's all."

"I don't want to discuss that shit this morning," replied Lo.

Helena didn't respond. Instead she slipped away through the doors to the dining room, perhaps in search of plates, perhaps escaping Lo's mood. Lo poked harder at the potatoes. She hoped that Helena hadn't said anything to Will about his skipping her graduation all those years ago. No, she wouldn't do that. She had guessed right, though—the old betrayal had been on Lo's mind all night as she tossed and turned in a sweaty, alcohol-induced delirium.

It had taken her years to scrabble back after sacrificing her youth and her dreams to fucking Ben's onerous and expensive PhD on Japanese warrior culture. She had always found him so cultured and sensitive—before he graduated, dumped her, met someone else, and moved to Tokyo. So sorry, Lo-san. She'd grieved and moved on. Finally Lo had gotten around to focusing on Lo. At the ripe old age of 32, she had had her law degree in hand. After years of standing on the sidelines watching Will receive all the accolades, she finally had something to show for herself. The degree ceremony was held at the Beacon Theater in downtown New York City. Lo bought tickets for her family. It was a near perfect night— except for the one empty seat. Jake said it was out of Will's hands. Something big had come up at work. The Ruurdaan attack began two days later. No brother, no law degree, no future.

Lo kicked the door of the kitchen cupboard, rattling the glasses within. The glasses shivered and shimmered on their stems.

"Morning, Sis." Will ducked through the back door. His head brushed the kitchen ceiling. He was awkward in the kitchen space, hunched like a big man in a small car. In spite of herself, Lo laughed at his bizarre sarong, which she now saw was a tablecloth.

"Morning, Bro. Nice outfit, nice artwork."

"Thanks,"

"Those tats look expensive."

"Exorbitant. Painful too."

"The price of vanity. Did you sleep well?"

"Not really. I was semi-conscious for about six hours. I kept getting disturbed by animal noises and gun-shots. I know you told me on the way home that there are dangers lurking beyond the perimeters, but I thought you were just trying to scare me."

She had been trying to scare him; didn't mean it wasn't true.

"What you heard was the midnight-to-six shift doing their job," she replied. "We have traps everywhere, pods constantly thrash the boundaries with their beams, and we have sniper teams that do their thing all night, every night. It's safer than it sounds.

Every now and again something gets through, but rarely anything we can't handle."

Will smiled and said, "I'll tell you one thing I don't think I can handle any more, and that's the booze. Helena is trying to rustle up some old Ibuprofen for me. As soon as I put my bodcoz back on it will start to treat my ailments—headache, acid stomach, trembles—but I'm enjoying letting my skin breathe free right now. I haven't experienced sunlight in a very long time. I guess that's pretty obvious, right? I look like a ghoul."

Lo smiled. "You look better than I feel."

Will returned her smile and said, "I'm not entirely surprised. You were matching me drink for drink towards the end of the evening, and I think your last words before your pal Pat carried you home were 'gimme another fucking Jägermeister, bitch.'"

In spite of her age, Lo blushed like a foolish young woman. Then she remembered the party winding down, walking home together. She punched her brother in the arm.

"Very funny. We ran out of Jägermeister years ago. And you know I don't swear. Still. We drank a lot of rot-gut. My stomach is gurgling like a waste-tubical."

Will looked at her quizzically. "What's a waste-tubical?"

"The pod toilet. A swilling, sucking porta-potty that attaches to your ass and squirts liquid waste wherever you direct it, like fertilizer."

"Nice."

"Yeah, it sounds kind of like this…"

Lowering her eyes to the kitchen bench Lo began gently squeezing the ketchup bottle with her mind. Gurgle, sputter, squirt. The pair were still laughing when Helena stepped back into the room, clutching a large bottle of long-expired Ibuprofen. She lit up at the sight of them, as if she hadn't seen Lo laugh in a hundred years. Lo quit smiling.

"Who wants eggs?" Helena asked, gently pressing a couple of pills into Will's hand before sliding over to the stove and beginning to crack eggs into a bowl.

"Those potatoes smell so good I feel faint," said Will. "Adding eggs may send me over the sensory edge. I've hardly had any real food in months."

"What do eat in your new world?" asked Helena.

"Pretty similar stuff actually," said Will, "just alien varietals."

"Is everything similar on the...Orbitals...right?"

"Yeah, Orbitals," said Will. "Well of course there are quite a few differences—more technology, different landscapes, entirely different histories—but in the fundamental ways things are similar. Life centers on meeting our most basic needs. We have a services and commodities economy. Orbiters eat, drink, sleep, and shit just like every other human."

"How the hell can people who don't come from Earth be human?" asked Lo.

"There are many different human cultures out there. A hundred and nineteen that we have identified so far. Earthans are part of a big intergalactic family."

"*Earthans*," said Lo. "It's weird hearing you call us that. And the idea that we are not the only humans? How can that be? What about Darwin and Dawkins and that woman in Iceland who found the fish with the strands of proto-human DNA? I thought she proved we evolved out of the primordial soup. What are the odds of that happening a hundred and nineteen times?"

"Miniscule. But it happened all the same."

"So what? The Ruurdaans were right, and there is a God?" said Lo.

Will answered without hesitation. "I don't believe so. Nor do most Orbiters. They think we are the product of some kind of intelligent design. The most credible scientists say the planets were all seeded at the same time, then manipulated by the same hands at various times over the millennia. The question that keeps the researchers in business is *who* stirred all those petri dishes? And why did they stop stirring? *Did* they stop stirring? And where are they now? Are they going to show their faces one of these days?"

"If they show their faces here I'll fucking kill them," said Lo.

"Of course," said Helena, "and I'll roast their corpses to make bacon. That's how we do things around here. For now though, we'll have to make do with just potatoes and eggs." With a flourish she laid two steaming plates of breakfast on the table.

Lo ignored Helena. She flung herself down on a chair in front of one of the plates of food and started hungrily shoveling food into her mouth. Will waited while Helena dished up the last plate of food. They then sat down together. Lo saw her brother and her wife exchange knowing smiles. Annoying. Mouth still full, Lo began to lay out the day's plans. First she would take Will on a tour of Saugatuck. Then she would spend the afternoon tending to business while Will and Bob met with a long roster of women, as promised last night. After that, maybe dinner at the Mess. Lo still had plenty of her own questions for Will, but hopefully they could squeeze their talking in around the rest of their schedule. Will was agreeable, as she had expected.

"Okay, then" she said, scooping up the last of her eggs, throwing her silverware down and pushing her dirty plate away. "I'm ready to get going. How about you?"

Will said, "Almost. First I'd like to help Helena clean up. Then I'd like to quickly change into my bodcoz before we head out for the day. Fifteen minutes?"

"Make it ten. Don't forget sunscreen. It's going to be hot. Helena will get some for you. And you'll need your keys or whatever it is you use to unlock your orbicraft. We'll start there..."

Will, in the process of standing up from the table, stiffened and coughed.

"I'm sorry, but that's not possible."

Lo started, even though she had half-expected this. She had so badly hoped he would just take her on board and show her his ship.

But no, he was going to prove more loyal to a bunch of fucking aliens than to her. He *was* going to let her down.

Will extended his hands in apology, eyes screwed up in a plea. "Please don't take this the wrong way, Sis. It's not remotely personal. Nobody can board without approval. Bob and I have been bio-scanned and chipped. The ship knows us. However, even Bob has to be in the presence of an authorized crew member to board. It's a safety measure. The orbicraft will expel any unknown the minute they try to board. I wish I could override the system, but it's just not possible. I hope you understand..."

Lo cut him off. "Oh I understand alright. Yesterday I allowed you to come sailing into our town in a spaceship, welcomed you with open arms, virtually no questions asked, defended you to my people, and now you won't even let me see your ship."

Lo's anger was visibly rippling the air around her. The table began to rattle. She waited for Will to make more excuses, but it was Helena's voice that broke the tension.

"Give him a break," she said. "We err on the side of caution too. Think about your own response yesterday. Can't you understand why their ship would be protected?"

Lo breathed in. She had raised her fighting hand in anger, ready to—what? Fling her breakfast around the room? Break something else? Hurt her brother? She breathed out. Helena was right. Will's refusal rankled, and she was right to question it—but she understood strict security measures better than anyone. Carefully interlacing her hands, palms down, on the table, she stilled both herself and the quivering breakfast provisions.

"Fine," she said. "I won't throw you to the ferals for this. However, if *I* can't board your orbicraft then *you* can't board your orbicraft. Not until I say so. I'm beaming a message down to the dock as we speak. No one goes near that ship without my approval."

Lo squinted as if beaming. In truth she had given her orders last night. No access within fifty feet of the orbicraft for anyone but the technical crew who had spent the last ten hours trying to open it. She stopped squinting and looked at her brother.

"Just go and get ready, Will. It's almost 7:30. You're not the only thing…"

Suddenly Lo stopped talking and froze, listening intently. Gesturing to Will and Helena to get on the floor, she slipped her hand into the weapons glove on her hip. Then she carefully pushed the back door open and slipped out onto the deck, keeping her back to the wall. The noise had come from around the side of the house where the old driveway ended in a junkyard of pod parts and other old Ruurdaan equipment that Lo was yet to master. The crunch on the gravel was light but distinctive. Back pressed to the wooden boards of the cottage, Lo glided on almost airborne feet to the corner of the house. Surveying the area, she saw no obvious signs of disturbance. She continued down the side of the house, armed and ready. At the front corner, again, nothing. Lo began to wonder if she'd made a mistake. Then she heard the front door slowly creaking open. She shouted out, "Stay in the house. I've got this covered."

No reply. Lo reached into her holster and gloved her hand before leaping out of the shadows, up into the branches of a large red maple on the front lawn. Peering across to the porch, Lo saw that the front door was open, but the screen door was closed. All she could see through the dull gray mesh was the outline of two people, one with distinctively large and pale white feet. Someone pushed Will through the front door and out onto the porch, an outstretched arm wrapped around his neck, a brown hand holding a switch-blade to his carotid artery. The attacker was invisible behind Will's bulk.

Lo shouted from the tree. "Let him go, and I won't kill you."

"Stand down, or I'll kill *him*, said a mocking male voice.

It was a familiar voice. "Reid…?"

Lo watched her son push Will before him down the front porch steps. She sprang down onto the overgrown front lawn. About twenty feet separated them now. Lo kept her glove hand firmly pointed at the tanned brown hand and the knife. "Reid..."

"So much for the security round here. I found an Orbiter in our house."

"Take it easy, kiddo. That's my brother," she shouted back.

"Oh yeah," replied Reid, "and you're my fucking daddy."

Lo sighed, head pounding. Reid was not going to make this easy. She should know, she was the one who'd taught him how to stand his ground. Unfortunately, she wasn't about to give him a chance to do any harm this time—whether he liked it or not. She fired a careful, precise stream of energy at the glinting metal of Reid's knife. In under a second, the knife turned molten around the edges, burning Will's bare neck as well as Reid's raised hand. It was a calculated action. The damage wouldn't be so bad, and they did have a doctor on hand.

"Why are you always testing me, Reid?" she said tightly.

"You should be praising me for what I did," Reid shouted as he slumped forward, onto the ground, pulling Will down with him. He thrust his injured hand into the cool, dewy grass. Will rolled onto his front and did the same with his neck.

Lo didn't rush to their aid. She left that to Helena, who flew out the front door with her medical kit the minute Reid dropped his knife. Instead she flung herself up and over the porch railing and into one of the damp Adirondack chairs growing up out of the long grass. She took a moment to breathe in the early morning air, feeling it fizzle as it went all the way down. What a start to the day. First Helena. Then Will. Now Reid had made her lose her cool for the third time this morning—and the umpteenth time this year—giving him even more justification for hating his authoritarian other-mother. No doubt Helen was also upset by her handling of the situation, and preparing to say so in some well-meaning way. Who knew what Will would make of the extended family dynamic. Lo didn't really care. A lot more was at stake here than minor injuries and wounded feelings. If everyone under her protection survived another day, then Lo thought she could feel pretty damned good about how she was living her life.

6

Will couldn't believe that Lo had burned him and Reid—and for nothing—because any first year psych student could tell the kid wasn't going to use that knife. Actually, Will had been rather enjoying his rugged embrace with the young Tarzan before Lo came charging to the rescue. The smell of him! Damp, dark earth. The color of him! Deep redwood brown. Those amber eyes, bottomless with suspicion. Right now he was squinting at Will like some backwater homophobe. It was textbook; the macho knife-waving, the young hunter get-up, the simmering anger towards the two moms. Poor confused young warrior. What was a young man's role in this Sapphic super culture? Seriously. Will sympathized with the kid.

He and Reid both lay splayed across the grass. Helena treated his burns sparingly with a rusty tube of Walgreens burn cream, apologizing that medicines were in short supply. Will was vaguely surprised to find that Lo couldn't just wave her hand and heal him. Not omnipotent then. That was a relief, given her capricious temperament. Will wasn't entirely sure why she seemed so suspicious of him all of a sudden. They'd always gotten along so well. He'd had a way with his baby sister and had enjoyed how much she idolized him. Now he had the feeling she was still angry with him over the way they left things thirty-three years ago. Could a woman really hold a grudge over something like that for so long? He was an ivy league psychiatrist, and he still couldn't answer that question. All he knew was that in his mind he couldn't have done it any different...

Two nights before the Ruurdaan invasion, he and Jake had been scheduled to attend Lo's graduation in New York City. At the last minute Will had been asked to stay back to review reports of a strange mass of spheres approaching Earth and advise on how to prepare for a probable first encounter. He had called Jake to say he'd been put on a special project and wouldn't be home for a couple of days. He asked Jake to pass along his apologies to Lo and the family. He said nothing about the spheres. His job required a high level of discretion. Later, in the shuttle, he had thought about them all celebrating without him, blissfully oblivious to what was coming. He was glad he'd said nothing and allowed Lo to enjoy her moment of glory. Boy had that girl earned it.

Lo had always been smart and tenacious, the kind of person who saw things through—even if that meant straggling in from a regatta two hours after everyone else—and she should have been a defense attorney, like she'd planned, by the age of twenty-three. Instead, that sponging pseudo-intellectual Ben had talked her into working as a paralegal while he took ten years to finish his PhD in Japanese literature. Ben had dumped Lo the day he got the post-doc in Tokyo, said he needed a fresh start. More like a cute Japanese girlfriend. Apoplectic with rage at the betrayal, Lo had actually asked Will to have Ben put on the DHS watch-list. He didn't do it. Then she fell apart and spent a year having unsafe sex with men she met in pick-up bars. Will knew all this because she always told him and Jake everything. Jake had really cared. It was Jake who persuaded Lo to try for her law degree again, told her it was never too late to chase your dreams. He was right, too, everyone's beloved Jake. Lo was on her way back up when the spheres hit.

And although those spheres had taken her down, she'd surely clawed her way back up again here in Saugatuck as well. Mayor, no less. Girl done good. Will hoped he might be able to turn her power and influence to his advantage, by building his hometown into a friendly entry-point for future Orbiter settlers. Admittedly that fantasy was a long way off at this point. Perhaps he should just settle for making sure she didn't hate him when she found out what he had planned. That was the whole point of spending today doing whatever she wanted of him—building up that little bit more trust with these women, winning them over to the idea that

Orbiters could be good people too. The rendezvous with Retske up in Madison would just have to wait another day.

In all honesty, after what he'd heard from Lo, Will was dreading meeting his fellow settlement program colleague. No doubt she blamed him for the trouble with the Unans. She *had* told him she thought they would struggle to adapt. Like he'd said at the time, though, why would it be especially hard for a Unan? What Orbiter wouldn't struggle to adapt here? And given the fact that Una was a cross between a crumbling Beijing and a large multistory parking garage, Will had imagined the Unans would be grateful for the luxuriant natural beauty of New England—all those creeks, coves, and rivers, all those lovely flowers and trees and cute animals. He'd clearly imagined wrong, just like he'd imagined the situation with the surviving women completely wrong.

The surviving women were a genuine shock. He'd heard something about the wiring but nothing about the special powers. He'd been expecting desperate creatures who would weep with joy at the sight of a few strong men. If Lo's group were in any way representative, then he suddenly understood why thousands of Orbiters were struggling in settlements across the globe. They weren't wanted, certainly not if they started trying to take over too forcefully. Even Janine, the blonde woman who had opted not to shoot them upon landing, had said to him, "I'm totally psyched to have some fresh male company—just as long as you all keep on behaving like gentlemen." Then Lo came around the corner firing lightening out of her fingers. No wonder Reid was so fucked up and angry. That kid needed a male ally, one who couldn't restrain him with just their eyes. Well, Will needed an ally too. Perhaps a point of leverage existed there...

As soon as Helena finished treating his stinging neck, Will leaped to his feet and said, "Let's not make too much of this little misunderstanding, guys. It's not a big deal, not to me anyway. Reid's response was totally understandable. Guy comes home to find a weird-looking stranger in his house, of course he's going to rush to protect his family. He did that job well, too—had me immobilized in seconds."

Will looked over and saw Reid shake back his long brown locks as he lifted his head and shoulders from the ground. The kid was paying attention.

Lo called out from her position slumped in the Adirondack chair, "Hey, don't indulge the little punk. I told him you were my brother. He should have let you go."

Will replied, "Sorry Lo, but he has a point. Saying that I'm your brother doesn't make it true. Maybe you were under duress. Reid was right to stay defensive."

Reid had pulled himself up into sitting position now and was glaring at Lo.

"Hear that, Lo," he said. "Even the freakazoid says I did the right thing. Stop interfering with my decisions. You're not always right. You're just always lecturing."

Will laughed. "No kidding. When we were kids she lectured her Barbies."

Lo struggled not to crack a smile as she said, "I was teaching them to play nice with each other. I didn't want them turning into mean girls. They needed my guidance."

Will rolled his enhanced eyes in unnatural circles, a trick that was worth nothing at home but gold dust here. They all laughed now.

Reid offered Will his hand. "Sorry about scaring you there, Stretch."

It was an unoriginal joke, but Will smiled with all his teeth as he shook the offered hand. "Funny guy." He helped Reid back up onto his feet, slouching to de-emphasize the height differential. "That's one hell of a knife you've got there."

"Yeah, Lo gave me the blade for my sixteenth birthday last year. She owes me, now that she's melted it—and I'd actually prefer a gun. You should tell her a guy needs a gun if he's to protect anyone properly." Reid paused for a half-second to enjoy the looks on both his mothers' faces before continuing. "If I'd known who you were, I wouldn't have... I mean how was I to know you were my uncle. Step-uncle. Whatever. Lo told me all about you when I was a kid, about Cape Canaveral and the astronauts, but I always imagined this dead guy..."

Will kinked his fair, spikey head. "Don't I look kind of like a dead guy?"

Reid laughed. "Nah, you don't look *that* bad."

Will's laugh was sincere. "So are we all going on this tour or what?"

Reid gave a cool little nod.

Lo said, "I don't know. If you still won't show me your ship..."

"I thought we already agreed," said Will. "You can't go on the orbicraft, I can't go on the orbicraft. I'm fine with that for now. We can negotiate something else later."

Lo shrugged. "Maybe, maybe not. Let's see how things go..."

Will hoped he had bought himself enough time to develop a new plan.

"Much as I'm loving the breeze, I can't go about in this tablecloth all day," he said, moving towards the beat-up steps of the cottage. "I need complete sun protection at this point in time. Can you give me two minutes to throw on my bodcoz,"

"There's some ancient sunscreen in the bathroom cupboard. Grab that for your face," said Helena. "And throw the tablecloth in the washing basket. I'll wash it while you're out. Perhaps you'll want it again tonight. I'll redress your wound then too..."

Was there a question in her motherly concern?

"He doesn't need any of that, Mom," interjected Reid.

"Thanks, Helena, but there's really no need," said Will, fleeing through the rusting screen door. "I'll leave it in my room and use it again when I get back."

Four minutes later he reemerged onto the porch—safely ensconced in his enhanced and reinforced bodcoz, operations control still attached and working. He wouldn't be taking the coz off again in a hurry—certainly not around his pumped and trigger-happy sister and her cronies. He thought he still knew Lo—and how to play her—but then before yesterday he thought he knew a lot of things. It wasn't that he doubted himself, just that he suspected absolutely nothing was going to be as easy as he'd expected.

7

The three of them made their way up the back garden, past the vegetable patch, and through a dense thicket carpeted with old leaves. The thicket ended at a six-foot green hedge, which stretched into the visible distance.

"You still haven't built that gate you promised," Lo said to Reid.

"Because we don't need it," replied Reid.

With that, he took a running jump at a pole wedged into the ground, grabbed it at shoulder height and vaulted the hedge like a pro-athlete. Lo looked at Will, grinned, then jumped—up, down, up, and over the tall scraggly boxwood—like her feet were on springs. Will was considering his options when he felt a force trying to pull him through the air. Lo was doing her thing again—without bothering to ask if that was okay with him. Feeling the bodcoz automatically resist his sister's assault, Will touched his chest and lowered the defensive shielding. Lo gave one more small tug and Will felt himself pulled roughly over the hedge. She landed him off-kilter on his feet.

"Slippery character," Lo laughed. Her eyes weren't laughing; they were thinking.

Will said, "Thanks for the lift."

On the other side of the hedge, Will had expected to see another backyard and more houses like Lo's running down another crumbling and overgrown street. Instead, he found himself at the top of a gently sloping park. Lo caught his confusion and smiled.

"Your memory is correct. There used to be about twenty cottages on this street, small houses on big blocks of land. We knocked them down to make a safe nature reserve, my favorite of all our soft projects. There's even a creek, a man-made tributary—see over there—it runs into a pond and fountain much closer to HQ."

Will understood the pride in her voice. He whistled as they made their way through a landscape of wild woods and man-made arboretums, dark valleys and sunny meadows. He saw a group of women digging in new flowerbeds and a couple of others paddling in the shallows of the artificial creek. Will took heart from their friendly waves.

After a few minutes walking on soft dirt paths, the impressive neo-colonial features of HQ came into view, the river glinting in the distance. Slowly the gardens became increasingly formal, flattening out into a more typical suburban park, crisscrossed with brick paths and dotted with benches, statues, swings, and other garden features. A small amphitheater had been dug into a shallow grassy incline, complete with eight curved rows of concrete bleachers. Images of summer repertory theater, cover-band concerts, and minor local protests flickered through Will's mind. Between the amphitheater area and HQ lay Riverside Avenue, still a flat and serviceable road, yet eerie without any traffic, just one battered old jeep visible alongside the Boat House's old service entrance.

Instead of heading toward HQ, Lo led the group right down Riverside Avenue, toward what used to be a favorite haunt of his — the strip-mall that backed onto the river between the Boat House and the Saugatuck Bridge. In Will's day the strip had been home to a handful of unremarkable businesses: a take-out pizza joint, a cheesy gift shop, the printing and photo place, a veterinary clinic, and the dry-cleaners. The gift-shop and the print-shop had been razed. The other buildings looked like they were being used for storage. The Mansion Clam House was still on the corner. Once a local institution that served obscene portions of lobster and steak, Lo said it was now a clothing exchange. All the strip buildings were still surrounded by parking space, the old white lines still visible. Only now, instead of cars fighting for every square inch of tarmac, about thirty big glass bubbles, each the size of a large helicopter stripped of all appendages, crowded the space. The strip-mall had become a pod lot.

At no point in any of his mission briefings had Will been told that Earthan women could fly the Ruurdaans' old pods. The first he knew of it was yesterday when he saw Lo's sidekick—the big homely woman called Pat—flying around in one. Then he saw the pod on Lo's driveway. It was pretty impressive really. He whistled in appreciation.

"Cool yeah," said Reid, coming up close by his side. "You should see them when they're all up in the air at once. And the things they can do: back-hoe, mold glass, power an electrical generator, shoot these weird pulse-fields. Want to see inside one?"

"Absolutely," said Will.

"Not happening," snapped Lo.

Reid looked confused.

Lo said, "Didn't you hear what I said this morning? Will won't let us see inside his ship—so we're definitely not showing him inside ours."

"I *can't* show you my orbicraft," said Will. "You need special ID."

"So how did the Orbiters rescue you?" said Reid.

"Um, they created an ID for me on-site," said Will. "We could do that for you too, but only in the special transit unit of our explorer vessel. It's parked about a seven hour ride away. Could we get there via pod?" He was banking on that being impossible.

"I don't think so," replied Reid, visibly deflated. "We don't fly them much higher than helicopters. And anyway, only the strong-wired can fly them. And not even all..."

Lo cut Reid off. "We could take thousands of pods into space if we wanted, but why would we? We're good here. Out there in space is where the assholes live."

If she was trying to big-up their air defense capabilities, she was wasting her time. He had already worked out that not all the women in Saugatuck were super-powered—otherwise yesterday they would have all been more terrifying and less terrified. He had also just summed up her little air force: thirty pods, parking space for forty. That didn't necessarily indicate the full number of fliers in town, but it was a pretty good clue. The women were well-defended against small attacks but would struggle against larger and stronger forces. Lo was right to be paranoid about security, but Will didn't think this was the time to tell her so. Hell, no. He diverted the conversation by pointing away from the pod-park—beyond the old bridge over the Saugatuck river—and toward the group of rambling interconnected wooden shacks that once comprised the Saugatuck General Store.

"I kissed my first guy there," he said. "Greg, the deli manager. Out back in the cool room. He didn't come out until after he had three kids. What's the place now?"

"It's still the general store," replied Lo. "Eight hours a day, seven days a week. Hand-milled flour, fresh butter and cheese, seasonal fruit and veg. Nothing exotic—the odd can—but everything we need. We even keep frozen meat and fish in stock. We're proud of how we produce and preserve our own food. It wasn't always like this…"

Will could imagine. As they walked toward the old building, along another stretch of well-maintained tarmac, he wondered out loud. "How do you get the power for lights and freezers? Is that something you can do with your wires, generate electricity?"

Lo smiled. "Enough to run a town generator? No. We were left with some small emergency generators, but they could never meet all our needs, particularly in winter. We ended up coming to an arrangement with the Norwalk sub-station. The Ruurdaans spared a number of utility workers—about thirty of them in Norwalk—just as long as they kept the power coming. After the occupation ended those guys cut deals with quite a few communities around here. Power for food and weed—that's us. Power for booze and hard drugs—that's some other bad-assed motherfuckers. Power for electric sex—that's for those who don't have anything else to give. It's not a beautiful barter-system. Forget the eco-dream. It's a grubby little business."

Reid had been walking alongside, listening and nodding like he knew it all but was letting Lo enjoy telling it. Now he suddenly began waving wildly in the direction of the old Saugatuck Bridge. A solid ten-foot iron gate stood in front of the bridge, something that hadn't been there in Will's day. Next to the gate, was an old lifeguard's post, set into a concrete block which was in turn set within a tall wooden shelter structure. A pod perched on top of the whole ugly mess, nestled there like a snow globe on a stand. Will had seen the peculiar structure as he flew in the day before and laughed. He wasn't laughing anymore. Sitting inside the makeshift observation post was a thirty-something woman with a crime-channel face—pitted skin and indistinct putty features. Will recognized her from the night before—finger pointing, face scrunched in anger.

"That's Marie," said Reid. "She's like my second mum." The kid studiously avoided looking at Lo. "She's married to old man Nunn. He's technically my Dad."

Will tried not to show his shock. Lo pursed her lips but said nothing.

"James and Marie Nunn? Used to run Nunn's Nursery?"

Reid answered, "That's where we grow most of our food, all the stuff that can't take frost, plus stuff we want in winter. And our pot. How do you know about it?"

Will tried not to smirk at the thought of Nunn's Nursery having morphed into a pot farm. It used to specialize in prize-winning roses named after Republican first ladies.

"When I was a bit younger than you, I used to sail and swim with James Nunn. Our gang even got tattoos together. We went our separate ways when we went to college. He got into some kind of trouble, cheating or gambling, something like that, and came home to get himself together. That's when he started working for his Dad. The local girls all thought he was the second coming of Brad Pitt."

"Who's Brad Pitt?"

"He was a baby-faced actor with flared nostrils."

"You're kidding me?"

"No, I'm not. Around here Marie Levitt was considered lucky to have landed such a treasure. His good looks, her money; they were minor local celebrities. You know, when I saw Marie last night, I didn't recognize her. She's looking pretty tough these days."

"She is pretty tough—lucky for my Dad. She saved him from the Ruurdaans. Wrapped him in foil to deflect their sensors, hid him in a boat just off Block Island, then used herself as a distraction. Marie's good people. She's been teaching me how to climb shit this summer. It's amazing the things you can climb if you just know how."

With that, Reid was off and running toward the ten-foot iron gates protecting the bridge. He shimmied up the gate like there were footholds instead of a sheer metal plane, grabbed hold of the ledge, and straddled the top of the bridge. At that distance he made Will think of Mowgli, a childhood hero. Marie cheered like a mom, but Reid's eyes were fixed firmly on him. Will gave a loud hoot of admiration. As the kid began his descent, Will became aware of Marie staring at him. Once she had his attention, she diverted her glance to her raised finger, which she then pointed at the ground in front of his feet and began wiggling like she was counting heads very fast. In response, the pavement rippled and raised up in a buckled line, as if a line of submerged fireworks were going off. Will leaped back as tarmac began to hit his legs like shrapnel.

Lo shouted up to Marie, "Very cute, but cut it out already, and clean it up."

Marie laughed roughly and moved her hand back and forth as if over a lump of clay, pressing the pavement and earth back into an even smoother surface than before.

"I think she's trying to impress you," joked Lo.

Judging from the dents the flying tarmac had made in the legs of his bodcoz, Will thought Marie Nunn was trying to do something entirely different.

"Let's go see something else," he said.

8

Reid worked hard to keep up with Lo and Will. Fit as he was, his legs were not long like his uncle's or super-sprung like Lo's. Just one more downside to being a natural. The three of them were walking super-fast down Riverside Avenue, in the direction of the old train station. This was one of the few places in town where a road was still a road, the sidewalk still a sidewalk. Riverside Avenue led from HQ to the old Exit 17 checkpoint, which was pretty much where the perimeter fence started and also his personal boundary, at least as far as Lo and his mom knew.

Reid had been past the checkpoint plenty of times on dares. Some interesting abandoned houses remained beyond safe territory, way bigger than in Saugatuck and often with better loot. Just a month or so back, he and Ned had scored a spear-gun. It was too bad all the beaches were off-limits; he would love to go spear-fishing in the Sound. Perhaps one day before the summer ended he and Ned could get out past the river checkpoint and sneak in some spear-fishing. He should suggest taking Will on a boat tour then take it too far. Reid had heard how it was between Will and Lo. The guy might appreciate doing something unauthorized.

Right now, though, Lo was totally in charge—frog-marching them past an old wooden commerce building with the windows all boarded up and a faded sign over the entry-way that said, "Saugatuck Artisanal Dairy."

Reid called out, "Hey Lo, aren't you going to show him the dairy?"

Lo didn't even slow down as she said, "He's not interested in that."

Will stopped. "Sure I am. Don't tell me the artisanal cheese guy survived. He sure made a mighty brie. He also used to teach weekend workshops on sustainability and local food sourcing, so I guess it's possible he found a way to survive."

It was all news to Reid, and who cared anyway. "I don't know about that—hardly any guys survived and none of them make cheese—but this place *is* still a dairy. My friend Ned lives in an apartment upstairs. His mum's the dairy manager."

Lo had turned back to join them. "Let's just keep going," she said. "What I really wanted to show you is a couple blocks down, the area around the old station."

"But it's just a pile of garbage now," said Reid.

"Exactly," replied Lo, marching forward, with the two guys trailing her once more. "I want to show him some of the less wonderful things in town. That station used to be this little town's everything, you know. There must have been, what, Will, a couple thousand people who took the train to and from Manhattan every day?"

"At least," said Will, who was staring at every little thing. "Maybe four or five thousand. Mostly guys in suits. Some women in suits. All pretending they loved taking the train to work."

Reid had heard about the old days and how Saugatuck was really just a slice of nowheresville between Exit 17 and the real town of Westport. Lo said it was where rich-people-with-mansions-and-beach-houses and wannabe-rich-people-who-owed-their-ass-to-the-bank bought supplies and stored their boats and went to places called dive bars and got drunk with the locals after work. Mom said it had been a cute little village where people pulled off the highway for great fish and even better Margaritas. Reid wasn't sure who was right. He had seen pictures of home when it had been packed full of wooden houses that were really businesses called *commerces* doing things that Reid didn't totally understand, like vacation rentals and portfolio management. Most of them had been turned into firewood by now, so they can't have been too important.

"Is it better now or how it was then?" Reid asked Will.

"Hard to say," replied Will. "It's a lot greener and quieter now. No buzz from the interstate." He pointed to the low hill of rubble that used to be a highway overpass.

Lo spoke up. "We dozed part of it straight away to stop uninviteds crossing the river. Then we kept going because it was fun and that thing was a goddamned eyesore."

Will smiled. "It was all onion farms around here once upon a time. Looks a bit that way again, semi-rural, prettier than I remember."

Onion farms? Onions just grew wild everywhere. In this part of town the vegetable plots were filled with important food—potatoes, yams, pumpkins, spinach—and animal yards everywhere. If you didn't know better you'd think that's all that happened here. They were almost past the old Futura labs building on the far side of the road now, but Lo still hadn't said a word, just like she hadn't said anything about the gas station, which looked like it was closed but was actually something they were all proud of, still running on supplies they managed to squeeze out from places in the wilderness once in a while. Mom said that most survivors would kill for their resources.

Suddenly Reid got it. Lo didn't want to tell Will everything even though he was her brother and she had defended him both last night and this morning. That was Lo for you: schizoid, always changing the rules to suit herself. He wouldn't say anything, though, not about the gas, or the labs and especially not the Inn. He had been taking the oath of silence since he was ten and had six personal rewards to prove it. He was wearing one of them now; a special trust watch called a Rolex that had the date and the time and a count-down function and never failed. Right now it was 10:37.

Reid saw Will starting to look all curious at Mom's research building, so he distracted him. "I bet you never walked down this road before. I bet you always drove. Nobody walked anywhere, right? They were all fat. We learned about it in school. I've only driven once or twice myself, in empty cars we found with some gas left in them. Driving is awesome."

"Awesome is right. I used to drive a Mercedes convertible. My blue baby. Top down at the beach on a warm night. Beyond awesome. I'll never forget that car."

"Who needs a car when you've got a pod," said Lo.

Why did she always have to be better than everyone else? She wasn't better than him in every way After all, naturals could do some things that Lo couldn't—like have a proper baby. Reid wasn't exactly thinking about that yet but he planned on having about ten kids when he was ready. A *real* happy family.

They passed through the road-sized cutting in the rubble of the overpass and emerged out the other side. To their left, pasture ran down to the river, which was booby-trapped from here to the Sound. Reid knew a lot about how to make a good booby trap. Straight ahead was the dump. It stretched for almost half a mile from here to the fence and the Exit 17 checkpoint: twisted piles of wire and metal, rusting cars, old baths and toilets, great mounds of glass. Massive.

Will said, "Wow, that's quite the collection you got there."

"There was no point in saving the station," said Reid as they turned away from the river and began walking along Station Road toward Exit 17. "Trains are a thing of the past, not the future." Then realizing the words sounded like someone else's he added, "Junk's got to go somewhere."

"We needed a place close by where we could keep reusable junk," said Lo. "We drop our waste into a pit way back of this pile and press it deeper with our pod beams. Nice huh? We call it alien composting. We learned it from the little silver people."

"It's not disgusting like the old landfills then? I can't smell a thing. Nice work."

"No need for congratulations. It's not so hard. We just clean up after ourselves. It's not the same everywhere though. Some people can't clean up, and others can't be bothered. They don't see the point of looking after this devastated planet."

"How about because our generation doesn't want to inherit a shit-sty," said Reid.

He didn't like how Will and Lo smiled at each other. It wasn't a stupid comment.

"Let's show him the lumber yard," said Reid. "We can walk down to the checkpoint and back around that way. I love the lumber yard. It's one of our most interesting places."

"You know your grandfather liked to tinker with wood," said Will.

"Yeah but he's not my biological grandfather, so it's not in my blood," said Reid. He'd been thinking about that a bit. Lo was not his biological mother, so Will was not his biological uncle. More like a step-uncle. Better than no uncle at all though.

"So you don't like to make things, fix things? You seem like you might…"

Reid was glad that Will could tell he was pretty handy. "Actually, I do like to build stuff. I'm thinking of being a carpenter as well as a security deputy. Maybe later I could show you some of my projects. I helped build out the dock last summer, and me and my friends are working on a deck for the rock pool up river. Then there's the stuff I did on the river checkpoint…"

He turned to Lo. "Hey Lo, how about I show Will the river checkpoint later."

"Absolutely not," said Lo, super sharp. "There's nothing of interest out there."

He should have thought before he spoke. The checkpoint was close to the Inn. The lights might glow or something. Maybe there'd be noise. Shit. He touched his Rolex.

"Yeah, you're right, it is kind of boring," he said.

Lo looked relieved. Will seemed oblivious, just busy looking at everything.

"Maybe it would be more fun to see the rock pool," Reid added. "You can swim."

"That sounds great," said Lo. "Will would have loved that when he was young."

"Sure," replied Will. "A swim sounds wonderful. Space is so dry."

They had reached the end of Station Road where the Exit 17 perimeter fence began. Reid could tell that Will was amazed by the fence, cars melded three-high and stretching in a long line on either side of the huge wooden checkpoint—which Reid also thought was impressive—like a massive tree fort on top of a double set of gates. The fence was the big deal though. At school they had learned about the Perimeter project—five years and exactly 4,895 cars. The fence was over two miles long from end to end, and shaped like a tire lever. It went from a little cove just beyond Exit 17 all the way through the woods to the checkpoint on the old post road. The rest of Saugatuck's borders were shaped by the Westport shallows, the river, and the Sound. The place was pretty close to impenetrable, excepting by air. It was also pretty small. Reid wished they'd built the fence out further, made the town bigger. It wasn't like they didn't have enough cars.

"How does the fence work? Is it just a barrier?" Will asked Reid.

He was about to explain when Lo raised her arm and pointed at the fence. Electric sparks flew from every surface. A slight burning smell hung in the air. Lo waved up to the pod that was parked on the checkpoint roof. "Only me," she shouted, like the duty guard hadn't seen her coming ten minutes ago and she hadn't been blinking out messages the whole time. Someone with spiky red hair waved back, probably Ruby. Reid had tried it on with Ruby a while back, but she'd just laughed at him. He still liked her anyway.

"Are you kidding me? It's totally electrified," Reid said. "There has to be someone who can channel their electrics into metal on duty at all times. There are also ten checkpoints. They're all slightly different so nobody can learn to get past them too easy."

Lo gave him a look.

"What, you *showed* him."

Annoyed, Reid ran for the tower and clambered up the ladder on this side. It was virtually impossible to climb the other side— even a great climber like Reid—so he only took trips when someone was on duty who wouldn't tell Lo that they had let him back in. Going outside was worth any lecture that a softie like Janine or Leslie could give him. He didn't plan on living his entire life stuck within a couple of boring square miles. Happy to be up on deck, he waved back down to Lo and Will.

"Get down from there," Lo shouted. "It's not a play house."

Reid ignored her and looked straight out over the perimeter fence to the broken and abandoned I95 exit ramp. Not even a jeep could drive down that these days. To his left lay the Norwalk Road. That was the road his mom took once a month when she did her medical clinic. Lo wanted her to stop after what happened to Dina. Reid understood why she wouldn't. His mom had a lot to give. Being a valuable member of a community wasn't all about security and flying and heavy lifting.

Something caught his eye. It was a small bristly thing, mottled brown all over with sharp little ears and a blunt snout, sniffing something on the ground at the edge of the old road. It looked like a puppy of some kind.

"Hey, there's a pup," he shouted down to Lo and Will.

"I said get down from there," repeated Lo.

Reid saw the trees around the Norwalk road suddenly start shivering. Lo must have told Ruby to thrash them in case a feral pack lurked nearby. No wild dogs started howling though. They weren't usually out during the day—which is why the dog squad worked nights. As far as he could tell, the puppy was alone. Maybe its pack had all been killed during the night. Reid was so tempted to go and pick it up. Of course Lo would tell him off if he went outside, even for just a few minutes, but with Will there she might go easy, just to look nicer than she really was. He knew he shouldn't—but the puppy wasn't more than fifty feet from the checkpoint. Ruby had his back. It would be fine. Reid climbed over the railing and dropped down onto the road.

Down on the road he took it easy, gently whispering to the frightened puppy, which looked like it might have hurt its paw. That was no surprise. Broken glass was everywhere along the exit ramp. They'd put it there specifically to hurt feral things. Reid tried coaxing the puppy out. It only looked about two months old, fragile and shaky. He'd love to take it home. Lo didn't like having dogs around, said their noise and smell attracted the ferals, but she let a few lucky people keep them because his mom said a pet was a normal thing to want, and didn't she want people to feel normal every now and again. So his mom would definitely allow it, and she did still win *some* of the battles at home. Making up his mind, Reid crept over and took the puppy's warm body in his right hand. It whimpered a little but didn't bite or anything.

He turned and looked up, waving at Ruby to open the gate. Lo and Will had climbed up onto the observation deck now, the same place he'd been a few moments ago. Reid smiled up at them. "It's friendly," he shouted. "I don't think it's feral yet. C'mon Lo, let me have him, her, I don't know, let me check." As he went to turn the puppy over in his hands he heard a rush of sound from the tangle of vegetation further down the old exit ramp. Snarling, growling, the whoosh of bodies passing through brush. He knew he had about two seconds. Shit, no switchblade. He pulled his penknife from his holster and began backing up toward the big metal gate.

"Ferals!" he yelled.

The brush immediately began thrashing. The fence gave off sparks. Lo leaped to the ground by his side and flung him behind her. He fell to the ground but managed to maintain his grip on both puppy and knife. He saw the flash of Lo's glove and heard the whimper of the first animal to go down. He knew that Lo needed time to recharge between energy bursts. He leaped to his feet ready to help defend her. She flung herself in front of him again, this time raising her right foot to kick out at a pair of snarling beasts that were almost upon them. One crashed back into the pack. The other sank its bared yellow teeth into Lo's arm. Reid slashed at it with his knife as Lo tensed her arm and flung it away. It slammed whimpering into the electrified car fence. Nothing else came, except the sensation of pulsing from above. Ruby was creating a temporary air barrier at the same time as she fired from her glove. One by one the ferals were going down, yet they didn't seem to want to stop coming.

Lo shouted at him, "Get rid of the puppy."

This time Reid didn't hesitate to obey her order. He threw the puppy back to the pack, who were momentarily distracted. Lo took the opportunity to shoot one more before Reid felt a beam turn the air around them to Jell-O and begin sucking them up toward safety. It was back-up, another pod come to assist. When their bodies reached the height of the observation deck Lo stretched out and grabbed the railing, pulling herself onto the deck. Then she reached into the beam and pulled Reid over too. Together, they fell back onto the wooden floor in a scrambled heap, almost taking Will down with them.

Lo was winded, but she raced over to the side of the deck and continued shooting at the pack. The wild dogs were now throwing themselves repeatedly against the car wall, seemingly oblivious to the electricity, which continued to throw them back. One by one she, Ruby, and the pod above shot them. The last five or so finally ran away, leaving twelve bodies at the foot of the gates. Reid saw the puppy limping around in the dead bodies, maybe looking for its own mother.

"You still want that puppy, Reid?" said Lo.

Reid wasn't quite sure if she was being sarcastic or not. Her tone was kind of unclear but she had begun raising her arm. Then he heard Will say "No," as he reached out to grab Lo's arm. Lo just flicked him out of the way, finished raising her glove arm and fired. The puppy's head thudded into the ground like a bag of water slamming into sand. Reid shouted, "How could you?" Lo ignored him and began blinking and screwing up her face as she messaged.

Reid saw the backup pod scoop up the body and turn to take it to the waste pit. Lo turned and stared at him, eyes blazing. She said, "Next week you're working two nights on the feral squad, Reid. Then maybe you'll get it. Now, let's get back to HQ."

Will and Reid both stared at the ground, avoiding an argument, another lecture.

After they had all climbed down from the lookout tower and begun their walk back to HQ—Lo wrapping and unwrapping a strip of her shirt around the wound on her arm as she pointed out the lumber-yard, the equipment supply store, the cannery, and various other town highlights—Reid looked over at Will and gave him a nod. He'd seen him try to stop Lo from hurting the puppy. Maybe Orbiters were alright after all.

9

It was only midday but they were all hot, sweaty, and tired by the time they got to Janine's condo. It was located in the Riverside View complex. Will could still remember the brouhaha over that place, which was located right next to the Boat House on the site of the old VFW building. The veterans had gotten a much nicer space in the municipal complex upriver, but it was not what most of them wanted. There had been a lot of foul-mouthed graffiti as The View went up. It didn't deter buyers though; all the condos were sold before completion, which as Will recalled had been scheduled for around the time the attacks began.

Janine answered the door to her ground-floor condo wrapped in a sheet.

Lo brushed straight by her, saying, "You're on security duty, not booty call."

Will caught a sly grin from Reid as they both followed. Inside the soft-featured space they found Bob lying on a huge canvas sofa, devoid of bodcoz or any other covering. He had the decency to grab one of the gold velvet cushions and place it across his groin, covering the bare minimum. Will noted once again that the guy didn't have a single gem on his skinny hairless pink chest—too poor to afford even the most basic enhancements. Luckily for him, some good things come cheap. Bob reeked of sex and pot. Will wondered for the thousandth time which stupid bureaucrat had decided to send a half-witted drug-offender on this mission.

"Hey y'all," drawled Bob, "Want to join the party?"

Lo replied by flipping the sofa, tipping Bob out of view.

"Hose him off and have him up at my place in ten minutes," she said, addressing nobody in particular as she strode back out through the front door.

"Your place?" asked Will, as they headed back across Riverside Avenue and up the broken old road to Lo's place. "I'd thought we'd be going to HQ next."

"You have interviews this afternoon, remember?"

"Won't they be at HQ?"

"No," replied Lo, "We can manage at home."

She was keeping him away from her command operations at HQ. Most important of all, she was keeping him away from his ship.

"No problem," he said. "I just want to build some trust between us."

"Then let me see the inside of your ship," replied Lo. "Prove you're really alone."

"You're kidding me, right? Of course we're alone. The orbicraft is small and cramped. But that's not the point, is it? And Lo, I already told you..."

"I know what you already told me, and I know you're lying. *I know you*, Will, and I hear it in your voice. I just don't know what you're lying about, or why."

"I'm no—"

She cut him off. "Oh, spare me..."

They walked on in silence.

As they neared the house, Will saw that big Pat was busy lining up a small crowd of fifty-odd women on the front lawn. Some remained standing; others were taking the opportunity to relax in the thick grass. At first glance Will was reminded of music festivals and farmer's markets: happy messy hair, honest scrubbed faces, unpainted lips, and unapologetically hairy bodies. However, when he looked closer the picture warped. Some of the women were partygoers he recognized from last night. In the bright light of day they had lost their candle-lit glow. Thirty years of pain and suffering stretched tight across those sparkling, unnaturally youthful faces. Will saw terrible fear and, even worse, desperate hope.

For a second Will wanted to save them all. He brushed the thought aside. He wasn't a psychiatrist anymore, and he had his own future to worry about. At his last bio control the life-monitor said he had a life expectancy of 139 years. Seven more decades. A whole second life. Will planned on spending it living in a cloud apartment on Crn and enjoying the advantages of the knowledge gem he had been promised upon his return. Access to the eternal database wasn't immortality, but it was the next best thing: knowing everything there was to know, becoming one with the record. All the other ambassadors with their beautiful cerulean gems would respect him once he was fully cruxed. So the sooner he got done here and got the hell home...

But that was rushing ahead, and some things couldn't be rushed. It would be weeks before the explorer turned around and headed for home. He did have the time to stop a while and build a relationship with this community, make peace with his sister. What was one more afternoon? Maybe he'd even come back for the drop too, although it was not expected of him. He did sincerely want to make this situation work for his sister and her people. Will tried to convey that genuine sincerity as he moved toward the crowd of waiting women, leaving Lo to fall behind him. He breathed out and let empathy overtake his entire body. Maybe these women could feel emotions?

As if in response, he heard Pat bellow, "Stop carrying on like you're in a movie about the second coming of the lord and sit down already, Tootsie."

She gestured at an Adirondack chair on the lawn. Memories of summers past. He wondered if Lo was experiencing any of that same nostalgia. Fireflies in jars, cherry cola.

"Listen up," she said. "Pat's in charge now," and strode off towards the house.

Pat slapped him on the back so hard he felt it through his bodcoz. She said, "Okay, Wilberforce, here's how this thing is gonna work. Each woman has a designated fifteen-minute slot, just like it used to be at the doctor's. Don't go over. Don't cut anyone short. If you need a comfort break just give a holler, and I'll escort you to the john. Chow will be brought out from time to time. And don't worry about safety—I'll never be more than spitting distance away."

Will looked up and winked. Pat said nothing, just coughed, spat, and adjusted her crotch like a baseball player as she spread her stance a little wider. Then *she* winked. Will made a note to himself to stop winking. It just wasn't working. At that same moment, Reid came running out of the house and pretended to rugby-tackle the big gal. Pat roared with laughter as she allowed the kid to leap all over her. Reid roared back as Pat shook and shuddered like a dog just out of the water until he lost his grip and went flying through the air to the grass. After picking himself up, Reid trotted over to speak to Will.

"Sorry, Will, but I have to leave you here on your own. Lo says I got to go stay with Marie and James for a bit," he said. "Bummer. I wanted to show you the pool I told you about. Maybe Lo will be over the whole checkpoint thing by tomorrow?"

"Sounds awesome—" began Will.

"Sounds distracting," said Lo, appearing without warning behind the Adirondack chair, Helena by her side. "Get the hell out of here, Reid, I already told you."

Reid gave her his middle finger, jumped on an old bike lying in a shrub, and pedaled off down the lawn, directly toward some women standing quietly chatting by the road.

As they all watched Reid leave, Will saw Bob walking up the street toward the group on the lawn. He had his bodcoz back on and his wet hair tied back in a ponytail. As Reid ploughed toward him on his bike, Bob stopped and played a little air guitar, like they were two stoner buddies of the same age. Reid responded by shaking his bike until it jumped, scattering the women in fear as he sped away down the old road.

"Be careful," shouted Helena.

"Stop mothering him," said Lo. "It's just keeping him young and dumb."

She didn't wait for Helena to reply, simply swung back to Will and said, "One last thing. I've been thinking about your personal security. You've got me and Pat. What more could you possibly need? So I'm going to take charge of that…"

Two seconds before he got her drift, Lo narrowed her bright blue eyes, pulled his control button sharply from his bodcoz, and slipped it in the pocket of her loose linen pants. The heavily magnetized control came away easily under Lo's gaze. She must have been evaluating it awhile. Bob walked up just in time. Lo snatched his control from his bodcoz the same way and strode off down the lawn. Bob said, "Whaaaa?" Will just shook his head. What a wasted gesture. His control would never work on the orbicraft access doors without his bio-ID, and Bob couldn't board without his authorization anyway. All she'd done was throw her weight around.

"You have a wonderful day too, Sis," he called to her departing back.

Helena patted him on his shoulder.

"Give her time," she said. "She has trust issues."

"Don't we all?" said Will.

"Not like hers," said Helena. "I'm sorry, Will, but I don't think you have any idea. All of us are alive today because of Lo's courage to do things the rest of us didn't dare. Hard and sometimes bad things. We thank her every day for carrying that heavy load."

"I hear what you say," said Will.

"Hearing is not enough," replied Helena softly. "You need to know her pain."

Will shivered in spite of the warm summer air.

10

Over the course of a very long afternoon, Will and Bob each completed over thirty interviews. It was a champion effort, a team effort of sorts. Neither of them said much to the other, but they sat quite companionably side-by-side on the Adirondack chairs talking with a diverse stream of women. Very quickly one thing stood out to Will: irrespective of their differences, most of the women were ageless and childless. The wiring process had both given and taken away. Unsurprisingly, many of their questions were about fertility and children. Could the Orbiters help them have children? What would happen if they tinkered with their wires? Would they suddenly become old women, or would they simply reset the clock? Would Orbiter men be able to breed with Earthan women? Would they want to? What were Orbiter children like? Each asked more questions than Will could ever answer in a fifteen-minute slot, most of them unanswerable anyway.

Will told the truth wherever he could. Nobody knew exactly what the Ruurdaans had done to the women. The Orbiters had anti-aging technology that borrowed some of its premises from very early Ruurdaan science, but this was different; this was far beyond Orbiter understanding and science. Still, he liked to reiterate, perhaps they *could* unravel the mystery of the women's wiring, given time and collaboration. The Orbiters were willing to help Earth's women in any and every way possible—including trying to restore fertility. Some of the shuttle survivors (both men and women) had had children with Orbiters. Maybe he would know more after he talked with the integrated settlers in Madison. Maybe they had looked into the issue already. Will tried not to over-promise. The desperation in the women's faces moved him in spite of himself.

Occasionally he had an interview that was not about children. Some of the women wanted to know about Orbiter men and what relationships between Orbiter men and women were like (many and various). Still others wanted to know about Orbital culture (orderly and peaceful), about their technology (advanced), about space travel (currently limited beyond their own galaxy). One or two of them even asked him about his own experience, his escape from the Ruurdaan invasion (unpleasant, lucky). It seemed that for many of the women the invasion happened yesterday; those tended to be the same women who wanted to know if more Orbiters were coming. To be honest, Will was surprised that all the women did not ask that question, although he was grateful they did not. All in good time.

At some point in the afternoon he asked Pat if he was going to meet any of the men. Back before he left on the mission, he had been told to expect a few male survivors, and clearly some of the unwired women had given birth since the invasion. Pat told him that Reid was one of the "naturals," but she didn't elaborate. She also told him that the men had discussed it amongst themselves and decided to consider their position further before meeting the visitors. When Will asked if it didn't make more sense to meet the visitors before taking a position, Pat just shrugged and said, "This is a democracy." Wishful thinking.

All afternoon his simplest questions were met with polite and careful evasion. Nevertheless, through a series of fragmentary reveals, Will developed a strong sense of the women, their histories, concerns, and agendas. Marie Nunn stopped by after work to tell him that James had always been worth ten of him and not to think otherwise because of a bit of plastic surgery. Hard, bitter, terrified of further loss. Punkie Ruby declared that she didn't have a problem with tall hairy guys just as long as they believed in peace and equality and didn't wink at her. She was softer than she looked. Softest of all, though, was Leslie, the long dark sylph who had stood and quivered while Lo shot at him. "I'm sorry about how we met," she said. "I get freaked out about certain things. But I'm okay now. I'm much better. And I wanted to meet you. Family is so important. I have four boys, you know, waiting for me. You don't have anything you can tell me about that, do you? Where they might be?" She was still shaking a little. Will gave her the best lie in his entire repertoire, an old one regarding a very vague God and his mysterious plans. Leslie hugged him and said she hoped he was the first of many miracles. Sweet. Sad.

Straight after Leslie came comms chief Yaz, an athletic-looking black woman with a halo of hair and a voice like Tupelo honey. Yaz announced right up front that she believed all things happened for a reason. Earth's environment had most definitely needed healing. In a way, humans were just like vermin, running around destroying everything in their path. Maybe just enough of them had been spared to right the ecological balance. Maybe that's why their fertility was on hold too. Yaz had a feeling about it, couldn't put her finger on it exactly, just call it a strong sense. Her senses were what got her through the hard times. She'd always been good at reading people. Now she could read all sorts of things. That's why she worked comms.

"I'll be reading your mind soon enough, Will Warren," she said as she left.

Even the nicest of these women gave him the chills.

Toward evening, the sun going down in a blaze, curly haired Adrianna—the woman who had shot at Bob—appeared in front of him. She refused his offer of a chair. Instead she stood there, arms crossed, and said that if it turned out he was fucking with them or with Lo, she would kill him. Something about the way she said it made Will wonder at her and Lo's relationship. He was trying to think of the right reply when Bob fell backwards off his chair, which he'd been rocking like a fool all day. Everyone roared with laughter, even Adrianna. Will noted that this was the second time Bob had fallen off his chair today. The same thing had happened when Marie came around shouting and threatening earlier. Why thank you, Bob.

Will was especially grateful because the guy had no obligation to help. His only remit was to do his time in Madison, yet here he was winning hearts and minds in Saugatuck. Bob never seemed to weary of the same sad questions about the wiring and the infertility. He chatted away like an old friend. Always ready with a goofy disarming smile, he was also quick to clasp sparkly hands and exchange long emotional silences. In spite of all appearances to the contrary, Bob was a natural diplomat. Will even turned to him when they were done and said, "I'll tell them you conducted yourself well. Perhaps they'll pick you up early." Bob just shrugged and smiled.

It was after ten by the time Pat sent the last of the women home, the sky long dark, the lawn lit by lanterns that drew thousands of mosquitoes. Earlier he'd rubbed a stinking herbal insecticide on his face; now he felt sticky and dirty in the cooler evening air. He was about to ask if he could take a shower when Janine arrived to collect Bob. Will asked him if he was okay with that, being treated like a prisoner, no privacy, but Bob declared himself totally happy to spend another night in the blonde's custody. No surprise there. The two of them wandered off arm in arm into the impenetrable darkness that had fallen.

That left Will alone with Pat and a couple of shadows lurking in the foliage. When asked if Lo was coming home soon, Pat said she was tied up, it might be a long night, and he shouldn't wait up for her. Still wasting her time trying to get into the orbicraft then. He kept his thoughts to himself as Pat said, "You must be tired, pumpkin. Get some shut-eye. You have another big day ahead tomorrow, starting with the town meeting in the morning. I expect that the men will be in attendance at that event. Then there's a council meeting in the afternoon. I'm sure Lo will want to talk to you about options in advance of that... Current thinking is we should just call Madison to come and get you, worry about the ship later, but maybe overnight you'll come up with a workable idea of some other kind. That would sure be a nice gesture toward your sister..."

"I'm going to take your suggestion and get some sleep," said Will.

"Fine," said Pat. "Just stay in the house, don't be trying to sneak off anywhere, and holler if you need me. I'm on duty till eight, so don't you worry your pretty little head about safety or nothing—I'll be here enjoying the beautiful night, real close by."

"Sounds romantic," Will said as he turned and headed for the house.

He thought he heard Pat swallow an old-fashioned chortle.

It had been a very long day. Will made his way inside the cottage, ducking through the front door and heading straight for the tiny upstairs bathroom. He got out of his bodcoz and scrunched himself into the shower cubicle. Struggling to get enough water, he contemplated the issue of taking Lo onboard the orbicraft. Should he reconsider? There certainly wasn't any technical problem; he could take anyone he liked on board simply by capturing a bio-record on his access gem (small yellow, left pec) and registering them with the ship. Under normal circumstances he wouldn't care about letting Lo see the inside of a ship she could not even begin to understand, let alone operate.

The problem was allowing her to see the cargo—five thousand small glass drug-balls filled with a quivering live brown culture. Vroom72, a drug that adhered to flesh and was absorbed in seconds, a drug that killed 90% of users within 72 hours, a drug that addicts would take even knowing it brought near-certain death, was the Orbitals' only real answer to Retske's problem with the Unans. He had considered telling Lo the truth. Maybe she would be grateful for some Vroom72 that Saugatuck could use as a defense against Unans. She'd already killed a few herself. However, she was so unpredictable. She might just as easily get her panties in a knot about a pacifist culture that distributed killer drugs to its undesirables. Will didn't imagine that women like Helena and Yaz would be impressed by killer drugs either. Best the question just never arose.

Will considered just lying about the cargo. Lo didn't know what Vroom72 was, and she might believe him if he said the glass balls contained medicine. Then again she was a good lie detector. Will feared she would demand to test the stuff in those bio-labs she had pretended weren't there this morning. Worse still she might try zapping away at the drugs for no good reason while she was onboard. He was ninety-nine percent sure she would be powerless on the orbicraft but better safe than sorry (look what a mess he'd already gotten himself into by assuming he could just fly in here and fly on).

That left only his other plan: taking the Vroom up to Madison as quickly as possible. It shouldn't take him more than an hour, tops. Zip on back. There'd be a bit of a stink here over him taking off on a trip without asking—but he'd remind them of the importance of freedom of movement in a democracy. They did still seem to care a little for personal liberty. The fact that he'd lied to everyone was a little trickier to explain. Hopefully he could smooth that over by pretending to be scared of them all. He'd also cave. He'd show Lo the orbicraft. Then he'd tell her and the rest of them about the settlement program. The benefits. The possibilities. They'd come around soon enough. And if they didn't, he'd just leave and that would be the end of the whole damned homecoming for him. Forewarned.

After putting his bodcoz back on, Will slipped into the bed in the spare room, throwing off the tartan coverlet even though his body temperature would be regulated. He barely registered his surroundings—a basket of graying towels in the corner, watercolors of old beach scenes, a dog-eared copy of *The Artist's Way* on the side-table—before he crashed. He slept deeply, awakening only briefly around midnight to the sounds of Lo and Pat opening his door a crack to check on him. Lulled by their unintelligible whispers, he fell right back to sleep and dreamed he was back at the Lilith music festival in the summer of 1998, listening to the Indigo Girls and getting high. It was the summer before he went to Harvard. He was the most popular guy he knew, and he was going to achieve great things. Only one small thing gnawed away at him. He hadn't told his parents he was gay yet, because he wanted to be sure himself. After spending the weekend dancing, flirting, and sleeping with the hottest of Lo's friends, he was pretty sure. He liked them all fine; they just weren't his destiny.

11

At 4:00 a.m. Will felt the small alarm in his left eyebrow vibrate. He tapped it with his hand, then eased out of bed as quietly as possible, lumping the bedclothes behind him into a sleepy-looking pile. Tiptoeing over to the door he listened for sounds of anyone awake. He heard nothing except the rise and fall of sleeping bodies. Reaching into the neck of his bodcoz, his fingers found the paper-thin sheet of fabric that nestled there and rolled it all the way up and over his bristle of blonde hair. It was like wearing a latex hoodie. Blinking, Will called up his operations projection screen, which opened into the darkness before his eyes. He checked the status of his invisibility and sound-dampening systems. Confident all was in order, he ran down the stairs, slipped through the front door, and set out for the dock down at HQ.

Jogging, Will managed to cover the ground between Lo's house and HQ in four minutes. As he rounded the corner of the building, he was disappointed to see that the orbicraft no longer sat at the end of the dock. It had somehow been towed across to the other side of the river—he thought that was the old Levitt dock—and therefore next to his old family house. Lo had said that whole area was unprotected and dangerous now, but that wasn't going to stop him. He'd swim if the woods were impassable. Will headed off on foot towards the bridge. Although the bodcoz did its job, there was still an almighty creak when he bounced down from the makeshift gate onto the bridge itself. Sound dampeners only work so well. Whoever was up there on the guard post jumped out of their seat and scanned the area, but Will held the hood over his face for a few stifling minutes then slipped away. Lo should never have allowed them to retain their suits.

When he reached the other side of the bridge, Will saw lights out to the right of him, in the direction of the old Saugatuck

Golf Club and Inn, perched right where the river met Long Island Sound. He was not entirely surprised. First, he'd seen something there as he flew in. Second, Lo was no liar, and the blanks in this morning's tour were hopelessly revealing: her unwillingness to allow him access to the water; an incredible denial of any knowledge of what had happened to everything on the other side of the river; a transparently tall story about the Inn being booby-trapped. Will suspected some kind of defense installation. Although he knew he should veer directly left and get within the force-shielded confines of the orbicraft as soon as possible, curiosity got the better of him, and he set off right, down the gravelly path leading along the water toward the Inn. This was clearly a new path, more like a dirt road. You couldn't even walk along here in the old days—this would have been the front lawn of a smattering of big houses—yet this was now some kind of functioning vehicular thoroughfare between the old Inn and the village. With each step the lights seemed to get brighter until he found himself squinting against the glare.

He passed a couple of old houses as he walked, all in darkness but well-maintained, their lawns sloping to the road. So *some* people were living on this side of the river. As he got closer to the source of the light Will suddenly realized that he was heading toward an enormous mound of those Ruurdaan pods the women flew. He knew where the old Inn should be, just beyond the bizarre bubble installation, but he couldn't see it because of the great peaked mound, ten pods high at the apex and completely covering what used to be the eighteenth hole. The glowing complex emanated a lot of light, not only upwards, but downwards and sideways. Strange cracks of light glowed through the surrounding green grass. Were there also pods underground?

The mound shined so brightly it must seem like a beacon to anyone flying above. However, when Will looked up he saw that no light penetrated the enormous silver cloud hanging like a great wad of metallic cotton candy in the night sky. The cloud hovered low over the podded area, almost touching the tree-tops and filtering all that bright light so that it dissipated into nothing. Shielding? As he contemplated the cloud, Will became aware of a low humming sound almost below his field of perception, a low atonal hum with the odd break. Chanting?

Will kept walking. When he was within a football-field length of the pods, a girl appeared without warning a few feet up the path in front of him. She was about eight years old, the same age his niece Mira would have been when the Ruurdaans invaded. But this wasn't Mira. This child was dark where Mira had been fair. Something else was different about her too. Her clothes might be old, but she looked fresh and new, right down to the small shiny silver dome, like a miniature yarmulke, that sat atop her bald head.

Will stopped and shivered. Was this even a child? She sure looked like one, but normal children did not go out wandering alone at the crack of dawn. Will listened intently for adult company but heard nothing except the low buzz coming from the pods. He was still trying to work out exactly what was going on here when the child started walking toward him. Will quickly made to move aside and let her pass—he was invisible, not immaterial.

However, he found that he could not move to the side. It was as if something else invisible, like a big gel mattress, was blocking his path. Will tried to speak to the child, who was now right in front of him. He had barely formed the "h" in "hello" before he felt his lips clamp together involuntarily. He began breathing deeply through his nose. As he struggled to control his panic, the child flicked her head in a strange circle, ripping the invisible hood from his head. He was now pinned, silenced and exposed. The strange girl stared coldly at him and mouthed something, although Will heard no sound. He strained to read her lips.

go—away

As her thought flashed through his mind, he felt his body released from the invisible grip. Without thinking, he began to speak. "It's okay. I won't hurt—"

The girl moved her head sharply up and down. Will felt his hand jerk up and down involuntarily; one, two, snap. He grunted as an excruciating pain shot up his arm. She had broken his wrist, right through his armored bodcoz. Will didn't waste a second. Clutching his damaged arm to his chest with his good hand, he swiveled on his feet and ran in the direction of his ship.

12

Lo watched as Will ran toward the bridge. When he got close enough, she stuck her foot out and sent him flying. Will yelped as his hand connected with something hard.

"I hope it hurts like hell," she said, stepping out from the shadows.

"I think my wrist is broken."

"Yeah, I think so too."

Lo gave her brother a moment to process the situation, waiting until she saw the realization pass over his handsome face, now pink and sweaty with pain and exertion.

"Yes, I can see you. That ridiculous invisibility cloak may work where you come from but it's not much good round here."

Seen through her enhanced eyes, Will's bodcoz was glowing just as surely as if he'd dipped it in fluorescent paint. Not only could she see his suit, she could also identify the gemstone cross tattooed on his chest and a series of wires running throughout his body. It wasn't an extensive network like hers, but it was not entirely dissimilar; he was a satellite view of Saugatuck at night, and she was a satellite view of New York. Both were lit up like Christmas trees under the skin.

"You can see me?" said Will, slow to accept the truth.

"Duh."

"Could everyone see me, even the guards?"

"Pretty much. The woman on duty said she smelled you first. Smell is her thing. If it was Yaz she would have sensed your mind. You can't hide anything from us."

"How long have you been following me?"

"Not long enough. After you left, I raced over to your ship to wait for you. I wanted you to almost make it, think you'd gotten away. But you didn't show up. The guards beamed to say you'd detoured towards the Inn. I'd gotten this far when I heard you running back. I didn't see what happened, but I can imagine. The children are even more scared of intruders than we are. You're lucky you're still alive. I should have stopped you at the bridge."

"Yes, you should have. And how about some warning signs and fences telling people the area is dangerous. Beware of the Children! If those are in fact children?" Will looked up into her eyes in angry inquisition, holding his wrist before her for effect.

Lo just shrugged. "You talk like this is the old America. Fences around our swimming pools and signs saying watch out for slippery conditions. Wake the fuck up. We are trying to protect the children *from* dangerous intruders, not the other way around. Everything north is booby-trapped. The old river path is the only way in from Saugatuck. You would never have made it past the bridge if I hadn't told the guards to let you be. I thought you were desperate to reach your ship. It's your own fault you went snooping."

Will nodded, his pale face a little shiny, his pained grimace barely creasing the mask. "Maybe you're right, but do we have to have this discussion here? My wrist is killing me. I need to get to the orbicraft. The medical system will fix it pretty fast."

She cut him short. "You can forget about going anywhere near your ship. Helena will patch you up later, but first I want some explanations. How can you control that body suit of yours when I took the controls away? Where's the hidden control?"

"It's just something internal to the coz—heat, visibility, defense—it responds to sensors in my body. If I'm cold, it heats up. If I blink a certain way, it glows. Blink another way, and it becomes invisible. It's nothing special by Orbiter standards."

"Tell me more about the sensors," said Lo. "Are those gems on your chest sensors? I can see the wiring from here, even inside your bodcoz. Green glowing lines."

"You can see that?" Will looked surprised. "The entire system is supposed to be shielded. When the technicians at home do their evaluations, we have to go inside special equipment, a bit like an

MRI. But that's beside the point. I mean, what's going on around here? Who are those children?"

Lo smelled his fear. Yet he was still doing all the asking and none of the telling. Would he ever tell her the truth?

"Walk with me," she said.

"Where," said Will, now even more nervous.

"You'll see when we get there," said Lo, turning and walking back along the path. Feeling his reluctance, she swiveled back around and made a scooping gesture with her hand. Will rose a little from the path. Lo turned and moved forward with her hand stretched behind her. It was a bit like pulling a resistant animal through the air on a leash.

"Your suit defenses are only so good," she said to him while they moved along as one. "They only protect what lies within. That's why you were scared to come out from your force-field yesterday, isn't it?" Will didn't answer her. "And just in case you're wondering, no, I'm not like the children—I can't entirely bypass your shielding—but I can move the cocoon you're resting in."

Still no response. Lo turned to see Will dragging through the air, his eyes closed tight against the pain of his wrist. "I wasn't even leaving," he began.

"Just stop bullshitting and start walking." She released him abruptly.

Will yelped and stumbled. "You scare me," he said as he began walking.

"You should be scared," replied Lo. "You've put me in a terrible position with your lies and your snooping. Now you've seen the children, you can't simply leave."

"I was having trouble leaving already," said Will.

Lo shrugged. This was a situation of his own making.

They trudged in silence back over the bridge, through the gates that the guard opened for them, past the Mansion Clam House and back towards the pod park. It was becoming light now, the sky was streaked blue and red. It was going to be another scorcher of a day. Lo remembered mornings like this, almost fifty years ago, when she and Will were both on the rowing team. They were both competitive—Dad lived for their sporting victories—but of course Will always brought home the most prizes. She had never resented his successes then, only the way he pushed her aside in his pursuit of them. She resented him now, though—for barging in here like God's gift, lying to them all about his agenda, toying with their emotions, and assuming that he was dealing with a bunch of naïve and gullible women. The latent sexism of it was staggering. Most of all, though, she resented him for trying to run away without saying goodbye. But it wasn't about her opinions and feelings anymore. It was about the security of Saugatuck.

Within minutes, Lo pulled up in front of one of the spare pods, parked roughshod on the tarmac next to the river. She turned to face her brother, who looked feverish.

"We're about to go for an unusual ride. I can fix your arm before we head out—or we can wait and let Helena set it later. If I do it now, you'll get immediate pain relief and the ride will be easier, but I can't guarantee my work. I'm not a doctor, and I don't know how the wrist-bone is supposed to look. I will do my best to set it straight, but..."

Will replied without hesitation, "Just do it."

Lo wasn't sure if it was the pain or his ego talking.

"You'll have to get the suit out of the way," she replied.

Will peeled back the left sleeve of his bodcoz and eased his broken hand out, supported by his good arm. His efforts were plaintive, but Lo stayed firm. Focusing her gaze on the wrist, Lo tried to see the bone within the skin. Although she regularly used her enhanced vision on the job—checking things at a distance, evaluating machinery and structures, even the earth beneath their feet—it was less often that she peered inside a human body. Lo could see the outline of the bone as well as the distinctive ridged line marking the break. No wires. Concentrating as intently as possible she waved her finger over the area, smoothing the line, fusing bone and flesh alike. Will looked pained and faint but didn't cry out. She gestured at him to flip his wrist, which he did without too much trouble, then repeated the procedure to be sure. When she was done Will waved his hand around in the air.

"It feels strange," he said.

"Ingrate," Lo replied.

Will smiled wanly and said, "Thank you."

Gesturing to the nearest pod Lo said, "I'm sorry about this bro, but now I need you to completely remove your suit and step over to the pod."

Will's eyes widened. "What?"

Lo replied calmly, "You wanted to see the Inn. We're going to the Inn, this time my way. But you can't wear that suit. It frightened the children. You need to take it off."

Will backed away, protesting, "It was just a stupid detour. I don't need to know anything, and I'm not interested in meeting any more of those so-called children."

"Well that's too bad. You've already seen too much. You need to know what's at stake here. Get your suit off. Please don't make me force you."

"Just let me take my ship and leave."

"Get the suit off," said Lo, sadly shaking her head and pointing her gloved hand at a place close to his left foot. She discharged a thin energy current that created a Lilliputian earthquake as it thumped into the ground, sending Will tumbling.

Sadly shaking his own head, Will stood up, placed his hands on his sternum, and pulled them both firmly apart, arching his impressive chest forward as he did so. There was a quiet hiss as the coz split open in two pieces. Will drew each piece off separately, like peeling off long gloves. Then he stepped completely naked toward the pod. Lo tried not to look at his hairless body. She didn't need to see every detail of his enhancements. Instead she stared at the sparkling tat on Will's chest—a beautiful mix of starry constellation and stretched Celtic cross.

"The tattoo is incredible. Are they real gems?"

"Yes. They're not exactly rubies and sapphires and emeralds, but they are their equivalents on the Orbitals. The pattern they form is called the orbital crux."

"It's gorgeous. But it looks like there's a piece missing in the middle. There's a space between all the smaller stones where it looks like there should be one big stone."

"Yes. A special blue stone called a dwyvt goes there."

"Why don't you have one?"

Will hesitated, then replied, "The stones are expensive. I can't afford it yet."

"Oh. Purely aesthetic value then? But what about all the wires behind the gemstones. How exactly do your enhancements work?"

"I honestly don't know," said Will. "It's all advanced alien biotech to me. The wires monitor and manipulate various bodily functions. The gems are like a medical console—they provide readouts and can be used to make medical adjustments. The crux is what's keeping my sixty-seven-year-old body in the condition of a thirty-year-old jock."

Lo thought for a moment. The parallels between her wiring and Will's wiring were intriguing. Perhaps the Orbiters really could help them understand what was going on with their own bodies? Something was bugging her, though. Something about what Will said was not quite right. Old men, young bodies. Got it.

"Bob doesn't have a crux. How is he staying young?

"Bob is like most regular Orbiters—he goes to the local medical clinic for anti-aging treatments. He has his drugs with him on the orbicraft—without them he will start aging normally—but they won't give him as good a result as the full treatment regime back home. He'll probably lose a few years of his life on this trip. But then that's part of the punishment for the drug offenses. He's doing time in more way than one."

"I think Janine is easing his suffering."

Neither of them laughed. Lo leaned over and pressed her hand to a fine star-shaped etching on the glassy hull of the pod. The star shape was formed by many intersecting lines of superfine silver thread. At a distance it looked like someone had thrown a rock at a windshield; up close you could see that the splintering followed a pattern. As Lo moved her hand over the shape, the splinters expanded to create a smooth aperture. Lo reached in and pulled out a length of silver mesh. She pulled and shaped the strange fabric until she had created a large metallic mesh net.

"Get in," she said.

"It's like a fishing net," said Will.

"Better to think of it as a hammock," replied Lo.

"Is that the only way you can take passengers?" asked Will.

"Of course not," replied Lo. "But until I know more about all your controls, I'm not letting you near the inside of my pod, especially not when I'm trying to fly."

"You've just taken away my bodcoz," said Will.

"I still have concerns about that crux," said Lo, gesturing to her brother to step into the sack. "Who knows what secret talents you're not telling me about?" She thought he looked edgy as she said it, but he didn't reply, simply threw up his hands in a gesture of hopelessness and reluctantly stepped into the space that Lo had created in the mesh.

"Squat down and face away," she said. She didn't want him looking at her from behind, seeing how she controlled the pod, knowing how everything worked.

"You can't be serious."

"Don't resist," she said. "The net will hold you comfortably enough if you let it. Otherwise you may get stuck in a miserable position for the whole flight."

Will squatted.

Lo released her hands and watched as the net shriveled up around Will's body, slowly pulling him toward the pod. His features strained against the net, which held firm. His hands and feet were pressed outward, as if he was trying to push his way out. He looked like a piece of modern art: *man in net attached to bubble.* She could have arranged it so his head was free, but that would not have been as safe. And besides, they would only be five minutes.

"Are you sure this is safe?" asked Will

"Relax. I've transported truck-loads of people in the net," said Lo. She chose not to tell him that most of those people were dead. Lo had regularly used the nets for transporting bodies back in the days when she was the head of a Ruurdaan waste-management crew—back when the Earth stank of decay for months on end—and after that too—in the years when raids were as common as rainy days.

"Then hurry up," said Will. "My knees are already starting to seize up."

Knowing that might be true, Lo pressed her hand against a different silvery star-shaped etching on the pod. The star stretched into a small-person-sized aperture. Lo flung herself up and into the pod. She slid into the smooth plasticized groove of the seat. The interior of the pod warmed and shimmered as it adapted itself to her. Getting into your pod always felt a little like settling into a gel pack, cooling in the hot months, warming in the winter. Comfortable, comforting. The pod was Lo's second home.

She moved her hands over the control mounds and felt the pod gently begin to lift. Calmer now, in the comfort of her pod, Lo tried to straighten things up in her head. But she couldn't help imagining Will's fear as he felt himself dragged up behind her—steamily warm from the energy vent that lay pretty close to his head at the back of the pod there—so she just focused on making the flight as smooth as possible. If Will thought that treating him like an enemy was easy for her, he was wrong. It hurt her in a deep place.

13

As the dawn light brightened, Lo directed the pod upriver, in the direction of the once upscale town of Westport. Moving at 20 mph it was still only minutes before the flats began, demarcating the zone of destruction caused when the sphere hit. *Flattening* was the term everyone used for what the spheres did, although there were some distinct geographical differences to the flattening phenomenon. In New York City the flattening had created a mile-deep sink hole that ate up the Hudson, the East River, and five miles of surrounding inhabited areas. In coastal cities like Bridgeport and New Haven, the flattening had expanded the river, creating shallows that extended for miles over lifeless tarmac floors. In smaller Westport, the spheres' impact had been more contained, creating flat plains of low-lying rubble but mostly sparing the river.

What were once thousands of homes and businesses were now one big fat splat, hilly in the odd place where a taller building might have stood, but mostly flat. The plain spread out in a fifteen-mile radius around the old downtown, splattering a little around the edges, like fires do, sparing one home then engulfing the one next door. Saugatuck survived, just out of range, downstream. Today, the river still snaked through the southern part of the flats, occasionally spilling over the flattened land in a shallow puddle, or breaking into tiny vein-like tributaries, but mostly following its original channel. Around the edges of the river signs of rebirth had begun—reeds and weeds—but in general the flats were devoid of life, the earth smothered in a layer of molten plastic and concrete and metal.

Lo suspected that Will had seen it before he landed, but he hadn't said so, and she wanted to make damned sure he saw now. They had been his people too—family, teachers, friends, an entire community. Here and there you could even see them—the dead—outlines of once-people forever imprinted into the surface. Lo usually avoided the places with faces. Not today. It was because of these people that she fought on, because of them that she killed puppies and shot at anything that moved or she didn't recognize, and that she couldn't afford to trust her own brother. Somebody had to survive; there must be a next generation. It couldn't be over, there had to be more...

Flying low, she took them back over the other side of the river, past the place they called "Harold's Grin," past the crumbling old river mansions, past the shabby remains of their own family bungalow near the old Bridge Road. Lo wondered how Will was taking it, down below. Could he even begin to imagine the choices she had had to make—including shutting out other survivors by booby-trapping this entire side of the river, northwest of the bridge? Seeing it, would he realize why she was not going to spare him just because he was her brother?

Gliding down toward the Inn, little sign of the old golf course could be seen, no bunkers, no perfect greens. However, the area remained relatively clear of dense vegetation—park-like. The pod complex itself, which was clustered around the old eighteenth hole, was invisible from the air—although you'd certainly know about it if you tried to fly into its airspace. The adjacent Inn remained clearly visible. Once a place for vacationing New Yorkers, it was now home to fifteen full-time caretakers: the nannies.

The nannies tended to the children's every physical need, almost as if they were still Ruurdaan slaves. There had been many discussions about other ways of caring, but the nannies insisted. They seemed to think that they were running some sort of special school, albeit one where the children ran the show. There had long been women who questioned the way things were done at the Inn and worried over the nature of the children who lived there, but nobody had the heart to challenge the nannies, who'd given their entire lives to a belief that the children were the future. What would they be without the children? Barren cyborgs? Although the physical nature of Saugatuck had changed over the years, the Inn remained central to its psychology. If HQ was their beating heart, then the Inn was their womb. It was sacred ground.

Lo was careful before approaching the old gravel driveway that lay between the Inn and the complex. The bright lights and movement told Lo that everything was as usual. Nobody paid any attention to their arrival. The children, entirely comfortable with pods coming and going, remained oblivious to anyone but themselves. The nannies appeared not to be awake yet.

After landing the pod with only the gentlest of bumps, Lo jumped onto the bright green grass. She released Will, heard him thump to the ground. She leaped out of her pod and ran around to find Will attempting to stretch out and disentangle himself from the net. She saw with a shock that his body was encrusted with dead insects—the scourge of summer and getting worse every year. Lo went to help but he shook her off and began dusting and scraping the insects from his naked body. His face was a grim and dirty mask, his mouth a hard line. Lo thought he was deliberately thrusting his hairless naked groin at her. She looked back into the pod, found a grimy old pareo and threw it to him.

"Here. Not that it matters. The kids are oblivious to things like clothes. Hell, they're usually oblivious to people. Carly only freaked out on account of the bodcoz. They've never seen anything like your suit before, especially not with the invisibility technology. You must have seemed like a scary stranger lurking in the bushes. Things should be different without the suit—and with me. The children are usually harmless."

As he wiped himself off and wrapped the filthy cloth around his waist, Will said, "You're kidding, right? That Ruurdaan kid I met—if that even was a kid—she could've just as easily snapped my neck as my wrist."

With a jolt she realized his mistake. "Are *you* kidding? That wasn't a Ruurdaan. That was one of *our* children. *Carly*—James and Marie Nunn's girl."

Will screwed up his face in disbelief. "The girl I saw had a silver cone on her head. No hair. Metallic veins popping out everywhere, like she was filled with mercury. She also looked about eight years old. The Carly Nunn I knew would be closer to forty at this point in time."

"That's right," said Lo. "She's forty-one. They froze the children too."

"She looked just like all the images I've seen of Ruurdaans."

"Only superficially—the cones, the metallic infusion, the small faces and bodies. The real Ruurdaans were more stunted and bloodless. Pointy-featured. These are just children with a few Ruurdaan wires screwing them up. There are forty-three of them living in this complex."

"If they're normal children, why don't they live with families in houses?"

"By the time we found them they'd already spent three years away from their families, being raised by Ruurdaans. We don't know why they kept these children but we think they were experimenting. The nannies tell us that they once cared for other children too, pure Ruurdaan kids, but those children all died of the plague. It's hard to get the nannies to talk about it though, they're the most traumatized of us all. That's why we don't know for sure what the Ruurdaans did to our children, just that it was different from what they did to us women. We do know the children were wired into the Ruurdaan network, and as a result began behaving a bit like Ruurdaans, praying and computing the whole time. We joke that they're looking for the ultimate algorithm for God—then we worry that it's not a joke."

Will tried to look deep into her eyes, but she looked away, avoiding his pity. "Shit, Lo. I'm so sorry. It's horrific. I had no idea. There was nothing about children in my briefing."

She shrugged. "I'm not surprised, if the Orbiters are basing all their information on what they know from their experiences in Madison. To the best of my knowledge, they don't have any children there. That doesn't necessarily mean there aren't any. Nobody with any brains would advertise the fact that they have children. The only place I know that is open about their kids is IBM City, and that's only because it's hard to keep a secret when there are twenty thousand people involved."

"Why would people feel they need to keep their children secret?"

Lo sighed. She was surprised that a psychiatrist couldn't work it out.

"Get a clue, Will. *They look like Ruurdaans.* That scares people murderous. Some think the children will evolve into Ruurdaans one day—Ruurdaans with mature powers."

"Okay so people might be scared of them, but *how* exactly could anyone actually hurt them? That kid just bypassed my suit's defenses. They also have your protection, not to mention the air-shield, the dome-cloud, or whatever that thing is."

"It's a dome with a cloud in the middle. We don't know how they did it."

"Exactly. They do have significant defenses of their own."

"Some survivors already found a way around those defenses. The children aren't entirely self-sufficient. They can't survive without people to feed and care for them."

Will's face told Lo that he got it, but she gave him the details anyway.

"There used to be another complex like ours at the old Green's Farm Academy."

Will nodded. "I remember it, private school up near Southport."

"That's the one. Well, about fifty women and fifty children were living there, all very open. I tried telling them, but they kept welcoming strangers, no security protocols. They lasted six months after liberation. The *avenging angels*—that's what they called themselves—murdered the women and threw poisoned food into the pod complex. The children died slowly and painfully. I believe our children experienced their agony—they were agitat-ed for days. After that we taught our children defense. We talked to them about stranger danger. We established security protocols for food and drink service. Of course the children said pretty much nothing, but we soon knew that they understood us. That dome was built in less than a month. The domes stop anyone from seeing the children before the children see them—which is exactly what happened to you."

"They seem to have incredible skills, Lo. I can understand why some people believe they're not children—especially now that they're older. What exactly do they do here?" asked Will, waving his arm at the complex. Lo knew the scene was hard to absorb. One little silver person in each transparent silver pod, working away at consoles, perhaps attending to screens of some sort. Children playing with some kind of alien computers.

She shrugged. "It's hard to say what they're doing. They barely acknowledge us. We think they're engaged in some form of communal calculation—that's their way of praying. They also clearly communicate with each other, indicating what to do and when—like they're institutionalized. We've seen no signs that anyone is in charge, or giving orders, and yet they all stop for food at set times. The nannies tell them some things, like when to go to sleep, but they only do those things that suit them. They follow a regular exercise schedule. They allow us to bathe them. Some of them come to us when we call. Sometimes they even speak to us. But there are no guarantees. It's like raising a group of autistic children. We've tried for years to break the patterns, get them outside, playing or swimming or even just exploring, but nothing has worked. We've even tried not serving them, withholding care. That's how we learned about telepathic screams, the kind that give you nightmares, the kind that make your ears bleed."

Will shook his head. "No normal psychological strategies are going to work. The children's dysfunction is literally hard-wired. Aversion therapy—electric shock treatment—might work, but I don't know how you'd manage to do that, and maybe you wouldn't want to…"

Lo kicked at a tuft of grass, looking down as she said, "Oh, we want to. Enough of us, anyway. We've talked a lot about different techniques over the years. Last time we communicated, IBM City thought they'd finally come up with a plan that might work. We're not in a great rush to try it here in Saugatuck though. Yes, we want our children to become more human again and have real lives, but we'll only take drastic measures if they're guaranteed to work. We're scared of hurting the children or doing anything that would incite them to hurt us."

"So you *are* scared of them."

"Maybe a little—children sometimes lash out."

"Tell me about it."

"You scared her."

"She broke my wrist."

"They don't always know their own strength."

Will shook his head. "You're making excuses—and making me nervous. I've seen enough. I get the point. Now can we go back? I still want to attend your public meeting this morning. But look at me. I need to shower and dress. Please, Lo."

Lo wasn't moved. "There's still plenty of time. And before we leave I want you to meet Mira. Do you remember Mira, Libby's kid, on Aunty Maggie's side?"

"The pageant princess?"

"Yeah, awful that was. Poor kid. Anyway, she's expecting us."

"How can she be expecting us?"

"Do you really need to ask?"

Lo shut her eyes and sent her message to Mira. A single word: *come.*

She looked over at the complex and saw a star-shaped aperture on one of the pods open into a window. A small silver-capped girl poked out. She waved, like a regular kid might, perhaps more mechanically. Lo waved back. Mira flew out the window and through the air. She flew to within five feet of their faces, but didn't land. Constantly fluttering her feet to remain airborne, she made peculiar

little humming noises as she circled Will. Lo had seen this before—Mira was behaving like a sniffing dog. Will remained calm
in his stance, but his voice was taut.

"Hi Mira," he said, "Remember me, Uncle Will?"

Mira ignored him and continued to flutter, peering closely at
the gem-studded crux on Will's chest as she did so, moving her
tiny pretty hands about in the air as if she was feeling his breasts
and typing on a computer at the same time.

Will said, "She's freaking me out, Lo. What's she doing?"

Lo threw her hands in the air. She had been wondering the
same.

Mira's humming became ever higher in pitch as her hands
hovered around Will's crux. Suddenly Lo's mind was flooded with
Mira's thoughts. As she had done many times before, Mira tried to
explain the inexplicable to her. Not feelings, but practical things
beyond Lo's ken. Mira was telling her what she understood about
the technology of Will's crux. As the concepts came into focus Lo
began barking them out to Will.

"Comms. Defense. Authorization Codes. Signal Blocking.
Medical Monitor. Data Recording. Visual Analysis. Portals. Information Systems. Spatial Analysis."

Lo stopped and said, "You told me your crux was a medical
device."

"It is," said Will.

"And the rest?" said Lo.

"Listen to her. There's no weaponry. Nothing that would harm
any of you."

"I'll be the judge of that," replied Lo.

"Please trust me," said Will. "I'm not here to hurt you or anyone else."

Lo stared at the crux. She was struggling to take it in, the full
extent of the powers lurking within those gems. Why hadn't he
told her? Was he planning on using all that technology against
them? Was he communicating with the Orbiters right now? Telling

them how to get past their defenses? Lo felt her wires begin to fizz with fear and rage. She was overloading. Her brain was hurting. Will was hurting her.

It wasn't just him. Mira's humming had turned to a buzz. She'd asked a question, and she was waiting for Lo to respond. Bzzz. Bzzz. The pair had built an understanding over the last thirty years, but Lo knew that Mira's attention span was short. The girl wanted to return to her pod. It was now or never. Lo made her decision.

do—it—carefully

The pretty little girl then raised both hands and shot a small but intense hail of light-beams into the gems studding Will's chest. A sharp burning smell rent the air. Will screamed. As he crumpled to the ground in agony, Mira flew away, face expressionless.

Lo's whole body felt like it was on fire too. She leaned down and whispered in her brother's ear, "It'll be alright. I'm taking you straight for help. Helena will patch you up. Mira only shorted your wires. The rest of you will be fine. Just some flesh burns."

She rolled Will back into the net lying on the ground, jumped through the open aperture into her pod, fired up the controls, and sped homewards. It was just after 5:00 a.m.; the light was turning. Waving at the bright-white tower of glass bubbles as she lifted off, Will huddled groaning in the net behind her, Lo floated a message out to Mira: *love—you*

Her reply was as usual: *love you too*

Then she added something extra: *everyone safe now*

If only that were true.

14

Marie watched from an upstairs window as Lo flew away with her brother strapped to the back of her pod. The Inn was silent, except for the whirring of rickety old ceiling fans. She'd only awoken because Carly had zapped her to warn of intruders. She wasn't sure how she felt about what she'd just seen. Will Warren most definitely needed to understand the rules and realities of Saugatuck, but she still didn't think they should encourage violence in the children. The women were the protectors. The children were the protectees. No matter what anyone else said, they *were* still children. If you covered up the silver pinpricks on her skin and put a wig over that silver dome, Carly would still look a lot like the snub-nosed child of her third-grade picture.

Marie was wearing her last pair of worn-out Hogwarts sweats—the ones they'd bought three-for-two on the trip to Universal Studios, Orlando—and her moth-eaten *Mommy Rocks* tank—the one Carly had given her on the very last Mother's Day. The dingy white top had pictures of diamonds scattered under the pink words. There used to be little pink beads stitched here and there. Those were long gone. Most things delicate and precious were long gone.

She looked around for some day clothes to throw on. It was hard to see in the dark, and the small room was a cluttered mess, filled with leftover fragments of Carly's other childhood, the one before the pod complex. Once every three or four months the nannies told her to clean the room up, said it was a health hazard, but she always ignored them. It wasn't as if anyone else was using the room; there were fifteen nannies, six living moms, and thirty-two rooms. Marie was the only one of those women who lived somewhere else as well. In the early days, James would quite often stay out at the Inn with her, but after about five years he said he'd had enough of pretending that anything was normal about Carly. Didn't Marie understand that she would never play with toys again? Marie almost left him over that. She almost left him many times, but if she left him, who would she be? She was Marie Nunn. He was James Nunn. They were the parents of Carly Nunn.

And this was Carly Nunn's room. There may not be a place set aside for her in their place on Bradley Lane, but here she would always be their little princess. Once a month, Marie went out "shopping" on the old post road, looking for clothes, toys, and other items that Carly might enjoy. Carly always rejected her gifts when she presented them to her at her pod, just dropping them on the ground like her hands didn't work. Marie didn't mind any more. She would just pick up the item and add it to Carly's collection. What a great surprise the kid was going to get when she finally woke up from her situation. The bed alone was home to five *American Girl* dolls, two *Frozen* comforters, an *Elsa* robe and slippers, a *Hello Miss Kitty* backpack filled with *Fancy Nancy* books, and numerous plush toys. The toys on the beds were the things that made Marie feel closest to the old Carly and she slept with them scattered around her. The rest of the room was filled with many more things Marie hoped Carly would enjoy one day, including the complete *Harry Potter* series, numerous craft kits, and a great selection of jewelry and hair accessories that a young girl might like.

As she squinted into the dark, looking for her clothes, Marie felt Carly's mind penetrate her own. *All gone—all safe.* She looked back out the window, focused her eyes, and zoomed in on Carly's pod. Her daughter waved at her. Marie waved back. *See—you—breakfast.* Carly responded with an echo. *See—you—breakfast.* Marie sighed. She was awake. Carly was awake. It would make sense for them to both go have breakfast together now, just throw something together in the Inn kitchen, enjoy some private together time. But Carly became agitated if Marie broke the routines. Breakfast was a group meal in the dining hall at 8:00 a.m.—three hours from now. Scrambled eggs and bread. Fruit and fruit jam. Milk. Always the same. The children tended to reject variation, and Marie had stopped bringing food treats long ago.

The question now was what to do until breakfast. Marie knew that she could do a lot to help prepare for the town meeting—and Yaz was probably already awake and on duty at HQ—but first she thought she should speak with James. Her husband had wanted her to join him at home last night for a group discussion about *the developing alien situation*, but Marie had opted to watch over the children with some other moms and the nannies. It might seem a long time ago now to some, but what those avenging angels did to the Green's Farm kids still haunted her dreams. In spite of all her watching and worrying, though, it was the kids who had looked after themselves last night.

After changing into a crumpled pair of khaki shorts and old Nunn's Nursery t-shirt, Marie crept downstairs and out the back door to where her pod lay on the gravel next to the kitchen garden. It was true she treated this place like her own personal hotel, but nobody minded because she gave so much of herself in return, bringing in most of the supplies and maintaining the property to a high standard. It was also she who established and oversaw the running program—twenty-seven years strong now. Sure the children were awkward and refused to run in anything but a set pattern, but they did complete their circuit every morning after breakfast. Perhaps they didn't need it, perhaps their Ruurdaan wiring protected their muscles, but this kept them fit for sure, and added a human dimension to their stunted lives. What was it Carly had said to her all those years ago when they got started—*running—feels—good—in—the—body*. Once upon a time, Marie would have begged to differ. However, in her wired incarnation she loved running five miles with her Carly every morning. Running together felt good in the soul.

As she flew away from the Inn, out across the river, Marie saw that the spaceship was still in the river. Still here, then. She flew straight on over town to their duplex on Bradley Lane, just back of the Exit 17 checkpoint. They'd moved there about fifteen years ago, along with some of the other mothers, the mothers of James natural children, the ones he called *the future*. Some of them were test-tubers, like Reid. Others were just regular little bastards. Marie didn't really mean that—in fact she was friendly with most of the kids and the moms. The world had changed, and her marriage had changed with it. If she had wanted a divorce, James would have given her one—but what was the point—their marriage didn't stop either of them doing what they wanted, and Marie liked the thought that there would be a family structure awaiting Carly when she got better.

Oh, sure, Marie knew that a lot of the other women thought James was a jerk. Maybe he was, but he was her jerk, and they understood each other. She supported and protected him. He stuck by her side and made her feel like his number-one wife. Not the one he wanted to sleep with, maybe, but the one he trusted and respected the most. Her father had treated her mother exactly the same way, like the boss mamma. Marie was sure that if it wasn't for the Ruurdaans, hers would still be a very happy family of five.

Trisha and Kyle had been at school the day the spheres hit. Their school was now the outer edge of the flats. Back then it was a series of buildings on a couple of acres at the far end of Riverside Avenue, up where the post road hit Westport proper. Nunn's Nursery was very close by, just a quarter mile closer to Saugatuck, its greenhouses built into a small hill. Carly had been at home with strep throat that day, resting up with her grammy on the other side of the river, over by the Warren place. Marie had been working in the greenhouses. Back then she had worked every hour of every day trying to make Nunn's Nursery support their standard of living. James had been in the office that day, probably watching porn online, or surfing for a new BMW convertible or planning a night out in Norwalk with one of their six pretty young garden hands, his usual idea of work.

Marie would never forget the thud of the sphere that broke almost every pane of glass — like a meteor had just crashed next to her. Cut and bleeding, she had run for the office, grabbed up a dazed and confused James, ordered him into the jeep and headed for the school. The road ended about two hundred feet up River-side Avenue from the nursery. River water was already flowing across the flat expanse that was all that was left of businesses, houses, people. Marie had turned the car around and headed for their family house. She then dropped James at their boat, docked right next to the general store, told him to load up with emergency supplies and wait for her to come back with everyone. She hadn't seen him again until three years later — when he straggled in from the sea, emaciated, disturbed, but saved by the foil-covered emer-gency blankets she'd bought them all one Christmas. He'd mocked her for them at the time.

Now, as she landed her pod in the old turning-circle outside their fake-colonial enclave, Marie saw that all four adjoining Nunn households were dark. James was clearly sleeping easy in spite of the developing alien situation. He was supposed to be pulling an all-nighter preparing for the town meeting. Lazy old fool.

Marie ran bare-footed up the path, unlocked the front door with a beam from her gloved hand and slammed it closed again behind her as she raced into the house. In case he hadn't gotten the message, she shouted, "James, wake up," as she began flicking her hands in the air, turning on every light switch in the house. She didn't waste any time with pleasantries either when the old man appeared in the kitchen doorway, groggy and muttering, "God damn it, Marie, it's half-past five in the morning."

"Are you alone?"

"Yes," he replied. "You know what I was doing last night. I had the guys over to discuss strategy—which we did. We're ready to march that Will Warren outta town."

"That's big talk coming from a man who hides in the hole with his girlfriends while his wife is out there covering his age-spotted ass."

"Are you still angry about the thing with Merryn Weintraub?"

"She's fifteen."

"She wants to have a baby. Actually, she wants to have a lot of babies. She wants to be a surrogate for as many women as possible. I find her noble."

"No. You find her nubile. She's underage, James. And before you even say it, yes, there is still such a thing. Sixteen is the age of consent in this town. Maybe we're more relaxed if the parties are the same age—but not if we're talking about a dirty old man."

"You're just a broken record, Marie. You don't even try to understand my position. I say no far more often than I say yes, and I say yes because I want to help."

"Just shut the fuck up, James. I'm not interested in all that right now. What are we going to do about Will Warren? How are we going to protect the secret of the children?"

James nodded. "We talked about that tonight, amongst the guys. We think it's pretty clear that you security crew gals need to destroy the spaceship and remove Will Warren and his buddy to somewhere far, far away from here."

Marie nodded. It was exactly what she'd been thinking. "So are you ready for the meeting this morning then? Are you ready to tell Lo how the men feel? Your buddies at least. Half the other guys never show their faces, and the young ones seem to like the idea of new blood. So your group really needs to speak out. I'm scared that Lo will keep taking half-measures because it's her brother. Her judgment is off."

"You usually side with your old buddy, Lo."

"You know we have a lot of history. But this is about Carly's safety..."

"You have my full support."

"What does that mean, James? In real terms?"

"Well the guys and I made some placards..."

Marie sighed. Where would she be without her man?

15

The only good alien... So read the placard some old geezer was holding aloft as Will and Lo crossed over the road from HQ and walked down the main path in Saugatuck park. Will noted for the first time that every red brick had a name etched into the surface. So many names. Behind him he could hear the comforting chatter of Pat, Janine, and Bob. They were all headed for the small town amphitheater, moving along in a sea of women's bodies. Will observed a distinctive halo of black hair up ahead, bobbing above all the other heads. It was Yaz, the woman who thought she could read people. This morning she was busy organizing a huge crowd gathered on the concrete benches of the amphitheater and the surrounding grassy slope. A couple of young guys were helping set up a dais. Will recognized some women from the interviews. A couple waved and smiled. Most stared and whispered, whether for or against him, he couldn't tell. Lo jerked her head to the right a couple of times, indicating the old guy walking alongside them with the placard.

"Your old pal," she said.

Will looked closer at the speckled brown corpse with the bug eyes. James Nunn. He looked closer to eighty than seventy. The guy used to look and talk like he was a Kennedy, although all he really had in common with them was Irish coloring and a lack of respect for women. He used to be a vicious homophobe too. Now, apparently, he was a vicious Orbiter-hater. All too predictably, he was not doing his hating alone. Two sparkly hard-faced young women and another beer-bellied older man were with him, carrying painted signs that read *Remember Dina; Sorry, We're Full;* and *Send them into Orbit.* Will didn't like to think that his future lay in the hands of people like this. It was going to take more than charm to get out of this situation.

When they had landed back at HQ after leaving the pod complex, Lo had carried him, enveloped in a cocoon of air, into simply furnished sleeping quarters, probably for crew in need of a quick nap, and laid him gently on one of the beds. Helena had been there as promised, ready to tend his wounds. She was wearing old doctor's scrubs, as if ready for a messy job. Through the throbbing pain of his chest, Will heard Helena berate Lo for what Mira had done. It was the only time he'd ever heard Helena raise her voice. The diagnosis was ugly too—extensive highly localized second-degree burns and potential nerve damage around the pectoral muscles. Helena had apologized profusely as she treated him: sorry for the pain, sorry that Lo used Mira to inflict violence, so sorry. Lo shouted at her, pointing out that he was caught snooping around the children, was more way powerful than he had admitted, and had lied to them for suspicious reasons. He'd tried to protest through the pain, but Helena had shushed him. She finished treating him in silence, whether angry, hurt, or contemplative he couldn't tell. She'd treated him like a delicate child, though, and when she was done she taped a small strip of twelve Oxycodone to his leg, well-hidden by the sheet he was wearing in place of his confiscated bodcoz. Will was especially grateful for the painkillers. The burns throbbed and seared.

Will had no idea how bad the damage was, but he feared that comms, authorization codes, and medical monitoring were all gone. There was certainly no pain relief. Visuals seemed to be working, but he could not access media files or utilities. He had no idea what else was working. That freaky kid had totally fried his crux. Not that he could really blame the kid—Lo had unleashed her as surely as if she were a trained Rottweiler. She seemed to feel justified because he hadn't revealed every detail of his personal technology to her—which was precisely because he worried she might react like this. Lo was more than just a loose cannon—she was a paranoid president with a fully loaded arsenal.

Now, as he walked alongside Lo to the dais, Will stopped thinking about what was beyond his control and focused on any angles he could leverage. Lo may have thought that giving him nothing but an old sheet to wear like a toga would diminish him, but Will thought he could work it. As he walked, he opened his palms to the crowd. It was the way all Orbital diplomats presented themselves. Will was reminded of his earliest days attending council events on Crn. Nobody trusted, respected, or even liked him. The shuttle story dogged him. But he'd said the right things, slept with the right people, done the right dirty—and within two years he was an ambassador. Will knew he had the kind of resiliency that you just couldn't learn, the kind you inherited from people who had come to America without shoes and coats. He could also feel the Oxycodone giving him the strength to take on this bunch of cowgirls.

"Are you ready," he said, turning to Bob. "That's quite a fan club."

"They're alright," Bob replied. "I like a world with a lot of chicks."

Will saw Janine kick him. Bob would barely feel it, as he was still wearing his bodcoz. Today it was a mellow green, still overlaid with the big peace sign on the chest. Will had already asked Lo why Bob could keep his bodcoz and not him. Apparently Bob had not yet attempted to escape supervision or otherwise acted hostile. Will suspected Lo was just using Bob to make a point—as if selective violence was justifiable and random mercy a sign of benevolence. He questioned both her judgment and her leadership. Yet this was clearly her town. The crowds parted as she walked; they were all waiting on her words. They clearly valued Lo's strength and certainty. He could only hope that some of them secretly harbored nagging doubts about her dictatorial and paranoid tendencies. If he could just build himself a strong minority of supporters... It was difficult to imagine though, looking out at all those hard young faces.

Today's crowd was much larger than the one that had greeted them on the first night, perhaps five hundred strong—more than half the population. Clothes were light in anticipation of another hot summer day. Shorts and tanks. Faded summer beach dresses. Will faced a sea of hair and breasts and glittering skin. The odd older woman was in the crowd, most notably Helena with her distinctive gray bun, but most were twenty- and thirty-somethings. Reid was with a small gang of teenaged friends, male and female. Will had also noted a couple of men standing together amongst the women. There was even a child in a stroller (a *natural* as he now understood these third-generation offspring were called). The crowd spilled out of the amphitheater and across the rolling lawn. Some of the women had brought blankets to sit on, reminding Will of rallies on Capitol Hill.

Other people were clearly planning on listening in at a distance—Will noticed broadcasting equipment set up around the low podium at the center of the amphitheater. The women must be operating some kind of radio network. Will wondered if he could use it to contact the explorer, or maybe even Retske up in Madison—to call for a rescue mission. Then he remembered. The Orbiters hadn't used radio-waves to communicate in eons. Only two rescue possibilities existed: repair his own equipment somehow or wait until he missed the rendezvous and the explorer sent a team to look for him in three or four weeks' time. There would probably be no visiting Madison or the other fifteen proposed drop-sites now, but that was just too bad. Personal safety took priority. Will smiled around the crowd and sought eye contact. The best thing he could do right now was wage a hearts-and-mind campaign here in Saugatuck.

Will was happy about the hard wooden chairs that had been set up for him and Bob on the podium. He didn't look so tall and alien when seated. He observed carefully as the women finished their preparations. Yaz ran around strategically positioning the security crew. Pat stood just below and to the right of Lo on the podium stairs, arms folded, face like a faithful bulldog. So the security was not all for his benefit. Perhaps not everyone always agreed with Lo. Will already knew that Janine did not. Looking around, he saw that the blonde was now seated on the benches with a group of sparkly young friends. They weren't really young of course, but their energy was youthfully upbeat—unlike Lo's jaded old gang.

Will saw that Adrianna and Yaz had taken up guard positions on either side of the podium. Yaz shut her eyes and nodded. A second later, Lo stepped up onto to the podium, gesturing to those sitting on the ranks of benches to scrunch up and make room.

"Quiet everyone," she boomed, throwing her voice like she had a megaphone.

The crowd stopped talking.

"Alright then ladies," she said, "so it's been two days since our guests arrived. Some of you have already had a chance to meet Will and Bob, and I understand those conversations went well. Some concerns were raised, but most of you reported feeling safe with the men. I too think we are generally safe with them—so long as they remain alone. However, I have some grave longer-term concerns. I've also had the opportunity to speak at length with my brother. Those conversations did not go well. They made me see that Will is lying to us all about many things—including his technological capabilities and his purpose here in Saugatuck. In fact, I've come to believe that my brother is here helping the Orbiters colonize our region, perhaps even our town."

Oh, shit. A roar of dismay arose from the crowd. A shrill voice stood out above the rest. "I knew it," shouted Marie Nunn. "Just like in Madison."

"No wait…" Will tried to stand up and speak but invisible hands held him fast. He looked around to find Adrianna glaring at him, hands outstretched and clenched.

"Let Lo finish," Yaz and Pat shouted to the crowd, almost in unison.

"Thanks," continued Lo. "You'll all get a chance to speak in a moment."

"Why are they still here?" shouted someone. "Let's just remove them to the Bridgeport Shallows and be done with it."

Lo raised her hands. "A little calm, ladies. I already said the men are no danger right now. All technology threats have been defused. They have no weapons."

A small group of women stood up and started shaking their fists at the podium.

Lo stared them down. "I said they're not an immediate danger, alright? Just settle down and listen. I'm trying to address your security concerns."

The crowd remained restless, but Lo pressed on.

"For the time being the men are under guard—and I trust my guards—but, we can't expend our security resources on them forever..."

Will saw that Reid and his friends had stood up. Reid shouted, "You're not even giving them a chance. I've met them both. They're good guys. We need more guys around here."

Will raised his hand and acknowledged their support. Reid held up a strong fist and flexed his muscles, not that those muscles would be any use against Lo.

Lo gestured for everyone to sit back down. "Calm down, all of you, and listen. You did vote for me to make decisions for you—but that's not what I have in mind here. Even in the toughest of times we've always honored democratic process. That's why I'm giving these two a chance to explain themselves to you this morning. After they've spoken there will be time for discussion and suggestions. We'll take the best ideas to the council and draw up voting ballots."

"Let them stay here," shouted Reid.

"Create a real prison," shouted someone else. "Let them stay here in custody."

"They'll just attract more Orbiters. We have to get rid of them."

"Drop them up to their friends in Madison."

"Drop them outside the gates with the dogs."

"Oh, give them a chance to speak, will you? They're not going to come down there and get all five hundred of you at once." That was Pat, and the sound of her voice seemed to help calm the mood.

Lo said, "Yes, let's hear from the men first, then make a decision."

As the crowd slowly quieted, Will looked to see how Bob was taking things. The lanky Alaskan was sprawled out on his small wooden chair, head nodding at nothing in particular, as if in agreement with everyone. Will gave him a sideways glance and pointed down at him with his finger, low enough for discretion he hoped. Bob should speak first so that, if necessary, Will could mop up after him. Taking the hint, Bob rose from his chair and ambled towards the front of the stage. The crowd fell completely silent. Bob gave everyone a lopsided grin and shouted.

"Hello everyone in Saugatuck. I'm not much of a public speaker, so I'm going to keep this brief. Thanks for letting us be here and giving us the chance to speak with you. As they say in Aleut—that's the native language where I'm from—*qagaasakung*. Now I know you expect me to tell you what we're doing here with the Orbiters and all that, and I wish I could, but the truth is I don't really know shit. I just hitched a ride home after too many years away—and not by choice. You peeps have no idea how good it feels to be home. The food is awesome, the place is beautiful, the weather's great, and Earth ladies are way lovelier than I remembered. What else is there to say? I'd like to stay here if you'll have me. I'm a trained biologist, and I would definitely like to try growing coffee here. That could make a nice change from mint tea."

Then he just sat back down.

Will laughed in spite of everything. Some of the women even began clapping politely. Janine began clapping wildly and was soon joined by her friends. Reid and Co. whooped like cattle rousers. However, most of the crowd still looked worried and angry.

Adrianna said loudly, "What the fuck?"

Lo finished her thought. "What I'm hearing is that there are quite a few morons among us who are more interested in reopening Starbucks than safeguarding our town for the future." Will noticed that she was staring at Pat and Yaz, looking for support.

"Yeah, get real," said Pat. It sounded half-hearted.

"Let's not lose focus here," said Yaz.

Lo gestured to Will. "Yes, let's move on," she said.

Will stepped to the front of the podium and raised both hands to the crowd. "Thank you for your attention," he said, aiming for polite formality. "I am deeply grateful to have this chance to speak on behalf of myself and the Orbiters."

Hissing and hooting competed for airtime. Will tried to ignore it.

"Before I talk about the Orbiters though, let me echo Bob. I've had an amazing couple of days back home here in Saugatuck. A-mazing. I'm not going to lie to you though and say it's all been easy. Lo is rightfully protective of her community, but as a result I have felt afraid."

"I'll give you afraid, you mongrel." Will looked for the source of the shrill female voice. Marie Nunn. He was beginning to wonder if he'd ever offended her personally.

Someone else yelled, "Save it for later, Marie, let him speak."

He pressed on. "As I was saying, I have become afraid to speak about the Orbiters and why they decided to send a few brave men to help the women of Earth rebuild. I desperately wish to explain the situation, but it's —"

"Let's just throw that one into the Atlantic without a vote," shouted someone.

"With concrete slippers," shouted someone else.

"What kind of talk is that?" It was Helena, standing up suddenly in the crowd.

Out the corner of his eye. Will saw Lo signaling to her security crew to tighten crowd control. It was ironic, given the state of his chest, but Lo was now protecting him. The crowd continued to murmur and jostle, but Helena had quieted them just enough that he was able to continue. "I can't speak of the Orbiter settlers if the very mention of them endangers me and my colleague. Note I said settlers, not colonists. I know what you all fear, but I can absolutely assure you that there is not going to be another invasion of Earth. There are only very small numbers of Orbiters who are interested in coming here. And only if they're invited..."

If only Retske had done her job. After settling Madison she was supposed to have gone around soliciting settlement invitations from surrounding towns. Will knew it would've been a challenge once the Unans started wreaking havoc in the area and that Saugatuck would probably have sent her packing. Nevertheless, it would have laid the groundwork for his arrival, saved a lot of misunderstanding.

"The Orbiters that want to come are good people. Or should I say, good men."

A good number of the crowd booed, but Will also heard a couple of cat-calls. That buoyed his spirits. If he could just catch that slender thread of enthusiasm, sell it on...

"The men will bring the skills necessary to rebuild this whole area: roads, gas stations, hospitals, factories, media services. Imagine the return of a national infrastructure."

"Who says we want one," shouted a woman in the front row of seats.

"I want one," shouted another, "I'm sick of this small town."

"He's just selling you a pipe-dream," shouted another. "What do you think they've got in Madison that we haven't got here? Television? Facebook? Twinkies?"

Will shouted back. "I'm not saying it would happen overnight. It will take time, resources and numbers—but don't you want to try? What you've achieved on your own is impressive. What you could achieve with the Orbiters' help would be incredible."

Light applause. The balance was shifting. Then he heard Lo boom.

"The only thing the Orbiters have done around here so far is kill innocent people."

Jeers again rippled through the crowd.

"I admit there've been problems" replied Will. "However, I'm confident I can sort those out. All I'm asking is that you give a few decent Orbiters a second chance."

"Yeah, like a fat chance," someone yelled.

"Bury 'em deep," shouted a male voice.

"Shut up, shrivel-dick," yelled someone else.

"Ladies," shouted Will, but the women didn't stop.

"We don't want to live on the planet of the apes."

"They'll overrun us within ten years."

"It's just another way of invading."

"I've had a lifetime's worth of aliens."

Will searched the crowd for gestures of support. Reid and his friends were arguing with a small group of women, and Janine and her friends were trying to shout over the noise. It wasn't going to be enough. He made a desperate decision.

"Children," he shouted. "The Orbiters can give you children."

16

The crowd were silent, expectant.

"What?" said Lo. "What did you just say?"

Will scrabbled fast. "I didn't want to mention it before I evaluated the situation myself, but I know that the Orbital settlers in Madison are working on reversing the sterilization. The last report we got from those guys, about a year ago, included news of two pregnancies. I can't confirm the birth of two babies, but I'm optimistic. So, yes, children. Your own children."

At least half the women began cheering and hugging each other. Others looked stunned and disbelieving. Then came the questions...

"Are the babies healthy?"

"Are the women okay?"

"What's happened with their wiring?"

"Do they still have their powers?"

"Are they aging? Or staying young?"

Will didn't have a clue. The last he heard, just before he left home nine months earlier, was that the first attempts at Earthan/Orbiter procreation had all gone horribly wrong. Nevertheless, it was true that the Madison settlers had been trying. Maybe they'd succeeded in the intervening period? It wasn't impossible.

"In theory two healthy children should have been delivered by now, but..."

Will didn't get to finish because the crowd erupted. Clearly this was the first these women had heard of any pregnancies or births in Madison. Either there hadn't been any live births, or Retske hadn't sent out birth announcements. Seeing the reaction of this crowd, Will could imagine why — the thought of hundreds, maybe thousands, of women descending on one small settlement seeking fertility treatment was terrifying.

"Oh my God, this changes everything! This is wonderful."

It was a young woman wearing a faded pink tennis dress and holding a piece of old plastic like a bullhorn. She had probably been preparing to abuse him three minutes ago.

"Oh my God, if it's true then we have to consider letting them settle here. It's not about the men. I don't care what they're like if they can give me a child."

The crowd rumbled with tension, reactions flying in all directions.

The woman in the pink dress continued, "It's all I've thought about since my own died. I just want to hold a child of my own once more. And don't any of you even think of saying we already have children. Our precious few naturals aren't mine, and neither are the children at the Inn. Those aren't even children anyway, not anymore."

Will felt the tension fill the air like static.

"They're eight-year-olds," screamed Marie Nunn.

"They're forty-year-old time bombs," hollered someone else.

"If it would help, I'm sure the Orbiters would also be happy to evaluate the children," ventured Will. "They don't know much about Ruurdaan technology, but…"

Before he could finish, he was rugby-tackled to the ground by Pat.

"What the…" he began, before seeing exactly what.

Someone had thrown a half-full cooler at the podium at killer speed. The cooler had been captured by a beam—midair. It now hung like a frozen fountain of broken plastic, scattered bottles, and droplets of liquid. Just behind the podium and on the fringe of the crowd gathered there, he could see that Ruby was using two hands to hold the mess in the sky while looking for somewhere safe to deposit it.

"Air-shield," he heard Lo shout.

Suddenly all the crew began waving their hands up and down like crazy in front of the podium. Objects flew at the small stage from all directions, but they slammed into the air barrier and slumped to the ground. Will saw Adrianna pulling small missiles out of women's hands and another woman engaged in a mid-air tussle with Marie, who was attempting to throw handfuls of coins—not entirely unlike a hail of bullets. Will was grateful to find himself face down on the podium under the reassuring heft of Pat. He saw Adrianna use her left foot to pull Bob's chair to the ground, Bob still in it.

"Calm the fuck down, everyone," screamed Lo.

The crowd simmered down and the missiles stopped altogether.

"And put your weapons down. If anyone is killed here today I'll charge the perpetrator with murder, you hear me? We are not vigilantes. We do things right."

Will sensed that she actually believed her own bullshit. She really needed therapy.

"That said, I've had enough of these guys causing trouble, lying and manipulating our emotions. If there's any truth in what they say about the children I'll make sure to get the information from Madison myself. We don't need these two to tell us anything. We need them where they can't hurt us—which is why I've come up with a humane plan to get rid of them..."

The crowd fell silent. Will felt sick. He was still lying under big Pat.

"What I propose is that we remove Will and Bob to some place way beyond our borders—further than usual—I'm thinking Bermuda. It's isolated but not wilderness. The last time I was there—admittedly about forty-five years ago with my parents—it was also pretty nice. I have no idea if there are any survivors on the island, but I know it's a survivable environment. If I throw their bodcoz and some weapons down after them they should have more than a fighting chance."

Will pushed Pat off him and sat up. Bermuda was probably also run by powerful murderous women. Without the tracking codes in his gems, or the comms controls that Lo had confiscated, he and Bob would never be found.

Lo continued. "Our tech team estimate the mission will take around twelve hours, round trip. I'm not going to lie. It's a risky trip. Not many of us have spent twelve continuous hours flying. We don't know what's out there. It will be a voluntary mission."

Ten hands flew into the air. Lo gestured for them to put their hands down.

"Thanks for your support, but we need to vote on the plan before I start putting together a crew. I'll also need volunteers to move that orbicraft still sitting in our river. We should dump it as far out in the ocean as we can safely manage. It's a potential beacon to other Orbiters."

Janine stepped out from the crowd and said, "You say there's going to be a vote, but you're talking like it's already decided. Well, maybe not everyone agrees with you, Lo. We should really consider other options. We're talking about two unarmed guys."

"Yes and some of us might want to hear more about the children…"

Lo rounded on the group furiously. "I already said we'd discuss options before we vote. I already said I'll make contact with Madison about the alleged children. Don't you dare suggest I'm not thinking hard enough. Will is my brother, for fuck's sake. You think I want to do this? But if we don't make it clear that we will respond with force to *any* attempts at Orbital colonization, then we will have nobody but ourselves to blame when aliens start landing here like they did in Madison—all smiles and where's my bedroom."

"And what if they did, Lo? How would that really hurt us?" It was Janine.

Will saw electric sparks of anger flash out of Lo's clenched fists. "Are you kidding me? You can't think how alien colonists could hurt us?"

"Things are different now. We're not defenseless anymore." Janine looked over at Bob—lying on the podium with his head resting on one bent arm—held out her hands and began lifting them up and down. Bob's body rose and slumped at her command. It was a gentle demonstration, and Bob made only the mildest of complaints. "Hey."

Some women in the crowd clapped. Most remained silent.

Lo shouted out, "Nice trick, Janine, but that's only one strong woman against one unarmed man. Do you think those are going be the real odds?"

Before Janine had a chance to answer, Will leaped up and shouted, "Janine is right. We're not dangerous to you. You're way more dangerous to us. Just look at this..."

Will ripped his toga down to his waist, exposing a mess of bandages. As he unraveled them the extensive burns on his chest came into view; singed skin clinging to half-molten stones, raw and weeping networks of red lines. A number of women cried out in shock. Even Pat and Adrianna had the decency to turn their faces away.

"Let me explain," said Lo.

"Save me from her," whispered Will. He hung his head and held his hand out towards Janine's crowd. "Help me get to Madison. I can get medical help there."

"Shut up, Will." Lo was raising her gloved hand.

Will saw advantage there too. "No," he shouted. "Please don't hurt me again."

He felt Pat clamp her hand on his arm and saw Yaz moving to speak to Lo.

All of a sudden the sirens began to whoop. Everybody froze. Lo held her hands up for quiet and closed her eyes. She began nodding and shaking her head. The others all started shaking and nodding too. Some kind of mass messaging. Suddenly a collective shockwave seemed to roll out over the crowd. Half of them turned and started to run.

Lo shouted out to the rest, "Full scale alert. Battle stations. Orbiters in the river."

Will thought fast. The chances that this was a rescue party from his own mission were extremely low. It was probably more of the Unans. Too bad he had no ship, coz, controls or access to the Vroom72. As he was considering running towards the river, Pat picked him up and dumped him over the edge of the podium. Reid caught him before he fell to the ground.

"Come with us," he said.

Will went with Reid, trailing bandages and bunching the toga around him as best he could. He felt for the Oxycodone taped to his side, the only thing holding him together right now.

"Where are we going?" he asked as he, Reid, Helena, and about forty other naturals slipped away into a passage beneath the podium.

"Into the hole at HQ." Reid replied.

"Hiding is fine by me," said Will.

Reid gave him a look. "I'd rather be fighting."

"Yes, of course."

"There are many different ways to deal with danger," said Helena.

"Absolutely. What will Lo be doing?"

"Fighting for us to the death," she replied.

17

Lo beamed a single command to her crew as they scrambled for their pods: *remove*. All forty fliers knew to proceed immediately to the river, begin plucking individuals off boats attempting to enter Saugatuck, and remove them to nearby Cockenoe Island. Nothing more, nothing less. The women were to refuse all entreaties or calls for negotiation, but also not harm anyone unless they were attacked, in which case they should use full force. There would be a cooling down period before Lo and her negotiators approached the island to talk to their attackers. This rigid protocol was born of bitter experience. Nobody wanted a repeat of the Cockenoe removals of Year 8.

The Cockenoe removals had occurred about eight years into the Saugatuck settlement. Back then they still dealt with things on the fly—no protocols, no chain of command. One night, two powerful feral women had been caught attempting to raid the fledgling marijuana crops. In the ensuing tussle Pat's partner Beth Ann had been killed, her neck snapped like a twig. The ferals were subdued using a controversial technique—cut-and-wet—shorting a woman's wiring by making small incisions all over and dousing them with water. After the two women lost consciousness, they were removed to Cockenoe and left to sting for three days. Everyone was just mad as hell, and nobody was in the mood for talking to them.

Cockenoe was a nice enough little island—a jagged-edged crescent of land about a mile out from the mouth of the Saugatuck river, no more than thirty acres, and renowned for its wild roses and white-shitting black cormorants; however, it was no place to spend an extended period of time without food, water, and shelter—especially when injured. Hungry, thirsty, hurting, and terrified, the two women had finally decided to swim for it, even though they must have known that wires and salt water don't mix. Both died in their own electrified brine, halfway back to the mainland.

Nobody felt right about it, not even as they buried Beth Ann. The line between Saugatuckers and ferals had gotten a little too thin. The women decided to create a security system with rules and protocols. They banned use of the cut-and-wet technique except under the most extreme of circumstances. They approved the use of removal to Cockenoe as the first line of defense. They also voted for Lo, until then simply their unofficial leader, to become their official commander-in-chief, answerable only to Helena (who was to be appointed their first mayor) and the council. On the same day they buried Beth Ann, Lo put out two military orders. First, she ordered the flag flown at half-mast above the Boat House. Second, she ordered the bodies of the dead ferals swung from a tall post just beyond the shallows of Cockenoe beach.

"We must terrify all comers," she'd said.

"We must do that which is necessary," Helena had agreed.

"We will do whatever you need us to do," Pat and the others had cried.

Well, here they were again...

Memories of terrors past always rushed back when Lo faced a physical threat. Those memories strengthened her resolve. Today as she released all her pent-up energy into the pod, readying both herself and her machine for battle, she was channeling the spirit of the twenty-six women they had lost since the women first came together all those years ago, a raggedy bunch of survivors staggering forth from various abandoned Ruurdaan work-units around the area, some coming home, some just looking for a safe-haven. These days others might think it was safe enough to talk and flirt with the enemy at the door—but never Lo. She would always remember Beth Ann, she would always remember Dina, she would always remember the twenty-six, and she would always remember those bloody rotting bodies swaying over the pretty white sands of Cockenoe.

Racing to the flotilla, which had gathered in deep water between Cockenoe and the mouth of the Saugatuck, Lo and her team executed their standard battle formation—forty glass bubbles moving together, at speed, in an inverted V—reminiscent of the Ruurdaan invasion itself. Lo already knew the general nature of the threat— sixty boats, the front ones bunched together like a floating city, the others bobbing behind like a watery wagon-train. Even if each boat held only two people, which seemed unlikely, that made a hundred and twenty potential enemy combatants. Lo figured on at least two hundred. She had no idea what kind of weapons they were packing, but she was glad she had called the whole crew out.

Leading the charge, Lo homed in on the lead boat, a newish-looking twenty-eight-foot Sunseeker. She directed her beam at the tall, bald guy at the helm. He was wearing a worn khaki bodcoz and waving. Echoes of Will. Lo didn't hesitate. Lifting him high, she flew across to Cockenoe, where she dropped her cargo safely on the long strip of grainy white beach. Although Lo could hear a dull cacophony of voices calling from the boats—*we just want to talk, we're not here to fight, we have families with us*—she refused to open her sun-roof and listen to them, just dove in on her next target.

For some reason, however, her beam could not get full traction on the tall pony-tailed red-head at the back of the lead boat, as if he were slippery. He appeared to be digging around in a box of guns. Infuriated, Lo put every bit of power she had into the beam. That enabled her to get a partial hold of the guy, although much more awkwardly than usual. She began pulling him up out of the weapons store and into the air. However, instead of rising neatly, the guy just jerked up a few feet then fell sideways into the water. It was lucky he didn't fall into the other boats, or between the cracks. Lo looked around. All her fliers were struggling with the same problem: people wobbling mid-air, people flailing in the water, even pods struggling to stay airborne. Only three Orbiters were visible on Cockenoe's sandy strip of beach. A couple more of the aliens flailed in the water. The rest remained on their ships shouting; they must all be wearing Orbiter defense technology. Contemplating the best way to deal with the resistance, Lo swooped back down over the lead boat, lifted the entire weapons chest, and flung it in the sea. Then she pointed a finger at the hairy Orbiter crouched down by the aft seating, peeking out. He was next.

Lo considered calling the pods into groupings of three. Together they could wrestle one or two key targets off the flotilla. Those individuals could be used as leverage to scare the rest away. They didn't have to get every Orbiter onto Cockenoe, just persuade most of them to leave. They had developed a technique that involved throwing and catching targets while they were trapped in the beam. It had proved an effective deterrent in the past. Lo was just about to give the order when one of the boats at the far end of the group started firing.

A barrage of bullets hit a pod that was already struggling to maintain altitude as it grappled with a resistant target. Although Lo's crew were strong-minded, they were not advanced telepathic fliers like the Ruurdaans; it was always a challenge to maintain full control of the pods while deploying their various functions, let alone under battle conditions. Lo watched in horror as the struggling pod began to fragment. The flier had lost control of the invisibly fine mesh of wires that dictated the integrity and flexibility of pod glass. The flying sphere that moments ago was as hard as a bullet itself was now as fragile as a Christmas ornament. Lo zoomed into action, scooping the cracking glass bubble into her beam as it plummeted to the sea. She managed to slow its descent, but she could not save it. The pod disintegrated upon impact and began to sink, leaving a woman with a beacon of red hair paddling unprotected in the water. Ruby appeared uninjured—her glass had held just long enough—but it had been a close call and she was not safe yet.

Sweeping down to the water, Lo scooped Ruby up in her beam and flew her across to a safe spot on the mainland, a rocky outcrop in front of the dense woods that blocked all views of the Inn. Then she drew back toward the mouth of the river, away from Cockenoe, beaming out the only possible order as she went: *pull—back.*

Her crew all immediately dropped their targets and pulled back to await instruction. Lo reassessed. Way up the river she saw a large group of boats had gathered around the checkpoint just beyond the bridge. Brave women, all ready to fight, even without the power of the pods. She didn't need them yet. It wasn't worth them risking their lives coming out here. She forced out another beam: *ground—hold—position.*

Then she used the very last of her comms power: *wave—big—all.*

Her own pod dipped as she struggled to maintain control, but her crew responded immediately. They all spun back toward the flotilla, casting their beams in the water as they went, creating great waves that rocked the ships together like toys in a bath. The firing stopped immediately, and people began falling into the swollen seas. Lo instructed some of the women to lower the strength of the waves—*less*—and the rest to get the bodies in the water over to Cockenoe. Then Lo used her smoke-maker to create a message in the sky. It was a trick the fliers used for parties and birthdays, a positive reutilization of the smoke-maker's original Ruurdaan purpose—routing concealed humans out of small places by blasting them with rank red smoke that clung luminous to their skin. Today Lo wrote: *leave and live.*

When she was finished she looked over at the flotilla. Some of the Orbiters were shaking their fists but others had their palms face-up to the sky pleading for mercy. Nobody was leaving though. Lo pushed out a new order: *Adrianna—whirlpool.*

Adrianna's pod peeled away from the group. Flying directly above the flotilla she directed a single beam into the water near one of the larger unattached boats. Carefully building up height and speed, Adrianna created a great swirling whirlpool in the dark sea, flinging two people into the water at speed, like tea from a spinning cup. One of the bodies began to sink, at which point Adrianna stopped, swept low, dragged both casualties into her net, and spun off to Cockenoe. Lo hoped the people were alive—but they fired first. She wrote a new air message high above the boats: *leave or else.*

The flotilla responded by firing off a few rocket-propelled grenades. The Orbiters must have raided a military supply station or abandoned naval ship. Shit. It was the one thing Lo had always feared but never really expected, old-time war toys. No one left on Earth had seemed capable of conducting any kind of organized military assault, and she had always believed their wires trumped conventional weaponry. Now she and her crew had absolutely no clue how to defend themselves against the incoming missiles— twisting and turning metallic footballs with fins. They would have to learn as they went, and pretty fast at that.

She watched in horror as one of the warheads exploded close to the checkpoint at the mouth of the river. Another two detonated on Saugatuck Shores, where a few groups of people lived in abandoned McMansions with rolling lawns and their own docks. Lo had warned against straying so far from the security of the tightly defended village, but some just couldn't resist the temptations of the big houses and the water views. At least twelve of the houses were occupied. Now Lo saw that the hits had torn a wing off one house and decimated an old tennis court. Lo hoped the inhabitants had heeded the warning sirens and sought safety. So much for the deterrent power of the waves and the whirlpool. Enraged now, Lo gave new orders: *harder—higher.*

The fliers began roughing the seas around the flotilla to tropical storm level. Many of the Orbiters had anticipated this and lashed themselves to masts and railings. It actually made them less safe. If the tangled and tied conglomeration of boats capsized, there would be many deaths. Lo hesitated as the storm built, unsure how far to take things. These people had only themselves to blame, but…

A hail of about twenty different missiles let loose into the skies. Ready this time, the crew rushed to retrieve them before they could make landfall—desperately casting their beams in the direction of the hurtling hunks of metal. Some of the fliers were successful, diverting the missiles deep into the sound, but most of them were not. Missiles slammed into various parts of the shoreline. If the Orbiters kept firing like this, one of their missiles would eventually hit something that mattered. Lo watched in horror as Pat dived for one last low-flying missile, caught the end of it with her beam, then lost control, dragging behind it like a superhero trying to halt an asteroid. Her pod trailed the missile as it skimmed the river, then bumped along the surface of the water before smashing into the jetty of what had once been the most expensive property in town.

Lo rushed to Pat's pod, now marooned upside-down in a patch of reeds and covered in broken pieces of wood. Landing precariously on the remains of the jetty, Lo flung her side door open and leaped onto the exposed bottom of Pat's upturned pod. Steering the glass bubble with her feet, like an acrobat on a balance ball, she slowly rolled the pod back upright. She ripped open Pat's sun roof. Reaching in with both arms, she gently pulled Pat out, vaulted over to the nearby lawn, and laid her down. Pat's head was bleeding, and her eyes were closed. Lo leaned in to listen for her breath. Then she sent a message: *okay—home—Leslie.*

As Lo sat waiting for Leslie to collect Pat, her mind raced. Pat might be okay, but the situation was not. She beamed Adrianna: *write—ceasefire—talk.*

Then, struggling now, to her crew: *ceasefire—climb—wait.*

The pods all began rising high in the clear blue sky. Adrianna began painting her letters—*c-e-a-s*—even as two more missiles thumped into the shore. One bounced off the invisible dome at the Inn, another into the rocks where Ruby had been standing not five minutes earlier, before being rescued by the ground force. Lo gave it until Adrianna finished her lettering before she ordered the destruction of the flotilla: *t-a-l-k*.

The missiles stopped coming. All was quiet as Adrianna rejoined her crew. Lo waited a little longer. Pods and boats alike bobbed peacefully in the mild summer breeze, which blew away the red sky-writing. Lo ordered her crew back to the checkpoint, all except Adrianna, who she called to come get her with the net. Adrianna swooped in and hovered. Lo put her hand to back of the pod, pulled the net out, and stepped in. She crouched and allowed herself to be strapped into position on the back of Adrianna's pod. She loosened the netting in front of her face and wiggled her ass against the glass until it created a comfortable groove on which to perch. Then she stretched her legs out for comfort, digging into the netting for purchase. Now she would be able to speak freely with the Orbiters — inside the pod that was impossible — but the dense metallic mesh would still offer a small degree of protection. Twisting her neck to see ahead, she assessed the situation as they raced over to the big red yacht flying the white flag.

Lashed to the mast of the red yacht was a tall scrawny blond with strangely pretty features. He might have looked feminine were he not so grizzled from sun-exposure. He was surrounded by the detritus of his damaged ship — scattered red leather cushions, upturned tables, smashed glasses, bloody smears on the wood. Lo tried to remain focused. A lot more than minor damage and a few injuries was at stake here.

Adrianna lowered the pod until they were on the same level as the deck of the yacht, but about a bedroom's length away. Lo was now almost facing the Orbiter.

"Are you in charge?" she yelled.

"No," the blond shouted back. "Our leader is on another boat having his injuries treated. If you are willing to wait, he can make his way here in about five minutes."

Lo squirmed uncomfortably in the net. She didn't want to give them any more time. "Too complicated, and I don't have time to wait. Go and find your leader now — wherever he and his grenade-rocket-launcher are hiding — and tell him to come to our checkpoint — that barge you almost sank with your missiles. Tell him to come alone, on a single open boat."

"Nobody told us about any checkpoint."

"Our checkpoint is for authorized visitors traveling in authorized boats."

The dirty pretty boy ignored her as she spoke into the button on his dirty gray bodcoz. After a second or two he said, "We'll send someone. But there must be a show of good faith. You must also send one of your people to us. An exchange."

Lo didn't like it, but she had expected it. Someone would have to volunteer.

"We'll meet you at the halfway point for an exchange in ten minutes."

The blond nodded. "Ten minutes will be enough."

"It's all you've got," she said, beaming Adrianna. As the pod swept away she also sent a short message to Yaz: *exchange — volunteer.*

Lo knew that Yaz would understand. Yaz was perfect for the swap. She might not be able to fly, but she could cast and receive book-length messages. She also had a way about her that might just work better than muscle. Yaz had used diplomacy to wangle her way into Saugatuck even after they'd frozen their borders. One day they had all just started picking up the same beamed message — Yaz saying she'd heard them thinking and liked how they thought. After a short meet at Cockenoe they'd let her in. Yaz was one of the cooler heads in town, perfect for this job.

As soon as Adrianna had dropped her back at her pod, she headed for the checkpoint meeting with the leader of the Orbiters. Flying back out over the water, she was pleased to see one of Saugatuck's sparkling blue bow-riders speeding toward the designated green buoy. The Orbiters' dirty white speedboat was just departing the flotilla. Good stuff, Yaz. Fast work. However, when she focused in more closely, Lo was horrified to see it wasn't Yaz driving the boat. It was Reid. Before she had time to try stopping him, she felt Yaz zap her. Lo allowed her friend's thoughts to flood her head.

Sorry, but he fought me to do this. I didn't want to use real force against him—that turns the naturals against us. They have their rights, Lo. Reid has a right too. I know it's dangerous, but it might also be the making of him. He needs a chance to be a man.

Lo looked down at her son speeding to the flotilla. If anything happened to him, she was going destroy every Orbiter on this planet and then destroy herself. She beamed Yaz: *if—anything—happens.*

Maybe she should have let the kid fight the wild dogs along-side her this morning. Helena kept saying he needed some sense of agency. Reid had been angry and out-of-control since learning two years ago that his father was James Nunn. On the one hand, he was desperate to make a connection with his sperm-donor father; on the other, he was desperate to prove he was nothing like him. And he blamed Lo for his distress and confusion over the situation—no thanks to Nunn's constant whining that she was a tyrant who controlled his wife and everyone else in Saugatuck. Lo had tried to give Reid confidence-building work: leading construction of the new river pool and teaching the smaller kids basic survival skills. Reid thanked her by sleeping with younger members of her crew, refusing to tell her his plans, and doing stupid things like go-ing outside the border on treasure hunts. Oh, yes, she knew about that. Now this...

Lo's pod literally steamed as she shot into the checkpoint, trailing a great cloud of vaporous static. The speed had ener-gized her. Pulling up to the spacious, purpose-built pontoon, she leaped out of the side aperture onto the wooden boards, leaving the pod lolling in the sea, at risk of taking on water. Women from other boats and pods rushed to retrieve and moor her craft. Way too many women were clustering in boats around the checkpoint;

they must not hinder negotiations. She beamed a quick message: *everyone — stay — back.*

Various craft began maneuvering upriver as Lo inspected the pontoon. It was sparsely equipped, but an old trawler was pulled tight against the back side to provide some facilities. Looking out to sea, she could see that the exchange had already happened; a single dirty white speed-boat was coming their way. For better or worse, Reid was on his way to meet the Orbiters — and their leader was on his way to meet her.

18

Lo took a moment to ready herself for introductions, legs apart, hands on hips, the fingers on her right hovering two millimeters away from her weapon holster. Her feet, as always, were bare. The wiring in their soles was all the protection any of them needed. She was wearing low-slung denim shorts and a tight gray tank, cropped to reveal the elaborate spider's web of wiring covering her belly button. Lo knew her body brooked no arguments. She encouraged them all to revel in their bodies. Wire-pride, wire-power.

She didn't budge an inch as the leader of the exiled Orbiters docked his boat, clambered onto the deck, and walked toward her, his footsteps slow and careful. He looked just like the Orbiters who had killed Dina—huge and furry, the hair on his head hacked out of a bale of black straw, camouflage bodcoz covered in leather, rope, and metal bits. Every surface of his body bulged indecently. His face was just two bloodshot eyes poking out of a matted nest. The only smooth skin visible aside from a slice of nose was on his dark-brown forehead—and that featured a raised gash. Talk about the old man and the sea—this guy looked like he'd been sailing on a pirate ship his whole life and drinking with Hemingway every night of it.

Just before he reached her, the hirsute behemoth stopped and cracked a warm smile, revealing two neat rows of gleaming white teeth. He bowed deeply from the waist. Rising, he extended a big hairy hand and said, "Zgyzg-Dm—but your people call me Lurch." His voice was thick and low with a light Russian inflection, just like the blonde sidekick. Odd.

Lo thought for second, then placed her own tiny hand in his great paw.

"Lo," she said.

As the guy squeezed and placed a second hairy mitt on top of her hand, Lo felt a surprising frisson pass through her body, creasing her stomach and fizzing her wires. She pulled away fast and hoped he hadn't felt it too.

"So, Lurch," she said. "What the fuck?"

Lurch replied, "I don't quite understand."

"Sorry. Let me rephrase that. What the fuck are you doing here? Why the fuck did you attack us? And when the fuck are you leaving?"

Lurch didn't blink. "We came to speak to the ambassador."

Lo was not particularly surprised, but she gave it a moment so it might look that way. A light sea breeze had sprung up, offering some relief from the blazing mid-afternoon sun. It was tempting to give Will to these guys and get Reid back as soon as possible, but she worried that he might reveal the secret of the children, or give them information that would help them break through Saugatuck's defenses. Will was also still her brother.

"Which ambassador? We have so many."

"I do not know who they sent, so I cannot tell you exactly who I seek. I just know that our tracker-systems detected an orbicraft— and Madison was expecting an ambassador…"

Lo blinked against the bright sunlight.

"What do you want with the ambassador?"

"We wish to discuss our situation," replied Lurch

Lo scoffed. "If that's all, you could have just asked."

"I would have just asked. I am asking now. Why do you think we were sitting there waiting? We were waiting for the chance to ask."

"You stormed in with two hundred violent thugs."

"I came softly with two-hundred refugees."

"You came with a trunk-full of grenades and rocket-launchers."

Lurch shrugged. "Some things are necessary. We are scared for our lives most days. Scared, hungry, exhausted. Which is what I wish to discuss with the ambassador. This is their responsibility, our situation. We know this is not your problem. But you have the ambassador..."

He had a point. They had the ambassador. And Will had already said he was here to resolve the Unan problem. Perhaps this would be easy enough...

"If I agree to arrange a meet with the ambassador—supervised for everyone's safety—will you leave when I ask you to leave? I mean immediately, just go?"

"After we have all our people back, then yes, we will leave."

So polite, so hairy.

"Even if you don't get what you want from the ambassador?"

"Yes. I understand that our needs are not your problem. We will be grateful for the opportunity to talk. And we will leave when we are done."

"When I say you're done."

"My apologies, when you say I'm done."

Was he being polite? He'd better not be mocking her. Lo gestured toward the only furniture—a weather-beaten wooden table surrounded by surprisingly new-looking aluminum chairs. "Okay, so take a seat while we go get the ambassador. Would you like a drink while you wait? There's usually something in the cooler."

"I would be most grateful for a drink," said Lurch.

As he moved to the table, Lo reached beneath it and opened the old Igloo cooler. Inside was a pleasant surprise—a crew-member's packed lunch.

"Water, apple juice, or home-brewed beer?"

"Beer, please" said Lurch.

She put a scuffed green bottle on the table, along with an old Tupperware container filled with boiled eggs and vegetables. Lurch hesitated before the slatted-back aluminum chairs. Lo raised her hand. "Let me fix that for you." Projecting a soft warm beam through each hand, gently pulling at the metal frames, she carefully made the chair wider and longer. The legs wobbled as she worked, and the final result was crooked and unstable, but it was now sized for an Orbiter. Lo wondered how these people got by in everyday life on Earth, too big for everything.

"Thank you," said Lurch, as if bending chairs were a normal courtesy.

Lo grunted by way of reply—and beamed Yaz to hurry up with Will.

Silence reigned. The boats just beyond all floated in quiet tandem, so quiet that Lo could hear the waves lapping against their hulls. A lot of whispering was coming from the women, but it was the low tzzz of almost-dead insects in a window frame. Lurch shifted uncomfortably on his chair from time to time, lightly scratching the wooden surface of the pontoon. He kept dipping his hand in and out of the Tupperware container like a sneaky, greedy child. He ate quickly and neatly, without making any noise—strange delicate manners for such a great hulking creature. Lo watched him closely as she lolled on another chair, her feet flung high on the wooden table for comfort's sake.

Lo coughed. "I have a question."

"Of course..."

"There under your bodcoz on your chest..."

"It is nothing to fear," replied Lurch. "It is only my crux." He put his hand to his chest and popped his coz open, revealing the same kind of body art her brother had on his chest, only with one big difference: amid a sprinkling of diamonds in the middle of the cross was a sizeable octagonal blue gem, deep cerulean blue.

"Is it a weapons' control system?" asked Lo.

"Of course not. Orbiters don't have weapons. We had to borrow yours, did we not? We have some defense equipment, but nobody anticipated the level of violence..."

Lo ignored him. "So the crux works like a force-field?"

"Not usually, no," said Lurch. "A crux contains things like communications controls, internal-monitoring, pharmacological administration, authorization chips, and a range of enhancement tools, nothing that poses any danger to you."

He sounded like Will. She said, "Tell me about the big stone in the middle."

"The stone itself is called a dwvyt but it has become known as 'the knowledge gem,'" replied Lurch. "It can be inscribed with a great deal of information. Fully loaded and activated, it provides personal access to the Orbital data store—a library of shared Orbiter knowledge—a living record of the communal mind. Unfortunately, most of my crux gems, including the dwyvt, were deactivated when they sent me to Una. I still enjoy some crux functionality—medical is working—but in general the system is useless."

That sounded too honest. Testing, Lo asked, "What is Una?"

"It is a planet of exiles. The Orbiters call it a prison planet—except that half the people there haven't done anything criminal—they have merely challenged Orbiter norms."

"I'm not interested in alien politics. Back to the crux. Do you all have them?"

"No," replied Lurch. "Only high-credit individuals can afford to purchase the smaller gems—and the knowledge gem must be earned. The High Council has granted less than eight thousand of the big blue ones since they were first developed about seventy years ago."

"So how did you get yours—and what the hell did you do wrong?"

"That is a long story. Perhaps another time," said Lurch.

"You're all so secretive, aren't you? Just tell me something straight for once. If you guys have wires, then why don't you have powers like us? Or do you have powers?"

"No," said Lurch. "I am afraid we Orbiters have not mastered any kind of telepathy. The Ruurdaans were extremely advanced bio-technicians—but we don't want to advance like the Ruurdaans—perhaps you can understand?"

Lo got the feeling he thought he was talking to a child. Should she tell him she was sixty-five years old? As silence fell, Lurch pulled his bodcoz back over his great hulking body and went back to eating and drinking. Lo looked over the sea in the direction of the Inn. How would Mira respond to Lurch's deactivated crux? In thirty years of caring for them, the women of Saugatuck had never really come to know the children, no matter how much they claimed otherwise. Lo wondered who would come off worse in an encounter between forty children and two hundred Orbiters. Perhaps Will had a point—perhaps *they* were the scary ones.

Rocking back on her chair, the warm afternoon sun beating down on her head, Lo suddenly felt like she might nod off. It had been one hell of a day, the heat was enervating, and she was exhausted. Could she trust Lurch enough to shut her eyes for a second? Peeking at him from under drooping lids, Lo felt strangely comfortable with the man-creature she had been exchanging weapons fire with half an hour ago. At the very least, she didn't fear him. Giving in to physical need, Lo allowed herself to slip under for a few seconds, lulled by the sound of her own breath. Then she heard the roar of the speedboat.

19

Lurch hoped he had not mistaken the initial electric charge between him and the Earthan, Lo. Whatever strange personal vibrations attracted women to him, despite his being ugly and approaching his 150th birthday, they might help. He had heard tales of the women of Saugatuck with their super powers and their flying security force—tales of the mangled and blind fools who had dared trespass beyond their fortified borders. Even in repose the taut, coppery woman with the metal-flecked body was aggressive.

Lurch hadn't believed the hype. Most of the Earth women he had encountered were damaged, skittish creatures with limited telepathic ability—either that or mad animals lost to reason. Flying seemed unlikely. Imagine his surprise when he saw all those glass pods charging at him out of the clear blue sky. And when the women had started plucking his people off their boats and flinging them roughly onto the beach, he was indignant. But when they started making cyclones and throwing them into the sea, he was terrified. He had had no choice but to fire the missiles. He knew both sides had suffered injuries, but his action had ultimately saved lives.

As he assessed his current situation—stuck on a pontoon with an angry, powerful, and semi-rational woman, within firing range of her fearsome posse—he was glad to hear the roar of the speedboat carrying the Orbiter ambassador. Although he had lost faith in the Orbiter system long, long ago, he would still be grateful to be in the company of another hypocritical pacifist.

When the Earthan speedboat docked, Lurch was shocked to see the familiar face of Wl-Wrrn. The Wl-Wrrn he knew was not one to stray far from the floating-cloud comforts and privileged buzz of the Crn orbital, let alone put up with six months of travel in the cramped rattle-trap that was an explorer. The High Council must have either bribed him or forced him here to do something about his ill-conceived settlement program. Lurch was glad. The smooth-talking Earthan deserved to experience the paradise he'd been selling. Lurch looked forward to a very honest discussion with his old acquaintance.

However, today Wl-Wrrn did not seem the imposing self-promoter of Lurch's memory. He struggled to get from the boat to the pontoon, as if sick, or drugged, or otherwise indisposed. He looked wrong too. His usually smooth handsome face was drawn in pain, and his torso was thick with bandages under a dirty old toga. Lurch didn't understand how Wl-Wrrn had been injured and lost his bodcoz. It wasn't easy to disarm an Orbiter in a brand new coz, and nobody in their right mind would just take one off. Not in this world.

Lo stood up abruptly, folded her arms, and said, "Will, this is Lurch, leader of that bunch of asswipes over there in the river. He's desperate to talk to you."

She turned to Lurch. "I hope this is the ambassador you wanted. He also happens to be my brother—in case you noticed the resemblance. Not that it matters here."

Lurch *had* seen it. The wide colorless mouths and sharp little blue eyes, the small fine bodies, the pale golden coloring. Exquisitely exotic.

"Thank you, Lo. I am already acquainted with Ambassador Wl-Wrrn," he said, standing and bowing deeply, hands facing outward in the Orbiter gesture of acceptance.

Although he was unsteady on his feet, Wl-Wrrn managed an even deeper bow to Lurch. It was a surprisingly polite acknowledgment of his former status. Perhaps Wl-Wrrn still felt that there was a use for him. "Ambassador Zgyzg-Dm," the short blond Earthan said. "It's been too long. What a pleasant surprise to see you here."

Lurch smiled and replied, "I do not think that you can be so surprised, Ambassador, not given that you sent me here."

"Just exchanging courtesies," replied Wl-Wrrn.

"What?"

"Semantics, old history, not interesting," said Will. It sounded weird.

"Interesting to me," said Lo, her face an angry question mark.

"I have more pressing concerns right now," said Wl-Wrrn.

"Fair enough," said Lo. "We can return to that point later."

"Can we sit down, please," said Wl-Wrrn.

Lurch gestured at his own distorted chair and saw the gratitude in Wl-Wrrn's eyes as he slumped down into it. He looked down at the remaining chairs, then back up at Lo. She nodded and repeated her trick. "When you're ready, ladies," she said as she sat down. Lurch assumed she was using sarcasm again. He really didn't understand it.

He turned to Wl-Wrrn. "I am requesting to use your orbicraft, Wl-Wrrn."

Wl-Wrrn shook his head and said, "No way, Zg. Not possible. It's not working at the moment. Say. I tell you what. Why don't you take me to Madison on your boat, instead? We can work something out when we get there. What do you say, old pal?"

"Whoa," said Lo.

"I am also thinking *whoa*," said Lurch. "He's not making any sense."

Lo pulled a face. "He's just acting the fool to get your sympathy. And you can forget about taking him to Madison on your boat. My brother is not free to go anywhere right now, especially not Madison where he has alien friends who might help him. And we still don't have the complete truth out of him about his plans for Saugatuck, the whole thing with the Orbiter settlers. He's not leaving my sight."

"I know about his plans," said Lurch. He was more than happy to tell her.

Wl-Wrrn looked at Lurch and shook his head. Lurch wasn't quite sure what that meant, but Wl-Wrrn's wishes were irrelevant.

He felt no obligation to the ambassador whatsoever. In fact, he might not even need him anymore. He had suddenly realized that he might have a better chance of getting the orbicraft from Lo than from her brother.

"Tell me about his plans," said Lo.

"Will you give me the orbicraft if I do?" said Lurch.

Wl-Wrrn muttered, "Don't trust her. She can't do anything for you. Deal with me. I promise I'll help you if you take me to Madison. Anything, Zg, anything."

Lurch didn't respond immediately. He wasn't quite sure what was going on here.

Lo said, "Just ignore him. I think he's taken too many painkillers. He hurt himself yesterday, and we gave him something a little strong."

Against his better judgment, Lurch chose not to mention that if Wl-Wrrn was wearing his bodcoz he wouldn't need any Earthan painkillers. He nodded instead.

Lo continued. "What do you want his spaceship for?"

"We want to go home."

"Why do you want to go home? Did you not come here voluntarily?"

Both the question and her gaze had a strange intensity.

"Oh, no, it is not quite like that. Those of us who were already exiles did sign up for the settlement experiment. At the time anything seemed better than the planet Una. However, with no way back, we feel like prisoners once more—and we have not adapted well to the new environment. My people find it inhospitable. In spite of your naturally beautiful Earth with all its plants and creatures and weathers, we miss our own overdeveloped planets. My heart and my work lies with those flawed orbitals. I miss having *the knowledge* surrounding me. All this nature and no civilization. It hurts."

Wl-Wrrn just nodded, head hanging rather loose. He seemed almost vroomed.

Lo said, "I have no problems with the fact you don't like it here, and I'm happy to help you leave, only there's a problem. That orbicraft is pretty small. How do you plan to get all your people home with it? Is it bigger on the inside?"

Lurch smiled in spite of himself. *Bigger on the inside than the outside.*

"You are right," he said. "It is very small. It is not capable of intergalactic flight. I and one other will fly back to the explorer waiting in orbit. We will depart with the bigger ship when it leaves in a few weeks' time. Back home we will demand an inquiry into the settlement program and hopefully stop it. I have powerful friends who will support me. We will also insist that the Orbiters send a BPC to collect all the unhappy settlers."

"Sounds like a plan," said Lo. "Only, what's a BPC?"

"That plan's never going to work," said Wl-Wrrn, springing to life for a moment. "You won't be allowed to stay on the explorer. And even if you were, nobody at home would listen to you. You're considered a dangerous Unan now. Chipped and ready for the jammer. I don't see the logic of your repatriation proposal, either. The Orbiters can't send a BPC here for a pickup. Physics dictate it's a one-way system. You know that."

That was more like the slick ambassador Lurch knew. However, as Lurch started to respond, Wl-Wrrn slumped back into his chair, apparently exhausted from his outburst.

Lo spoke. "What is he talking about—jammers, BPC?"

Lurch said, "The jammers are penal control devices. All Unans are chipped to respond to their acoustic energy emissions—which turn your brain into one great scream. Up in Madison, Retske managed to expel over five hundred of us using just ten jammers. They are illegal almost everywhere on the Orbitals except Una, but they're standard equipment on any BPC—big people carriers—carrying Unans to the new settlements."

"Tell me more about these BPC. How many people do they carry? And where do you think they're going to land? Or are they the ships that bring the boxes?"

"I see you know a little something about how things work. The BPCs don't land. They *are* the ships that carry the boxes. Each carrier holds about twenty thousand settlers. They cannot land without special docking stations, so the settlers are dropped from just beyond Earth's atmosphere. Boxes are preloaded with coordinates. There are settlers everywhere on Earth. We just happened to be deposited outside Madison."

Lo nodded furiously, gnawing her lip. She even comprehended things aggressively. "If only two thousand were dropped in Madison, then where are the rest?"

"Mostly on the western coast of this continent. They are trying to spread us out."

"So there are more coming. How many more are coming?"

"There will be another twenty thousand in the fourth drop. Twenty different towns in this area have been chosen. There will be one thousand settlers per town."

Lo let out a small cry. "No. Please don't tell me…"

"I'm sorry, but it's the truth—a thousand are destined for Saugatuck."

Lo looked across to her brother, now completely out of it. For a moment Lurch thought she was going to do something, then she turned back to him. "When?"

"I don't know—I am just a settler, not an organizer—but I think very soon. That must be why your brother is here—as part of the team overseeing the fourth drop."

"The *fourth* drop? There have already been *three* others? Sixty thousand!"

"Again I apologize that I am the one who must tell you this, especially as it is not a happy story. Sixty thousand have already been dropped. Only about forty-two thousand of them are known to have survived. Settlement was a disaster in China, South America, and England. Eighteen thousand died in those places: inadequate survival skills, disease, Earthan savagery. Another thousand were accidentally dropped in the Baltic Sea and left to drown. The most successful settlements were on this continent. Seventeen thousand survivors. Your brother will have more specific figures for you—when he awakens."

Lo ignored that, although she did briefly glance at Wl-Wrrn—maybe not with concern. "How do you know so much? Are you in contact with your home world?"

"No, not really. Otherwise we would not find ourselves in this predicament, would we? The Orbitals are too far away to send messages, but the explorer missions have brought news—only once a year, and the ambassadors are secretive, but still I hear. An old pilot friend—Captain Syd—flies the missions. I also have friends left in Madison. They may be too scared to leave because of what lies beyond the security fence, but they are not too scared to send messages. Everybody has issues with the settlement program."

"What did they expect, coming to a ravaged planet like this?"

"Ask your brother—he is the one who promoted it as 'Paradise on Earth.'"

Lo's face stiffened. She turned and waved her hand at her brother, shaking the air around him so hard that all their chairs rattled. Wl-Wrrn flopped around like a rag doll, at first shocked awake, then staring at his sister through dazed and confused eyes.

Lo's voice was cut crystal. "Is what he's saying true?"

"What? You let that kid burn me. I didn't know what you would do if..."

He had been burned? Lurch watched in horror as Lo swirled her hand through the air, hoisting her brother into the air. Wl-Wrrn pushed down, and the chair fell gently into her beam, hanging below him in the air. Both man and metal roiled helplessly in the maelstrom. Fury contorted Lo's sparkling face. "I think you need to wake up, bro."

Lurch felt compelled to intervene. "No more violence. That is not the way."

Lo said nothing, but she lowered the dancing figure to the height of their heads. The chair fell to the ground. Lurch thought the moment had passed, but then he saw Lo drag Wl-Wrrn through the air until he was hanging over the water. Then she dropped him into the sea. She shouted, "How do *you* like being dropped, Will?"

A small flurry of cries arose from the nearby boats, but nobody moved. Lurch watched until Wl-Wrrn safely surfaced, rolled onto his back, and began floating with his arms outspread, almost as if enjoying the dip. The guy could clearly swim. Lo blinked away, talking to her pals down her wires. Lurch said nothing, just waited for her to speak.

"You had better not be lying to me," she said when she finally looked up.

"I never lie," said Lurch.

It was true. It was his one simple credo. It was why he was here.

Lo looked deep into his eyes for a moment, then said, "So take the orbicraft and go. I'll escort you there just as soon as we get our exchange guy back. Fly away to that explorer in orbit. Get on board if you can. Send the message that you all want to go home. Tell them not to send more. Say that we don't want you. Say whatever you need to say. Say that we are killer savages who like to drink the blood of Orbiters. But before you go, I have one more question for you—is it too late to stop the next drop?"

"I don't know," replied Lurch. "To the best of my knowledge, you cannot turn a BPC around. But perhaps it is not too late to redirect the drop, perhaps to California where the settlement program is more successful. I am certainly willing to try to convince the crew to do so. And not just for the benefit of you and your people. I'm worried that if the boxes drop here you will mistreat more innocent Orbiters."

Lo said nothing. What was there to say? It was pretty clear what she was willing to do. Burn, drug, and shake. Throw people into the water.

Lurch put his hand out. "Do we have a deal?"

Lo ignored his hand. She said, "Before we shake on any deal, let me be very clear. If you do anything except fly straight out of here and never come back, then I will hunt down your flotilla and press it to the ocean floor like a rubber ducky in a bath. Got it?"

Lurch understood only one thing—threats made her feel safer.

"Understood. May I go ahead and instruct the flotilla? They will bring your boy straight back. The procedure at the orbicraft should be very simple. All I need is an authorization chip to access the controls. Wl-Wrrn has one. He just needs to release the door. I will then take the orbicraft over to the flotilla, say my goodbyes, pick up a passenger, and head straight to the explorer. Should I tell the Orbiters to come back down and retrieve Wl-Wrrn? Will you authorize that?"

"Are you crazy? We're keeping him here until all our problems are resolved."

Wl-Wrrn was not his problem. "Okay, but first he has to open the orbicraft."

"Why can't we just use his authorization chip. That's his control button right?"

"No, the control button operates the bodcoz. Pilots have embedded authorization chips for the orbicraft. It's a security measure. I used to have a working one."

Lurch unzipped his bodcoz and pointed to a small green emerald in his left nipple.

Lo went pale. "Oh shit," she said. "There might be a problem. There was a misunderstanding—some damage to my brother's crux—I don't know."

Lurch thought he knew. "I need to see the damage."

Lo looked down at the water, reached out and pulled Will back through the air onto the pontoon. She rushed to place a towel under his head—as if she suddenly cared. Lurch suspected she was running off a conflicting barrage of instincts most of the time.

"Lurch wants to look at your injuries," she said.

"The water was so refreshing," said Wl-Wrrn. He sounded feverish. "You know I think I might have some serious internal system problems. It feels like the heat is set to super-high in there. Perhaps Zg can help. He worked on the knowledge systems back when he was still a great citizen—way back when—which means he's way too old for you—not that he would go for you anyway— just in case that's what you're thinking."

Was that a blush Lurch saw spreading across Lo's skin? He bent down and began peeling back the bandages from around Wl-Wrrn's chest. What he saw took his breath away: the half-molten gems, the singed black skin, the red raw web of burns radiating out from the crux. No wonder the man was half-delirious—with pain-regulation gone he would be in too much agony to function. How could his own sister have done this? She was no better than the worst of the Unan criminals.

"Can you help him?"

"Maybe... The flesh wounds must be very painful, but they are not life-threatening. They would heal sooner if we could get his medical gem working—but I cannot do anything without the right equipment," said Lurch. "They have the equipment on the explorer ship—but that is not possible as things stand—and also at the Madison colony. Retske and the others might let me in to use their medical center if I am with Wl-Wrrn. Is that a possibility, given the situation?"

Lo was emphatic. "Only if you're accompanied by a security team. I'm not letting Will out of my sight—he's our only leverage point with the Orbiters—and I'd like to keep my eye on you too. It's an idea, though. I do have questions for the Madison women. They've been virtually silent since their boxes of aliens arrived—just sending around the occasional scary note telling us all to watch out for criminals on the rampage. We've been keeping our distance."

"So we can all go together? How many boats will we need?"

"No boats. Pods."

"As you wish. I am grateful for your assistance."

"Iwannoogonoo," muttered Will.

Lo raised her eyebrows. "You say he's alright, just hurting a little."

"Hurting a lot, but as long as there is no infection, he should be all right."

"Then we'll go tomorrow," said Lo. "I want Will lucid before we begin discussions with Madison. I also need to make some calls. We can't just arrive. There are security protocols, and I need to inform my own people. That will take time. You can spend the night here at the checkpoint. I'll send women with food, whatever you need."

The woman had some nerve. "That is a kind offer, but I am afraid I must decline. I need to return to the flotilla to speak with my own people. Perhaps you would consider visiting us with some of your people later? You would see another side of Orbiter culture. Let us share something of our societies, even if just for one evening."

Lo cocked her head sideways and gave him a look that he feared was the wrong kind of curious. He smiled politely but turned and began to wrap the bandages back around Wl-Wrrn's devastated chest. He could do nothing more to help the ambassador today. When he was finished, he rose from his haunches, stood before Lo, and bowed deeply, palms up.

"It has been a pleasure," he said, something Retske had taught them.

"Oh, I wouldn't go that far," replied Lo, again with that sideways glance.

She didn't even know she was doing it. Shameless creature— barely civilized—just like the rest of this doomed planet. Lurch sighed and began signaling to the flotilla.

20

The sun was long gone by the time the women gathered on the flotilla. Stars flickered high in the sky, almost bright enough for a natural to see by. The main boat was a large motor-cruiser, but space was still tight for the ten visitors and the jostling stream of Orbiter men strangely eager to meet the savage women who had tried to knock them into the sea just hours earlier. Male and female bodies brushed and banged together in a myriad of ways not usual in these times. How everyone felt about the experience remained to be seen.

Helena and Lo were alone in the bow. Helena was listening as Lo rushed through all the practical details of the plans to go to Madison. Apparently, Lo expected Helena to deal with the political fall-out from today's developments while she was gone. Factions were forming, not entirely along fault lines that Lo had predicted. Helena knew that confusion and tension were to be expected. Nine hundred women were not going to come to immediate consensus just because they shared the same kind of bodies. The women of Saugatuck might look fairly similar—youth has its own homogenous quality—but their histories and experiences differentiated them in ways that ran deeper than the simple fact of womanhood and wiring. The usual: religion, sexuality, class, family background, children, experiences with men. The less usual: role in the Ruurdaan occupation, level of wire-power, experiences of violence. All these factors would come into play as the women struggled to deal with sudden change. Helena knew that the arrival of the alien men would not easily be stopped—and that it would irrevocably divide their community. But she was no longer interested in telling the women how they could or should respond. They needed to start working these things out for themselves.

"Take a deep breath," she said to Lo. "You're getting way ahead of yourself. We don't even know exactly what issues we're dealing with yet. Nobody can control the unknown."

"I'm not asking for your opinion," said Lo. "I'm asking you to stand in for me while I'm in Madison. Keep us unified. You know you still have the people's ear."

"For the thousandth time," replied Helena. "I'm done with politics. It's time for the next generation to make their own world. I just want to find peace."

"You can look for peace once we know we're all going to survive."

One thousand and one. "Survival is *your* biggest concern, Lo, not mine. If you think about our situation from the point of view of universal responsibility rather than individual—"

"Now is not the time for this, Helena."

"Now *is* the time. It is time to eschew violence, to show compassion. To evolve."

"So this is what it's come down to, then? I can't even depend on you in a crisis."

"Now you're being dramatic. You know can always depend on me, Lo. I'm here with you now. I came the moment you sent for me."

"You only came because Reid decided to stay out here for the rest of the day. You're here as a mother, not my wife, and not for the sake of Saugatuck."

"Listen to yourself, Lo, judging, accusing. I am on your side, hon."

"Prove it. Take over the leadership again while I'm gone."

Helena sighed. How much longer were they going to remain stuck in this damn loop? Hell, it had been at least a couple of years already. She reached up and rearranged the pins in her hair. It was a breezeless night, but the ride out on the speedboat after the truce had blown her hair everywhere. It was time to cut the whole lot off, forgo that old vanity, but something about her dark gray mane made her feel proud, proud to be a natural, proud to have aged.

"It's time to allow some of the other women to take their turn up front," she said. "We need a natural cycle of change in our society. The young ones coming up need to see that happening too. Otherwise, what do they have to live for, to work toward? We must evolve."

"Sorry to interrupt." It was Lurch. They had asked him to give them ten minutes. It had been fifteen. Helena saw Lo straighten up in the big man's presence.

"Yes, alright. Just let me finish." Lo turned back to her. "To be continued, okay?"

"Okay." Helena wasn't going to argue with Lo in front of Lurch. This wasn't his business. However, she saw a look of complete understanding in his eyes anyway. She had spent the last couple of hours with Lurch, and one of the most important things she had learned was that he didn't need to be told every little thing.

Lo said to him, "So what's the plan, then? Name badges and warm white wine?"

Lurch said, "I think that is a joke. I am afraid I do not understand all your Earthan jokes. My apologies. When you are ready, there are some people I would like you to meet. I do not want you to judge all Orbiters by a rough old *smooshian* like myself."

"*Smooshian?*" Was that his nationality?

"It means troublemaker in Russian."

Helena had to laugh. Lo gave her a look.

"Why *do* you all have Russian accents?" asked Lo.

"Our teacher was Russian—Retske—you will meet her tomorrow in Madison."

"So do you all speak Russian?" Helena didn't quite understand.

"Not really. We were assigned to this continent, so we learned English."

Lo said, "Yeah, well you all sound weird."

Now Lurch laughed. "Weird suits me just fine. Now please, come meet my people. They are better than me in so many ways, and more representative of Orbiter culture, I think."

"I hope so," said Lo. This time Helena didn't laugh. Lo's defensiveness was wearing. Helena understood it. God knows she once shared it. Anger had been fuel. But that was the past.

The three of them maneuvered around the deck towards the wider back section of the boat. Adrianna was talking to an attentive clay-colored man with solid black almonds for eyes and a tangled claret afro. She came up to his armpit. Leslie, perched on an upturned cooler, was shyly talking to a Nordic-looking blond with twinkling green eyes the shape of mail-slots. Helena had met both men a couple of hours back, but Lurch stopped and introduced them to Lo. Blr was the scraggy blond, Rans, the fiery mixling. These two guys were smooth and hairless—not like Lurch and their other hirsute colleagues.

"Hey lady," the blond said to Lo, "So you decided to drop in after all."

"He enjoys Earthan sarcasm," said Lurch. "Another smooshian."

"We're all smooshians," said Rans , "if your definition of making trouble is speaking out against an authoritarian system you believe is wrong."

"We don't need a lecture," said Lo. "We run a successful democracy here."

Helena wasn't sure that was true, but she was still glad Lo cared enough to say it. Words have the power to move—although not in the same way as action. Janine sidled in front of Leslie, clearly competing for Blr's attention. Two days ago, she and Leslie had been inseparable; today, it seemed that sisterhood had nothing on the promise of a man. Helena regretted that, but she was not about to say anything. They would learn—or they would not.

Janine was questioning Blr. "Are there any women on the flotilla. Or just men?"

Rans answered. "We are exactly 147 men, 34 women, and 2 childs."

"*Children,*" Janine corrected. "Whose *children* are they?"

Rans said, "The *childeren* belong to Orbiter women. They were both born in captivity. Here on Earth."

Helena could feel his gravity. For all that they smiled and clustered in sociable circles, these men had serious faces, cautious mannerisms. They wore faded, worn bodcoz, and deprivation showed in their lean hungry faces.

Lo asked, "So, where *are* the women and children?" Helena had also wondered about the absence of women. She'd already spoken about it with Lurch.

"Like I told Helena, most of our few women companions are Earthan. They have the wires but they are not strong like you," said Lurch. "In fact they are afraid of you after what happened this afternoon—so most of them are at home in their boats. Perhaps later they will join us, once we have all become more comfortable."

Helena was surprised to hear Leslie speak up. "Your women shouldn't be afraid of us," she said. "We are still women just like them. Many of us were once mothers too. If God didn't want us to help your people he wouldn't have brought you to our door." Helena felt her heart rise into her throat. She'd been counseling her once a week since Dina's death over a year ago now. Lo had been concerned that Leslie would lose her powers, her means of survival. Helena had worried that she would lose her faith—the one thing that had always kept her going.

"Nobody is helping any goddamned fucking aliens," said Lo quickly. "We're just making whatever arrangements are necessary to get them to leave without a fuss." She turned to Lurch. "Before you people leave, though, I *would* like to meet an Orbiter *woman*, get her perspective on your culture. Let's hear one of your women tell us you're a bunch of great guys."

Lurch didn't hesitate. "Helena asked me the same thing earlier, so I have anticipated your request. I have already spoken with the one Orbiter woman who sails with us and she's agreed to meet with you. I was just waiting until you were ready."

Adrianna stuck her head into the conversation. "Sound's great. Let's go." She must have been listening all along, guarding Lo. Over the last six months or so Helena had noticed that the town firecracker could often be found lurking around Lo. One day they were tight colleagues; the next day they were just *tight*. Helena thought that if anything had actually happened between them, Lo would have confessed by now—and yet she still got a strange feeling every time she saw Adrianna horsing around with her wife. It wasn't a feeling of jealousy, more one of concern. Adrianna lay just on the right side of feral. Great at working, flying, and fighting. Fun for drinking, dancing, and wild antics; impossible in any kind of discussion. Adrianna had refused all offers of counseling over the years. *Fuck talking, bitches.* A woman like that would keep Lo warring for the thrill of it. Helena tried to let the thought go. Angry and impatient thoughts just impeded empathy and understanding.

Lurch broke her reverie. "I am sorry, but you cannot all meet Byllyn at once. Too many, too much. I will not have her scared. I will just take Lo and Helena this time. If that goes well enough, then perhaps she will agree to meet more of you."

Lo said, "We're not in the business of scaring other women."

Leslie said, "We are the ones who get scared."

Adrianna said, "Speak for yourself, Leslie. Some of us don't have the luxury of fear." She turned to Lo. "Just beam me if you need me. I'll be right here checking out all the cock."

Leslie and Janine both looked at the floor while Lo coughed.

Lurch was clearly confused. "Checking the cocks?"

Helena laughed out loud. "I'll fill in the gaps in your English on the way," she said to Lurch, stretching her hand out to indicate that he should lead the way.

Lurch led them scrambling across a nest of intertwined boats. Away from the bright lights of the main boat, Helena became aware of shadowy figures scattered across the flotilla—of many eyes looking their way. Lights flickered in most of the boats. Lurch had told her and Reid that the Orbiters had a unique technique for recharging batteries, giving them power that didn't require gasoline. Since then Helena had seen only the occasional glimpse of her son, smiling and waving from the ships way up front, the power base of the flotilla, she assumed. She had long known that he suffered from a lack of male role models. Only now did she see quite how much. She wasn't yet sure about these men but she was happy that Reid was having an experience outside the female enclave of Saugatuck. Who could blame him for not wanting to spend his life huddled behind a car fence? Change always entailed risk, but change was the nature of life. She hoped she wasn't an idiot for trusting her son to these people of the flotilla, but her time spent with Lurch today had given her a safe feeling that had nothing to do with weapons or words and everything to do with his quiet observant patience.

Just as she was starting to worry about Reid all over again, Helena saw a tiny blonde head suddenly poke up from under a tarpaulin at the back of a small white cabin-cruiser. Helena felt her heart lurch; the child, the boat. She and Robyn had bought a small Bayliner just like this the month before their civil ceremony. Their honeymoon had been ten days puttering round the Thimble Islands, Robyn doing the driving and Helena navigating. All too soon they'd both had to get back to their residencies at Yale. That was the summer before the invasion. Helena knew that the boat would have a tiny kitchenette with a table that folded down, seats that doubled as extra sleeping space, and a tiny double bed wedged into the bow. There would also be a head that doubled as a shower and one storage cupboard. It was no place to live for long periods of time, but it was a cozy play-house for a child. Helena and Robyn had planned to have two children, one each, probably with the help of Robyn's brother. Robyn had been with him the day the spheres hit—shopping for anniversary rings in New York.

"Papa!" The squealing child popped out from under the tarpaulin completely, pulling herself up onto the boat railing with confidence. As best as Helena could tell, it was a little girl, around the height of a four-year-old, yet with the chubby features and mannerisms of a young toddler. Her golden skin was covered in fine blonde hair. She was a fuzzy kewpie doll.

"Papa," the child squealed again.

"She calls us all Papa," said Lurch.

"Cute," said Lo.

"No, sad," said Lurch. "Lil's father died nine months ago in an attack on our fuel supply station in Black Rock. Women like your-selves—only feral—I think that is how you call them."

"Yes," said Lo. "We've lost a number of people to the ferals over the years too. They're nothing like us—those women—they were lost to humanity thirty years ago."

Helena said, "What *is* humanity? Who knows anymore?"

Lil broke the silence that followed. "Fishy, Lil, fishy, Papa."

"Those are almost all the words she knows," laughed Lurch as he reached the edge of the boat and scooped her up in his huge furry arms. "She is telling you everything about her day. Luckily she missed the fighting, playing down the hatch. All she cares about is the big fish she thinks she caught this morning. Big fish, huh?"

He rolled her about gently in his arms.

"Big fish," echoed the child. "Big fishy."

Suddenly the tarpaulin flew off with a whoosh, high onto the roof of the small cabin. Before them stood the first Orbiter woman Helena had ever seen. Unsurprisingly, she was almost seven feet tall, big-boned and firm-fleshed. Surprisingly she was not wearing the ubiquitous bodcoz. Instead she was sprinkled head to toe—although not in enough quantity to cover her protuberant bald pubis—with what appeared to be a fine misting of gold dust inter-mingled with an explosion of tiny gems. Her large pale head was bald too, ringed by some sort of golden, sparkling projection. The halo illuminated a soft-featured face, achromatic except for the eyes—startling citrine ellipses. Helena and Lo both stared.

"This is Byllyn," said Lurch. "Please do not stare, although I understand why you do. Byllyn is a high-born courtesan. She is considered something very special at home, but here where nobody knows her kind she feels shy."

Byllyn crossed her arms over her small soft breasts, bent forward in a gentle bow, and smiled with just those queer eyes. Helena experienced a sudden feeling of effervescence in her lungs. Once upon a time in mythology, people fought wars over this kind of radiant beauty.

"Lil shy," shouted Lil, banging on her own chest. "Lil."

They all laughed, and Helena's breathing returned to normal. She said, "Hello, Lil, I'm Helena." "Lil, Lil," said Lil. Helena laughed again. Even Lo cracked a smile.

Byllyn gestured for them all to climb down into the boat. She produced water and a bowl of what looked like small dried pieces of fish. The boat was small, yet it still felt comfortable and adequate. Playthings were scattered around, like you might find in a home. The setting was undeniably domestic, even if Byllyn was outwardly not. The women sat together talking while Lurch played with Lil—who didn't seem to tire of being hoisted up over his big shaggy-bear head then dropped back down like a rag doll. Helena tried to absorb something of Byllyn's aura as she listened to Lo ask a series of clumsy questions.

"So how did you end up here, Byllyn, I mean if you have a special status at home, and home is as wonderful as my brother says, then why would someone like you ever leave?"

Byllyn's voice was like ice in a glass of Stolichnaya. "It was not my choice. I was a drug addict. Vroom. It is not easy being loved so much and expected to give so much love in return. Vroom helped me love when I was tired of loving. But it made me sick. I lost myself. I did bad things just to get more Vroom. I refused rehabilitation. That destroys your soul too. How can I love if I have no soul? So they sent me to Una. There it was even harder to love. All those terrible men. I took so much Vroom my muscles began to waste. Then they came and took me. I don't know who. Probably my father's assistants. I slept for a long time. And then I was here, with Lurch and his people, free from the Vroom after so long trapped. I like it here with them, even when life is hurting. I still give love, but I give it only as I wish. It is my gift once more. Would you like me to love you one time? I feel that you are special too, lady-with-wires."

"Thanks," said Lo, blushing. "But no thanks."

Byllyn turned to Helena, "And you, gray-haired lady, how may I help you?"

Helena could not remember the last time anyone had asked how they could help her. She helped others. It was what she did, who she was, and always had been.

"I'd like to come back and talk some more," she said.

Lo gave her a strange look. "What I really want to know before we leave is how you find the Orbiter men? Do you feel free to speak in this situation?"

"Of course," said Byllyn. "These are my friends. But I don't like questions. They already asked me so many, the women like you in the white place. They tired my spirit."

The white place? Helena wanted to ask her more.

"If you don't like questions then we won't ask any more," said Helena. "But may I come back and talk to you about the different ways of love and healing in our world?"

"This kind of talking is of interest to me, yes."

"Perhaps just a couple more questions about what happened in…"

"Not now," said Helena.

"Yes" said Lurch. "That is enough for now. Byllyn needs time to get to know you. If you can't see that she feels safe here with us, then I feel you lack understanding." It was as harsh as Helena had ever heard him. He put Lil down, ruffling the hair on her arms as he did so. "I'm sorry, but I have to go now little one. I have to put all the lights out and make sure that everyone is going to sleep. I'll come by later to make sure that your light is out and you're asleep. If you get enough dream-time tonight, then maybe we can fish together in the morning."

The little girl began shouting again, "Lil, fish. Lil fish."

"Lil bedtime." Byllyn rose from her seat and bent forward in front of them all as she scooped up her daughter—revealing a great flash of her most intimate parts, also jewel-studded and gold-dusted. Helena saw Lo look away. She did not.

Lil squealed as she was carted below deck. Byllyn turned back just once to smile at Helena. "I hope we meet again, gray lady. I would like to share our thoughts."

Helena reached out and lightly touched Byllyn on her sparkling arm. It felt like rolling her fingertips over a braille board. She knew how that felt, she'd worked with a blind woman once. It had made all communication physical. She felt no need for words now. She moved her fingers back and forth across Byllyn's arm once more, then followed Lo and Lurch, both of whom stood ready and waiting to help her out of the boat.

As Lurch steadied her with his big hairy right hand, she heard Lo ask, "So are you and Byllyn an item?" Her heart lurched a little as she waited on the answer.

Lurch said, "We are friends. Not that our relationship is any of your business."

Helena felt ropes of tension in his arm. Lo just kept going. "Everything is my business. I wonder why you took me to meet someone who you knew wouldn't answer any of my questions. She told me nothing."

Lurched waited a moment before answering. Helena sensed suppressed anger. "In the Orbitals it would be considered a great privilege to lay eyes on such a woman, let alone speak to her. Byllyn told you a great deal. You just didn't hear her."

"Oh sure I did. I heard what she wanted to tell me, not what I wanted to know. Tell me, Lurch, does your friend still work as a... *courtesan?*"

"You ask all the wrong questions," said Lurch.

Helena knew he was right, and yet she still wanted to know that answer too. Lurch didn't oblige. He said, "The only way you can learn about us is to spend more time with us. It is not my job to enlighten you about the complexities and subtleties of our culture. I am not the one promoting the Orbiter settlement program. That is your brother. Ask him your questions."

"Lurch, I feel honored to have met Byllyn," said Helena, and she wasn't just trying to soften the conversation. "Do you think she was serious about meeting me again? I sensed an affinity between us. I would love to learn more about her view of the world, spend some time together. As I told you earlier, I'm a doctor. I am sworn to respect the privacy of others."

Lurch began, "I believe that you will respect—"

Lo cut him off. "That's not the only oath you've taken, Helena."

"Oh, grow up, Lo," she snapped, immediately regretting any hint of disloyalty her outburst might convey. "I'm sorry," she continued. "I understand your point, Lo, although it is not necessary for you to make it. We're all just a little tired. It's been a long and stressful day."

She was happy to see that they were steps from the main boat now. The rest of the women were watching them approach, probably awaiting their instructions. Lo was distracted by the sight of Janine demonstrating her powers by dancing a candle in the air. The moment had passed. No doubt Lo would want to argue about it sometime, but thankfully not right now.

Once she was home, Helena planned on discussing her impatient outburst with the Dalai Lama. The relationship was something she very much kept to herself—and yet she knew that it was something she could and would tell Byllyn. Byllyn would totally understand why she had begun to talk to their cow as if she were the hotline to Buddha. It was, and it wasn't, a joke. Talking to the Dalai was really just praying out loud. Helena felt compelled to do that these days—express her spiritual desperation—yell for otherworldly help. Otherwise she wasn't quite sure how she was going to get through it, watching herself age while everyone else around her remained young, approaching her own death with no sign of meaning in this whole damned mess of a world. Every day lately, and especially now that she could feel the winds of change blowing so very hard, Helena feared that she just might have reached the limits of her own endurance.

21

Reid was waiting to greet them, eyes shining. He rushed over, the happiest she'd seen him in months. Seeing him so pumped up, she just couldn't bring herself to chastise him for his behavior this afternoon. They could discuss his stupidity at a later date, in private. Lo knew not to humiliate her son in public; she was a whole lot more sensitive than people credited.

"How cool is this flotilla? The guys are cool too. I've been talking a lot to Blr. He's an astronomer. He learned to navigate by our stars, just using whatever information he could find in old books and maps he gets from abandoned boats. Amazing. And Lurch is an inventor."

Lo looked at Lurch, who just smiled. She'd never thought to ask what he *did*.

Reid rushed on. "You should see the things he's rigged up. Machines that recharge batteries without needing another power source. Maybe we could even try and trade something for one. I could work on that deal for us. These guys know me now. We got rapport. I mean we have loads in common. We're all trying to make good stuff with whatever crappy broken stuff we've got. It's like everyone has to be an inventor these days, that's what Rans says. Rans is a physicist, and he's working on theories of gravity so they can land big ships from space without making craters and killing everyone, but he also has this hobby where he wraps big structures with messages. He got in trouble for it back home, but I told him that sort of thing wouldn't be a problem here. Nobody cares. We say what we like here, right, Ma?"

Ma. Reid hadn't called her that since they'd told him the circumstances of his birth on his sixteenth birthday. After that he began spending more and more time with James and Marie and the other mothers and all the half-siblings living on Bradley

Lane. Reid might not have much respect for his father, but he still seemed to like him better than Lo. Thanks, kid. Teenagers.

"Reid, it's great you've hit it off with the Orbiters, but you know these guys are only staying until I get back from Madison, right? They can't hang around here, attracting others…"

Reid shrugged. "Maybe I'll go with them, see something more of the world…"

Lo expected Helena to object, but she just stood there smiling and looking calm. It had been like this for a while, Lo always having to do the hard parenting work…

"You know what, Reid? I think that we're going to talk about this some more back home. Right now, I need you to get in the naturals' boat. I've agreed that another delegation can come out to meet the Orbiters. We need to make the switch. You can drive if you'd like."

Lo looked around for the rest of the group as she beamed a message to the wired. It was time to leave. The women began saying goodbye and moving towards Saugatuck's boats. The only two who didn't move were Helena and Reid. Lo stared Reid down.

He glared back. "I'm not leaving," he said. "Blr says I can spend the night on his boat. I want to learn about the stars. This is the best thing that has happened to me in my whole life." Like they didn't teach astronomy in school. Lo continued to glare.

Helena touched her on the shoulder. "It's all right, Lo. I'll be here to keep an eye on him. I'm staying too. These people need medical assistance. There are injuries from today and other issues as well—I'm seeing a number of allergies to Earthan foods and some clear cases of malnutrition. If it's all right with you, I would like to send for a couple more clinic staff tomorrow—they can help with examinations and testing, and they can bring supplies with them. I'll send a list."

Lo said sharply, "We need you more, Helena. We have our own injured."

Helena replied, "You know that everyone at home is alright, Lo. Please. Just let me do this. Don't fight me. I love the idea of sleeping here out on the water. It's not something we usually dare to do—we terrified wireless, powerless, women. I am also interested to take this opportunity to hear more of Byllyn's story, to get some perspective on her people."

Lo felt a pang of jealousy sear through her wires. "Byllyn barely seems capable of normal speech, let alone perspective, Helena. You need to come home."

"Byllyn is just damaged from the years of drug abuse. I might be able to help her."

"Fine," said Lo. "Help her all night long, then. Don't even think about Pat, who has a concussion from being shot down this morning, or Will, who is sleeping off the overdose of Oxycodone you gave him. And certainly don't think about me..."

She knew she was being petulant and unfair. She had no interest in Helena that way anymore. It was unfair to deny her the comforts of someone else. Still...

Helena just said, "I will be here if you really need me."

Lo nodded. What was she going to do, drag her off?

"Just one last thing before you go, Lo. There's a woman with a badly broken femur bone. I could try to make a cast, but it's a difficult bone to treat, and your way is much faster..."

Lo nodded again. Helena had put her on the spot.

Lurch pointed to the nearby hatch. Lo scrambled after Helena, with Lurch following. Downstairs the mahogany and leather interior had been adapted for practical purposes. Polished tables and chairs served as a work space. The kitchen appeared to be a small laboratory and the bedroom in the bow of the boat was set-up as a makeshift first-aid station. A woman lay moaning on the lowest of three bunks. Lo could see the problem from ten feet away—a splint was tied tightly to the area between knee and hip. The visible skin was badly bruised. Something had smashed onto that leg with a great deal of momentum.

"She got caught between two boats in the maelstrom," said Lurch.

Lo walked over to the edge of the bunk and addressed the woman, a dishwater blonde with a rabbity face, eyes watering with pain and fear. "Are you okay with me doing this?"

"Anything. It hurts so bad."

Lo looked at the woman's sparkling skin. She was wired. She should be able to fix her own leg; no need for lying helpless as an injured animal. Lo understood this kind of woman, though — half of Saugatuck had been like her in the beginning.

"This is going to hurt some too. Try biting your finger."

Lo lowered her glove-hand over the damaged thigh, focused her eyes on the area of the bandage, and began slowly drawing her fingers back and forth across the injury. The woman groaned, but Lo didn't stop. Two minutes later, she turned to Lurch and Helena and said, "It's still going to hurt because of the bruising to the surrounding tissue, but the fracture is repaired. She can try walking on it now, but probably best to wait until the morning."

"And you thought I was the doctor," said Helena, smiling at Lurch.

"I did not know that the powers could be used for such good," replied Lurch.

"Like you said earlier, there's plenty we don't know about each other," said Lo.

She turned back to the woman and grabbed her shoulders.

"Try looking at the injury yourself. Use your eyes. You have the power."

"Not me. I could never. Thank you," murmured the woman. She still reeked of fear. Fear spread. Fear was their greatest enemy. Lo pulled the woman close into her arms for a moment, closed her eyes and pressed the air between them with her mind, trying to pass on her strength. There was no connection. This woman may as well be unwired.

"Just try. Focus your thoughts. I'll do it with you. You *can* do it."

The woman began to cower, as if Lo were the one who had hurt her. A victim forever. Lo knew better than to pressure her any further. She leaped up from the bunk.

"I'm done here, and I need to get going," she said to the group. "Lurch, meet me at the checkpoint at 9:00 a.m. tomorrow. Helena, enjoy your night on the water."

Both Helena and Lurch started to bid her farewell, moving simultaneously to bow, to kiss. Lo didn't give them a chance. She pushed past them, made her way up on deck, then scrambled across the smaller boats to where her pod sat waiting on the water.

HQ—five—meet, she beamed Pat as she jumped into the pod.

She opened the throttle of her mind and burst into the starry night sky like champagne shooting from a freshly popped bottle. She knew how to use her powers.

22

Will woke from a dream involving Lurch and a green Unan mud-pool to find Pat yanking the catheter out of his swollen member. Then she pulled the drip from his wrist. A small gash split Pat's eyebrow where she had hit her head yesterday, but otherwise the great lump of a gal appeared fine. Although Will was pretty sure Pat wasn't a trained nurse, he was grateful that someone was looking after him. Lifting his heavy head and looking around, he decided he was at the old Weingartner clinic, once famous for breast enhancement. He could see a clutter of medical equipment, clean white work units, and that he was lying in a hospital bed. A big mug of tea and a muffin sat on the pull-tray beside him — further evidence that Pat had a nurturing side. However, the clock on the wall said 7:13. There was nothing nurturing about that.

Pointing to a dingy white towel on the end of the bed, Pat said, "You've got fifteen minutes to shower and dress. Bathroom is next door. Burn cream is on the sink. Skin suit is hanging on the hook behind the door. Do you need help with your bandages?"

"Thanks for the offer, but no. If I'm getting my bodcoz back, then no bandages are necessary. Is Helena here?" He felt something of her presence in this place.

"She's out on the flotilla," Pat said on her way out the door. "Helping people who got hurt yesterday. Now get yourself in that shower, sweet-cheeks. We got a big day ahead."

Will was very grateful that he could still feel the packet of Oxy-codone taped to his leg — six left by his calculations. He reached down, extracted one, slipped it into his mouth, and gulped it down with a slug of tea — definitely just one this time. He shouldn't have taken so many yesterday, but burns hurt like hell. If rationed carefully enough, the remaining pills would see him through until the medical staff in Madison could fix his medi-controls. In his mind's eye, Madison was a civilized enclave equipped with medi-controls, system-repair-bots, Unan jammers, and force-shielding. The very thought of it motivated Will out of his fog and into the shower. Although it was cool, Will relished the feel of water on his skin. He didn't give a damn about summer water rations. He cranked the tap as far as it would go.

The sooner he got to Madison, the sooner he could be heading home. In addition to the cloud apartment, his deal with the High Council included a personal assistant and a regular seat at high table. After thirty years of small apartments, shared assistants, and scrounging about for dinner invitations, he was looking forward to the new privileges. At the time he cut his deal, those privileges seemed like more-than-fair payment for a long but simple PR trip home. Unfortunately, however, the trip was turning out to be nothing like the blow-through he'd envisaged. It was going to be a challenge simply to get his ship back before departure—let alone deliver the Vroom72 to Madison, help distribute it to roaming gangs of Unans and make sure that any already-inhabited settler destinations were prepared to welcome their unexpected Orbiter guests.

As far as Will was concerned, any problems with disgruntled settlers and native Earthans were now secondary to his own problems. Retske would have to distribute the Vroom72 herself. She was the one who had begged the last settlement-support mission for help. Well, he'd come, hadn't he? He just hoped she stood ready to help *him* now. It was certainly her duty, and her gems would still be generating visual, oral, and sensory records—the kind of thing that would be reviewed at a later date. Thinking about the practicalities of official obligation, Will realized for the first time that he himself was no longer acting on the record. All his recording gems had been melted. Perhaps that was one gain from his terrible encounter with sweet little cousin Mira. There would never be any official record of how he conducted himself here on Earth.

Just as he had started enjoying the thought that he was no longer accountable for his every word and deed on this ill-fated mission, Will felt a hand reach into the shower from behind him. It slid right under his hairless armpit and reached directly for the tap. He jumped as Pat shouted, "Hey! I think you've used my allocation of water for a month, you stupid dickwad. Get the hell out of the shower now. What do you think this is, the Beverly Hills Hilton?"

"No," retorted Will. "And stop ogling me like I'm a Chippendale."

"You'd need a better tan and bigger equipment for that line of work," said Pat as she clumped out the door. She was softening to him.

Will sighed with relief as the last few dribbles of water ran down his fried chest. The pain was already noticeably duller. Thank you, Helena. He toweled off and pulled on his bodcoz, enjoying the relief its soft inner skin brought to his wounds. He set the color of his bodcoz to a dirty bronze that reminded him of his old sailing and swimming trophies, the color of the nameplate on his door at NASA. Then he yelled to Pat, "Ready, honey-buns."

It was a new day, and things were looking up.

Within ten minutes he and Pat were slipping around the side of HQ to the great lawn, where a flurry of activity belied the early hour. Will saw that his ship had been towed to the other side of the river, possible only because Will had been stupid enough to turn the defense shield off to appease Lo. Sure, nobody could enter or fly it without the authorization codes embedded in his melted access gem. However, the ship was no longer totally invulnerable. It could be—and had been—moved.

The dock where he had landed three days earlier was filled with smaller boats this morning. At least thirty women bustled around the boats. The same number again dotted the lawns, almost like it was the start of a regatta day. What appeared to be registration tables had been set up in the middle of the lawn. Women gathered around them—obviously signing up to go out to the flotilla. Will saw Yaz standing behind a table, busy with lists. Pat waved as they walked past, toward the pod-park. Yaz waved back, although she did not smile at him. Many of the women stared, but none approached. Just as they reached the arch in the hedge leading to the pod park, however, Will heard a hissing sound.

Pat turned and bellowed at a woman with a waist-length braid, "Hey, cut that crap out, Crissa. This is not high school." He thanked the big gal, but she just shrugged.

Things were just as busy in the pod park as they were at the dock. Will saw Lo, Janine, Adrianna, Bob, and Lurch standing around. They were clearly all waiting for him. He waved to keep up the courtesies. Nobody waved back, although Bob did nod. Today Bob's bodcoz bore a ridiculous projection of a Hawaiian girl with a cocktail on the front. He must have limned it himself. What the hell was he thinking? Will would be glad to shake the guy off when they got to Madison. He could hardly believe he had spent all those months stuck on the explorer listening to the details of his many skanky sexual encounters. Enough was enough.

"Right," said Lo, as soon as they were close enough, dispensing with any kind of greetings. "Bob is going to be riding shotgun with Janine, Lurch is with me, and Adrianna gets Will. I want my brother where I can see him, but I don't want to hear his fucking voice."

"Are you sure I shouldn't be going with you?" asked Pat.

Lo looked at her and said, "No, I'm not sure — but I need you here."

"Whatever you need, Lo. Keep me posted while you're in beam range. Send me a message when you get to Madison using their radio. If I don't hear from you every four hours, I'm sending a rescue party. Roger that?" She smiled.

"Roger that," replied Lo. She smiled back.

Pat turned to say goodbye to Will: "And you, Gaylord, you behave yourself."

"Roger that," he replied.

Nobody smiled.

Next came the indignity of getting into the pods. At first Will was grateful to be spared the scary and uncomfortable net, but as it turned out, inside the pod was not a whole lot better. Not only were the pods designed for one person only, they were designed for short Ruurdaan persons. The pods were rounded and smooth inside, like melting ice-cubes. It was clear from various markings and bulges that the sphere had multiple openings, but Will experienced it as a continuous glass surface. The pod's controls were molded into the rounded front panels of the sphere, responsive, he knew, only to hands with wires. The only apparent form of seating in the pod was a half-moon groove in the center glass bench. It was a tiny groove.

Although it appeared virtually empty, Will knew that the pods were in fact all extraordinarily complex machines. They had to be more comfortable than they looked—and surely they must expand to fit others when necessary? Apparently not, though. When he did as Adrianna asked—squeezed in behind the glass bench—the space proved just as tight as it looked. Will was forced to spoon the woman, head under one of her arms, folded knees under the other. The glass bench did give a little, allowing his body to sink into position; however, it was still cramped and overly intimate. Adrianna's curls tickled his neck. Her body smelled damp and salty, like she'd been swimming that morning. Will stretched his cramped legs as best he could.

"Get your feet away from the fucking control panel," she barked.

He missed Pat already.

Fortunately, the ride was faster than Will had been expecting—under ten minutes for what used to be a seventy-minute drive doing one-twenty up the I95. Adrianna was quite the pilot. She swooped and looped through the air with the confidence of an eagle, showing off, maybe, but impressive nonetheless. Will's main complaint was that he couldn't see anything through the glass because his face was awkwardly turned toward Adrianna's firm dancer's thigh. It would have been interesting to see the flattened shallows of Bridgeport and the new coastline.

"You're quite the fly-girl," he said once they'd flattened out.

"What?" replied Adrianna.

"You know, a fly-girl, like they used to call women pilots"

"When was that? In my day we called women pilots, you know, *pilots*."

"Forget it," said Will. She was probably too young to even remember a time before women in active service. Or was she? It was impossible to tell with these women. Adrianna might be pushing seventy, but she didn't look a day over twenty-one.

He tried again. "You have the legs of a dancer, Adrianna."

"Thanks, I think. Actually, I did used to be a dancer. A pole dancer."

Will was not sure what one said to that in this day and age.

"I imagine you were very good at your job. Tell me, do you miss the men?"

"No!" replied Adrianna. "And just in case you were thinking it, no, I am not interested in your Orbiter men—ugly-looking freaks—so far they've brought nothing but trouble."

"So the trip out to the flotilla didn't change your mind," said Will. He was curious to know how it had gone out there on the water. How bad were the Unans traveling with Lurch?

"I have to say, I liked them a whole lot better than I like you," replied Adrianna.

"Well that's more positive than Lo's attitude. Clearly you've recognized that there are some important differences betw—"

Suddenly Will felt himself spinning upside down. She was doing something crazy with the pod. Some kind of three-sixty. He could feel the breakfast muffin up near his solar plexus.

"Sorry, I didn't mean..."

"I know what you meant," said Adrianna. "Don't even think about trying to manipulate me. And show a bit more respect for your sister, asshole. If it wasn't for her, most of us would be long dead. I might not always agree with her, but I'd kill for her if she asked me to."

It was a quiet ride after that.

23

They landed on broken tarmac in a small clearing surrounded on three sides by a jungle of hogweed, kudzu, and other invasive plants. On the edge of what had once been the post road stood an old sign. *Route 1.* A big white board with large red letters was attached to the top of the sign. STOP HERE. Ahead of him lay a long visible stretch of cleared road. About thirty feet away from the pods the road was blocked by a scrappy wire fence bedecked with glow sticks and fairy lights. Will knew what the others might not—those were Orbiter shielding rods and cords. The strange, messy fence continued into the scrub on either side of the road for as far as Will could see, past a rundown old cottage with a worrying message painted on it: BEWARE OF DOGS.

Will wondered if the defense shield reached high enough to stop pods from entering. That fence barely looked fit to repel intruders approaching on foot. Looks could be deceiving, though. Orbital defense technology fed on force. Their own power was the main reason the women hadn't managed to breach the orbicraft's force-field. It had also caused them to be stymied by the limited shielding Zgyzg-Dm's people had deployed in the battle yesterday. Will was grateful the women did not understand Orbiter technology—it meant that he should be safe once he was inside that perimeter fence and back with his own people.

As they clambered out of the pods, Will saw a couple of tall and lanky Orbiters waiting for them by a shiny khaki box, about the size of a large shipping crate, that was set into the fence. It was a drop box, clearly repurposed. The men didn't come out to greet them, instead gesturing them all in. Taking the hint, the women encircled Will, Bob, and Lurch. Adrianna, Janine, and Lo used their gloved hands to thrash the surrounding vegetation, cutting down scrub and slashing long summer grass. "Run as fast as you can," Lo said to the men. As the women continued to thrash, Will, Lurch, and Bob sprinted to the dark-green box and clambered through the knee-high opening. Will was through first. The women followed right behind.

The group found themselves alone inside a metal freighter crate, stripped of everything but a pull-down bench/bed/table, supply box, and cleansing station. The women seemed curious. Will was keen to get out. Cramped spaces of any kind took his thoughts back to the shuttle. It had been terrible on the explorer all those months, ghosts lurking in the stale air. The only thing that had made the trip to Earth bearable was the stim-sims, which allowed him to wallow in the illusion that he was elsewhere; he'd taken the full interactive Orbital history course. Old fears besetting him, Will scanned the drop box for an exit. He found a trapdoor in the back side of the crate, pushed it open, and hurried out onto the other side of the broken and weedy highway.

The two Orbiters waiting on the other side were wearing gleaming white bodcoz made out of what looked like thin white ceramic snakeskin. Pure—as Will had expected. "Welcome," they said as each member of the group came through. The women looked shocked at their appearance. He remembered feeling the same way the first time he encountered the Pure—skin and hair whitened from the bleach pools. Freaky. Will wondered if these guys were still white from when they left home or whether they had recreated the bleach pools here in Madison. No wonder Lo was struggling to wrap her mind around the idea that Orbiters were human. Tall rubbery dolls, hairy Yetis, and now strange white ghosts. Oh well. He was actually happy to be here with the weird old Pure. At least they accepted the general rules and principles of the Orbital hierarchy—they would listen to him, help him, maybe even take instructions.

Will pushed himself forward. "Ambassador Wl-Wrrn, Settler Support."

"Yes. We expected you three days ago."

"Slight delay. May I ask, is Ambassador Rtsk-Fdrvsky expecting me today?"

"She is expecting the whole party. Please follow me."

For once nobody argued.

They walked down what was left of Route 1 for about twenty minutes until they reached the turnoff for the town proper. Will was shocked to see how nature had taken over this once busy strip. Shops and businesses were so overgrown with bittersweet that they were starting to collapse under the weight. The road itself, once a generous two-lane highway, now looked like a long weedy driveway through a dense forest. After the turnoff, though, the tangle of vegetation began to thin out, giving way to a landscape more reminiscent of the grounds of a neglected stately home. Proceeding down an avenue of freshly painted white Victorians—complete with ginger-bread trim and wrap-around porches—Will began to see signs of human habitation, first clothing on a stoop, then freshly dug plant beds. Here and there a large khaki drop-box clogged a driveway. Perhaps some of the Orbiters still slept in them—it would be pretty uncomfortable in the old houses unless they were fully adapted for tall people.

Two thousand Orbiters had joined the four hundred Earthan women here in Madison three years ago. Although rumor had it that seven hundred of the original settlers had struck out on their own since then, that still left more than fifteen hundred people living here, most of them Pure by the looks of things. It had never been Will's goal to sell the Earth settlement program to the Pure, but for some reason his pitch had resonated with those guys. As it turned out, the High Council had also been thrilled to hear they wanted to relocate to Earth; Pure religiosity made other Orbiters uncomfortable, and nobody was pleased about the way they had taken over the White Lakes area of Gllryn, stealing the crystal and ruining it for ordinary tourists.

Will felt the shock of the others as they slowly realized what the Pure had done here in Madison. Every single house was painted or stained white. That was not so unusual in a New England land-scape. It was the extent of the surrounding whiteness that was truly extraordinary. As they had walked along, the gray-colored tarmac of the old road had slowly given way to a gummy white surface. The gravel and dirt alongside the road had become chalky. Even the green of the grass began to look abnormally delicate and pale — blanched. The trees were still green where they hit the sky, but the trunks were all white-washed. A wide variety of white flowers bloomed prettily along the underside of porches and in beds around the edge of the town green (which was also blanched). And then the people...

Even from a distance, Will could see that the delegation await-ing them in the center of town was half Orbiter and half Earthan. They might be different heights, but they were all the same ghostly white from head to toe. The men had shorn white heads, just a few bristles here and there. The women had long white tresses, cur-tains of peroxided straw. Will knew from experience that their faces would be powdered with chalk, their lips painted with white paste.

Will heard Bob whisper to Janine, "No wonder your people are scared..."

Will snapped, "The Pure are members of the Orbital collec-tive. We're pledged to accept their choices and here to assist them with their integration, not insult them."

"Just saying, dude. It's not what I expected."

"Well it's this or nothing for you, Bob, so improve your attitude."

Bob fell back in step with Janine and Adrianna. Will turned to Lurch and Lo, seemingly stunned silent. "I thought you were in communication with these people," he said to his sister.

"I admit it's been a while..."

Lurch interrupted in a hushed whisper. "A while? It has been this way for over two years. Retske converted about a year after we dropped. She expelled my group six months later because we re-fused to convert and complained about the allocation of resources."

"Well I'm sure she has a story to tell as well," said Will. "I look forward to..."

Before they had a chance to speak further, they were upon the delegation.

An emaciated and dusty white Earthan woman about seventy years old stepped forward. The heavy gold chains hanging on her white kaftan told them all that this was Gail, the mayor of Madison. Nothing else about her was mayoral though. Her face was like a dried and moldering prune, white with dark hollows. She wobbled unsteadily toward them and fell into an exaggerated bow—like an inexperienced Orbiter girl—only this was no girl. A very large man and a tallish woman hovered on either side of her, clearly worried she might fall. Will started as he recognized the woman helper—her bodcoz was set to porcelain, her thick mane of once-black hair was now white, her face chalked like the rest—it was Retske. His fellow ambassador and another big, thick, doughy-lipped white Orbiter held the shriveled little woman steady so she could speak.

"Welcome to Madison, home of the Pure. I know most of you already but I don't think you know our new deputy mayors— Retske and Jrm. Perhaps you can all introduce yourselves. I'm bad with names." Her voice quavered through parchment lips.

Lo, Janine, and Adrianna exchanged glances but nevertheless put their hands out and began exchanging greetings. Will followed suit. Lurch merely bowed slightly, began nodding around in a circle and said, "It is a pleasure to see you again, Gail—although you are so white I hardly recognized you. Retske, Jrm, peaceful greetings."

Retske smiled and replied, "It is good to meet in peace." Her Russian accent was as thick as the day they first met, thirty years ago, at an early press conference on Crn.

Jrm said, "I am glad you and your people are well, Zgyzg-Dm. We have missed you and the contributions you made to our community. If you ever wish to rejoin us as members of the Pure, we will consider your applications in all seriousness." Jrm sounded Russian too—like so many of the settlers who had learned English using Retske's language feeds on the trip out.

Lurch replied, "Those are good words, Jrm, but you made your real feelings clear when you set the jammers on my group as you drove us into the boats. Some of us still experience migraines. Lil talks about the needle in mama's brain."

"Byllyn must have told the child that—she can't know how a jammer feels."

"Nobody should know how a jammer feels, not in a civilized society."

"You don't seem adversely altered by the experience, Zgyzg-Dm."

Will thought he should move things along. "This is a great opportunity for transparent dialogue on the many issues facing settlers and hosts. I have promised the High Council a very detailed report that represents all views equally and fairly. I—"

"Yes, yes," said Jrm, waving his words away. Nobody else seemed interested. Retske was glaring at Lo, who was telling Gail what she really thought.

"Holy shit, Gail. Is that really you under all that talcum? I mean I know it's nine or ten years since we signed the alliance treaty in IBM City, but we wired don't change that much. No offense but you look like something floured and ready for the pan."

"Now, now," said Retske. "There is no need to be insulting."

Adrianna ignored her and added, "I don't get it, Gail. You looked pretty normal when I dropped off the medical supplies you requested four years ago."

"I flew that mission too," said Janine, "and everyone here was still normal."

Jrm and Retske spoke over the top of each other. "Respect please. Everyone here looks perfectly normal to us. The women of Madison have simply chosen to become Pure. Better than normal. They are stronger and happier now."

"Oh yeah?" said Lo. "*How* strong and happy are you, Gail?"

"Very happy," warbled the shriveled white husk of a woman.

Will saw Lo's face twitch with doubt. Then she shrugged and said, "You know, at the end of the day, it's not my business what kind of weird shit you've got going on here. We're still in the alliance together, you haven't violated our agreement, and you responded to our call. That's about the strength of our commitment to each other, no more, no less. So let's quit with the niceties and get down to business."

Retske nodded and said, "Certainly. If you could explain that business for me. The radio messages were not entirely clear. Something about the ambassador needing medical assistance?"

Lo nodded and pointed at Will. "His technology is damaged. We need to fix the gem-chip-thing that controls access to his orbicraft. He can't get in right now. Can you help us?"

Retske and Jrm didn't answer. They looked across at Will. He burst open the bodcoz and showed them the mess that was his chest. Retske breathed out so hard the air whistled. Jrm knelt and cast his eyes over the damage. He said in a phlegmy voice, "I've never seen anything like it. Most of the gems are melted. Are your retinas still working? What about other systems?"

"The eyes seem fine," replied Will. "The rest I'm not sure about. I can't access any records or controls, but the damage seems quite localized. I was hoping we could repurpose some of the system controls. I just need to fix the authorization codes. As soon as I'm back on the orbicraft, I should be able to repair more of the damage."

"I don't know," said Jrm. "We have the equipment and some spare gems—but it would take time, and there are no guarantees. As you know, the biotech work we do here is different. What happened to you, Wl-Wrrn?"

"Just a little misunderstanding," said Will.

Lo was staring at the ground. Retske's eyes widened.

He said to Retske, "Would you like to talk privately?"

Lo answered, "No way."

Will raised his eyebrows at Retske—who took the hint. "I *would* like to speak with the ambassador in private," she said. "Perhaps as we walk to the meeting house? Jrm can lead the way, and I will follow with Wl-Wrrn. No, don't look concerned, Lo. I respect our mutual commitment. But Wl-Wrrn and I are old colleagues. There are things we need to say to each other; things that pertain only to us."

Lo nodded her reluctant agreement. She stepped aside to allow Will to join Retske. Jrm set off down the road, in the direction of a blockish white building. Everyone else followed, Lo with Adrianna, Janine with Bob, and Gail escorted by a couple of Pure. Will and Retske fell back to what was only a slight distance. Will hoped that none of the wired had super hearing. He hadn't heard about anything like that, but who knew...

He began in a whisper. "Thank the Orbits you're here. I need your help. Things went very wrong in Saugatuck. They think I'm some kind of alien infiltrator. They've had some bad experiences. The Unans attacked them. Most of them don't want settlers."

"I had a feeling. Exactly what kind of help do you need?" asked Retske.

"Major system repairs and not just my authorization codes. Personal shielding is critical. I also require safe passage back to the orbicraft. You must have some kind of defended transportation. I need to get back to my ship and board it alone. Once I'm on board, your obligations are over. I'll be okay from there."

Retske thought for moment then said, "Would you return directly to the explorer?"

"I would certainly like to, but as I'm sure you realize, I have other duties. The fourth drop is due in three weeks. The designated settlement sites require advance assistance—at the very least they need to be informed so they don't attack the incoming. Given that you yourself have done zero prep work, I will need to visit eighteen towns in as many days, prep them myself."

Retske stopped walking for a moment, grabbed his arm, and looked at him.

"You don't want to do that, Wl-Wrrn. It's dangerous out there."

"I think I already know that, Retske."

"I hope you have a jammer on your ship."

"So it's the Unans you're most afraid of?"

"We are worried about everything and everyone, but yes, especially the Unans. They understand our technology. They have their own defenses. They buried one of our people down a mineshaft. A bodcoz alone won't get you out of that kind of situation."

Will grimaced. "I'm very sorry. The Unans seem to have been a disaster. I'll make sure that the settlement program doesn't send any more of them—if and when I manage to get back. In the meantime, however, I have something with me that may help you with the Unans."

Retske raised her white eyebrows.

"My orbicraft is stacked full of Vroom72. I had always planned to deliver it here and maybe even help with distribution. Most of the trouble-makers you exiled are Unans right? And most of those are ex-junkies who would kill for a little Vroom. You know how addictive that stuff is. I'm sure if word got out that it was available at your fence..."

Retske looked shocked. "Vroom72. You think I should poison the Unans?"

"You sent transmissions begging for help. You've already used the jammers."

Retske shook her head. "Vroom72 is a step too far. It would make me no better than the Unans themselves. I'm surprised you would condone it. Or maybe not..."

Will resented the inference. "Fine," he said. "Don't dirty your own hands with the Vroom72. Let a dirty guy like me do that job for you. But please help me get back to my ship. You have a moral obligation to help. Aside from which, if you don't, you'll be stuck here with me—and I outranked you last time I looked. You are still loyal to the government, I assume?"

"Don't you dare challenge my authority here," said Retske. "*I* am the one stuck taking care of all the Orbiters *you* sent to this half-savage place. You're here about three years too late!" She began walking away from him at quite a clip. Will had to increase his gait. He grabbed her arm and said, "I apologize, Retske. I know the settlement mission has proved challenging. You've done well just keeping all your people alive."

Retske shook his hand off her arm, but she slowed down. When she spoke, her tone was more conciliatory. "Are the repairs and access to the ship all you want from me?"

"Pretty much. I will take care of—the rest—myself. There is one small *other* thing though. I want to take the courtesan Byllyn home with me. Her father has requested her return now she's been three years off the Vroom, and he's heard there's a child. It's not a top priority, but it would be a nice success story for the settlement program. Royal family member home and off drugs after spending time in the healing environment of Earth. Is she still here, or did I hear that she went with Zgyzg-Dm's group?"

"She's no longer with us," said Retske, "We wanted her to stay, but she made her own choice. Maybe you can persuade her to go home—maybe not. Don't let her anywhere near that Vroom though. Three years clean is nothing to an addict."

"It was just a thought. I'll take it up with Zgyzg-Dm. My own situation is far more pressing. You have to either persuade Lo to give me my ship back—or help me get it back without her permission. If I have to wait until the rest of the team realize I'm missing and come looking for me, there will be no time left to assist with the drops. No time to distribute the Vroom. The Unans will remain and the settlements put at risk. And if the settlement program fails, there goes any reward you might have been promised for all your hard work."

Retske said, "Don't act all secretive about the reward, Wl-Wrrn. I know we were both promised a knowledge gem."

"And I think we've both earned them, don't you?"

Retske smiled. "I don't share your ambitions anymore, Wl-Wrrn. Can't you tell? I don't care about knowledge gems and meals at high table and cloud apartments on Crn or any of the things I used to believe were important. I have come to love the simple work I'm doing here. It has made me...*pure*. I have no wish to return to the Orbitals."

As she said it, Will suddenly became conscious of something that had been there in the air all along—the strong whiff of bleach. Pools of the stuff must be nearby, perhaps in the brackish tidal ponds that lay between here and the beach. Retske was lost to the whiteness.

"I accept your decision to become a permanent settler, Retske, but it is still to your advantage to work with the Orbiters, and to help me. After all, I am still going to be the one determining how many Pure settlers the program sponsors. I will also decide which supplies are allocated to their dispatch. I'm sure you'd like more Gllryn crystals."

"Yes, certainly—but those things aren't the only considerations. I'm sure you heard what I said to Lo? We do have a mutual assistance agreement with the Democratic Alliance towns—and those people can get here a lot faster than you if we desperately need help. We have to build allegiances here on Earth if the settlement program is going to survive in the long run."

Will lost his composure for a moment. "If you're referring to the so-called political alliance that Lo claims to have with IBM City, well that is obviously a joke, Retske. There's no credible government around here—just lynching committees and..."

"Nothing here is a joke, Wl-Wrrn."

"I didn't mean..."

"I know what you meant."

"I'm sorry. I'm worried for all of us, the small group who are already here and the twenty thousand on their way, many of them Pure. Are you going to help me or not?"

"Maybe. We'll see. I don't know."

They had come to an intersection. The old traffic lights had been painted white, as had the old brick bank they had just passed. There was, of course, no traffic. The road was bleached white. Directly opposite stood the old grocery store, still operational, selling what, white foods — wonder bread and cool whip? Kitty-corner stood an ornate house set in extensive white gardens.

"That's our place," said Retske. So she and Jrm had their very own white house.

Over on the farthest corner of the intersection was the big white building. Half-way down, Lo and Lurch had come to a halt in front of a wide-stepped entrance. The others had already disappeared inside its great square mouth. The large modern structure clearly predated the invasion — but to the Pure arriving here in Madison, it must have seemed almost preordained — a brand new white city hall and library. Will wondered if they'd even had time to open the place before the Ruurdaan invasion. At a moment like this, he almost wished those amoral little bastards had just flattened it, flattened everything. The resettlement of Earth would have been so much easier on a clean slate.

24

Inside, the building was fresh and functional. The group—eleven of them, including two Pure bodyguards—were gathered in a large plain meeting room. They were seated around an enormous conference table with matching chairs that had all been stained white and modified to accommodate bigger people. Retske told them that the water in the jugs was purified, same as the overflowing bowls of big creamy-colored strawberries. Janine looked over to Bob to see how he was coping. He looked how he always looked—amused. After spending the last three days joined at the hip Janine had come to believe that Bob was really Northern Californian at heart. He was easy-going, he was fun and considerate in bed, he thought she was smart and attractive, and he believed that everyone should just try to get along; he was a gift from the gods, was what.

Janine knew that the situation was very serious right now and that the potential arrival of thousands of alien colonists was more a threat than an opportunity. She wasn't the stupid cheerleader some people took her for, just inclined by nature to look on the bright side. It was the women who judged her who were the fools if they thought she didn't hurt too. Some mornings she still woke up thinking she was sprayed tight in the skin covering, about to begin another day trying to do the impossible, zapped until her eardrums nearly burst if she didn't. Some of the women in town stayed in bed on days like that, but not Janine. Those were the days she dressed her very best, painted her smile on, and went out there ready to take on anything. As a flight attendant she hadn't had the luxury of a bad day. She didn't allow herself that luxury now. Her attitude had always been her greatest strength—she wanted to be the kind of person who made others feel like the plane wouldn't crash while she was in charge, and if it did, well then it would still be okay, with last smiles and kind reassuring words, not terror and screaming.

Lo knew all that about her too, and even though she mostly ignored her, she had let Janine take care of Bob for a reason, let her come on this mission. Not many of Lo's crew could fight and fly *and* put a whole room at ease. Janine was proud to be that kind of person. A people-mover. TGIF. The park project. Getting the shut-ins to come out to Thanksgiving at HQ. Instituting the Wired Olympics (one day she dreamed they'd all come, strong-wired women from everywhere, ready to show each other their stuff). Janine liked bringing people together in spite of their political differences. Her friends all said she had real leadership potential—if she would just put her mind to the more difficult political challenges. That was easier said than done.

Take now, for example. Retske and Lo were talking about the exact same thing that they'd all just talked about on the walk, the exact same thing they'd all talked about for the last three days. Janine knew she should try to process the details of the discussion, knew their future was probably hanging on the line, but Bob was raking his toenail up and down the inside of her bare foot, and she was distracted by a pleasant tingle between her legs. Terrified of what Lo would say if she caught them fooling around at a moment like this, Janine kicked Bob off and tried to concentrate on the discussion—but the tingle remained, fogging her brain. There hadn't been much romance in her life these last thirty years. So many of the other women had settled into happy relationships with each other, but Janine never could; she was just too straight. She was not the kind of woman who would stoop to using James Nunn or becoming one of a harem or chasing after teenage boys, either. Well okay, maybe occasionally that last one. Back when, you used to read cases in the paper about older women who went with teenagers. Teachers who had taken advantage of their young pupils. Female sex offenders. Things weren't that simple anymore.

"We must stop them," Lo was saying. Janine knew that Lo was probably right about the Orbiters in general, although perhaps a specific number of the new arrivals, specifically Bob, should be allowed to stay. The situation reminded her of when the government went after Ronaldo, her old next-door-neighbor without any papers. His lawyer had asked her to write a letter to the INS saying that he had been a good neighbor, which of course she did: he was a great neighbor, fed the cat for her when she was flying. She had celebrated with his family after he won his case. The following year she voted Republican even though she usually voted Democrat—because her brother's landscaping firm was put out of business by illegals. Janine remembered feeling bad about both things: writing a letter for an illegal when her brother couldn't get work, and voting against a neighbor whose wife sewed her curtains for free. These were the reasons Janine still avoided the more difficult political stuff. You couldn't support everybody.

Retske asked Lo a question. "How do you know the settlers won't prove useful to your community?" Bob had asked her the same question. What if the settlers could all do things like Bob— grow coffee, develop frost-resistant foods, offer relationships?

"No chance," said Lo. "We don't have the resources for any more people, and we certainly couldn't accommodate the needs of the Pure. We're not into white."

Janine certainly agreed with that. The Pure were creepy.

Lo turned to Will. "What are we getting? Unans or Pure?"

"Each group offers a mix of Pure, Unan, and other volunteers, three hundred some of each. We reduced the group size this time so as to minimize the impact on existing inhabitants."

Okay, so a mix, not too many. Personally, she thought it sounded reasonable, even potentially desirable. If those people contributed, they could easily expand the boundaries, stretch down into the empty houses on Saugatuck Shores. If they were decent people who could be trusted to respect the secret of the children, it might work. If you looked at IBM City, you could see the strength in numbers. But what if all the immigrants were men? Some men would be very welcome, but a thousand might be intimidating. Overwhelming even.

She raised her hand and said, "Will there be men and women, or just men?"

Lo looked surprised. Lo had been looking at her that way for thirty years.

"A quarter of every group will be women. We know the all-men groups don't work."

"How very, fucking, thoughtful," said Lo.

Retske objected. "I would prefer it if you didn't swear. We're trying to keep every aspect of our environment pure—including our language."

Lo said, "Point taken. Now, about the imminent fucking invasion…"

Retske looked furious, but all she said was, "If you do not wish to accept Orbiters into your community, then you can just direct them to a more suitable nearby location."

Janine and Bob had talked about this, very casually of course, nothing out of turn, nothing top secret. Bob agreed with her. Take the people who fit with you and suggest other places for those you can't accommodate, like they used to do in Chi Omega.

Lo scoffed, though. "So it would be okay to redirect them up here?"

"Well no, not here. We too would struggle to accommodate so many new settlers at once, even those of our own faith. We are already concerned about supporting a thousand more. Believe me, we understand that aspect of the problem all too well. We also want Ambassador Wl-Wrrn to return home with the message not to send any more settlers until we ask for them. The program *must* slow down. I think that all of us here agree on that point."

Will nodded enthusiastically. "Oh yes, I'm going to support you all the way on this issue. Earth is a huge planet—there are plenty of other places to dispatch settlers." Janine agreed. As she'd already said to Bob, *there's always the Midwest, it's easy to grow things there and there's definitely a lot of empty space.* Perhaps that was a little naïve of her, but Janine knew that getting bogged down in reality checks turned women into emos. She'd seen it over and over, not just after the invasion but before as well, women scared and hopeless and negative.

Lo scoffed again. "My brother says all the right things, but don't trust him. He'll say anything to save his own skin. He'll never tell the Orbiters to stop sending settlers. He's the architect of this program and totally invested in keeping it going. No way will he speak out against it. No. Our best chance is to send Lurch. I don't entirely trust him either, but we know he's not scared to speak his mind, and we know he has people here that he cares about."

Janine hoped everyone *would* agree to send Lurch home. She agreed with him and Lo that it wasn't okay just to dump people on Earth without asking first. Bob agreed with that too. He said who wouldn't agree? Now even Will seemed to agree. In fact, Janine didn't understand exactly *who* thought it was an acceptable idea to just dump boxes full of people on Earth. Nobody seemed to have asked that question, or had they and she'd missed it?

Retske spoke up. "I have no problem with the idea of Ambassador Zgyzg-Dm returning home and speaking out against certain aspects of the settlement program. It is true that the Unans and the Pure should never be mixed. At the same time, I cannot agree to help anyone physically coerce an Orbiter ambassador into opening his ship just so they can steal it."

"Why not?" said Lo.

Janine thought they both had a point, although of course she sided with Lo.

Suddenly the tall creepy white guy called Jrm spoke up. "We will not commit criminal acts, even for a just cause. We are Pure in mind, body, and deed."

Lo said, "And word. Don't forget word. And we're not asking you to commit a criminal act. All we're asking you to do is fix his authorization system—he asked you to do that himself. So just do it and let us leave. What happens then is between us and him..."

She looked down as she trailed off—and Janine knew why. It was obvious. Lurch would have to knock Will out if he wanted to use his body tech to gain control of the ship. If they let Will remain conscious, then he would be able to just turn on the ship's defenses and eject Lurch back out into Saugatuck. He said he wouldn't do that, but everyone knew he would. Still, knocking him unconscious after everything they'd already done to him seemed brutal.

Retske stood up and put her hands on the table, like the discussion was coming to an end. "I'm sorry, she said. "No more arguments. We will not help you steal Wl-Wrrn's ship. We cannot risk our relationship with the settlement program. We depend on the Orbiters for supplies. Until we can live independently, we do not have the luxury of independent political action."

She then swung around to Bob—of all people—and said, "I have one last question for *you*, Bob, whoever you are, sitting there with no opinions. Why can't you open the orbicraft? Are you damaged too?" She obviously thought he had the same technology as Will, which he did not. Janine had checked every little inch of his body and had found nothing. She'd even tried peeking inside, but all she saw was a human body, just slightly different, though, because Bob's heart was on the other side. Bob told her that one percent of all people were born that way. It was a special abnormality. Sometimes he had wondered whether he was destined to be one of those who made first contact.

Bob quickly pulled his foot away from Janine and sat up a little straighter. He smiled his lovely white smile at Retske. "That's an interesting question—am I *damaged?* Well, not in the way that I think you mean. Not physically. I don't have the kind of parts that get *damaged*. Not like Will. The Orbiters wouldn't give me a taste enhancer, let alone authorization chips."

Retske and Jrm both looked confused. Will leaped in to explain.

"He's not part of the diplomatic corps. He's a community service volunteer—drugs offense. I should have mentioned it earlier. He's been assigned to the Madison settlement."

Janine thought Retske and Jrm looked horrified. Bob winked at them and said, "No offense, guys, but what else do you think would persuade me to come here, half-way to Assville."

It didn't come out particularly funny. Janine gave him a kick under the table.

"I mean, I'm a biologist," he added, "I work better in a lab situation..."

Retske stood up and said, "Right now your situation is the least of my worries. We'll deal with you, same as the ambassador, once official assistance arrives. The explorer team will eventually come and collect him. It's standard procedure in the case of a missed rendezvous."

Lo looked like she was about to start throwing her powers around, which Janine hated, but then got control of herself and said, "I'm not going to pretend this is acceptable, but I'm going to follow dispute procedure rather than stand here arguing with a bunch of ghosts. As soon as we leave here, we're heading straight to IBM City to talk with Candace and her governing team. They can decide whether or not you have violated our alliance treaty by refusing assistance in a time of crisis. They can decide if you should be required to help. I mean, if you didn't have that fence of yours, Retske, then you might share our sense of urgency..."

"I'll pretend I didn't hear that threat," said Retske.

Janine wasn't sure what to think. She'd never been asked to fight an ally before. She looked across at Gail, who reminded her of desiccated coconut. About ten years back, Candace had miraculously persuaded Lo and Helena to host a limited outreach event. Gail and five other women from Madison had attended a special alliance skill-sharing day in Saugatuck. Even back then, Gail had not been particularly strong—she couldn't fly or communicate telepathically—but she'd been determined to learn. The security crew, led by Lo, taught her group how to create a defensive wind screen. It had been a fun day, a memorable day. Janine had flown Gail there and back, the two of them squeezed together in the orbicraft. They talked about the importance of continuing to grow in their new lives, of never letting hope go. Janine had liked Gail.

It was as if Lo had read her thoughts...

"One last thing before we go, Retske," she said, pointing at Gail. "Is everything all right with the original women here? I'm looking at Gail, who used to be young like the rest of us, and now she looks at least sixty. She doesn't seem right in the head, either, and we're talking about a woman who ran her own internet tutoring company and was the youngest ever member of the board of education in Madison. What the hell has happened to her? Is it the bleach?"

Retske said, "We were waiting to tell you, or should I say, Gail was waiting to tell you. The mayor is still perfectly capable of speaking for herself."

They all looked at Gail, who nodded, her white hair wispy around her head.

"It is totally my choice," she said, in a warbled old voice.

"What?" asked Lo. "What's your choice?"

"A baby," said Gail. "I've had a baby."

Janine felt a rush of energy pass through her wires, a silent gasp. She'd been wondering when Lo was going to ask about the rumors, although rumors were all she had thought they were. Well, now they knew that Will had been telling the truth. And this changed everything.

25

As far as Will could tell, Branca was a normal baby: pink in-side his white swaddling, two blue eyes, squashed thumb nose, cherub's bow for a mouth. Will had no interest in babies, even babies born miraculously to infertile women, but this one might just prove useful to him. Perhaps Janine, Adrianna, and Lo would look at him differently now that they realized he'd been telling the truth about the possibility of reversing their infertility. At this exact moment, however, nobody was interested in anything but the miracle baby — who was delivered to the meeting room in a bleached white carriage — evoking images both biblical and theat-rical. Lo and Adrianna were playing it relatively cool, but Janine just gushed and gushed and gushed.

"Oh. My. God. This is so amazing?"

"We've got it, Janine. You're amazed," said Adrianna.

"Explain the science," said Lo. "I want to know what you did to Gail."

"It's an imperfect science as yet," replied Retske.

"Orbiter science is hard to explain to Earthans," said Jrm.

Will wondered again just what Retske saw in the big stick of chalk. He hoped that Jrm was not the father, not one of those creepy father-to-them-all types, like James Nunn.

"Is the baby definitely all right? Who is the father?" It was Janine again.

"The father is definitely Pure, so how can the baby not be all right?" Jrm looked too sure.

"I had sex with a lot of different men," said Gail, her face crinkled and happy. "They said it was the fastest way to get a baby. The men were nice. And I got a baby."

The women exchanged glances. Lurch looked pinched. Who were they to sit and judge Gail? Gail was the one truly happy person Will had met since he arrived back on Earth.

Janine asked, "Are there others?"

"Gail is one of twenty volunteers," said Retske.

"So, are there more babies?" asked Janine

"Branca is the only live birth so far."

"And how are the other volunteers doing?" Lo's tone was sharp.

"They share in the joy of Branca's birth."

"I'm sure they do," said Adrianna.

Lo raised both hands. Then she turned her hands around as she said to Retske, "Thanks for showing us the baby. You've given us plenty to think about. But we're not here to discuss babies. Right now we have a flotilla of aliens in our river. You say you can't help. So I need to get to IBM City to discuss the situation with Candace. It's a shame that's how this meeting has to end, but thanks for the hospitality anyway. I have a feeling we'll be seeing each other sooner than either of us would really like — so let's keep it friendly, eh?"

Lo gestured for her group to leave. Janine, Lurch, and Bob began moving towards the door. Janine seemed reluctant.

"But I have questions about the baby," said Janine.

"We can come back and talk about the baby once our mission is complete," said Lo. "Otherwise, we're just allowing ourselves to be distracted, and every minute brings thousands of goddamned aliens closer to our door. Do you understand?"

Retske helped out. "The women of Saugatuck will be welcome again. We will be happy to discuss the ways in which purity confers fertility at any time. We always seek more of the right kind of settler, and we are always open to our fellow women of the alliance."

Lo snapped. "Save the recruitment pitch for another time, please. Right now we're facing the horrors of another invasion and, unlike you zombies, we're trying to do something about it."

Retske just nodded as Lo shooed Janine forward. The blonde might be argumentative, but she was still very loyal. Bob followed, as if he too was a Saugatucker now.

Will sat back down in his seat. Lo glared. He shrugged. He was not going with them. Next thing he knew, however, he felt a draft under his arms that lifted him out of his chair. As he stumbled to his feet, grabbing the table for support, he heard Lo cough.

Will turned to Retske. "I want to wait here for the Orbiters to come and get me," he said. "I assume that you will at least offer a fellow ambassador diplomatic shelter."

"That much I will do," she replied. "I'm sure we all still believe in free agency."

Lo snapped, "Don't make this political when we have a real security issue on our hands. Will must remain under my supervision. If he stays here, he'll pressure you into making those repairs so he can help drop more Orbiters on our heads. Then he'll run home and tell everyone how great everything went. And where will that leave us, Lurch's people, Earth…?"

She knew him too well, or at least a side of him.

"What he does and where he goes is entirely his choice," said Retske.

Will tried to explain it to Lo one last time. "I'm sorry, Sis, but your plan to send Lurch back to the Orbitals to stop the settlement program is beyond hopeless. The explorer crew won't even allow him on board. The rest is never going to happen. You should let me speak for you. You have a much better shot of getting through to the Orbiters with me than with Lurch."

"He's wrong," said Lurch. "I have my supporters."

Lo waved Lurch quiet and said to Will, "I stick to my deals, *brother*. Lurch isn't the one who has lied to me and tried to trick my people into allowing themselves to be colonized."

"So you're putting the word of a stranger—a criminal—over your own family?"

Lo said, "Yeah, I guess I am. Now, are you going to walk out of here with me like a man, or are you going to make me carry you out like some victim?"

Will thought about it for a second. "I'm not leaving here with you, Lo." He didn't dare look at her. Instead he looked at his last great hope—Retske—who exchanged glances with Jrm but said nothing in his defense. If he survived this mission, Will was going to make sure that Madison never received another single box of bleaching agent, let alone real Gllryn crystals. He would also make sure the High Council repatriated Retske. Two weeks away from Jrm and the bleach fumes, and she would realize what an idiot she'd been. She would be forever in his debt—but she would never sit with him at high table and *never* experience the knowledge.

Will dared to look up into Lo's eyes. Her gaze felt almost as if it were pricking his retina. He started to protest, but was halted by a sharp stabbing sensation at the base of his skull. He crumpled over as a needling pulse drove through his nerve endings. Then everything went blank.

26

Lo watched as the girls loaded the slumped body of Will into the back of Adrianna's pod. She hoped he would wake up soon; the longer he was out cold, the more likely the others were to feel sorry for him. Believe it or not, it was Helena who had taught them how to stun — after a feral woman was killed by accident when one of the crew threw her too hard. It was tricky precision work that required a detailed understanding of brain physiology. Back in the day, her and her soon-to-be wife had celebrated her mastery of the technique, another glorious victory against the bastards that had tried to zombify them. Now, Helena would probably just get mad when she heard that Lo had stunned a defenseless Will.

At the moment, however, Helena was the least of her worries. Babies and Pure folk were also low on her list of worries — although she knew she'd have to address those issues in the near future. Right now her main objective was getting rid of the Orbiters already on their doorstep before others just like them, only better defended, started arriving. The flotilla still scared her, but she was confident that she and her crew could handle those guys; one thousand shielded boxes filled with criminals and white creatures was another story entirely. Candace and IBM city *had* to help her stop these people coming, *had* to help Lurch get the drop diverted.

For the flight to IBM City, Lo decided to pair up with Bob. It was an opportunity to evaluate Will's fellow survivor. Retske was right that he had been strangely quiet. Janine said he was just a regular guy, but Lo wasn't just going to take Janine's word for it. Janine, after all, still believed that everything was all going to be all right in the end. Like they weren't already bang in the middle of end-times, clinging to the precipice of existence.

Lo felt surprisingly comfortable with Bob's lanky body snaked around her. His bodcoz was cool against her skin. She'd felt horribly flushed flying up to Madison with Lurch — perhaps because he was more like a bear rug than a man, perhaps because he exuded pheromones. Bob was younger and leaner, boyish like an aging surfer. In a way, she felt more comfortable being close to him than to Will; he was more her idea of brotherly. That said, she really didn't like the current proximity of his nose and mouth to her groin crease. Bob kept twitching both; his beard and moustache tickled her exposed thigh. If she'd thought about the issue in advance, she would have worn jeans instead of tiny twill shorts. She shifted her ass to the right, pressing Bob's head between her thigh and the curved glass shell of the pod for a minute, then released him.

"Stop making facial expressions on my body," she said.

"Sorry," he said. "I've got an itch I can't reach. It's driving me crazy. And hey, Lo, thanks for not leaving me there. I'm a lot happier with you ladies. You're way more sane."

"Don't thank me. Thank Janine. She's the one looking out for you."

He was a fool for feeling safe. Lo hadn't decided what to do with him yet, and Janine had no real say in the matter. If Janine wanted to make decisions, she should run for election. Bob chattered on, oblivious, creating a warm moist sensation on her thigh.

"No diggity. Janine is good people. You're all solid. But, hey Lo?"

"Yes?"

"How'd you do that?"

She knew exactly what he was talking about.

"How'd I do what?"

"Put your brother's lights out."

"I didn't do that," said Lo. "He fainted. Bleach fumes, maybe."

There was an uncomfortable pause while the lie settled. Looking for a distraction, Lo mentally squeezed the throttle of the pod, propelling them forward with the elegance of a G6. The pod sped up, and she shot out over the top of Adrianna and Lurch's pod, also moving along at quite a pace. Lo was tempted to initiate a race — expend some of that nervous energy firing through her wires—scare the shit out of the guys—but today was no time for crap like that. So she dropped back and let Adrianna take the lead. Adrianna was a navigational natural. She would direct them along the fastest route to IBM. Lo estimated it would take them at least forty-five minutes. Janine was not quite as fast as herself and Adrianna—and it was tough concentrating with an oversized guy crammed inside your pod, his body pressed around you like dough.

She said to Bob, "What do you care about my brother? He's not your friend."

"You're quite the perceptive lady, aren't you?" said Bob. "You're right. Wl-Wrrn and I—sorry, Will—are not what you'd call buddies. Somebody just stuck us two home-boys together for the ride back to Earth. Maybe they thought it was a nice idea—or maybe nobody else wanted to room with us. We got along well enough on the way out here—talked a lot about nothing to pass the time—but if I'm being totally honest, I think the guy's a horse's ass."

Lo pushed her own ass backwards, bumping Bob against the glass. She meant it like a friendly punch in the arm. Bob didn't respond. Perhaps she'd been a bit rough.

Lo said, "So tell me what exactly you know about my brother, the horse's ass. You must have learned quite a lot about him on that long trip out here."

"Nothing I didn't already know from media projections back home," replied Bob.

"That sounds like media in the air?"

'Exactamundo. Think electronic visions that are everywhere all at once, in the air, in your brain, on your walls, wherever you want them to be, and sometimes places you don't want. It's cool technology. A lot of people are addicted to it, watching and participating. Wl-Wrrn is well known for his projections, so I knew who he was long before we hooked up for the ride here."

"What exactly does my brother do in these projections?"

"Oh, I think you know already—he flogs settlement—persuades political exiles and religious freaks to move to a whole other galaxy that doesn't have any technology. No gems, no stim-sims, no controls over nature, food, bodily functions, nothing. It's not easy getting people to come here, you know. The Orbiters way prefer culture to nature, but your brother somehow convinces them they want to emigrate to a cultural waste-land with a shit-load of wildlife. He's the "Paradise on Earth" poster boy. Kudos to him, I say. Turning all that bad publicity around."

"All that bad publicity?"

"Um, like maybe you should ask him about that yourself."

"I'm asking you."

"I'm not sure…"

Lo allowed the pod to drop. They began descending faster and faster towards the vast canopy of green below, punctuated only by the odd glint of unidentifiable silver, gray, or white. Once-were-things. When it hit the point that she herself was ready to puke, she pulled them out of the dive and back up into the blue summer sky. *Woo—hoo*, she beamed Janine and Adrianna, just in case they were worried. "Woo-hoo," she wailed at Bob, just in case he thought that was accidental. Bob was breathing heavily into her leg; his grip was tight as a latex glove.

"You were saying something about bad publicity?"

"Yeah, okay," said Bob, peeling himself away from her body, his voice more serious now. "It's about how he survived. There have always been rumors…"

"How do they say he survived?"

"Well, after the attacks we were left floating around in space for about five months—me with the Alaskans, Retske with the Russians, Will with the official Americans. The situation was okay at first, but then the supplies started to run out. By the time the Orbiters picked us up, there were body bags on every shuttle. They put the rest of us bags of bones into some kind of induced coma and took us back to the Orbitals. It was a month before I came to in the recovery center."

"Will, too?"

"I don't really know. We were never together. However, news projections about our rescue were everywhere. Some of them said your brother killed everyone else on his shuttle—even though they hadn't run out of supplies yet. The Orbiters were horrified. But they had no real proof. The bodies had—you know—and it was hard to tell. And even if...I could kind of understand it. I mean we had to—shit—it was horrocious. Maybe he went insane..."

"You just said there was no proof?"

Bob said, "There wasn't—and I know he fought them over the rumors—and somebody must have believed him because otherwise he could never have become an ambassador."

The pod was silent except for their damp breathing. Lo changed the subject.

"Is it true that you have a family back in the Orbitals?"

"Yeah. Two girls and a boy."

"And a wife," added Lo.

"Relationships are different on the Orbitals," said Bob.

"Whatever. Have you told Janine?"

"We're not all liars, Lo. On the Orbitals I'm guilty of being a pot-head, and back here maybe I'm your idea of a cheater. Those are my worst crimes."

"Whatever. Do the Orbiters really hate nature?" she asked.

"Yeah," replied Bob, taking the hint. "They're not used to it. Life is all artificial in the Orbitals. It's hard to describe, but it makes me think of yellow cheese and water-beds and buying power tools at the mall on a freezing cold day—comfortingly artificial."

"But you grew up with nature, didn't you miss it?"

"Miss Alaska? Are you shitting me? I never went outside. It was cold, and you could hear the wolves howling. I hear something a lot like it at night in Saugatuck. I can deal, but your average Orbiter settler is going to drop a load in their bodcoz when they first hear that sound."

"Charming."

"You don't understand, Lo. They're totally unprepared."

"Oh I understand. Do you think I was prepared?"

"I admire everything you ladies have achieved. I'm in awe."

"I'm not sure this is going to end the way you hope."

"It will if you have a heart, Lo. I'm just a lonely guy, far from home, missing his comfortable plastic unreal life. I need a sanctuary, a little civilization."

"You Orbiters are so full of shit," said Lo, swooping down over the thick green woods of old Westchester County toward the only clearing in sight. "It's like listening to the BS channel."

"I'm just trying to reach you," said Bob.

"Enough," said Lo. "Twist your head and look down. Armonk. IBM City. Civilization."

She would be glad to get out of the pod. It was getting very uncomfortable.

27

As they swooped down towards IBM City—the pyramid on its main operations building still proudly dominating the view—Lo was struck by changes to the surrounding area. It had been a couple of years since her last visit, and in that time, a refugee camp had sprung up on vacant ground opposite the fortified front gates. The old overflow car park had once been home to hundreds of abandoned pods. The pods were gone. In their place were tents and caravans. Dotted among the habitations were small vegetable gardens, lines hung with washing, assorted vehicles—mostly racing bikes and motorbikes—tables, barbecues, and a significant number of inflatable wading pools. Upwards of a hundred people could be seen milling around; their height and their tight camouflage-colored bodcoz suggested that these were more of Madison's missing Orbiters. Many looked up and waved. Lo didn't wave back, although scanning behind she saw Janine doing so. Lo realized how much she missed the solid presence of Pat.

It was unclear if it was safe to sweep down in front of the gates as usual, so Lo instructed her entourage to *hover* while she beamed a message down to the guard station: *Saugatuck—safe—land.*

She took a deep breath, exhaled hard as she concentrated, and tried to add a little more: *Candace—expecting—whoaaaaa.*

Shit, two words too many. The pod dipped and veered wildly, causing Bob to *whoaaaaa* too as he clenched like a monkey around her. Righting the pod, Lo heard the unexpected sound of male cheers. They clearly didn't know how she felt about Orbiters. She also received an unexpected beam: *Steady up there. Yaz radioed already. Candace is expecting you at the gate. Fly beyond the fence and land up by the main ops building.*

Amazing—a complete message. This was what both she and Candace desperately wanted for all their wired women. It seemed that Candace was beating her to the realization of that ambition. Beaming her own basic message to Janine and Adrianna—*fol-low*—*me*—Lo swept over the expansive entrance gardens and double-wide driveway to the parking lot in front of the ops building. Although at least sixty pods littered the space, there was still plenty of smooth tarmac to spare. Lo landed on an empty space right next to the front door of the ops building. That would once probably have been Gini Rometty's parking space. Lo remembered all the excitement around the appointment of the first female CEO of IBM. She'd been on the cover of *Time*. The things that used to matter...

As the group piled out of their pods, Candace appeared alone on the front steps of the ops building. That was Candace for you— no guards, no ceremony. Lo felt a rare surge of joy at the sight of the big-boned redhead, her great mass of curls spilling over a flowery kaftan. She and Candace rushed into each other's arms and hugged so hard that Lo lost all sense of anything else for a moment. They had worked together the whole three years of the occupation—mostly as flying trash-removers, but sometimes as the dreaded overseers—slowly helping transform the Fairfield University campus into a Ruurdaan city. At nights they and the other women fliers had huddled together on the ground next to their pods, sleeping as best they could, comforting each other when they couldn't. It was Candace who had first encouraged Lo and the others to try expanding their powers. It was Candace who had taught her the true key to survival. *Believe.*

After the Ruurdaans died they'd both set off for home—Lo with a small group of women to Saugatuck, Candace alone back to Armonk where her sister, Mindy, had worked as a computer programmer at IBM. The plan was to search for surviving loved ones and take it one day at a time from there. In the same amount of time it had taken Lo to turn the ruins of Saugatuck into a working village, Candace and her sister had turned the old IBM campus into a small working city and a fledgling regional political center.

By any standards it was a remarkable achievement. Twenty-thousand survivors, nineteen and half of them women. Lo knew of nowhere else that had managed to rebuild on this scale, at least not in the northeast.

If they ever wrote history books again, then IBM would be early Rome, the civilized center of a savage, unpredictable world. Lo always loved coming here to this oasis of order. There had even been times when Lo wondered if she shouldn't just step down and move to IBM City, find a new purpose in this purposeless life—but then she would start worrying about Helena, Reid, the women, and the children—they needed her, they were her purpose.

Today they all needed Candace.

"I can't believe the news. What are the chances?" said her old friend, one arm still squeezed tight around her shoulder, the other indicating Will. "My God, you look so alike. Is he all right, though? He seems kind of dazed. Should I call for medical assistance?"

"He'll be okay in a minute or two. He's taking pain killers, and he banged his head getting into the pod earlier," replied Lo. "He just needs to stretch out in the fresh air."

Candace nodded. "Good—I'm glad you're not here because you have a medical emergency—but I get the feeling this isn't just a social visit either."

"No, I'm sorry," said Lo, "it's not. We have problems, all of us, big problems."

"Do I need to sound the alarm?" asked Candace.

"No," said Lo, surprised. "The threat is not..."

"Then we have time for greetings, old friend," replied Candace.

"Well, yes, maybe, but we do have really big problems."

Candace smiled at her, tilted her head at a funny angle, and squeezed her shoulder even tighter as she gestured at the old car park and the reinforced fence three hundred yards beyond.

"Are you talking bigger problems than that?"

Lo took her point. "I'm sorry, you're right. How are you? What is that?"

"People who don't like it up in Madison," said Candace.

Lurch, who had only just stretched back to his full height, coughed. "I know most of them. They are generally decent, just unwilling to live under unjust rule — be it Orbiter or Pure. Perhaps I can advise you regarding specific individuals while I'm here. The sooner these people are inside your fence, the better. We are not born farmers or hunters. That is why my group went into the water. At least the fish are always guaranteed. I am Lurch, by the way."

He stuck his hand out.

"Hmm," said Candace, letting Lo go and reaching over to shake Lurch's hand. "I'm Candace. And fresh fish sounds good. Perhaps we could talk trade. Sometimes we have extra vegetables, and we have facilities for preserving all kinds of food. Plenty of glass containers!"

Everyone except Lo laughed. Glass and metals were a kind of Ruurdaan currency. Great piles of glass still marked those places the Ruurdaans had pitched camp, in the same way that new housing estates once attracted piles of earth, sand, bricks, and lumber. The glass had been scavenged from all over by teams of wired women they all called the glass collectors. The collectors had been particularly active at IBM. Lo had seen great mounds of jars and old windows lying in piles around the campus on previous visits — a useless reminder of three years of misery and terror.

She said, "I'm sorry, Candace, but there's nothing funny about the two hundred Orbiters parked in my river, and the thousand more that are planning to —"

Candace cut her off. "Sorry to cut you off, but Yaz radioed ahead with the details. I've called for a council meeting in ninety minutes. It's extremely short notice, but of course we'll do it for Saugatuck. In the meantime, I wanted to show you how we're dealing with our own refugee crisis. I'm not saying this is what you should do, not at all, but I do want to give you some insight into our current thinking and practices ahead of the meeting."

Lurch was quick to respond. "That sounds most interesting."

The others all nodded, even Adrianna, who never agreed to anything. Candace had a way about her. Lo shrugged at her friend. She needed help; she should also show a willingness to listen. That said, she would *never* let Orbiters this close to Saugatuck.

It took about a minute for them to walk to the security fence. They stopped in front of a massive set of iron-barred gates hanging between two new guard towers.

"Impressive new set-up," said Lo. "You're still a bit nervous then?"

Candace said, "Sure we are. Who wouldn't be? The wilderness holds its own dangers, and we're still getting to know the Orbiters. Maybe one day…"

"I understand," said Lurch, as the electronic gates creaked open.

The gates stopped moving almost as soon as they'd begun — leaving a foot gap. The group squeezed through one by one. Once they were all on the other side, Candace stuck two fingers in her mouth and let out a great whistle — silencing the gathered crowd. These Orbiters looked less hungry and desperate than Lurch's boat people, but they had a sense of expectation that she didn't like. Lo noticed that although Lurch exchanged bow after bow, he didn't speak to anyone directly or move to leave their group.

Candace raised her hand in greeting and said, "Hello again, Orbiter friends. As you can see, today we have visitors. I've invited them to observe our admissions process, show them what's possible in terms of integrating our groups, but we're short on time, so let's get down to it. Do you wish to send forward someone of your own choosing — or shall I conduct the lottery?"

"Lottery," yelled a big, hairy yellowish man, clearly some sort of group leader.

"It's better if you choose among yourselves," said Candace. "It demonstrates your ability to function as part of a group, to make choices and compromises."

"Just get on with it," shouted another hairy guy.

Candace remained expressionless, although Lo sensed a tensing of wires.

"All right—we'll conduct the lottery again."

Candace looked up at the guard towers and nodded. A barrage of marbles flew out the open window, dropped into a swirling celestial ring just above their heads. Without looking, Candace reached her hand into the maelstrom, pulled out the marble and yelled, "Eighty-four."

A lanky blond with the same strange mail-box slot eyes as Blr raised his hand and stepped forward. He pulled a small ticket from the sleeve of his moth-patterned bodcoz. Candace exchanged the ticket for the marble and shook his hand. Someone, somewhere, sucked the remaining balls back up towards the guard tower, where they disappeared as if into a vacuum.

Candace turned to the guy. "Congratulations to..."

"Xvr," said the Orbiter.

"Zervyer," said Candace. "Welcome to IBM City."

Xvr bowed deeply.

Candace returned the bow then turned back to the crowd. "We're happy to welcome Xvr as our seventy-second admittee. We still hope to admit at least fifteen more of you by winter—dependent on your continued cooperation—and we'll keep helping those outside as best we can. There'll be the standard daily meetings to discuss any pressing issues—today's will be at 5:00 p.m. as usual. But unfortunately I don't have any more time for discussion now. Thanks for your understanding. I look forward to seeing you all again, in person, next week."

The crowd began shouting questions.

"Who are the visitors?"

"What is Zgyzg-Dm doing here?"

"Why can't you take two of us at a time?"

"Tell them to put soap in the rations."

Candace just smiled, turned on her heel, and ushered their group back through the gates and up to the main building.

Following her, Lo exchanged a look with Adrianna, a look that she hoped said, "never in Saugatuck." Adrianna gestured at her head with her hand, in a loose approximation of a gun. Janine, catching the exchange, whispered, "You guys are terrible." Lo had a sudden horrible vision of Janine calling out lottery numbers down by Exit 17. She whispered back, "And you need to remember where your loyalties lie," before striding away to the ops building.

Inside it was almost like the Ruurdaans had never invaded. The lights were all on, revealing women working in a number of ground floor offices. The spacious marble foyer featured white-boards filled with announcements about computer workshops, disco nights, and clothing exchanges. Lo felt a twinge of envy at the normalcy of it—even though she knew that this way of living—trying to recreate all that had been lost—was not right for her people.

Candace stopped right underneath the glass pyramid and said, "Okay, so here's the plan. The rest of you will be escorted over to the civic center where we'll be having our meeting. You can take your time getting there, see whatever you would like on the way. You have an hour."

She turned to Lo. "You and I are going to walk over there alone."

Lo said, "That's fine with me, but my guys need a *security* escort."

Candace nodded. "I know you, Lo. It's already organized."

Before she could reply, Lo saw three mighty-looking wired women heading their way. Lo thought they would be enough. They reminded her of Pat. Lo hoped that Pat was coping with everything going on at home. What if Lurch's people... Just as she was starting to really worry, Lo felt Candace reach out, grab her hand, and yank her through the air.

"Quit chewing on your lips and come talk with me awhile," said her old friend.

Lo felt her body travel sideways out through an open side door and into "the city."

She sighed and gave herself over to a world where she had limited control.

28

If you never tried to leave the three-hundred-acre city of IBM, then you would probably never know that you were trapped inside a four-mile ring of ten-feet-high razor-wire fence—all fortified and electrified. The fence was mostly hidden behind landscaping. Inside the fence, IBM looked like a lush new university campus—very different from the quaint semi-rural village of Saugatuck. Here the human lines were sharper—neat asphalt paths intersected a mix of woods, gardens, and commons—and led to attractively utilitarian buildings surrounded by well-tended shrubbery. Lo didn't know where Candace was leading her, but she was happy meandering through the clean fresh landscape. If this was the future, it was all right.

Candace didn't give her much time for reverie.

"First things first, old friend," she said, turning to stare pointedly at Lo. "About your communication skills."

Lo tried to make her excuses.

"I don't want to hear it, babe. We've sent out an absolute ton of messages about the Orbiters to all members of the alliance— via email for those who are connected, also via radio, and we even sent a messenger to Saugatuck, maybe about a year ago. So imagine my surprise when Yaz radioed us about your troubles as if this was the first anyone had heard of these guys."

"It's not like we hadn't heard anything, just that…"

"I haven't finished speaking, babe. Our messenger came back from Saugatuck saying that you had promised to be better at staying in touch because of the Orbiter problem. Since then, however, all I have heard from you is the scheduled weekly radio transmission from Yaz."

"So that's good, right, we've maintained radio contact."

"It's the bare minimum, and you know it. We could share so much more."

All these years, and Candace still just didn't get it. Lo flung her hands into the air.

"How many times do I have to tell you, Candace? I'm sorry I don't keep in touch and sorry that we keep to ourselves, but there's no other way for us. The more we communicate, the greater the chance that bad people will find us and hurt us."

"That's a dated and paranoid perspective, Lo—and it's holding your community back. I also believe that safety is important—but it's not the only thing a society needs. What about intellectual and cultural development? What about social evolution?"

"Luxuries we can't afford. Same as always. Nothing has changed."

"But the world around you is changing," said Candace, "Sometimes it's better to be an agent of change than a slave to the status quo. Speaking of which, there's something I've been wanting to tell you, something we haven't announced yet because it's controversial."

Lo knew exactly what she was talking about.

"So you finally did it?"

"Yes, we finally did it."

As they were speaking, Candace led the way down a neat crisscross path through a copse of dogwoods and out onto an open playing field where a baseball diamonds were laid out in the short green grass with soccer nets at either end. In the distance Lo could see a low-rise building that had all the signs of a small school: playground equipment, colorful pictures in the windows, bags and balls scattered around. A small group of about six children sat clustered in the shade of a large oak tree close to the school building, reading their books along with their teacher. The kids all looked about eight years old. None of them had silver-foil domes on their heads, although their sparse hair only thinly covered the scarring where the wires had webbed their scalps. Lo shivered a little at the sight. Disconnected children.

Candace whistled. The children all looked up from their books. They didn't smile, but they did look curious.

"Good afternoon, children. We have a visitor today. This is my friend, Lo. Lo comes from Saugatuck, a town by the beach. One of these days I hope we'll all visit her and the children who live there. Perhaps have a swimming party. Say hi to Lo, everyone."

"Hi, Lo."

They sounded normal enough.

"So what are you all reading today," continued Candace.

"Harry Potter," chirped one small girl, shaking her head a little too vigorously.

"Do you like it?"

"It's awesome," replied the girl, continuing to shake.

"And you?" Candace pointed to a boy sitting quietly further away. He just shrugged shyly and looked down.

"Well, enjoy your wizards, then. Good afternoon children."

"Good afternoon, Miss Candace."

As they walked away, heading back down a quiet wooded path leading towards the old IBM hotel and conference facilities, Lo asked the obvious. "Are they normal?"

"Define normal these days," said Candace. "They're functioning, some better than others. At first we thought they were all going to be autistic, but over time they've become better socialized. The teachers have worked incredibly hard with them. We think there's a chance that they might lead something approximating a normal life."

"Have they been able to tell you what they were doing before?"

"No. The memories seem to have gone with the wires. They never speak of Ruurdaan things, even when asked. They still have some strange habits, though, and we think that they still try to communicate with each other—try and fail. That sometimes causes frustration. We haven't reintroduced computers yet—we're a little worried about how those might affect them. And we keep the pods out of sight as much as possible—in case they trigger memories, behavior. So far so good though. There are no real signs of Ruurdaan behavior."

"It's amazing, Candace. How did you do it?"

"I won't lie to you, Lo. It wasn't pretty. First, we heavily medicated their food and water. It wasn't easy coordinating things so that none of them realized in time. Then we performed the cut-and-wet technique under controlled conditions, with anesthesia."

Lo both grimaced and nodded. She and Candace had discussed deprogramming methodologies before. They were not for the faint-hearted.

"Did they all survive deprogramming?"

Candace paused as she leaned down to pick a big weed from the side of the path.

"No. They didn't. We lost quite a few."

"How many?"

Candace came upright, put her hand on Lo's shoulder, and looked into her eyes.

"Half died. Half survived. There are twenty-eight children remaining."

Lo felt a chill pass through her wires, in spite of the heat and humidity of the day. Only half. Saugatuck would never agree to those odds. She reached up and pressed her palm on top of Candace's silver-veined hand, still clasping her shoulder.

"Is your niece one of the survivors?."

"No, I'm afraid she's not."

"Oh, Candace, I'm so sorry. How is Mindy taking it?"

Candace shook her head. "She's not."

"What do you mean?"

"A couple of months back she left a note saying she was going to fly higher than she'd ever flown before. The guards saw her go up in her pod, but not come back down. We looked for crashed pods for weeks. Found nothing. I still look occasionally."

Lo said, "I should have come, I should have helped you look. I don't know how I missed your message. Yaz usually manages to get my attention if it's something as important as this."

"I didn't send any message," replied Candace. "I didn't want to tell you via some public radio message. I thought one day I would get to tell you in person. Today is that day."

Lo didn't say anything, just pulled her friend to her and hugged her tight. When they finally pulled apart, Lo reached out, wiped the tears from Candace's pretty freckled face, and pushed her hair back behind her ears. "You are the bravest woman I know," she said.

Candace started walking along the path again. They were between buildings, in a densely wooded outcropping of butterfly bushes. They could have been the last two women on Earth.

"Two of the nannies left and went to Madison. The rest hate my guts. I'm scared there might be more suicides. It's a terrible thing we did to the moms, Lo."

"You knew how they would react. How did the rest of the women take it?"

Candace said, "We grieved together, then we moved forward together. We did almost all vote to deprogram the children, even some of the nannies. We'd become scared of them, Lo, really scared. The number of incidents grew, and finally one came that tipped the balance. One night the dinner provided was lighter than usual. One of the boys slammed a nanny up against a pod and beamed *hungry* at her over fifty times. It took us ten minutes to talk him down. The woman had a mild stroke. She'd been looking after him for thirty years."

"I fear something like that happening in Saugatuck," said Lo. "The children's powers are growing, and our control over them is slipping. One of these days I think they'll hurt one of us too. I know we promised to protect them no matter what, but maybe that means making sure that they don't simply become the robotic end-product of a Ruurdaan experiment. How long do we just sit by and watch as they are slowly absorbed into the machine? I want to give them a chance at their own lives. But 50/50 odds? That's a tough ask. I don't know if I'd ever get a majority to agree."

"Maybe if more of you came and met the deprogrammed children?"

"Maybe when we have our other problems sorted out, Candace. Right now, though, those other problems are pressing. Remember those two hundred Orbiters I mentioned..."

"Believe me, I know how it feels to have all those people banging on the door. But you saw what we're doing here—it seems to be working. Drip-feeding the refugees in. Have you thought about integrating Lurch's people into Saugatuck?"

Lo turned to her friend in disbelief. "You're kidding, right?"

"No, I'm not. We were terrified of those guys, but we've come to realize that they're not much of a threat to us, not in small numbers anyway. And they've brought a lot of good things to IBM" said Candace. "They have extremely advanced technological knowledge, and they're helping us rebuild our infrastructure. Look over there, that's their work."

Lo looked where Candace was pointing, over at the far edge of the big lawn that had opened up on her right. It was a four-story office block with hundreds of old satellite dishes melded together on the roof. Post-modern, post-media—though clearly not art. A couple of tall guys were visible, wearing safety harnesses and tinkering away on the structure.

Lo was unimpressed. "What's the point of satellite dishes without satellites? The Ruurdaans destroyed them all. It's why our cell phones will never work again."

Candace said, "We don't know that for sure. Some may just be damaged or adrift. This maximizes our chance of finding any remaining signals."

Lo pulled a face. "Seriously? Whose signals are you going to find? The only people out there are the alien hordes. Your satellite sculpture will just help them pinpoint exactly where to drop their boxes. Why don't you give them all the alliance town coordinates while you're at it?"

"I think they may have those already. And anyway, our refugees tell me that not that many people want to come here. It's like asking for volunteers to populate Greenland. Besides which, we could use a few more people. It's not right, so few of us, and I am getting a little sick of this all-women, never-growing-old, nothing-ever-changing lark."

"Speak for yourself."

"I am speaking for myself—although I know that many of the women here agree. The Orbiters are sending mostly men— that will help redress an existing imbalance—and so far those men don't seem any better or worse than any other men I've known."

"How can you say that, knowing what the Orbiters did to us last summer?"

Candace said, "I know that some of them are bad, but we're not all perfect either."

Lo started to protest, but Candace held her hand up.

"We have to learn to make distinctions, babe. The guys that we've integrated into IBM are respectful. So far, so good. They also have some technical understanding of our wiring that might help us. If you've just come from Madison then you know that there is a chance the Orbiters can even adjust our wiring and reverse our infertility."

"Have you been there, have you *seen* what they're up to?" said Lo.

"No," said Candace, "They only told us yesterday, via radio. Retske said she had wanted to make sure mother and baby were doing well before telling the alliance."

"Bullshit. They weren't going to tell us until we forced their hand. They don't want anyone interfering with their experimentation— because it's creepy stuff. You need to get up there and see it for yourself, Candace. The baby seems fine—although who can tell yet—but Gail seems sick and lobotomized. And the town is overrun with religious freaks dressed in white and obsessed with purity. It's a bad scene, Candace."

Candace stopped for a moment and crouched down to pull a small stone from between her toes. They had reached a large glass house of some kind. Inside Lo could see women bending over work-benches covered in peppers, apparently deseeding them. As Candace stood up, she turned to Lo. "I'll head up to Madison as soon as your visit is over, Lo. Please don't rush off, though. I'm so happy to see you, you crazy old bitch, even if all you ever talk about is your own problems. You know you haven't even asked me if I'm in a relationship at the moment."

Lo kicked at a stick on the path. "Are you in a relationship at the moment?"

"Maybe. If you can beat me in a challenge, I might tell you."

"You and your challenges. How old are you, Candace?"

"Very old, but who cares, challenges motivate. Come on, can you do this, Lo?"

Laughing, Candace pointed her hands in a slanted line toward the sky, one stretched out high, one tucked low by her side, raised her right knee, and leaped. She flew ten feet into the air, paused a moment, then glided to a landing two hundred feet further down the path. She turned, slashed her arm into the air, and shouted, "Wonder woman!"

Candace had always been the same, making light in the darkest of moments. Did Lo once laugh more, too? Probably—before the years took their toll—although to be honest, she had been pretty angry even before the Ruurdaans. That was okay, though; anger was a pretty good motivator. Lo decided to take Candace's challenge. Flashing all her wires like an igniting sparkler, she shouted out to her old friend.

"Yo, call that a trick?"

She started somersaulting where she stood, building up speed with every turn. On the fourth turn she pushed herself off, propelling herself forward, directly toward Candace, like a human cannon-ball. The redhead dived into the nearest bushes. Lo continued on for another fifty feet, landing on the ground with a soft roll. Bounding back to her feet, Lo stuck her hands on her hips and waited for Candace to run down the path and join her. Just before Candace reached her, Lo whipped up a wind blanket. Candace hit the blanket at full force. She laughed as Lo tossed her up into the air like a small child, then caught her in her arms as she came down. She was a little heavier than Lo remembered, and the two of them crashed to the ground, both laughing now.

"I'd forgotten just how good you are," said Candace.

"I'd forgotten just how wonderful you are," said Lo, although she didn't say it out loud. Out loud she said, "So who's the new woman, then?"

29

Ten minutes later and too, too soon, they reached what used to be the IBM conference center, a low-rise building made of natural stone walls and wooden beams. Today the IBM City civic center (the ICCC) was swarming with women. They were clearly preparing for a celebration in the massive stone courtyard in front of the entrance: moving chairs, setting tables, laying out kindling in a large barbecue. Lo knew it was in their honor. IBM had always thrown a party when the women of Saugatuck visited, treated them like family coming home.

Lo liked to think that they returned the favor on those rare occasions when the city folk came to visit Saugatuck. However, it wasn't quite the same. In Saugatuck all visitors were supervised at all times, even friendly alliance members. The problem, of course, was the children. Everyone in Saugatuck knew about the IBM children, but only Candace and sworn-to-the-oath council members knew about the Inn. Although Lo would never regret their secrecy policy, it did affect their ability to connect with other survivors. Lo had once overheard one of Candace's council members referring to them as the shut-ins. That was unfair. Shut-in was the tiny community of Southport, right next door to Saugatuck, where the thirty-odd women who lived there all ran and hid in their basements when anyone tried calling. Saugatuckers weren't that kind of antisocial. Lo plastered a tight smile across her face. She mustn't forget she was looking for support here today.

As they made their way to the old hotel and through the foyer to Candace's office, Lo was struck by the presence of Orbiter men. She saw at least three of them—distinctive not just for their tight bodcoz and strange colorings, but for the fact that their heads almost scraped the ceiling. A couple even nodded and smiled at Lo. She refocused her gaze on the polished slate floors as she headed for Candace's office. Like everything else here, the office was comfortable and modern, with views of an inner courtyard filled with abstract sculptures. Candace walked over to an old coffee machine and pressed the button. Lo thrilled at the grinding sound that followed.

"Coffee?"

"Contraband. We ask the Orbiters to search for it on their travels. It's become a sort of currency. I'm not sure that we're doing the right thing making it so valuable. There've been fights over the stuff. If we refused it, that would all end. But it's coffee."

Lo gratefully took the cup and sipped. It tasted just as good as she remembered.

Candace sat on her desk as she gestured for Lo to take a comfortable seat.

She sighed before speaking. "Time to talk business, I'm afraid. We have about ten minutes until the council convenes for formal discussions. Before we do that, I have a couple of questions I want to ask you in private. It's a bit awkward, but I'm going to be direct."

"Fire away."

"I've been told that you physically attacked your own brother? And then I saw that he looked kind of groggy when he got off the pod. Did you hurt him, Lo?"

"Who told you that?" Lo was furious. Who was talking about her?

"Not that it matters, but it was Retske. She afraid of you."

"Yeah, well Retske should be scared. We could so easily just fly in there, high over their defenses, and start shaking the earth under..."

"What are you saying, Lo? Gail is an alliance leader; Retske is a fellow survivor."

"Retske is a chalk-eating freak supporting a scary science experiment."

"Are you hearing yourself, Lo? You're sixty-five-years old, but you sound like a petulant teenager. You're angrier than I've seen you in years. What's up?"

Lo flopped into the black leatherette armchair—like a petulant teenager.

"What's up? What's up!" She swung her legs over the armrest. "My brother came back from the dead and pretended he wanted to play happy family, but it turns out he's an alien ambassador conspiring to turn Saugatuck into some kind of human dumping ground. There's a flotilla of scary men in my river. What the hell do you think is up, Candace?"

"I know you have problems, Lo. But hurting and scaring people…"

"I don't *like* scaring people," said Lo. "I'm just doing what I have to do."

"Are you really, though? Or are you just lashing out?"

"I thought I could depend on your support, Candace."

"Personal support, always. Support for abuses of power, never—and especially not violence for personal reasons. I feel like you're driven by primal rage, Lo. And I worry about whether or not it's misdirected."

"Fuck you for lecturing me, Candace. You sound just like Helena."

"Speaking of which, babe, how are things at home?"

Lo paused a moment to finish her coffee. Had Yaz said something? She knew that people gossiped about her and Helena—the arguments, the separate lives, maybe even the other stuff, the lovers. Reid showed it in his eyes. Yaz and Pat had asked. Adrianna had commented. Not much went past their small group. Still, Lo liked to think that Yaz wouldn't gossip about her to Candace. She tried to stop being paranoid. What did it really matter how Candace had gotten the idea? She had always known that Candace would ask this question and that she would answer. Maybe she'd even been looking forward to the relief of saying it.

"I think my marriage is over. I don't love Helena anymore. I try, but it's not real."

"Oh, no," said Candace. "I'm so sorry. That must be very hard." She said it like she'd gone through the same thing herself, although Candace herself had never married. She had plenty of girlfriends; those relationships always faded into friendships. Candace had once told Lo that it was impossible to love a person properly and run a city at the same time. Lo had disagreed. She and Helena had rebuilt and run their town together—and doing so had been a big part of why they had loved each other. They weren't failing because it was too much work. They were just fading out—sort of in tandem with Helena's youth, beauty, and fire.

"Is it because of something specific?"

"It's hard to say."

"Is there someone else?"

"Not really, nothing that matters, but…oh, I don't know… Helena grew old, normal old, and I stayed young, abnormal young. We didn't change together. Lately I've found myself…"

"Found yourself…"

"Looking, okay. I've found myself looking at other people."

It wasn't just Adrianna, either. Her mind flickered to Lurch, his warm bulk.

"Oh, Lo," said Candace, "you poor thing. After a quarter century together. How confusing and distressing. It must feel like you've lost something very important."

Her face was so kind it made Lo want to run away in shame. She hadn't said a thing about how awful this must be for Helena. "It's not that big a deal, Candace. Not like the problems we've got with Orbiters landing on us from every direction. That *is* a very big deal."

Candace nodded. "It's all a big deal, but you're right, we have to resolve your political problems first. Our problems too, now. I just got a beam, and the council is ready. We'll have to put the personal stuff on hold until later. Is that okay with you?"

"Totally," said Lo, jumping out of the chair.

As far as she was concerned, there wasn't going to be any later. She loved Candace and respected her more than any other woman she knew, but she wasn't answerable to her, and she didn't share her priorities. The minute they had secured the assistance of the IBM council, Lo planned on doing whatever it took to make sure no aliens dared even think of gathering at the gates of Saugatuck.

Sorry, Candace. Sorry, Will. Sorry, Helena.

Better sorry than extinct.

30

The meeting droned on. For the first fifteen minutes she'd tried to engage. Then Adrianna realized it was all a repeat performance. Two hours later, her mind was on everything but the debate. What a waste of time. Friend or no friend, Candace and her council weren't going to help them. They did things differently here at IBM, more like the old way, as if there were still a point to any of that, trying to maintain the rituals of their dead society. Take for example this meeting room — all got up like it was the new Oval Office, complete with an enormous disc-shaped conference table. Twenty of them were seated around it, all pretty comfortable in their leatherette swivel chairs. The view was presidential, too — floor to ceiling glass doors and windows facing onto a fancy sculpture garden filled with a load of bullshit art. All this stuff gave a veneer of civilization to IBM City that might impress visiting diplomats and aliens — but not her. She'd never had any time for politics — only for feeling and staying alive. Fuck meetings. Fuck society. Fuck all these Dudley-Do-Rights.

The truth was they weren't all saints in this joint. In fact IBM City had quite the underbelly — shady types dealing in black market items, drugs, violence, and sex for sale. All that good stuff was a consequence of IBM's size rather than a reflection of its general personality. Put twenty thousand people together, and shit just starts to happen. Then someone has to step in and start regulating and controlling the shit levels. Councils, administration buildings, legal procedures, controls. Fuck that shit. Adrianna loved the way they still made it up as they went along in Saugatuck. Ironically, she felt free behind the fence. However, there were an awful lot of couples and not enough fresh meat in their small town — which was why she slipped over here about once a month. Lo knew, and she didn't like it, but the two of them had a lot of trust—and Lo had her secrets too.

Adrianna looked around the room at all the intense faces. So serious it must hurt. Of course, she was also well aware of the seriousness of their current situation. She just didn't give a shit about controlling everything, especially not destiny. Who was she to argue with what destiny delivered? Hell, she was a fifty-eight-year-old woman in a twenty-five-year-old body. She could kick most people's ass. She'd led a fucking interesting life. Surrendering to destiny wasn't all bad. That said, she'd fight destiny too if Lo asked her. Why the fuck not? She liked fighting, and she loved Lo. She'd loved her since the night Lo had first whispered in her ear in Fairfield, "We've got one of their weapons gloves. Interested in trying it? You seem like you might have the guts."

Adrianna had never known anyone like her, beautiful in that uptown way, fierce like she'd fought her way there from downtown. Before the Ruurdaans, Adrianna had mostly hung with pole dancers and drug addicts and her drop-out buddies from highschool. Back then her own little habit—E—was costing her every penny she earned and some. She was pretty damned close to going on the game. Then the spheres came. She was working that day. The Ruurdaans killed all the clients, took all the girls.

Although the Ruurdaans had ruined most everyone else's life, the weird truth was that they'd made Adrianna's. What the Ruurdaans did to her was part of a long continuum of shit in her life. Things could have only gotten better after the occupation—and they did. She found physical satisfaction in hard labor. She reveled in her new powers. She made real friends, the kind worth fighting for. She discovered the joys of women. It turned out she was suited to this life, danger and all. She didn't want to sleep cozy in her bed at night. She wanted to live hard, really hard. Political tactics—like getting the cooperation of Madison, sending Lurch back to Will's ship, and diverting the incoming Orbiters—those things were of fuck-all interest to her. She preferred physical challenges to verbal sparring. Words didn't win battles—not in this new world.

Not that anybody here cared what she thought, even though Candace addressed her with uber-polite regularity. "Anything you'd like to add, Adrianna?" Nobody really wanted to hear from her. They thought of her more like a soldier than a diplomat—which wasn't entirely wrong. Adrianna did do pretty much whatever Lo asked—whether she agreed with it or not. That was just their deal. Will had said a lot of stuff about Lo being a dictator and tyrant, but that wasn't it at all. Lo was their wild-eyed queen, and ruling Saugatuck was her hard-earned right. They all knew it, even the ones who didn't like it. Lo looked like a queen, she fought like one, and yes, sure, sometimes she behaved badly like one too. For the last thirty years Adrianna had fantasized about fucking her. And lately that fantasy had come pretty damn close to reality. First things got sour with preachy old Helena. Then the two of them started drinking a lot after work together, partying more, horsing around. Too bad Lo had suddenly gotten distracted by this latest bullshit.

And this *was* just more of the same bullshit, even if it did come in different packaging. The others seemed shocked at the thought of another invasion, but Adrianna had always known more shit was coming. It was her destiny. She was ready for it. She just didn't want to talk about it anymore. Could somebody wrap up this meeting already so she could go burn off some steam in the bars? No way were they heading back to Saugatuck tonight, not with the light lowering and navigation in the dark being a challenging business.

Adrianna didn't mind staying. She always had fun in the city. On one memorable occasion she'd even partied with Candace and a woman whose toes vibrated. Tonight she would try to drag Janine and Lo along—show them a spicier slice of life— but she doubted they'd be interested. Janine was still pathetically straight, and now she had her very own wiener. Lo was in savior mode, obsessed with altering their destiny. Adrianna was happy to let her try. She'd fight alongside her, whatever happened, whatever was decided. Lo just had to say the word.

Until then, though, fuck the future, shouldn't they all just live a little?

31

Lo knew they were screwed—and not just because Adrianna told her so while they waited for a final decision in the reception room. Those po-faced bitches that Candace called her council had been giving her plenty of clues the last two hours. To think that she'd led two of them out of Fairfield thirty years ago. What happened to "How can I ever repay you?" and "You saved my life"? Their gratitude obviously had a time limit.

Back in the conference room, most of Candace's council appeared to be checking for scuffs in their section of the table. Candace was smiling and making eye contact, but her demeanor was stiff. Lo looked at her and said, "Just say it already, no platitudes."

"We've considered your issues carefully," said Candace, addressing the whole group but looking directly at Lo. "All of them. We agree that the Orbiters can't just keep sending settlers without asking. If they do, then they should expect significant resistance. That said, we don't see why Will can't be the one to take that message home. He is the official ambassador, not Lurch. We must work with him and Retske, respect the Orbiters' official channels."

"But Retske won't work with us, she doesn't respect our official channels."

"Sure she does. She's already called to say so. Madison believes in the alliance. They just won't help you turn your brother into a key, render him unconscious, and steal his ship."

Lo shifted feet and said, "You're misinterpreting our intentions."

"Uh, huh," said Candace. "But anyway, the council has come up with a better idea. Will can simply stay with you until the Orbiter drop in Saugatuck happens. That way he can help you deal with the incoming settlers—take some personal responsibility. They will trust him. I assume you'll be asking them to proceed elsewhere."

"That's a fucking understatement," said Lo. "But..."

Candace didn't let her finish. "We think you should direct the settlers to Madison. We'll need to discuss the logistics with Retske. It's not going to be a good situation for anyone. Preparation is key. We can work out the details later. Once they've moved on, then Will should be free to go. He says that his team will come and collect him. I hope he's right."

Will and Lurch both started to say something, but Lo beat them to it.

"What about Lurch and his people?"

Lurch spoke up. "Indeed, what about me and my people?"

Candace turned to Lurch. "I'm sorry we can't help you return home, or even as far as the explorer ship. We'll do whatever else we can to help you, consider immigration, send supplies via our pods, but we can't help you steal Will's orbicraft, especially when doing so means using physical force against him. It's not the right way."

Lurch looked at Lo. Lo looked around to see if anyone else was going to speak. Adrianna, who'd appeared to be half asleep most of the meeting, now looked fit to explode. Will looked quietly smug. Janine and Bob were exchanging glances. The rest of Candace's council were nodding like wise fools. Nobody wanted to speak.

"You've left everyone speechless," said Lo.

"I'm sorry," said Candace. "It's an imperfect solution—but we've decided."

"You've decided just to leave us in it."

Candace replied, "Not at all, Lo. We're still offering support. We'll help you draft a comprehensive report on the issues to send back with Will. We have plenty of people on hand who are fluent in Orbitaal. If you and Lurch agree to stay the night, you can help us draft that report—plus a letter to Retske explaining why they must make plans to take the refugees from Saugatuck, and not just the white people."

Lo saw that Adrianna was glaring and shaking her head. Lo raised her eyebrows and shrugged lightly. What were they going to do, fight Candace?

She turned to Lurch. "What about you? Will you accept this decision? Will your people leave our river now? I've kept my end of the bargain. I think we're done."

Lurch stood and bowed deeply before Lo. "Thank you for all that you have done to help me and my people, Lo. Of course I shall honor my promise. I would still like to discuss the possibility that we remain in your area, but only if you wish to talk further."

Lo started to say that she did not wish, but something stopped her. Instead, she turned to Candace and said, "So there goes any chance of diverting the drop. Do you plan on being there to help us politely redirect the thousand people heading our way?"

Candace was quick to respond. "Now that *is* an alliance matter. You know we've already agreed to help if you ever come under an attack that you cannot handle. All you have to do is call, and I'll send fifty fliers. Hell, we have two hundred that can help if things get really difficult. You know we'll help you."

"Will you help us seal up the doors on those boxes and throw them out to sea?"

An audible intake of breath preceded a horrified hush. Some of the women shuddered. Lo saw Janine's eyes widen. What? Did they really think it was going to be all hand-painted redirect signs and polite discussions about the best route up to Madison?

Candace's voice was sharp as a Ruurdaan glass-cutter. "Don't even joke about killing innocent people—not unless you're planning on leaving the alliance—in which case you can forget about using our pod fleet." Lo had never heard her quite so angry, not at her, anyway.

Lo said, "I appreciate the offer of backup, but you *know* we don't like anyone flying around Saugatuck unsupervised. We'll only call in an absolute emergency."

She felt Candace rush to remind others—a message beamed through the room.

remember the children—careful what you say

Lo appreciated the old and deep loyalty in that message, as well as in the wave of support she felt coming from the rest of the council. Now they remembered. Saugatuck wasn't just a bloody-minded group of old women. They were guardians. Lo tried to catch the eye of each and every wired woman present, trying to consolidate those old bonds. They used to be in this together. Who knew, these days? Candace had started talking like this was the old America, where people had rights and a legal system existed to sort right from wrong. Dangerous idealism.

Lo knew when she was beat, though—and that was when you had to play dead.

"I'd like to say that this reunion has gone well, but it hasn't really," she said. "I'm not sure that I can depend on you the way that you could depend on me and my people. That's disappointing. That said, I know I can still depend on you to provide me with a decent feed. I'm starving, and I need a beer. Any chance of getting some refreshments around here without having to take it to a vote?"

One woman laughed. That's right, Lo could do humor too. A couple of the council members clapped. Candace smiled. Bob and Janine exchanged one of their glances. Adrianna relaxed. Lurch and Will looked relieved, even though they were both also losers in this situation. So this was the face of compromise. Weak. But what choice did she have? If her sense that bad things loomed in Saugatuck's future was right, then as far as she knew, IBM City was the last safe haven on Earth.

32

It was 2:00 a.m., and Adrianna and Janine were still out having fun. Earlier, Lurch had heard the women trying to cajole Lo and Bob into joining them—but both had complained of exhaustion and declined. Adrianna had nagged Janine into leaving Bob for one night. *Just one fucking night, girl. You're supposed to be my friend, not some alien fuck-buddy.* In the end, the two women had gone off in search of whatever passed for fun in IBM City: a sport called bowling, speed-dating, some old visual entertainment called *Mad Men,* and a party at a nightclub. Lurch didn't understand the specifics, but he got the basic idea. Young people partied in the Orbitals too. However, it had been about sixty years since Lurch had bothered with such social amusements, and he wasn't about to make an exception now, not even out of anthropological curiosity.

Opening the door of his room in the guest quarters, Lurch had to bend to avoid hitting the beam. After a quick glance around, he ducked down the hallway. Hair scraping the ceiling, he made his way to Lo's room, just around the corner. He had heard her and Candace bidding each other goodnight down in the courtyard just minutes earlier.

"No hard feelings, babe?"

"Don't push your luck, *babe.*"

He knocked gently.

"Yes? Who is it?"

"It's Lurch. May I speak with you?"

"You pick your moments. Hang on."

He listened to Lo banging around for a minute or so, then the door opened. She was wearing a white gown. Lurch had found something similar hanging on a hook in his door; it must be an Earthan custom, leaving clothing for you to exchange for your own while you stayed with friends. He had experienced something similar when he first arrived in Madison, regularly finding old men's clothing, big but not big enough, folded on the doorstep of the barn he and four others slept in. It still seemed dirty to Lurch, sharing cloth, even if you did clean it between uses. The bodcoz were much more comfortable and hygienic, but it would not be possible to manufacture them here on Earth for many years. Perhaps the Orbitals could send some child-sized bodcoz in future dispatches — and Lurch did fear that there would be many more of those.

Ducking into Lo's room, Lurch looked for a spot to sit comfortably. It was a spare and boxy room decorated with fake-wood floors and fake-leather furnishings. The window coverings featured images of pebbles. They liked that kind of fake nature in the Orbitals too. The only place he might comfortably sit was the bed, a big whitish square with a soft gray blanket folded neatly across it. He looked at Lo and raised his eyebrows. Lo looked back at him and nodded. Lurch seated himself with his back flush against the hard leather cushion that was stuck to the wall, feet dangling over the side. Basic and yet overly complex, these things the Earthans called beds. They lacked the light embracing comfort of an Orbiter cocoon. Lurch didn't understand why the Earthans hadn't created a better sleeping device during their age of technology.

Lo took a seat at the desk unit attached to the wall, swiveling the chair to face him. She glanced into his eyes then quickly lowered her gaze to a point on his shoulder. "So what do you want," she said.

Lurch did not waste time on small talk. "This afternoon was disappointing."

Lo nodded her head but said nothing.

"But that is not what I am here to discuss. I have come to realize that my people may not find their way home for many years yet. We must adapt, make new plans. Which leads me to what I wish to discuss. When we were waiting on the boats to talk with you, I noticed that you have many big houses at the edge of your town."

"Yes, I think your missiles hit some of them."

"My sincerest apologies. But that was long ago—yesterday—before we agreed to assist each other. I know that it is much to ask under the circumstances, but I must ask anyway. Those houses... They are somewhat separate from your town. We cou..."

"Out of the question," said Lo. "We are helping you leave, not stay."

"Wait. Please listen to my proposal. We could live there temporarily—those habitations will actually fit us—and help you make preparations for the drop. We know how the boxes work, how to open and close them, how to move them, how to beat Orbiter defense systems. With our help you might be able to move the Orbiters away from Saugatuck before they even land. If, as I fear, that proves impossible, then my people could escort the Orbiters to Madison. And then..."

"No, I don't think so," said Lo, but her voice was less forceful than usual.

Lurch leaned forward on the bed, elbow on one knee. "It wouldn't be forever. My people are determined to get home to their own galaxy in the end. But it is going to take time, and we need a respite from the sea. Look at me. The water is wearing me down."

Lurch waved his hand over his worn bodcoz and his sun-grizzled face. Lo's eyes traveled with his hand, then reverted to the same fixed point on his shoulder.

"If you do not want to do it for us, then do it for the sake of your own people—not just the women in Saugatuck, but all the other women out there who do not know what is coming. Imagine their terror when those boxes start falling. We can go out there in the pods with your fliers—like we did today—and tell those people what to expect."

"What makes you think I care about anybody else out there?" she said. "Candace can just send some warning messages around the alliance."

"But most of the towns scheduled for drops are not part of your alliance. They're not connected to any communications system."

"If we're all lucky, they will be abandoned towns."

"We should check. Do you not feel a sense of responsibility for others?"

Lo flared. "Don't you dare judge me. We helped you even after you attacked us."

"I know that you are a good people. Why do you think I ask you for shelter?"

Lo was quiet for a moment, then said, "Even if I did agree to let your people stay in Saugatuck—how the fuck would we feed two hundred extra mouths?"

He stifled a sigh. "My group can still fish, Lo. We can provide fish for the whole community—summer and winter. And we have access to fuel supplies at the old Black Rock marine refueling station. There are deep supplies there, unspoiled. You need special engineering knowledge and also machine-operation skills to retrieve the fuel—that is something else we have and are willing to share. How else do you think we get around?"

"I don't know. Alien batteries."

Lurch laughed out loud. He thought he saw a smile twitching at the corner of Lo's mouth too. "We wouldn't have much power if all we had was our xynth units—I think that's what you're talking about. The xynth is good for small things, lighting, charging our bodcoz, small motors, but we need Earth fuel for Earth boats, you know—gasoline."

Lo laughed back at him. "Oh, I think I know a thing or two about gasoline. Early on we managed to get our local station back up and pumping, but our original supply ran dry within a couple years. Since then we've been dependent on abandoned fuel tankers and supplies we syphon from old gas stations. Replenishing our fuel reserves is dangerous work, and the returns are getting smaller by the year. We are always desperate for more gas, especially, as you just pointed out, for the boats. So who knows? Maybe you do have something to offer. I could put it to the council, but I doubt..."

Lo sighed as she broke off. Lurch thought he knew why. Dreaming of fuel and fish, talking about sharing resources, imagining friendly neighbors: it was all a waste of time. The women of Saugatuck would never let a group of strangers move within spitting distance of their strange children, their secret children. Their not-so-secret children.

He broached the subject carefully. "I would appreciate any consideration you are willing to give my people. The men need a break from the relentless movement of the seas. Byllyn and Lil need civilization. It has been very hard. The child needs a proper home, somewhere to play. Even more importantly, she needs to learn. I imagine you have a school for the natural-born children — not the children at the Inn — children like Reid and his siblings."

Lo froze. Lurch said, "Please don't be afraid. Please don't do any violence to me. I know your greatest fear is that others discover the secret of the children — but it is too late — we already know that they are there. All of us. We have known from the first day. The missiles bouncing off the air-shield alerted us, and we used a specially modified drone to take a closer look. The children destroyed it of course, but not before we saw them. I did not mention this before now because I feared your reaction — but I believe the time has come for us to start trusting each other. We will not reveal your secret Lo. We want to build this relationship, share our burdens."

Lo's face creased with distrust. "If you wanted my trust, you would have said this much sooner. Instead you waited until you had settled in with us, pulled on a few heart strings, introduced us to your women-folk, made it harder for us to act against you."

"Of course I did. It doesn't mean I am insincere."

"Insincere! You're a total schmoozer."

"What is a schmoozer? Is that like a smooshian?"

"Ask Will, he's a Class A version of the breed."

"What is Class A?"

Lo laughed. She always laughed when he played the dumb foreigner. What did she think, that just because he didn't talk with an old American accent he couldn't understand the language?

"No promises," she said. "But I will present your proposal to the Saugatuck council when we get back tomorrow. I really don't know what we're going to do with you now. You may be right, we can't just kill all two hundred of you without a big old political fuss, but there are plenty of other possibilities that don't involve you guys moving in with us after just one date."

"Our people have so much to offer each other," replied Lurch.

"Do you ever talk like a normal person?" asked Lo.

Lurch smiled broadly as he replied, "I could if I fucking well wanted to."

Lo laughed, leaning forward in her chair and wheeling across the fake-wood floor to punch him lightly in the arm. Instead of wheeling back away when she was done, she stopped a moment and allowed her hand to drift over the outline of the crux in his bodcoz. As her hand swept over his gems, her white robe fell open across her own chest, exposing one small flat breast that reminded him of bread buns. She was so muscular and strong.

Lurch reached out, took both arms and gently moved them away from his body. He held her arms between them, looked into her blazing blue eyes and said, "My dear, lovely young woman. It has been a long day for an old man: 137 years old next birthday. I am glad that we have come this far in our relationship—you feel like the granddaughter I always wished I'd had."

The second his words registered, Lo shook off his hands and leapt up from her chair, blushing like a fresh Crn assistant. She raced over to the door, indicated that he should follow, and said, "I'll present your proposal to the council tomorrow,"

"Thank you," he said, rising from the bed.

"Yeah, but don't get your hopes up," said Lo, looking at the hallway. "There are a lot of women who are still keen to jet-propel your flotilla back into the middle of the Atlantic."

Neither of them laughed.

As he walked slowly toward the door, his head once again grazing the ceiling, Lo said, "Goodnight Gramps." He thought he understood.

And in spite of everything, he left feeling optimistic.

33

Lurch made his way back to his own room, turned on his invisibility sheath, then slipped back out the door and down the corridor to the room assigned to Bob. This time he didn't bother knocking, just knelt down and pressed his fingernail to the rudimentary electronic lock, quietly pushed the door, and slipped in. The room was identical to Lo's, except that the blanket on the bed was the color of the sea in winter. Bob was sitting at his desk. His hair was flipped back, all in one piece, and lying at a strange angle on the back of his head, revealing a small constellation of lights on a shiny dome. Bob's fingers were busy fiddling with one of the many gems embedded in his skull. It was a full skull-crux. Top of the line.

"I wondered when you'd show up," said Bob. His Earthan twang was gone. He was now speaking the most formal Orbitaal. "I hope you've been very careful. We're all skating on pretty thin ice with these women—add that to your Earthan metaphor bible."

Lurch smiled without showing his teeth. "I seem to be doing all right with them myself," he said, "and I am neither burnt nor reduced to masquerading as a half-wit."

"Just begging," replied Bob.

He ignored the comment, walked over to Bob's desk, and perched on the edge.

"I think we are safe. Lo has gone to bed. Adrianna and Janine are busy partying. There are no guards except the usual around the building perimeter. Nobody seems to be spying on us, at least not very closely. There are security cameras in the halls, and I am sure someone is monitoring them, but I made sure no one saw me come in here..."

Lurch ran his hands up and down his invisible body. "How much of me can you see?"

"Everything, but that's because my crux is fully operational. Don't worry, you're invisible. Not that it would matter. I checked the room. Nobody's spying on us in here."

Lurch remained invisible anyway. He noticed that Bob had reverted to English.

"I've never seen a crux on the head before," he said, also in English, a language he now almost preferred to his own, perhaps because it had given him new ways to laugh. "I have heard about it, though. They are the talk of the Unan black market. Undetectable even to security scans. The hairpiece cleaves to the area like an organism. Waterproof. Tamper-proof. Clever. I assume you have control sensors in your fingers to work the gems."

"Touch technology," said Bob. "I think of it as simply another language."

"They also say that only members of The Trust have access to them," said Lurch. "Certainly only a Trust member would go around pretending *not* to have a crux."

"I knew from the way that you were inspecting every inch of my body in Madison that I'd blown cover," said Bob. "What was it? I mean, I'm good. Wl-Wrrn spent six months on the explorer journey out here with me and still doesn't have a clue."

"You said something," said Lurch.

"What?" said Bob.

"You made a joke about Madison being *halfway to Assville*. It is an unusual turn-of-phrase, and it caught my attention because I remembered hearing it back on Crn. There was a man who attended our group's launch. He stood next to me during the departure speeches. He did not look like you, except that he was short. During one of the many speeches, about how the settlers showed great courage, going halfway to the edge of the known universe, I heard the short man mutter something to himself—*halfway to Assville*. I did not understand the comment, only that it was derisive. It gave me a bad feeling—that's why I remember it."

Bob nodded and smiled. "Who would have thought anyone was paying attention. Well-spotted Zgyzg-Dm—you might have made a good Trust man yourself."

"I beg to differ."

"Your English is impressive," said Bob. "A bit Russish but very articulate."

"It's all down to Retske," said Lurch. "Yours is better, though. More natural."

"So it should be, dude. I really am Earthan," said Bob. "I was the *captain* of that secret Alaskan shuttle, working covert space surveillance, *saw* those Ruurdaan fuckers en-route. After I was rescued, the Orbiters suggested I join the Trust. I was grateful for the opportunity. I also found I liked the work. It's never boring, and I find the anonymity totally liberating."

"You are a voyeur who dares not show his face."

"I am a loyal servant of the society that saved him."

"A society that puts political protestors on a prison hell planet with junkies and psychopaths and feeds them killer drugs when they get too hard to handle or sends them off to other prison planets hundreds of galaxies away?"

"Just be grateful for a society that doesn't believe in the death penalty."

"Una is the death penalty. Earth is the death penalty."

"And yet you're still here jabbering about your rights."

Lurch had had enough. He reached forward, placed his hands on either side of Bob's swivel chair, and said, "Enough small talk. Tell me what you are doing here, or I will start howling like a Unan fendrillyn. And when the women come running, I will tell them that you are an Orbiter spy with an entire arsenal of technology under your wig."

Bob snorted and pushed Lurch away. "Howl away. You'll only make your life more difficult than it already is. I'll tell Lo the back-story of every one of those scumbags living on the flotilla with you. I'll sour things with Candace. And I'll make sure you

254 / Jackie Hatton

don't get back home—ever. But let's not take things that far, Zg. Let's be friends"

Lurch grunted and sat down on the bed. "You still haven't said why you're here."

"I'm doing what spies do, Zg. I'm looking for the truth. You can't trust your average settler support ambassador to tell you a word of it, right?"

He flipped his hairpiece shut and shook his long hair out.

"We all know that Will is never going to take your message home. His livelihood depends on the success of the program. He won't reveal any of its problems or actively promote change. I, on the other hand, am relatively impartial. I *am* willing to take a message home—and believe me, I do plan to go home just as soon as I've witnessed the drops. I'll be taking the orbicraft—but not Wl-Wrrn. That leaves one spare seat."

Lurch straightened up. "Are you offering to take me with you, Bob?"

"No, I am most definitely not. Nobody wants to see or hear from you at this point in time. Give it another twenty years, buddy. However, the council would like to hear the opinion of someone who has lived here as part of the settlement program."

"Blr. Or Rans. Either could speak eloquently of our experience."

"Actually, I was thinking more of Byllyn and the child. Her father misses her. She's been off the Vroom for three years now, so it should be all right. She is also a very prominent name among the first settlers. People would listen to what she has to say."

"Byllyn cannot fully articulate the issues we are facing."

It was true, but it was not the whole truth. Lurch knew full well that Byllyn would draw a lot of attention upon her return, attention that might help them. It would also be wonderful for Byllyn to be able to raise Lil back on Crn, with all the privileges a child of that rank could enjoy. Although the child was thriving in the natural environs of Earth, it was not what most Orbiters would ever want for their children—life without any hope of ever accessing the knowledge. Lurch knew that if he really cared about Lil, he would let Byllyn go. But Byllyn, their Byllyn. The community would be bereft without her. And Lil. He would be bereft without Lil. But he needed to think of the others, too, all two hundred of them.

"She won't go with you unless I say so, and I'll only do that under one condition: will you make sure there are plans to retrieve all the settlers who wish to return home?"

Bob swiveled around his chair and said, "First, you're not in a position to set conditions, and second, retrieving settlers is hardly the point of the exercise. *However,* I do agree that offering a way home would radically improve the appeal of Earth settlement. The problem is that it will require an enormous investment to send the necessary equipment to extract settlers. Collecting those boxes isn't as easy as dropping them off is, you know."

He had known that from the minute he crawled out of his packing crate.

He said, "Wl-Wrrn and his program recruiters promised that pickup would be possible within five years."

Bob shook his head. His long hair flopped back and forth.

"I'll do my best for you, but I didn't create the program, and I don't run it. I'm simply here to observe how it's doing and help where I can—like take Byllyn back with me. I am pretty sure that I can arrange for the next support mission to follow up with your group—if that helps?"

Lurch weighed his options.

"When do you need Byllyn to be ready?"

"In two or three weeks. I'll let you know exactly when."

"I'll tell her to ready herself."

"I'm sorry that this is the only solution we have for you right now. I've always had a lot of respect for you, Zgyzg-Dm, in spite of everything. Your work on early crux technology was seminal— they say that without you, we might not even have the knowledge."

Lurch winced a little at the word. He missed the knowledge so much it hurt. "The knowledge was intended for everyone. Do people still fight for universal access?"

"Maybe on Una, maybe if they want to end up on Una," said Bob. "I'm sorry Zg, but you know the knowledge is only sustainable for a certain number of people, and that possessing it comes with great responsibilities."

"I know nothing anymore," sighed Lurch.

"I'm sorry, old man," said Bob.

"No you're not," said Lurch, bowing deep and backing toward the door.

"I'll be in touch," said Bob, not even standing, just dipping his head.

Lurch turned the doorknob and slipped out, down the corridor.

34

Lurch had one final piece of business. He crept into Wl-Wrrn's room, silent and invisible, leaned over the bed and gently shook the ambassador by the shoulders. Wl-Wrrn jolted awake, but Lurch pressed him back down into pillow. "Don't panic. It's only me." Will quit resisting and lay there quietly, legs sprawled diagonally across the bed, feet hanging over the edges. Lurch removed his hands, sat on the edge of the bed, and whispered into the dark.

"What a mess you've made of things, Wl-Wrrn."

Wl-Wrrn replied, "How can you say that, Zg? Retske and Candace refused to indulge your self-righteous lawlessness. I was doing victory laps in my dreams."

"You're still stuck here at the mercy of your psychotic young sister."

"Not for long, Zg. They'll come for me."

Lurch sighed. "It's unfair but true—they'll come for you."

"And you can forget about catching a ride with me when they do come," said Will, sitting up a little now. "Captain Syd won't take you home. Do you know how much trouble he'd get into for assisting in a hijack? Just forget about it. I'll take your message back to the High Council. I know changes are needed. In the meantime— try a bit harder to make it work, will you?"

Lurch said, "Would you consider taking Byllyn? I'm sure she'd be welcome."

He knew that this was probably a futile conversation. If Bob was really Trust—and Lurch thought he was—then not only was Wl-Wrrn going nowhere, but he had no bargaining chips left either. Nevertheless, Lurch thought it wise to cut as many deals as possible while he had the chance.

Wl-Wrrn said, "You know I might consider taking Byllyn and the child. There are many who miss her. She would definitely be welcome to speak about your situation in front of the high council. It's a thought, Zg. I'll consider it."

Suddenly everyone wanted Byllyn. Her father must have asked the explorer team to bring her home. Lurch should have realized that the minute Bob mentioned her by name.

He said, "Of course I need to talk to her first. I know she wants to go home, but I'm not sure how she would feel about returning without the rest of us."

"You could always persuade her."

"Hah. You clearly don't know Byllyn. I will ask her—but only because I think it might be good for her, and not because I'm willing to do your dirty work for you."

Lurch could see Wl-Wrrn in the darkness now, the outline of his white skin.

"Don't get personal, Zg. None of this is personal"

Lurch leaned over, pinned Wl-Wrrn to the bed, and spoke within an inch of his face.

"Not personal? I hooked into those body-regulators in good faith—and told my fellow Unans to do the same. I persuaded them you could be trusted. I told them you were trying to help us create a viable new society on a livable planet. I believed it. I believed *you*. Imagine how I felt when I crawled out of that dropbox—battered and bruised because the exterior defense shields had failed in the atmosphere—and found myself surrounded by a sea of white. Fifteen hundred of them and five hundred of us—and pretty soon they had control of the Madisonians and the jammers. You gave them jammers to hurt us with—you sleazy, dirty, used-planet *salesman*."

Lurch pushed himself away from Wl-Wrrn in disgust.

Will sat up a little on his pillow, protesting. "Don't blame me. At the last moment, all these Pure came forward, wanting to join friends and families. It was very inconvenient as most of the Unans were already comatose and loaded. However, High Council said they felt obliged to put citizens before criminals. So some Unans were bumped. I knew it was a bad idea, but who knew the Pure would treat you so badly? I didn't give them those jammers."

Lurch grunted. "You're such a liar. But I'm not here to argue with you."

"No? Then what are you here for?" said Wl-Wrrn, reaching out and running his knuckles along his leg, over the tattered fabric of the bodcoz, past his groin to his belly.

Lurch swiped the hand away. "Not if you were the last man on Una…"

"You didn't say that last time."

"I didn't know what kind of person you were…"

"Yes you did."

"I thought we had an understanding."

"Don't we?"

"You're so slippery, like a Gllryn water jelly."

"I know who I am, old man."

"Times like these, I really do feel like an old man."

"Let me change that," said Wl-Wrrn, pulling Lurch down to him.

As he felt himself drawn to that beautiful pale face, Lurch sighed and vowed to do better by himself and his people tomorrow.

35

They flew home at the first red streak of dawn and were relieved to find that the situation had remained calm in their absence. The Orbiters had remained out on the flotilla—although apparently one hundred Saugatuckers had visited the boats. The rest, they were told, had stayed in town arguing about what was going to happen next. Some of the survivalists had gone to ground. Pat had scheduled a vote from 8:00 a.m.–11:00 a.m. No excuses, no exceptions. Counting was scheduled to take place from 11:00 a.m.–noon. It was only 7:00 a.m. when they landed, but already small groups of women were camped in and around HQ, waiting for guidance, waiting to vote, just waiting for something to happen. Within seconds of landing Will was out there, working those small crowds, shaking hands with any of the women who'd let him, making his last-ditch pitch. Lo let him.

She had her own work to do. As Pat walked with her from the pod to HQ she explained that Lo was expected to give a speech just before the polling station opened, and again, later, to announce the town's final decision. In between times she had a back-to-back schedule of meetings. Everyone wanted to talk to her, before they voted, about the vote, after they voted. The council was there looking for information, Yaz was there looking for instruction, Helena was there looking concerned, Marie was there with her husband and their placards, Janine was there with hand-painted t-shirts that read, "Hearts+Hopes=Humans," Reid was there wearing a tattered old Orbiter bodcoz. It was a public announcement that Lo had lost her grip on her own people. It was a call to action. Lo spent the next four hours shouting herself hoarse: No way, at least not without conditions; No, hell no, not without a fight!

Around 11.15, just after the polling station closed, Lo said she was going to the toilet, but instead slipped off to the hammock down by the river. She needed a moment alone, truly alone, to rest her tired voice and mind. It was a cloudless day, already at least eighty degrees. The hammock was slung between two chestnut oaks, just a couple of hundred feet away from the bustling dock, yet secluded behind the reeds. It was not really like she'd run away. Everyone knew that in the summer months this was where Lo went to think. Anyone seeing her there would probably think that she was agonizing over the vote, the future. In fact, to her shame, she was chewing over her feelings of rejection. So many people had turned against her, even her own family. She knew that not everyone would be voting her way today. Then there was that embarrassing moment with Lurch last night. Clearly he didn't think too much of her either. He'd tried to let her off lightly, pretending he thought she was too young for him, but he knew damned well that she was really sixty-five years old, hardly some naive young woman. He just didn't like her that much, or in that way. Like everyone else, including her own wife, he was obsessed with that strange pseudo-visionary Byllyn. Lo had been extremely happy to hear that Will planned to take her royal glitterness back home with him. The last thing they needed in Saugatuck was some crazy goddess turning good hearts and minds to shit.

Lo glanced at the river. The orbicraft remained moored at that strange oblique angle on the opposite shore, guarded by two of her crew. Lo was still curious about the ship's interior and planned to ask whoever came to collect Will if they would show her inside— on the off-chance that her brother had lied to them about the conditions of access, just like he lied about pretty much everything else. As she contemplated the shiny cockeyed pyramid, a vision of Will and Bob arriving in their lurid bodcoz flitted across her mind. That event seemed like months ago, not less than a week.

Lo was pretty sure she already knew the two men's fate; Pat and Yaz predicted general consensus on that particular issue. Will would most likely be going home with Byllyn. Bob would most likely be staying. Both had promised never to reveal the existence of the children—not that it was such a great secret anymore. First it turned out, Lurch and his people all knew. Then Candace revealed that the children had long been an open secret in IBM City—visitors had seen and heard things. So much for their thirty years of isolationism. Clearly she hadn't been strict enough concerning movement in and out of town. Or maybe there had never been a point to being strict at all? Just as that particular thought started to get her blood flowing, her head filled with a buzzing sensation.

A slew of beams were bombarding her circuits. The results were in.

The trouble was so many messages were coming at once she couldn't understand any of them. Too impatient to search for one clear thread, Lo shut down, high-jumped her body out of the hammock, and landed upright on the lawn. Turning to face HQ, she literally shouted for Yaz—projecting her voice along a clear funnel of air to the comms office upstairs. With every window open on account of the stifling late July heat, that should work.

Lo walked up the lawn a ways and sat down at one of their indestructible picnic tables. Almost immediately she saw Yaz strolling down the lawn toward her. The tall, brown-skinned woman was wearing a billowy pair of pink silk shorts, a sheer tank-top, and bling-encrusted sandals. Usually Yaz favored old college running shorts and t-shirts. She said one of the things she actually liked about her new life was never feeling obligated to dress up. So what was with the getup? Had she dressed up like that with the men on the flotilla in mind?

Lo made a face at the outfit and said, "So Caribbean Barbie, what's the verdict?"

Yaz made a face back and said, "Don't you screw up your face at my outfit like that, girl. It's a big day today—historic, you said. I thought I might end up in a photograph or two."

"Sorry, you look nice. So are they in or out, the flotilla people?"

"Almost everyone voted no to permanent residence, but a slim majority voted yes to a three-month trial. A group has already formed to help clean the vacant big houses out at Saugatuck Shores. Pat is drawing up plans for a checkpoint between there and here. It's going to be a lot of work, managing two hundred extras on the edge of town. The families already living out there are pretty pissed about it too—as you can imagine."

"Of course. Part of me wonders why I even put this to a vote. I could have just put my foot down. But I'm already struggling against accusations that I'm some kind of Stalin. I'm not what you'd call happy about the end result, but my gut tells me I've done the right thing."

Yaz said, "You have done the right thing. And not just because it's a good political move, or because it's the compassionate choice, but because you let the women decide for themselves. Even knowing they would probably vote yes. Or did you think they would vote no?"

"I knew how it would go. If it had only been about the men, they might have said no—too intimidating—but it's not just about the men now, is it, it's about the possibility of children."

"I don't know, Lo. I have to tell you that I also voted yes, and honestly, part of my decision was about new relationship opportunities. I'm sorry, but it's true. Not all of us have been happily married for the last thirty years. And some of us can't help how straight we are."

"Sure, but aren't you scared these men are psychopaths who want to take over?"

"I am, but I sense they're all right, and there are only two hundred of them and we are very strong. It's going to be a test for us—but I think we're ready for this test."

"Maybe. But I'm also worried about what we have to lose. Thirty years together without men, so strong in our relationships, our commitments to each other. I worry that I'll look back in thirty years and have nothing but nostalgia for these terrible, hard years."

Yaz nodded, and her halo of hair bobbed in sync. "Tell me about it. But don't worry, Lo. We'll all fight with you if these guys start trying to take over."

"I fucking well hope so, Yaz, but history tells me different. You know how guys get all I'm in charge around here. Which reminds me. I assume we voted Will home?"

"Yes. As we expected—he'll be going home with Byllyn."

"Anything else?"

"Yes. Although the decisions went our way, the voices of dissent were very loud. You won't believe some of the obscenities people wrote on their voting slips. It's not going to be straight sailing from here. There's talk of breakaway communities and opposition parties and civic resistance. Marie is the biggest agitator. She's furious about everything."

"She's irrational because she's afraid for Carly. It's to be expected."

"I know, but you need to talk to her. You two used to be such strong allies—even after the problems when Reid found out James was his father—now it's like you're enemies. But she's still one of us, Lo. She's also very influential among the hardliners."

Lo shook her head in frustration. "I already talked to her this morning, Yaz. She's totally irrational. She says I'm enthralled by the Orbiters. She says that I'm more loyal to my brother than to Saugatuck. She even says that I'm motivated by some vendetta against James because of something in the past. It's all bullshit, but it's destructive bullshit."

"She knows that none of what she's saying is true—she's just trying to undermine you on multiple grounds. Otherwise it will look like she's only got a single issue."

"I didn't even mention the possibility of deprogramming our kids."

"Oh, c'mon Lo, the minute you told us about what Candace did to the IBM children, we knew it was going to be an issue for our future too. You did absolutely the right thing in telling us the truth—brutal honesty has always been one of your strengths—but it's an explosive development, and a scary one for Marie."

"I so nearly held it back for later. We have so much else to deal with first. We have to integrate Lurch's flotilla. We have to prepare for an invasion in two weeks' time. But when Marie asked how the children were doing, I just couldn't lie to her."

"You did the right thing—but it may have negative consequences this time…"

Lo shook her head again. "So they voted to hold elections early."

"I'm afraid they did. A huge majority voted to hold general elections in three months—at the same time that we decide whether or not to continue absorbing the Orbiters from the flotilla."

"Oh great. My future is tied to the behavior of a bunch of oversized hooligans."

"I know. It sucks. However, the thing that will really make the difference is how you handle the incoming. We need to peacefully and successfully move those people on."

"So nobody voted to just allow the aliens to invade us?"

"You know that was a no-brainer. Only twenty voted yes to a new open door policy. I have no idea who, possibly women who've been in contact with Madison these last couple of years and have some empathy for the Pure."

"That's a scary thought. Secret radio infiltration by the Pure."

"I wouldn't worry too much about it, Lo. Nobody sane is going to agree to let strangers land on them in big metal boxes then invite them in for a welcome dinner."

"I knew that nobody would vote to accept the thousand coming in the boxes, but it was important that we put it to a public vote. Thank God-who-only-a-halfwit-would-believe-in that I didn't entirely fuck up on that score."

Yaz laughed and said, "Hallelujah."

Lo knew that Yaz had abandoned her deep Baptist faith around the moment the Ruurdaans inserted the fortieth wire in her body, four hundred still to go. Now, Yaz stretched her silver-streaked hands out across the table and grasped Lo's own sparkling fingers.

Lo smiled but pulled her hands away. "Whatever it is, just say it, Yaz."

Yaz said, "Allow me to make just one personal suggestion, old friend. You've done well today, pulled us all back together in an honest way. But you have a family to answer to as well as a community. Helena and Reid are both still out at the flotilla helping the refugees. Everything is fine, but you should go and talk to them. So many changes in such a short time—and more coming—there are things that need saying."

Lo folded her arms before replying, "They sent their votes by proxy, Yaz. They could have come in to see me. Why waste my time on people who don't give a shit?"

Yaz shook her head in dismay. "We're talking about Helena here, Lo."

"Yeah, and there's not a lot to say, Yaz. It's over."

"Anyone who knows you both knows that—but have you told her? Has she told you?"

"Some things don't need too much telling."

Yaz scrunched her face in disbelief. "I don't think that this is one of those things."

Lo had had enough. She climbed out from the picnic bench. "You know what, Yaz? I know you mean well, but I just don't have time for personal shit today, and that's the honest truth. I'll see you later tonight, at the meeting that Pat has scheduled, okay?"

Yaz said, "Oh c'mon Lo. Don't go stomping off. You can spare five…"

Lo didn't stop to hear the end. She was already halfway to the pod-park. There were times for talking and times for doing. Yaz might be an all-around comms whiz, people-person, and wise counselor, but Lo was the one who knew how to run a town under threat.

36

In the late afternoon thirty-four pods gathered on the flats, just by the checkpoint on the post road. The old commercial strip was still home to an ugly array of abandoned stores and businesses, many which could have served as a solid base for Saugatuck's western border post—but the women had opted for the remains of the once-swanky Casa Spa. Nothing much happened there anymore, of course, although the spa still had plenty of nail-varnish to play with on a boring shift and comfy loungers that the crew dragged outside onto the old parking spaces in the warmer months. The women had built a tower on top of the substantial brick building, giving them an exceptional view across the flats. Straight ahead lay the wooded hill that ran down to Saugatuck HQ. To the right of the old spa building lay the long, heavy car fence, which ran from here to Exit 17. Immediately behind the post road lay nothing but booby traps. Beyond that lay the old towns of Weston and Wilton and Georgetown, and far, far beyond, IBM City. Nobody went beyond that particular border too often, though; the denser the woods, the more the ferals and bears you'd find.

On the other side of the post road, outside Westport, beyond the car fence, lay all the territory held by the Norwalk Power Station, about fifty square miles total. The territory had more stuff than people, and the Saugatuckers tended to still take what they needed when they needed it, but they did formally acknowledge that it belonged to Norwalk. Damned Norwalk—as in damned if Lo was going to bow down to their demands forever—and damned if she had any other choice at this point in time. Power was power. Lo had plans to meet the governing group at the power station later in the week. The flotilla group would add to their energy burden—but they also knew how to improve energy efficiency. Lo hoped that Norwalk would allow the Orbiter engineers to work with them to improve the power supply in Saugatuck—in exchange for free technical expertise. At best they would agree. At worst, they would cut off Saugatuck's power. For once, though, Lo felt she was going in there with some real negotiating leverage.

That was later in the week, though—many work hours away. Today Lo had called the security crew to a critical removals drill. Immediately after the meeting in IBM City a couple of crew members had been sent to Madison to retrieve one of the Orbiter drop-boxes. It had taken a whole day to drag the box back to Saugatuck, where it now rested slightly askew on the flats outside the checkpoint. It looked like it had been dumped in frustration, which was entirely possible. The box turned out to be bizarrely slippery. Trying to move it was like trying to press two magnets of the same pole together—not impossible, just painfully difficult.

Lo stood alone and watched as two fliers tried to move the box from the shallow edge of the flats to the empty expanse of the post road in front of the spa. In unison, the two pods raised the box, wobbling it slowly into the sky. Then they tried to move it horizontally. The box hung at a precarious angle as they dragged it toward the flats. It looked almost as if they were pulling at something snagged on the air. Eventually they made it the two hundred feet to the road. They dropped it like it was a dumpster that had got out of their grasp and the box landed hard on one of its corners, penetrating the soft hot tarmac before slamming onto its side.

Lo shouted into the sky, "Hey, I nearly got a concussion just watching that."

Ruby opened an aperture in her pod, leaned down as she came in to land, and shouted back, "You do better, Lo. It's like these things are greased bowling balls. You can't get a grip."

"I know," said Lo. "But we have to keep trying anyway."

Ruby landed and leaped out of the pod. "I'm fit to scream, Lo."

"I can't move them so great either," Lo said. "But if we can't find a way, then we're going to have to wait until they land then scoop the Orbiters up individually as they crawl out of the hatches.

That's way more personal than we want. If we can get the boxes away from Saugatuck, then we'll barely have to deal with the individuals in them at all. I'm hoping we can move them somewhere that leads to Madison. Maybe even the old Merritt Parkway. It's not a straight shot, and the road's overgrown, but it will take them all the way to their Orbiter buddies up north without hitting impassable water."

"The Merritt's a good idea" said Ruby. "But at the rate we're working, we'll need almost half an hour per box. Tell me again how much time you think we'll have."

"According to both Will and Lurch, it's a pretty slow affair," replied Lo. "The boxes should come down in rows of ten or so, each about five or ten minutes apart—a process of between five and eight hours. They think. Nobody seems to know for sure. The word *depends* comes up a lot. We do know they'll be coming in along the I95—that's apparently where Will suggested—thanks bro. The good news is they won't be able land too close to us because we broke the highway up years ago. The bad news is that anywhere else on I95 is still three miles away from the Merritt."

"Should we think about moving them somewhere closer?" asked Ruby.

"I sure as hell don't think so. We just have to keep practicing. Try again, Ruby."

"Yes, sir, Lo, sir." Very funny. She jumped into her pod and began rising.

Lo turned to see what everyone else was up to. Between stints working with the box, the crew were practicing mind lifts—lifting the heaviest things they could find with their minds. Lo saw abandoned trucks rising up and down, old cars being stacked like play things, dumpsters being hauled over the top of overgrown buildings. Adrianna appeared to be standing on top of the old Whole Foods shouting instructions. She looked rather magnificent, the most Amazonian of them all. She and Adrianna hadn't spoken much since before the disastrous trip to Armonk. Adrianna had beamed her that night to see if she wanted to go out—but Lo had pretended not to receive the message. She'd been staring at her often enough, but not really saying anything. Awkward. Now Lo felt a beam she couldn't ignore as the two of them made eye contact.

a moment—in private

Lo nodded at Adrianna and stepped over to a quiet place on the covered walkway outside the spa.

Adrianna jumped all the way from the roof of the Whole Foods to the other side of the post road. She was by Lo's side in another three great bounds. The challenges they faced were only making her stronger. Lo could not afford to alienate her now, certainly not over a bit of awkwardness.

"If we were all like you, the Orbiters would be too scared to come," she said.

"Yeah, well," said Adrianna. "Look, I was at the flotilla earlier—and the women working there tell me Byllyn doesn't actually want go home with Will. They say she's being forced."

What? Now Adrianna was also worrying herself about Byllyn? And the worst thing was, Lo had no idea what Adrianna was talking about.

"I hope nobody is saying that I'm forcing her. I fought for Lurch to go, remember? And, anyway, I thought Byllyn wanted to go. Don't they all hate it here and want to go home?"

"That's what I thought too. But Helena just told me that Byllyn is now saying that she doesn't want to go back on her own with Will. Lurch is putting pressure on her. He says someone has to go who can get the attention of their high council. A celebrity like Byllyn. But I've been thinking, Lo. What if I went in Byllyn's place? I reckon the Orbiters might think I was some kind of celebrity, at least exotic. I would be the first wired Earth woman they ever met. And I'm one of the strongest ones."

"I don't know," Lo began.

Adrianna cut her off. "I already discussed it with Will, and he's says it's an option. He doesn't like me much, but he thinks I would make a great souvenir. The Orbiters have no idea about the strength and extent of our wire power. They'd actually find me fascinating. And you know how hard I'll argue for our rights, Lo. I'll scream and shout and refuse to back down. They won't know what hit them. They'll be too scared to invade us. It's actually a brilliant idea, I think."

Lo was shocked that Adrianna would consider leaving Saugatuck. "We can't fight the boxes without you."

"I know. I won't be leaving until after the drop."

"There are always more battles, you know that."

"The rest of the crew are getting stronger every day. I can feel the fire in their wires. And there are wired women coming in from the flotilla who you might be able to teach to fly and fight. You don't need me that bad. You've never said so before."

"I've never had to say it before. Did you come here to make me beg?"

"Please don't make this hard, Lo. You know I deserve more than what I have now. This is a chance for me to take on a challenge of my own. Get out of your shadow."

"Let me talk to Will and Lurch and Byllyn and think about it," said Lo.

"Yes! Thank you! You'll see. They'll all agree. Just one last thing, though..."

"What?" Lo was distracted now. She hated to admit it, but Adrianna had a point.

"I've been thinking. I don't know quite how to say this. I'm not a big verbalizer like Janine." As she said it, Adrianna breathed in and out hard. Lo felt her energy wrap around her. It was certainly not verbal, but it was very powerful indeed. It was the same kind of melding that she and Adrianna shared all those evenings after work, those evenings of drinking and fooling around. Only it hadn't just been fooling around. Lo could feel that now. She could also feel the awkwardness radiating out of every nerve and muscle in her body. She was way too sober.

Adrianna said, "I know we've gotten closer, you and me, these last few months, and I'm going to miss you when I go. I was wondering whether, oh I don't know, maybe whether you wanted to go out on the water one night before I leave. Now that you and Helena..."

Now Lo felt herself become rigid. Adrianna must feel it too.

"What do you mean, now that me and Helena...."

"I heard on the grapevine you broke up?"

Lo kicked the tarmac. Her face felt like she was pressed close to a radiator.

"You heard wrong. And I don't have time for any of this shit right now, Adrianna."

She flung Adrianna's energy off her. She should never have let things go so far. Not with crew. She'd always worried her indiscretions would cause trouble, and here it was.

"Fuck you, Lo, you're as bad as any married guy that ever used me for entertainment," said Adrianna, her face ablaze. "But if that's really how you feel, then you'll let me go."

"I'll think about it, all right? I'll think about it. But not right now, Adrianna."

Watching Adrianna's muscled back as she stalked away, Lo wondered if the vote had triggered something in all of them—a hankering for real freedom—of movement, of dreams, of spirit. Lo wanted that too—she didn't run their town as a fortress for the fun of it—but she was a realist. She looked up and saw Ruby slamming the box into the broken front window of an old organic food market. Then she spent the rest of the afternoon pushing her crew to the limit.

37

That night she went out to the flotilla to find Helena. She found her with Lurch, Byllyn, Lil, and Reid—all enjoying a starlit dinner on Byllyn's boat—grilled fish and salad. The boat's old music system must still work too, because Lo heard one of Reid's moody folk CDs playing. Lo could barely look at Lurch after *that* particular lapse of judgment. She'd barely spoken to him since they got back from IBM. Helena was liaising with the flotilla now.

"Sparkle, lady, sparkle," said Lil, jumping up and hugging Lo's thighs.

"She does sparkle, doesn't she," said Helena, smiling.

"She calls all of you wired ladies that," said Byllyn. "But not me, which is strange, because I would say that I am sparkly all the time but you are in truth silvery, and only sometimes. Children have funny ways of seeing, though, don't they?"

Lo ignored Byllyn as she calmly peeled the hairy little blonde creature from her legs, placed her in her mother's indecent lap, and turned to face the others.

"This is all very cozy," said Lo.

"Yes it is, why don't you join us?" said Helena.

"Stop being so nice to her, Mom" said Reid. "She isn't very nice to you. Marie is right. She just does whatever she wants and ignores the rest of us."

The kid was totally confused. If Marie had gotten her way today, Reid sure as hell wouldn't be sitting here on this flotilla dining with what Marie called the eh-lee-yens. The eh-lee-yens would be off dodging stray cruise-ships in the mid-Atlantic.

"Did you participate in the voting today, Reid?" she asked.

"Yes, of course I did. We agreed I have the right."

"Well yes, we did, but are you eighteen?"

Reid sneered, "Whatever. So what that you allowed me to vote even though I'm only sixteen? Who says that eighteen is the voting age anyway? Who makes the rules around here? I've been talking to my friends about this thing called proportional representation, and we even think that naturals should maybe get two votes, you know, to make up for how the wired women dominate us unfairly."

First Adrianna. Now Reid. Lo felt the steam rising off her wires.

"Dominate you! We totally indulge you. Everyone, including me, has treated you like a little prince since the day you were born. We didn't want you feeling weaker than us. We wanted you to feel like a man. We told you how great you were. How strong. How smart. We let you run free. We let you vote. I don't need thanking every day, but…" Lo tried to think of a clever way to finish her sentence, but she was all out of gas—too exhausted to argue with an ungrateful sixteen-year-old boy.

Reid replied, "You don't get to *let* me do anything."

Lo kept expecting Helena to intervene on her behalf. Instead she was surprised to hear Lurch's thick Russian gargle. "Take it easy please, Reid," he said. "Lo has a difficult job—doing things and making decisions that weaker souls cannot. I would ask you to show some respect."

Lo appreciated it, but she also resented the fact that Reid was going to listen to it—just because Lurch was a man with authority. This was everything she feared for her community once the men came back—women straight back into the weaker roles.

Helena reached out and touched her son's arm. "Lurch is right, Reid. Give Lo a break. She needs our support, and you know she's tried very hard to accommodate everyone's needs and wishes. Don't use her as a scapegoat for your own feelings of powerlessness—your power will come, in time, with maturity, when you've earned it. You're earning it now—here—with your work on the flotilla. Be happy about that. Not angry. Nobody here should be angry."

Byllyn nodded vaguely in agreement. Lurch picked at his food, done with advising. Reid just sulked. All those years raising him, and it felt like she could die tomorrow and he wouldn't grieve for her. How the hell had that happened? She felt like crying. She scowled at Reid instead.

Funny little Lil pointed at Reid then pointed at Lo.

"No angry. No angry."

"I'm not angry," said Lo, "just a bit serious."

"Seeryeth," replied Lil, staring pointedly at her nose.

Everyone except Lo laughed hysterically.

"It's really not that funny," said Lo, which sent the rest of them into fits. Lo had never seen Lurch laugh before, his mouth a hairy black cave filled with white rocks. When the laughter stopped she said, "What's all this I hear about Byllyn not wanting to go home?"

Lurch replied, "I would say she is still deciding."

Byllyn replied for herself. "I would say that I am not still deciding. I will be staying here if I may be allowed, please. It is good here for me and my child where there is no Vroom, and nobody wants to love me unless I want to love them."

Lo got the feeling she was speaking to Helena, even though her eyes were looking at Lurch. Either way, it chafed. She said, "Don't get me wrong, Lurch, I'm very keen for her to go. I'm just worried that she's not right. We need a rep who can control Will, keep him honest."

"You see," said Byllyn. "I told you that I am not right for this task. I am not someone to keep people honest. My father says I inspire dishonesty."

"Of course you don't," said Helena,

"Of course you don't," mimicked Lo. She could no longer stop herself. "Seriously, Helena. Would you just listen to yourself? You hardly even know this fucking woman."

Helena looked away. The other three looked at their feet. What was this? Judging and shaming? Lo felt like throwing one of them somewhere.

Lil tugged at her t-shirt and said, "Fucky."

276 / Jackie Hatton

The kid was only looking for another laugh, but nobody responded.

"I said duck," Lo said to the child quickly. "Ducky, quack, quack." She swiveled back to speak to the group. "I don't care enough about any of this to fight you all over it. So let's just assume that Byllyn has decided to stay. I can live with that, as long as she stays in Saugatuck Shores. That means we're short one representative to go back to the Orbitals with Will. I have a suggestion. Adrianna has volunteered."

Lurch was quick to respond. "It should really be an Orbiter who goes."

Lo had expected that answer. "Respectfully, Lurch, having given you so much already today, I think you can concede this one this small thing. And anyway, I've spoken to Will, and he says that if it's not going to be Byllyn then it has to be one of us women. Adrianna is quite powerful. She should generate quite a bit of publicity. That means more chances to speak out publicly against the Earth settlement program. I've come to think that sending one of us is a good idea, better than sending one of you."

"Maybe," said Lurch. "Does what I think make any difference?"

"Better that we all agree. Think about it overnight," said Lo.

Get used to the idea, buddy.

She looked around and contemplated how to end this visit. Did she dare ask Helena if they could speak privately for a moment? Was she capable of having that conversation? Lo knew that Helena would never end their relationship herself. She was too loyal. Yet here she was out on the flotilla, not particularly concerned about what Lo was doing, hanging with Byllyn. Although Lo had little desire to be around Helena right now, she missed their bond. All those years, challenges, battles, victories. Lo looked across and glanced at her wife. Helena gazed back, comfortable, as always, in her emotions. When she spoke, however, it was not of Lo.

"I think it's a great idea for Adrianna to go. What a good choice. What a chance for her. It's also much better than forcing Byllyn to do something she doesn't want to do. Slowly but surely we are finding our way. Don't you think, Lo?"

"Maybe. I don't know. Helena, we need to talk in private."

"Yes, we probably do."

Lo felt a lightning bolt of fear shoot through her wires. Living without Helena at her back would be worse than living without the fence, worse than living without her powers. As Helena rose, Lo felt her stomach clench. She was not ready to have this conversation at all.

"Shit," she said, pretending to receive a beam. "It's Yaz. I'm needed back at HQ."

"Another time, then," said Helena. She was unreadable to Lo now. It was unbearable.

When Lo moved to say goodbye to the whole group, Reid turned his back and busied himself with observing the stars.

Helena sighed and said, "You can come by again tomorrow."

Lurch bowed and said, "I too would like to speak to you again tomorrow."

Byllyn said something inaudible and incomprehensible.

Lil popped her head up from where she was playing and said, "Mowwo."

Lo knew that a normal woman would probably find the kid cute. Lo found her terrifying. She was the portent of a totally unimaginable future, one that Lo had no hope of controlling.

38

On her way back, jumping lightly from boat to boat, Lo ran into the Orbiter with the back-slash eyes and the tangled mess of claret hair—Rans. She landed very close to him, having not seen him bent down, tying the tarp on the back of a small speed boat that lay in a dark hollow between bigger boats. His bodcoz was a deep terracotta today, almost the same color as his skin. It made him look almost naked, naked and back-lit. She thought of clay-painted savages dancing around fires. Ancient hunter-gatherers. Earth back when. She shivered. Then the metal on the Orbiter's costume glinted, small diamond-shaped slivers of garnet in relief, and she thought of savages in space-ships, savages falling from the sky in metal boxes. Earth now. She shivered again.

"Was your visit successful?" Rans asked in the same polite manner as Lurch.

"It was okay."

"These days for me, okay is in fact good," said Rans.

"I know what you mean," she said. She smiled thinly, considering her next move out of this tangle of boats. She had planned to dash along the speed boat's tarp and spring up onto the front of the sleek yacht moored behind, but now Rans had stood up and was blocking her way. She was tempted to yell at him to move, but he spoke first.

"It is not yet late. Would you be interested in coming to see my boat? It is at the other end of the flotilla, but it is very interesting, a *schooner*, I think it is called. It can move on the water quite efficiently even when there is no power. It has sails."

"I used to sail boats like that when I was young," said Lo.

"Is that a yes?"

Lo looked into Rans's strange violet eyes—rich and dark in hue like the rest of him. They dared her. Her eyes considered the way his body strained against the fabric of his bodcoz. In spite of his serious and polite manner this was a big raw man, a man who lived like her, day by day, on his wits. Lo hadn't been with a man who was her equal in many years, if ever.

"No offense, but you're not my type," she said.

"No offense taken," said Rans, stepping back. "I just thought we might both appreciate a break from our burdens. Are we not all curious? Our bodies so different. Not to mention our minds. You Earth women are all so violent and crazy." He smiled, his great stretch of teeth glinting in the moonlight; challenging.

"I'll give you violent and crazy," said Lo raising her hand and making a back-handed motion, sweeping air out from under the big guy's feet. Rans fell sideways onto the tarpaulin. As he went down, he reached out and grabbed for Lo's leg, perhaps seeking support, perhaps not going down that easy. Lo lost her balance and fell on top of him. She moved to pin him down. He rolled away, pulling her with him, one arm pressed over her, now pinning her down—or so he thought.

"Stop it, stop the violence. It lessens you."

"Say another word," said Lo, breathing heavily, "and I'm going home."

Rans answered her by taking her throat in his mouth. Lo wasn't sure if he was going to bite, or suck, or kiss, and she didn't care. As they rolled into a dark dip in the tarpaulin, she just abandoned herself to whatever the alien was offering.

Afterwards she gave him five minutes of her time, a post-coital courtesy.

"This was just a spur of the moment thing, and just the one time, okay."

"What? You didn't like it? You seemed to like it."

Lo was glad it was dark. "I liked it fine, thank you. But once was enough."

"Your preference is for the other electric women?"

"Yeah, probably," Lo sighed. It was easier than explaining why she wasn't interested in him. The truth was it wasn't about the wires in her body; it was about how the wires connected to her brain. Rans was not Lurch, he was not Adrianna, he was not anybody she wanted. She felt ashamed for having so little control over her sexual urges. But she also felt good, both relaxed and energized. She *had* liked it.

"Well, thank you anyway, for sharing yourself with me."

"You're welcome, were welcome. I mean, that's it . . ."

"I understand," said Rans. He was clearly not offended.

"So see you round then," said Lo, zipping her pants as she leaped up and rushed away.

39

An hour later she stopped by Pat's. Pat's place represented the outermost point of safety along the river, as far as most women were concerned. Even though it rested well within the security borders, it was still within sight of the flats. The women had razed everything else between Pat's and the flats, and the area was now given over to cow meadows. Pat loved her home on the edge of the civilized world as they knew it—not that she took particularly good care of it. The pale yellow bungalow hadn't been renovated since the 1970s, one of the few homes in the area that had missed twenty-first century gentrification. After they resettled Saugatuck, Pat had had her choice of local mansions, but she said this place reminded her of her dead parents. It was still crammed full of stuff from the previous owners: knick-knacks, books, fishing tackle, and badly stuffed furniture in grimy shades of burgundy and beige. It suited Pat well. Today it seemed to suit Will, too. Stretched out on one of the couches, antimacassar at his head, Will looked more comfortable in the company of Pat than Lo could ever have ever imagined possible. They appeared to have grown accustomed to one another.

"How you doing, bro?"

Lo was still angry with Will, but she needed his help with the coming crisis. For the two weeks they had left, Will had promised to spend every day going to different towns: warning, explaining, reassuring. He and Pat had been strategizing for the best part of the day on how to tell women who had barely survived one invasion to prepare for another. It was one thing to shout out a message from within the safety of an orbicraft force-field, quite another to go face to face and meet the women you had royally screwed over for the sake of your political career. He would probably deserve it if they shot the messenger—but Lo couldn't afford to lose her brother before he'd helped her deal with their own incoming. Hence the pairing with Pat.

Will looked up from his sleepy contemplation. "To what do I owe this pleasure, Sis? Congrats on the results of the referendum, by the way—your charismatic leadership style won the day."

"You know just as well as the rest of us that Saugatuck needs a general right now, and not some bullshit shrink."

"Oh, come on," replied Will. "It's a challenging situation for sure, but nothing you can't handle. Last time I looked, you women were the ones with all the power."

Will made the sound of wires fizzing, pzzt, fzzz, as he threw his hands around mimicking and mocking the women with powers. Laughing in spite of herself, Lo threw a beam at her brother, zapping a tiny hole in the couch near his shoulder."

"You're such an idiot. How the fuck are we related?"

"Maybe we're not. Maybe we're both aliens."

Lo laughed again. "Speaking of aliens, I need to talk to you about Byllyn."

"Um, what about Byllyn?"

"She doesn't want to go back home with you. She's making a big drama of staying with the flotilla. So Adrianna's volunteered to go in her place. Lurch says they'll go crazy over her at your high council on account of her powers. Is that okay with you?"

"It is most certainly not okay. Adrianna's a nightmare. But I'll do it anyway. At this point I'd take James Nunn if you asked me. I just want to survive this experience."

"Stick to our deal, and you'll be fine. Just a couple more weeks of taking instruction and you'll be home free, rid of me once and for all."

"You know I still think you would have made a good lawyer, kid. You take no prisoners. You smile when people go down. You argue for the sheer hell of it. I would have loved to have seen you on courtroom TV."

"Yeah? Like you would have loved to have seen me graduate? You're so full of shit, Will. You missed my graduation. You didn't even call. Two days later the Ruurdaans came. You must have known they were coming—you worked at NASA—and still you didn't call."

"I *couldn't* call, Lo. We were locked down. Calling would have been an act of treason. What would I have told you, anyway? We had no idea what those spheres contained or what they meant, and even if we had, we were powerless..."

"Forget about it. I'm over it. I'm not waiting on an apology."

"Like I'm not expecting you to apologize for what you did to my crux?"

Lo went silent for a moment. Then she rushed to say it all at once. "Shit, Will. I *am* sorry. I erred way too far on the side of caution. I was paranoid. I was right to be concerned, of course, but I'm still very sorry I hurt you. They'll fix you when you get home, right? When they give you the knowledge gem? There's no permanent damage?"

"I don't know. They'll fix me, sure. But I doubt I'll get the knowledge gem now."

"Why not?"

"Um, fucked-up program, hijacked ship, rejected settlers. Need I go on?"

"I'm sorry I asked. Tell me again about the knowledge gem."

"It's the big gem that fits in the middle of your crux. When connected, it links you to the shared knowledge of all others with the gem, past and present. I'm told you cannot overestimate the pleasure of knowing. Like I said, though, I doubt I'll get it now. A lot depends on how Adrianna goes over with the High Council. She may not be Byllyn, but she is certainly unique. I hope they consider her some kind of treasure. I hope she tells them good things about me. I'm going to work on her better nature the whole way home. But you already know that."

"Yeah, I figured," laughed Lo. "Good luck with that."

Pat wandered out from the kitchen bearing a pile of baked potatoes on a tray.

"Congratulations, Lo," she said, "I knew the women would never go against you."

"Thanks for the vote of confidence." Maybe they hadn't turned against her today. It was true, what she'd said to Will; they still needed her to fight for them. But one day that would change, maybe one day soon. Lo turned her attention to the tray. Grated cheese and sour cream. They'd been making their own dairy products for over twenty years now—using milk from the herd of eighty cows grazing along the river bank—but cheese and cream were still considered special treats. Pat set the tray of food down on the old laminated coffee table and said, "Dig in."

"I see that Will has you mothering and spoiling him," said Lo.

"We all have to eat," said Pat. "Feeding him beats talking to him."

They all laughed and got down to the business of eating. Listening to Will and Pat banter companionably, trying not to think about Rans, savoring the salty butter and tangy cream, Lo couldn't help but smile. In spite of everything, she had had a pretty good day.

40

Will awoke to the continuous wailing of the Saugatuck general alarm. As he struggled out of sleep he realized that Pat was shaking him and shouting like the house was on fire.

"Wake up! They're here."

"Who?"

"Your buddies in the boxes."

"Shit, so early?"

The settlement program predictions were off by two weeks. He wasn't surprised; he had always known there was no guaranteed ETA. BPCs sprung through space via a kind of sonic rubberband technology, the elasticity of which created time variables over distance. He had just plain lied when he said they definitely still had two weeks (maybe, hopefully, four). Call it wishful thinking. He hadn't lied about the rest of it, though: there was no stopping a drop once it began, it would be over within twenty-four hours, and he couldn't be entirely sure about the landing site. Will remembered pointing to the line of the I95 on maps. Maybe he'd pointed out Exit 17—his old home exit. That whole area of highway was broken down now. Will had no idea how that would affect the drop. He hoped that a captain with a good eye had chosen a better stretch of I95.

"How far up are the boxes?" he asked Pat.

"There are boxes already on the ground. Near the Inn."

He jumped off the couch. "Shit, no!"

"Shit, yes! We need to go."

They rushed out of the house and ran for her pod, parked between a couple of cows in the meadow by Pat's bungalow. She didn't need to tell him how to get into the pod. They had spent some time the previous day practicing flying as one, prepping for their tour of the proposed settlement sites, a tour that probably

wasn't going to happen now. A small part of Will regretted that—
he'd come to care a little more for the women here on Earth. He
couldn't say exactly why, although he knew that familiarity fostered bonding. Or maybe Pat fostered bonding.

Within seconds of taking off, Will heard the unflappable
woman gasp. He couldn't see much with his face pressed into her
grey sweats, just the dizzying drop below them.

"Stretch up and look ahead to the left," she said.

As Will craned his head, Pat maneuvered the pod to help him.
They were flying above the river near HQ, with a clear view past
the bridge and over to the Inn. Even though the light was only just
coming up, you couldn't miss the flock of metallic-green cubes. The
drop boxes were floating slowly earthward in haphazard rows of ten.
The rows stretched miles high into the sky, each row spaced a couple
of football fields apart. The boxes were coming down between the
old broken section of the I95 and the sound—gliding toward the
beach at the Inn, the old golf course, the Inn itself, and of course the
pod complex. It was like that old game Tetris made real.

Pat said, "Apparently the first ten are down on the point,
just where it joins the river path. I guess that's a clear spot. But I
thought you directed them to the I95."

"I did. Maybe it looks too overgrown. The path must look like
a road at a distance, and the golf course is clearer than the rest of
the area. Maybe the dome creates an extra illusion of space near
the Inn."

"You said they'd be landing on the I95, Will. You said it with
conviction."

"Well I was wrong, Pat."

"Yes, but this is *very* wrong, buster."

Will contemplated the situation in silence for a moment. The
good news was that the children themselves were in no immediate danger. Nothing was going to hit that complex—a Ruurdaan
domed shield was definitely strong enough to protect it. The bad
news was that some of the boxes might hit the dome itself. If

that happened, they would bounce out of formation, possibly even into each other, putting the nannies and the Inn itself at risk. The women needed to evacuate immediately—without the children.

There was still quite a bit of time to salvage the situation. In total, the drop was going to take close to twelve hours. Each box that landed would sit on the ground for a lull period—somewhere between fifteen minutes and an hour—while its systems registered landfall and inactivity. Then the doors would release, the air would pour in, and the Orbiters would crawl out. That complex disembarkation process bought a little extra time too. It was unlikely that even one Orbiter was out of their box yet. Nevertheless, they weren't adequately prepared, and the situation was suddenly a lot more complicated. Lo was going to have to call Candace.

"This is your chance to put things right," said Pat as they dropped into a tight space at the pod-park. "You gotta lead these incoming aliens far away from here. Truth be told, my heart goes out to them, but they ain't welcome in Saugatuck, and that's that."

"I understand," said Will. "I'll do my best. And Pat..."

They were almost disentangled now, half-falling out through a large aperture that Pat had opened on the underside of her pod. "The best of luck to you too."

Pat squeezed him tight, with everything she had. He wished he was half the person she was. He also wished he was safe inside his orbicraft shielding.

Outside the pod, the scene was chaotic—women and pods everywhere. Lo was standing on top of her pod, clearly trying to simultaneously intercept messages and survey her crew as they gathered. About twenty women were standing around and more were running into the area every second. Will asked Pat for the time: 6:12 a.m. The dusky blue sky was streaked pink and yellow. The air was still chilly and damp. Everyone was shouting over everyone else and against the wail of the siren as they waited on Lo.

The shrill voice of Marie was the loudest. "They're landing on the children. We need to go. If I don't get my instructions in two minutes, I'm going without instructions."

Ruby screamed back at her, "Don't be a fucking idiot. You won't be much help to Carly if you're dead. Wait for instructions, Marie. Organization saves lives."

"But I'm getting messages from the nannies. The children are terrified."

"The children are protected. The nannies need to get out of there," said Ruby.

"What's happening with the children?" shouted Leslie as she came running into the park." What if the dome fails? They'll get squashed."

"Leslie is right. Forget about waiting for orders," shouted Marie.

Will saw Pat moving toward Marie, ready to restrain her if necessary.

"You've got a right to your feelings," she said, "but let's do this right, Marie." She turned to Leslie and said, "Are you sure you're okay to go up there, hon?"

"It's the children," said Leslie. "I have to be okay." She was shaking.

Lo's voice boomed as if through a microphone, over the shouting and the wailing of the siren. "Everyone settle down and wait for my goddamned orders. Yes, we need to act—but we need to act strategically. I don't want anyone dying under the weight of a falling box. The children are defended by their own dome. Any boxes that hit the dome should just bounce off into the surrounding area. I've had a couple of reports via beam from the flotilla, and that's what they're seeing from their position—boxes bouncing mid-air and rolling to the ground. So far nothing has landed in the water—although I fear it's only a matter of time. We can't just fly in there and help, though. We need to evaluate the situation first. Wait till the sky above a particular area is clear. Then we'll do it like we planned, just a bit faster, even if that makes it kind of rough for the people inside the boxes."

"I'm not waiting," shouted Marie.

"Just listen to me, Marie. You can't go all the way into the dome, but you can fly reconnaissance—if you promise to maintain a safe distance. Break that promise, and I'll bring you back in myself. We'll start with four pods. You. Me. I need two more."

Every woman's hand shot into the air.

Lo selected Pat and Adrianna. One of the women complained, but Marie told her to shut up—everyone knew those two were the very best. Lo instructed the rest of the crew to wait in the hole until called to duty. Who knew where those boxes would start landing next. Yaz was the only one who would be staying above ground, manning the comms station. Lo finished up with a word to them all.

"Thank you all for getting out here so fast. Record time, guys. I'm proud of your skill and courage, and we'll celebrate it once we're free and clear of the Orbiter threat. Before that, we have one hell of a day ahead of us. So get ready. Beam your families and tell them what's happening. Eat enough to keep you going for a long stretch in the pods. Get mentally prepared. And never forget, ladies, we are strong, we are invincible."

The entire crew roared. Adrianna released a volley of lightning.

Lo turned and addressed Will.

"Okay bro. You're with me. Let's go check out your buddies in the boxes."

Will couldn't believe she was pointing at the net.

"You can't be serious," he said. "I'll have zero protection."

"You'll have me," said Lo. "I need you in a position where you can speak to whoever, *whatever*, starts crawling out of those boxes. You speak Orbitaal, which may be critical to a peaceful intervention. Lurch says it's near impossible to think in a different language when you're crawling half-conscious out of a drop-box."

"Take Lurch, then, if you think he knows how to handle the situation."

"Lurch needs to move the flotilla," said Lo. "Aside from which, are you not a fucking ambassador? What did you think you would be doing during the drop, sitting down the hole drinking coffee with the ladies? This is your mess, Will, and you need to face up to it."

"How about I ride inside the pod with you?"

"No, it's hard to communicate from inside and too tight for two in this kind of situation."

Will knew better than to argue. He stepped into the net, faced away from the pod, and sat down on the ground. Déjà vu of the very worst kind.

"Stand facing the pod this time," said Lo. "I've made some adaptations."

As she opened an aperture in the top of her pod and slipped in, Lo asked that nobody except Yaz or the other pilots in the air beam her. Yaz would keep them informed. The women began shouting messages of good luck. This was really happening. They were flying into a settlement drop. He stood up and faced the back of the pod as instructed, his arms loosely wrapped around the smooth glass of the pod. How the hell was this going to work?

Suddenly he found himself pulled tight to the back of the pod, the net holding him snugly, just his head free and clear. It was almost like riding piggy-back. He could both see over the top of the clear domed glass and through onto Lo's sparkling golden head. His feet found purchase on a couple of unexpected indentations in the glass. He had never noticed any bumps in the glass before but now, everywhere his body pressed the glass, it made way for his shape. He could even find flexible handholds. The pod protected him from the wind, and his bodcoz protected him from the sun. It was better than his first experience in the net, but it was still going to be a terrifying ride out to the edge of the drop zone—out where the river met the sea.

Lo began her reconnaissance by making very wide circles of the area then slowly closing in on the boxes that were slowly but surely landing on the grounds of the Inn, the golf-course and the beach. Some were falling perilously close to the river. Others had already struck the dome, slid off the invisible barrier, and landed on the ground in a strange jumbled ring. Boxes upon boxes, about thirty so far.

Will watched in horror as ten incoming boxes all struck the dome at the wrong angle and bounced away. Five landed in the wooded area near the Inn. Five landed in the river. For now they just bobbed on the surface. Will knew that as soon as the seals burst open, the boxes would begin to sink. They had no flotation technology — the same design flaw that had resulted in the deaths in the Baltic Sea. Will had raised the issue with the council, but they just told him to make sure future drops were not over water; flotation technology was cost-prohibitive. Will tried to put a positive spin on the current situation. Orbiters could swim. The shore was very close. But doubts quickly overwhelmed him again. What if the boxes sank to the bottom before the doors opened? What if the doors opened up onto the ocean floor? What if people were too groggy to swim out even if the boxes were facing the right way up? Will wondered what Lo was thinking. Were they just going to leave them there?

Then Will saw Pat's pod swoop down and start trying to pull the boxes from the water. Trust Pat to go risking her own neck for a few aliens she pretended not to care about. He could hear Lo screaming inside the pod. He was sure she was beaming too: *no — too — dangerous.*

Either Pat wasn't listening, or she wasn't listening to Lo. She grabbed hold of one of the boxes and dragged it through the water toward Saugatuck Shores, where she dumped it in the reeds. Then she went back for another. Will could see that another row of boxes were already getting close, half of them headed toward the grounds of the Inn, the other half toward the river. Pat should move. Lo clearly had the same thought. Will sucked in deep as she swooped up high and began nudging the incoming boxes with her beam. She was trying to push them toward the relative safety of the wooded area between the dome and the river—but she wasn't very successful. She pushed the first box she tried to move smack dab into another. Both boxes tumbled toward the dome, bounced, then crash-landed together on the driveway of the Inn.

Will banged on the rubbery pod glass. "No. You're screwing up the trajectories. The boxes will crash into each other, crash-land. The people in there might get hurt."

Lo shouted, "Shut up. I can see they're crashing. I need to concentrate."

The pod swept down to the water. Lo began dragging one of the boxes toward the shore. Pat and Adrianna followed suit. Marie began pulling a box away from the edge of the dome. Will doubted that was her instruction, but he understood her motivation. They worked in anxious silence. The next row of boxes was now about four minutes from their air space. Will's face felt cold in the cooler upper air and hot with fear at the same time. They were so close to the falling boxes. They were hopelessly outnumbered. They needed help. As if on demand, he saw the rest of the security crew—almost forty pods—charging up over the river. Bob was with them, strapped to Janine's pod. The idiot had probably volunteered to help.

Within minutes the entire crew was working to a system of some sort. Rescue pods retrieved boxes that had landed in the water and dragged them to shore. Defense pods pushed falling boxes away from the rescue pods. Another small group worked at moving boxes that were safely on the ground—tugging, wobbling, and heaving them up and through the air—about a half mile away to the interior edge of the old golf course. Those woods might be dense and unpleasant, but they were still within Saugatuck's booby-trapped borders. When the Orbiters came out of the boxes, they would be greeted, prepped, then sent further away. If they were lucky, their boxes would come later. Will knew all this because he could hear Lo talking as she beamed. But she had no real plan. Lo was working mostly on instinct now.

Meanwhile, the boxes continued to fall from the sky, littering the ground with shiny green metal. The slow-motion rain of cubes was strangely beautiful, Will couldn't help but observe. Shame about the disastrous landing. It was only a matter of time before someone got hurt. Sure enough, minutes later an incoming box clipped one of the pods. The pod staggered then dropped, rolling and spinning, toward the small beach in front of the Inn. Lo swooped, ducking and weaving, but she was too late. The pod slammed into the beach with a great thud, creating a deep crater in the sand. The flier had kept enough control that the shield held. They were lucky they hadn't hit one of the boxes; the beach was now littered with them, like someone was about to start a building project.

As soon as they were close enough, Will saw that the downed flier was Marie, slumped in her cracked pod. Lo scooped the fallen pod up in her beam and whisked the feather-light craft away. Flying as one now, the two pods sped back to the edge of the pod complex, passing through the dome as if it didn't exist. Lo dropped Marie softly on the lawn by the great tower of glass bubbles then darted away again. Clearly she thought Marie would be safe with the children. Will wished she would put him down somewhere safe—although not with those children.

Instead, Lo just kept flying, ducking and diving as the boxes dropped, with seemingly little regard for Will's comfort and safety. As she worked she seemed to get better at moving the boxes in the air, controlling their landings just enough to make the difference. However, she just couldn't move those boxes once they were on the ground. It was as if the people in them weighed a thousand pounds (Will had told her she wouldn't learn much from practicing on that empty unshielded box). Eventually she focused on simply making sure the boxes landed safely outside the dome without hitting each other. After about an hour of doing so she flew away to the checkpoint in the river, created a jagged fracture in the glass and asked him how he was doing.

"Are you all right," she yelled.

"No," said Will. "I'm terrified and uncomfortable."

"Join the club."

"Couldn't you just drop me back at HQ? I can help prep the ground crew. We're going to have to walk the settlers out of Saugatuck now. We need to create maps..."

"No. As soon as the first Orbiter crawls out of their box, I'll need you to talk to them."

"They may not listen to me, strapped to a Ruurdaan pod like this. I'll just scare them."

"I want them to be scared. They need to do what we say and get away from the Inn. They've spooked the kids. I'm worried that something is going to happen."

Will started to speak but Lo raised her hand. "I'm receiving a message from Adrianna. It's exactly what I feared. The boxes nearest to the Inn are starting to open, and the children are gathering around. We need to get there immediately. Get ready to talk. Tell the Orbiters to stick to clear roadways. Walk away from the water, through the golf course, until they reach Beach Road. Turn right and keep walking until they hit the car park at the town beach. We keep it clear for the pods. There's a nice strip of beach there, but they must be careful. Everything north of the old pavilion is booby-trapped. We'll send ground crew on motorbikes to guide them. First sign of any trouble though and the pods will be over there beaming their asses into the Sound. You'd better make that very clear to these people."

Will didn't have a chance to reply. Lo closed the fractured opening and dashed skyward. Within seconds they were hovering over the Inn. The children had all come out of their pods and were wandering around the boxes—which covered all the lawn space, most of the visible golf course, the old parking lot, the road through the grounds, and the small private beach by the Inn— absolutely everywhere. A couple of boxes even landed in the old club swimming pool. If it hadn't been for the efforts of the women, many boxes would have crashed into the Inn itself. Boxes poked out of the battered shrubbery and balanced precariously on the upper deck.

About sixty of the big metal crates already lay open on the ground; others were opening before their eyes. Tall figures in colorful bodcoz scrambled out of the hatches and staggered around the bizarre scene. White coz and chalky features identified the Pure among them. They all looked dazed. They didn't seem to comprehend the presence of the little people that had come out to greet them. Will thought that the average Orbiter would have learned about Ruurdaans in school—but the children didn't look quite like Ruurdaans—the way dolphins don't look quite like sharks. The people staggering out of the boxes looked more confused than scared.

Will banged on the glass and pointed downwards. He made what he hoped was a clear hovering motion with his hand and shouted, "Don't land." Lo swooped low and hovered over the greatest concentration of people. Will began to shout in Orbitaal.

"I am Ambassador Wl-Wrrn of the Earth Settlement Program. You have landed in the wrong location. Please start moving down the nearest clear path. Help is coming. *Please start moving immediately.* You need to move away from the children."

The Orbiters looked up, confused at the unfamiliar sight of a Ruurdaan pod, not quite understanding why someone was strapped to it shouting in Orbitaal. Will just kept repeating himself. *For your own safety—start moving immediately.* A few Orbiters began stumbling in the direction of the main road leading out of the golf course. The rest seemed too stunned to move. Will watched in terror as the children drew closer.

"Vlt," he shouted in Orbitaal. Then again in English: "Run!"

It was too late.

The Orbiter sitting atop his box probably felt quite safe up there on high, protected by his fluorescent pink bodcoz. He smiled and waved as a small girl wearing nothing but a floral swimsuit approached. The little girl raised her hand into the air. The guy's head flip-flopped from side-to-side. Will heard the bones snapping. Then the child threw his body through the air in the direction of the Sound, right over the top of the Inn. The settlers' bodcoz were supposed to have light defense technology, but Will already knew it was useless against the children.

Now the same small girl wandered up to another Orbiter, this time in white, standing in a daze on the ground by his box. Before the man could even begin to smile she had twisted his neck till his head pointed backwards. She then pressed his body deep into the ground as if pushing her thumb into putty. The child looked up and stared at them for a moment before moving on. She converged upon another hatch, just beginning to open, with another little silver-domed friend. They were all trawling around the boxes now, hunting their prey.

Will was about to start screaming in Orbitaal when he felt the pod swoop away. Lo began darting up and down into the groups of children like a mosquito. She quickly found what she was look-ing for—Mira. Today dear cousin Mira was attempting to smelt an unopened box down to its basic elements. Lo said nothing, but Will could see her body tensing in concentration. He didn't know what kind of exchange passed between the two. He just felt it as they were repelled a couple of hundred feet into the air, right past another row of incoming boxes. Even in his terror, Will knew that they had been lucky; Mira had spared them, spared them from smelting, burning, twisting, pulverizing, liquidizing, and whatever else the others were doing. He began to shake involuntarily.

As they hovered in shock, Will saw Marie leap out of her pod—still parked on the grass by the pod complex—and run toward a small, ruddy-featured girl wearing a pair of old dunga-rees. The child was busy compressing a white-clad Orbiter from head to toe, blood spraying her like she was squeezing a perforated bag of red paint. The child had a satisfied smile on her face. Marie shouted as she ran towards her. "No, Carly, no. You mustn't kill people. It hurts them. Come to Mommy. I'll get you more silver, like you asked. Mommy promises."

Carly turned, looked at Marie in puzzlement, picked her up, and flung her back into the great mound of pods the children called home. Marie landed funny; her head slammed back into one of the wired joins between glass bubbles. As her body slid to the ground, a bloody smear streaked the glass. Carly did not move to help her mother. Instead, she looked up at them and hissed, her breath rocking the pod like turbulence. Will screamed at the top of his lungs. Thankfully, Lo kept a cooler head. She maneuvered the pod away to a position of safety—away from Carly—and set her beam to work, drawing Marie's slumped body toward them. Within seconds the poor woman was floating ten feet below him. Will couldn't help but see. Her skull was smashed, and her body floppy. She was dead. She'd died trying to save Carly's soul.

Lo flew across to HQ and gently dropped Marie's body into the arms of Yaz and Helena, waiting on the lawn. Whatever they planned to do, it was an exercise in futility. Will shouted to Lo that it was time to give up. She was risking all their lives staying there. The least she could do was drop him off too. Within two minutes they were both back darting in and out of the boxes, attempting to pluck Orbiters to safety. Will sensed that Lo was not going to let those children kill just like they were little Ruurdaans, not without a battle. It was a losing battle however, especially after the Orbiters began switching on their defense systems. How ironic that the very systems that blocked the women trying to help them were totally useless against the children.

If you could even call these murderous savages children. Although they appeared to distinguish between Orbiters—who they killed—and Saugatuckers, including their nannies—who they just flung out of their way—their violence was beyond human pathology. Strangulation, crushing, decapitation, electrocution—it was as if the children were experimenting with their repertoire.

They took their time, nothing frenzied about what they did, but they kept a real pace. Will saw only one sign of empathy or conscience in the carnage. A group of children had gathered around an Orbiter mother and a child of about Lil's age, both in bright white bodcoz. Mother and child cowered in fear before the blood-spattered children. The children seemed to confer a moment before plucking the child from its mother's arms and throwing it up towards a hovering pod. Ruby caught the child in her beam and raced her away. The children then turned and ripped the mother limb from limb, throwing the pieces of her dismembered body back into the box, which they then smelt into a lump the size of an armchair.

Lo and her crew could do nothing to stop the children now — although they all kept trying. The nannies were all podded out of there. The fliers also kept trying to grab Orbiters before the children could get to them. Will shouted instructions at the opening boxes until his voice was nothing but a rasp. Eventually a small line of Orbiters could be seen making their way to the safety of the town beach car park. At least Will hoped it was safe. He feared that the children might begin to follow their prey. In fact the only thing he thought would finally stop them was sheer exhaustion. For now, though, the killing just seemed to energize them. They almost seemed to be competing to reach the next descending box.

About two hours after the first box had landed, without warning, Lo turned away from the drop zone and headed back to HQ, the rest of the pods following. As soon as they landed, he struggled to disentangle his cramped body from the netting and slumped onto the strip of lawn between the pod-park and the river. The left arm of his bodcoz was flecked with vomit from when he had seen a child press an Orbiter's head until the brains burst through top of his skull in an arc of blood and tissue. Will had committed violence in his own life, but this was something else — this was blood sport. He heard Lo's broken voice shouting to her crew.

"I called everyone in because we need to make a decision."

He looked up. Lo was standing on top of her pod. Almost everyone else was flopped on the ground. Women rushed to assist the weary crew, bearing damp cloths, food, and water. Will reached out for a glass of orange juice and a hunk of bread and called for a bucket of water to clean himself with. Lo pulled a glass of water through the air, slugged it back in one giant gulp, spat half of it back up, then continued.

"Okay, so we think we have about eight hours more of this shit to go. The big question is, do we continue risking our lives to save Orbiters, or do we just let this thing take its natural course? The children are currently beyond our control. I think they're going to keep going until they've killed every last incoming settler within whatever they perceive to be their zone. They're quite capable of killing us too. Don't think otherwise for a second. They've already crossed that line, and I think they'd do it again if any more of us got too close. So what do we do now?"

Lo paused, allowing the space for someone else to speak. Nobody said a word.

"Okay, so we've already airlifted about sixty Orbiters out of the drop zone. That's a real achievement, given how hard they're resisting our help. They're scared. As soon as we try to grab them they activate their defense shielding, and now they've taken to hiding in their boxes—which, as we all know, are a complete bitch to move. Will and Bob have shouted themselves hoarse trying to talk to them, but they're just not listening. They think those boxes are the safest place in the world. Only now instead of killing the Orbiters as they emerge from their boxes, the children are either smelting the boxes down to nothing or throwing them into the sea. If we want to save these people, we're now going to have to move those fucking boxes."

Again Lo paused, this time to shake her head and close her eyes for a moment.

"Let's talk hard truths. Marie is dead, and we've lost three other pods. Two are lying damaged near the Inn, but the fliers don't dare get out, and the children won't let us approach. When she tried, Leslie was thrown through the air almost as far as the checkpoint in the river. She got away with a broken arm, but she could have died. That's why I called you all in. I don't feel right about ordering you to risk your lives for a bunch of invaders we don't want here anyway."

A couple of the women cheered. Lo shook her head.

"On the other hand—you've seen them—those are real people in there. I feel sick thinking about what it's like to be crushed or baked or even boiled inside a box, or sink to the bottom of the ocean and slowly run out of air. How can we let the children just do that? It's like standing by and watching the Ruurdaans do what they did all over again."

Murmuring rolled across the crowd. Someone called out, "Don't you dare compare our children to the Ruurdaans. That's outrageous. They're victims."

Lo waved the point away. "That's a debate we definitely need to have later, but for now I just don't think I can stand by and let the children kill those unarmed people. I know that might sound like a turn-around, but for me this isn't a political issue anymore. We're dealing with a humanitarian crisis. There are women and children in those boxes. But I'm only speaking for myself now. You all have to make your own decisions—that will always be the way we do it here in Saugatuck. If you want to stand down, please stand down now. I won't judge you for it."

With that, eight of the women walked away from their pods— one of them crying that she was sorry, the children were evil, she didn't sign up to save aliens, she couldn't control her pod much longer, it was turning into a suicide mission. Another shook her fist at Lo and shouted that she was working for the aliens against their own children. One held her hands up in apology as she walked away, saying that she wasn't prepared to die saving strangers.

Lo shouted after them, "You don't have to apologize. This isn't easy."

A couple of the women turned and waved in appreciation. Most just kept walking.

The thirty remaining crew women stood firm beside their pods. Will was surprised to see that Bob remained with them, standing with his arm around Janine. He wouldn't have blamed the guy for abandoning the Orbiters to their fate. Who knew he was brave? Will didn't move either.

An awkward silence had descended as the eight left. Now Pat shouted loudly.

"I didn't vote to accept any of these damned aliens, but I'm still not gonna stand around and watch 'em get slaughtered. So just give me my orders, Lo. I want to finish this thing."

The remaining crew cheered loudly.

"Yeah, let's finish this thing."

"Those people need us."

"We can do this. We just need to dig deeper into our powers."

Lo seemed bolstered by their energy. She began shouting orders, back to her default personality. "Okay then. Pat, choose a team to go rescue our lost pods."

Pat shouted out to Janine and Ruby, who nodded.

Adrianna shouted, "Me too, Pat. I'm not scared of those fucking little weirdos."

Lo responded, "Don't think like that Adrianna. You *should* be scared of those little weirdos. They're stronger than us. And anyway, I need you to go out to the flotilla and see if any of Lurch's people will come out on the pods with us. The Orbiters don't seem to understand what we're saying. We need people who speak Orbitaal. And, everyone else—keep working in your teams to move the boxes to the nearest point of safety—but avoid the children wherever you see them, and keep beaming your numbers in to Yaz so that she can beam them to me. The minute we are done, we are getting the hell away from that, that, *killing field*."

"Let's do it," shouted Adrianna, leaping into her pod and taking off.

Will sighed and waited for his own instructions. No doubt Lo had no plans to release him from his involuntary duty. As the rest of the women began getting back into their pods and launching themselves back into the warm blue summer sky, he sighed and hauled himself up off the ground. As he moved toward the back of Lo's pod, she looked down and stared into his eyes.

"Like I said, bro. It's all voluntary from here on out. You can continue trying to save your adopted people if you like, but I'm not going to make you. Consider yourself officially free to go down the hole with the rest of the ladies who can't fight or don't have the guts to try."

Well, when she put it like that. Will stepped forward and into the net.

"Let's finish this thing," he yelled.

41

The next morning, around ten o'clock on another bright summer's day, Lo stood before a group of about five hundred women at the town amphitheater and reported on the situation. Not a single drop-box was left at the Inn or in the surrounding area. Most of the boxes were at the bottom of Long Island Sound—where the children had continued to throw them, empty or full, compressed or intact, until they were done at around two o'clock in the morning. About one hundred and fifty boxes had been moved to safer ground. That was largely thanks to IBM City. Candace and fifty others had arrived to help about three hours into the disaster. The help was appreciated, but it was still not enough. The work was hard and took coordination. Also, no one could hang around once a child arrived on the scene—the children could now fling a pod out beyond Cockenoe with one sweeping backhand motion.

. This morning the children were back at work in their pods as if nothing had ever happened. At daybreak Lo had allowed the nannies to approach them with milk and bread. They had accepted the breakfast and exchanged the usual morning greetings but refused to go on the regular post-breakfast run. When queried on what had happened, all the children had just beamed the same simple message: *all—safe—now.*

The nannies had chosen to let the subject go. They'd asked if they would be willing to bathe. *After dinner*, came the reply. The children bathed after dinner every day.

Every day except yesterday.

The only good news was that the Orbiter survivors were in the process of relocation to an abandoned home for the elderly just a mile or two down the road from the Inn—outside the border and well away from the children. The flotilla people were assisting. Just as soon as this meeting was done Lo would be heading there to evaluate the situation. Pat and Yaz would remain on hand to address all the many issues Lo knew the women would be raising. Lo hoped her people would understand why she was keeping this particular announcement short. The practicalities had to come first. She knew that there was so much more that needed saying—but the saying of it would just have to wait. For now the best she could do was keep her people informed.

Lo gave them the straight facts. Only 327 survivors were known; 674 others were presumed dead, most of them Pure Orbiters, one of them Marie Nunn. One of Candace's crew had also died when her pod crashed into the river and disintegrated. Another five were being treated by Helena for crash injuries.

There was just one thing she chose not to say out loud, a simple sum that they could all do right now if they wished, and probably would all do in time: $674 \div 43$.

Sixteen orbiters per child.

42

Two long days later, Lo was sitting at the meeting table in her office at HQ with Yaz, Pat, and Helena. Outside, the day was bright green and blue, prisms of light glinting off the weedy river and lush grass. It had been a beautiful summer. Lo could hear the buzz of activity down at the dock through the open window—Lurch's flotilla community were slowly but surely moving into town—and she could see the red spikes of Ruby's hair as she sat with a couple of other women at the registration tables on the lawn. The women were busy processing the Orbiters as they arrived—typing their details into laptops. The printing of any lists would come later. Paper was scarce and printer cartridges even scarcer. The muster would be a treasured document for the archives—noting that in Year 30 Saugatuck had admitted 187 new residents—144 of them Orbiters, 141 of them men.

Lo tried not to dwell on the strange sight of men around the place: reedy hairless blondes, thick hirsute brunettes, colorful hybrids. If she'd imagined for half a second that the flotilla people would be moving to town, she wouldn't have fraternized with that Rans. She dreaded running into him. It wasn't so much the awkwardness between them she feared as the thought of the other women noticing.

Earth to Lo, Yaz beamed with a little zap, making her jump.

Lo snapped to attention. Helena was saying something about trying to find old Adele CDs to play at Marie Nunn's funeral. Yaz was going to make the basic arrangements. Helena thought everyone should contribute something personal to the event: a poem, a picture, a story. Lo had agreed to sit with Reid, Helena, and James Nunn, like a proper blended family. Her personal contribution was a lie. Nothing was ever going to make them all family again. James Nunn was still nothing but a sperm donor. She and Helena were over, they just hadn't said the words yet. Reid no longer even acknowledged that she had once been his mother too.

Lo forced herself out of her funk. This funeral was important, and it wasn't about her. She didn't need Helena or Yaz to tell her that. The crew and the community needed to share their grief, express their feelings. That was how others began to heal. Lo tuned in to Yaz, who was saying that she had organized a plot for Marie in the memorial section of the gardens. There would be a small plaque and a new hybrid rose called Carly-Marie. That sounded nice—which was a lot more than you could say about the real Carly, the Carly who'd killed her own mother like she was a mosquito, the Carly with blood under her fingernails.

"So, where do we stand on the issue of the children?" she asked, cutting Yaz off.

"I hate to say it, but I think we have to deprogram them, ASAP," said Pat.

"My heart is heavy, but I agree" said Yaz. "However, we can't do it without clear majority support. Do you hear me, Lo? We have to at least listen to the nannies."

"They'll never agree, even after what's happened," said Lo.

"It doesn't matter. They just need to get their due process. A vote."

"But I don't know what the majority will decide. Not everyone saw what we saw. I've already heard people say that the children were just defending themselves. What if the women demand long investigations and research committees? I'm scared that if the children get wind of our plans they'll kill us before we try anything."

"So what are you suggesting," said Helena, "that we creep out there at night and lobotomize them? What would that make us?"

"I think Lo is right," said Pat. "The children pose a real threat."

"But…"

Helena was interrupted by Ruby, who rushed through the door without knocking. "There's unauthorized activity on the dock. Should I sound the alarm?"

The women jumped up and pushed through the French doors onto the front balcony. They all leaned out over the railing. Lo half expected another hail of boxes. Instead she saw the skewed silvery pyramid of an orbicraft down at the dock. The regular boats had been pushed from their moorings into the middle of the river; captains were shouting from their posts. There were no obvious injuries, though. Nobody had been hurt. It was a lot like last time, only this time Lo wasn't running down there shooting.

"Hold off on the alarm for a few minutes," she said. "But stand on alert."

It must be Will's colleagues come to collect him at last, thought Lo as the door opened and the gangplank unfurled. She expected some new variation on the Orbiter theme, tall and colorful. Instead she saw a bald, silver-suited version of Bob strolling down the strange metallic gangplank. Lo experienced a sudden blast of intuition. She glanced across the river and saw that the original orbicraft was no longer there. This was Will's orbicraft—the supposedly inaccessible one—now apparently piloted by Bob. As she was considering the implications of that, she saw the distinctive blonde features of Janine appear at the door of the orbicraft. What the fuck?

Janine was carrying a bunch of large clear bags filled with what looked like big liquid-centered marbles. She walked down the gangplank and threw the bags onto the lawn by the dock. Then she went back for more. Bald, silver Bob walked to the edge of the jetty where it met the lawn. He looked up to the deck and waved at them all, beckoning them down. The light caught upon something sparkling on his head. Lo got it at once. She looked over at Yaz, leaning further along on the railing. "Beam Adrianna out at the flotilla. Tell her to bring Lurch. Byllyn should come too. Where's Will?"

Pat answered. "He's with the settlers out at Evergreen Manse."

Evergreen Manse. Last week an abandoned old people's home just beyond the perimeter. This week a refugee center, just within the perimeter. Will had been working around the clock helping the traumatized survivors set up camp. He'd worked so hard he'd almost ingratiated himself back into the women's hearts. Pat seemed to think he'd found a conscience. Lo doubted it, although there was no denying his contribution. They could have actually used him a little longer. Was this it now? Was he finally leaving?

"Get a message to Evergreen and tell them to bring Will. His ride is here."

As she said it, Lo felt a strong sense of unease. How could Bob be Will's ride? If that was the case then they could have left at any time in the last week. It made no sense.

She beamed Janine, still busy moving bags: *what—happening.*

Janine glanced up and gestured with her head.

come—down—talk—me

said—what—up

heard—you—come—down

Now Lo knew something was wrong.

"Yaz, perhaps we should sound—" she began.

Helena cut her off. "Not this time, Lo. The women's nerves are already raw. Let's talk to Bob and Janine before we hit the alarm and initiate another crisis."

Lo said, "I don't initiate crises, Helena. I just get stuck dealing with them."

Helena shrugged and smiled like she didn't particularly care. A week ago Lo had been about the biggest thing in Helena's life. Now she felt like nothing and nobody. Byllyn and Lil had taken her place in Helena's heart pretty quickly. Lo knew she should be happy for her, knew Helena deserved the warmth and love she couldn't provide, but still...*one week.*

Lo saw that a curious crowd had started to gather on the lawn: women on duty, women who had come out to see what was going on in the river, Orbiters signing their entry papers. All thirty of them seemed to be looking around for guidance, looking for Lo.

"Who's coming with me?" she asked as she jumped over the railing, landing with a bounce on the lawn below. Pat followed, although not so gracefully. Yaz and Helena would have to follow via the stairs. Lo jogged out in front of Pat, parting the crowd, who were creeping closer to the dock by the second. To think that a week ago the sight of that spaceship had everyone cowering in their basements. Were they getting used to aliens?

Fifty feet from the beginning of the dock Lo hit a flexible force-field. She struck the surface with her knee and sprang back twenty feet onto the grass, landing a little awkwardly. Shit, the field was bigger than last time. Catching her balance and stretching back upright, Lo took in the situation. Up close she could see that Bob had a complete orbital crux on his skull, one with a big blue knowledge gem in the middle. The head art spoke of power and influence. It also screamed deception and abuse of trust. Lo suspected Bob was well-defended, but she raised her gloved hand and shot at him anyway. The beam reverberated around the field.

"Don't waste your energy," said Bob.

"Aren't you the surprise," said Lo. "Why didn't you tell us about your crux before now? You could have saved us two days traveling to Madison and IBM, plus a whole lot of other grief. I'm assuming that you could have opened up that ship all along?"

"Sure, but I had no interest in your political wranglings with your brother and the others. I didn't want to get involved in all that unpleasantness," replied Bob.

"So why are you even still here?"

"I came to see things. I've seen. Now I'm leaving."

"And taking Will with you, right?"

Bob laughed. Janine, standing behind him, smiled knowingly.

"Oh I don't think so, Lo. You ladies can keep that one. I'm here for Adrianna. I had originally planned to take Byllyn home with me, but I'm willing to honor your latest choice. You agreed upon Adrianna, right? She'll certainly liven up high table."

"Yes, but what about Will? Aren't you working together?"

"Hardly."

"I don't understand."

"Just call Adrianna and Will for me, please. I'll explain when the gang's all here."

His tone was polite, but the words were insolent. She was about to say something when Janine stepped forward and said, "Hey, what are you talking about? You said there wasn't any spare room when I asked about Leslie. How are we going to fit Adrianna?"

Bob shrugged his shoulders and said, "I'm sorry to have to tell you this way, Janine, but I am *only* taking Adrianna. It'll be easier that way. You've become too attached, and I'm afraid I can't offer you anything longer term. It was pleasant for a couple of weeks, but…"

Janine fixed her round blue eyes on Bob in a hard interrogative stare, her mouth quivering in anger. "Too attached! You said you couldn't imagine life without me."

Bob said, "I'm sorry if you feel misled, but you definitely begged for it, Janine."

Lo could see the sparking ends of Janine's wires. She was thinking so hard she was exploding. Lo hoped she was thinking about her court martial.

She heard Ruby shout, "You've been plotting with this guy? You desperate, stupid idiot. How could you? You should be kicked out of Saugatuck."

Other women in the crowd shouted their agreement, but even more of them began screaming abuse at Bob. *User. Liar. Loser. Scrote.* They were creeping ever closer to the drama, drawing in to a tight semi-circle around Lo. Lo saw one of the Orbiters, the blond Orbiter called Blr, pulling an anxious Leslie back, but others pressed in. Feeling claustrophobic, Lo flung her arms out on either side and indicated to the crowd to back up. Her arm movements generated a thick wave of air. The crowd retreated about twenty feet.

Janine remained frozen in place, staring at Bob. He raised his arms once again in an apologetic shrug. Lo thought she saw a hint of a smirk. Janine must have seen it too, because suddenly, in a flash of sparks, she flung herself at him. Lo wondered if she had a chance against an Orbiter with a working crux—inside a force field. She did not. One minute she was raising her hand, the next she was lying sprawled on the lawn at Lo's feet. As far as Lo could see, Bob had done nothing more than blink. She wasn't sure whether he had instructed the ship's defense system to spit her beyond the force-field, or whether the ship had done that by itself.

Janine picked herself up off the grass, flung herself against the force-field, and began screaming. "You promised you weren't just using me. You promised we'd be together." And then to the crowd: "I double- and triple-checked him. I didn't see anything, no wires, nothing. I don't understand how he fooled me."

"Remember how I told you my heart is on the wrong side?" said Bob.

Janine nodded.

"Mirroring camouflage," he said. "So don't blame yourself on that score."

"I don't blame myself. You suckered me all the way."

Bob shrugged as he gathered up the last bag of clear plastic balls lying on the dock and threw it over to the knee-high pile on the lawn. Lo exploded in fury at his calm arrogance. First she fired at the force-field, aiming straight at his groin. Then she tried throwing herself at the shield, all systems blazing, hoping to work some small rend into the invisible substance. Like Janine, she bounced right back to her feet on the lawn.

Bob laughed. "You'll hurt yourself if you keep that up—and she's not worth it."

Janine began sobbing her heart out.

"Shut up, Janine, you're demeaning yourself."

Janine shut up, scared now, as well she should be. Lo was burning up with rage. She turned to Bob. "Did Janine use her security clearance to help you?" She didn't really need to ask—but she wanted everyone to hear the answer.

312 / Jackie Hatton

"Of course she did. She liked what I was offering—a trip to a big civilized world with food and entertainment and consumer goods and a social life with men in it. Can you blame her for wanting out of the situation here in Saugatuck? I mean, it's not just a question of feeling like you're missing out—it's also about having your life run by a paranoid dictator."

Lo had been called so much worse. "That's easy to say for someone who lives their life behind force-fields. Go spend half an hour naked in the woods around here and then come back and say that shit to me." She turned to Janine. "And as for you, you sniveling traitor."

Janine said, "It wasn't like he's making out. He's twisting my thoughts."

Like hell he was. Swinging her glove hand wildly in the air, Lo grabbed Janine and dragged her up through the air. Then she flexed her hand in the direction of the dock.

"Have her back—she's sure as hell not wanted around here anymore."

"No," shouted a number of the women in unison. Lo heard Helena's voice.

Too late. Lo hurled Janine backwards into the force-field—which absorbed the heavy impact of her body and threw her back out again, hard. Janine slumped to the ground. For a moment she didn't move, and they all held their breath. A second later she groggily pulled herself up into a sitting position on the grass, her back up against the force-field.

"What the hell," she said to Lo. "I'm so sick of how you treat me. I've been risking my ass on your say-so forever. You choose me for every dangerous mission because I'm so good at what I do, but then you diss me because I'm popular. I've been following your orders for thirty years, Lo. So what if sometimes I draw the line at things like shooting at people. I think I've earned the right to make those kind of decisions for myself. I'm a fifty-five-year-old woman. I'm not some stupid bimbo."

"Not anymore. Now you're a treacherous bimbo."

"How dare you say that to me when you do the same thing all the time? You think we don't know, but we all know. Teenage boys, how sick is that? The guy at the power-station. God only knows how many Orbiters. I know you can't help yourself. I've seen you making eyes at Lurch. How is what I did any different?"

The crowd fell silent. It didn't matter that the accusations had no bearing on Janine's own gross misconduct. They had the potential to change the wind of opinion. Lo turned to Pat.

"Arrest her," she said. "The charge is breaking the oath."

She stared at Janine. "You can say whatever you like at your trial."

She turned back to Pat. "I'm serious, arrest her. She's betrayed us all."

For a horrible second Lo feared her deputy was going to let her down—but then Pat stepped forward, leaned over, and gently placed her hand on Janine's shoulder.

"Real sorry, honey, but you're under arrest."

Janine dissolved into a great heap of sobs on the lawn.

"Oh, just get her out of my sight," said Lo.

The truth was she didn't want her lying there gathering sympathy.

43

As Pat led Janine away, Lo looked to see how much support she had in the crowd. A number of her crew raised their fists. One of them even made a knife gesture across her throat. Adrianna spat on the ground in front of her friend as she stumbled by with Pat. Helena and Yaz, however, along with a significant number of the others, looked genuinely shocked and horrified. First those accusations. Then the peremptory arrest. Lo knew she was going to have a lot of explaining to do when the dust settled. For now, though, she would just have to front it out. Someone always had to lead.

Surveying the crowd, Lo saw that Lurch had arrived with Adrianna. Lo and Lurch had spent many hours working together these last couple of days, training the flotilla people to help the incoming Orbiters and discussing the logistics of integrating the flotilla into Saugatuck. They had also talked about his ideas for rebooting old medical and analytic tools and re-automating some key services, like sprinkler systems in the greenhouses and street-lighting. It had turned out Lurch really was a clever inventor. They'd gotten over the awkwardness of that night in IBM City, developed a respectful working relationship. Respect was not what Lo saw in Lurch's eyes now, though. Yeah, well how dare he, after how much she had helped him and his people? None of this was her fault. A week ago their world had been ticking along very nicely, thank you.

She looked across at the dock and shouted at Bob, "Why? Why do this to us?"

Bob replied calmly. "Don't blame me for the problems you're having with your people. Don't even blame me for the problem with the Orbiters. I didn't send them. I'm only here checking things out, considering the future of the settlement program, developing a better understanding of the situation here, making some native friends…"

"So why the big disguise? You could've just told us…"

It wasn't Lo speaking. It was Will, maneuvering his way to the front of the crowd. He looked very different than he had a week ago—ruddier, messier. His grey bodcoz was covered in builder's dust. His hair was disheveled. Everyone fell silent.

Bob greeted Will. "There you are. I was hoping to see you before I left."

"Answer my question. Why are you in disguise? I find that very odd."

"I wanted to make people feel comfortable around me. You included."

"Who are you really?"

"Nobody important, just an Orbiter—well okay, a Trust member—doing their job. Part of which is to tell you that you won't be heading home any time soon. You've been reassigned to Earth. I'm sorry about that. It wasn't my decision, and it's not personal."

Will's entire body stiffened. "I don't understand. I'm the face of the Earth Settlement Program. I'm critical to recruitment and strategy—back home."

"There are those who beg to differ, Wl-Wrrn," said Bob. "The High Council thinks you've become a PR liability. All you've done is sign up a bunch of Pure and Unans. You're very unpopular with regular Orbiters. And that's why the program is failing on the ground. You sent the wrong settlers. They're a bad mix, and the natives don't like them. At the rate this thing is going we're going, to lose half of every dispatch we send. And who can blame the women survivors? We're sending them our very worst. The mandate was to develop new potential Orbital habitats that might offer a viable solution to overcrowding—not establish a prison or religious colony."

"What's going to happen to me? Am I still an ambassador, an Orbiter?"

"Oh, sure. Don't worry. You haven't been fired, like I said, just reassigned. You're an Ambassador-in-situ now, same as Retske, although to be honest, I'm not entirely sure about *her* future. But anyway, *you* are going to be the first point-of-contact for incoming settlers, at any settlement of your choosing—maybe here?"

Will said nothing, just stared at the ground. His whole world was falling in, Lo could see it. Part of her wanted to help him. Part of her wanted to look away. She said, "There won't be any more incoming settlers, and he's not staying here. So you may as well take him with you."

"I don't think so," said Bob. "If he can't stay here, then he can go live in IBM City, which, let's face it, is a far better place anyway. But who says that you will be the one who gets to make that decision, Lo? I see your women fighting you on so many fronts. They don't like how you treat people, and I'm not just talking about us alien visitors. I mean, look at what you just did to Janine. Did she really deserve that—verbal abuse, an ass-kicking, and public arrest? Wasn't there another way? Seriously, if I lived in this town, I'd agitate to remove *your* ass."

Lo looked around at the gathered group. Many were shaking their heads in disagreement and Pat was shaking her fist, but there was no great roar of support for her.

"Fuck your opinions, you spy," shouted Lo. It was all she had right now.

"Please don't leave me here," said Will, lifting his head and looking at Bob. He seemed to be sweating, although it was still cool enough and his bodcoz should have regulated his temperature.

"With respect, Wl-Wrrn, begging won't change the situation," said Bob.

He turned back to Lo and gestured at the plastic bags. "One last thing before I leave. The globes you see there in the bags contain a drug called Vroom72. It's a variation of regular Vroom, the drug that destroyed Byllyn's life. Vroom72 is contaminated. Each ball provides an unparalleled high—and kills most users in about

72 hours. Hence the name. The Vroom should help you deal with any future problems with Unan criminals—at least half of them are addicts. You just have to throw them some of these hardened glass balls and they won't bother you again. Make sure you keep the balls away from direct heat and they'll keep for many years. Don't try to open them, though—Vroom is unstable and dangerous. It's a live culture and has a natural attraction to human flesh. Starts working with minutes. Very powerful stuff."

The women in the crowd exchanged looks. Some were curious, most were horrified. Killing potential criminals with some kind of living drug? What the hell kind of culture did that? Looking around, Lo saw Lurch step forward, fist raised and shaking.

"Shame on you, shame on all Orbiters," he said.

"Oh spare me your sanctimony," said Bob. "You've seen the studies. Even if you tell an addict that the Vroom you're giving them is contaminated, the hard cases will take it anyway. Nobody's forcing anybody to do anything they don't want. People *volunteer* to die of Vroom72."

He turned to Lo. "I hope the drug resolves any social problems caused by the Unans. I will personally make sure that the program doesn't send any more of those guys in future shipments. No offense, Zgyzg-Dm, but you have to understand—"

Lurch began shouting. Lo had not imagined that he ever shouted. "I cannot believe you would bring Vroom here. It is the scourge of our people, and you know it. Back home you would be arrested for distributing it. You're committing a crime."

Bob remained unmoved. "It's not a crime here, Zgyzg-Dm. The High Council has sanctioned the use of dirty Vroom in the settlements for defensive purposes."

Lurch strode across to the large pile of plastic bags, spat on them, then turned and stood with his massive hairy black arms folded as if he was on guard. "Nobody come near this poison," he said. "We're going to incinerate it."

"Hey, I'll be the one who decides that," said Lo.

"You need to heed my warning, Lo," said Lurch. "You do not know what you are dealing with here. If you were ever going to trust me, now is the time."

"I'm never going to trust you," said Lo. "I think you've been keeping secrets."

Nevertheless she turned to Pat. "I want this stuff removed to Cockenoe for safekeeping. Call in a few of the most skilled crew. The sooner, the better."

"Thank you," said Lurch. "You have no idea how dangerous..."

"Keep it safe," said Bob. "You'll want that stuff in the future, I know you will."

Lo had no idea what she wanted, now or in the future. Too many problems, choices, decisions to make. It felt like the wires in her brain were ready to fuse in a hail of sparks. She desperately needed time to process everything that was happening.

She didn't have time.

Out of the corner of her eye she caught a glimpse of something shining particularly bright. It was Byllyn, who had stepped out from the crowd and was now shimmering in the sunlight as she edged closer towards the mound of Vroom.

Lo beamed a message to Yaz: *Byllyn—Helena—away*.

She saw Yaz gently whisper in Helena's ear. Helena rushed to guide Byllyn away from the scene, back over to where she had left Lil happily playing on the swing in the old oak tree by the side gate. As she absent-mindedly began to push Lil back and forth, Byllyn continued to look across at the Vroom. Would she really do that to Lil? Take a drug guaranteed to kill her? The look in her eyes said yes. Lo beamed Adrianna: *help—guard—Vroom*.

Adrianna rushed over and joined Lurch in front of the pile of plastic bags. Lo swiveled around to face her brother, who had remained suspiciously silent on the subject of the Vroom.

"You were going to bring this drug into Saugatuck?"

Will's face was weary with resignation. "No. I was going to give the drug to Retske to distribute among the Unans who had fled Madison. The trouble-makers are probably all Vroom addicts. Even after many years there are withdrawal symptoms…"

Lo looked at him goggle-eyed. "How did you plan to identify the exact Unans who were causing the trouble? We know they're not all murderers. Byllyn is not a murderer. Is she?"

"Of course not. But the murderers are all Vroom addicts, of that you can be sure."

"I understand, but still, you're talking about giving killer drugs to potential threats. It's a step too far, Will. Surely you can see that. Lurch is right, those drugs should be burned."

"I'm surprised to hear you say it, Lo. I thought safety was your first priority?"

"Not this way, Will."

Will shrugged. "Your politics change hourly, Lo. I can't keep up."

Bob clapped his hands loudly. "Enough. You can argue about it after I'm gone."

He looked across to Adrianna, standing next to Will in front of the small mound of Vroom. Bob gestured to her. "Step over here, Adrianna so I can let you through the force field. We need to get going. We're expected back at the explorer in six hours."

Adrianna said, "Let me just say my goodbyes."

"No," said Bob. "You've been saying them for the last two days. Just get over here, or I'll leave without you." He began walking up the gangplank.

Adrianna moved in the direction of the jetty.

The women began shouting out to her. *No, it's too soon. I'm going to miss you. Take care. Love you. Make sure you come back alone. Don't do anything I wouldn't do.*

Suddenly Lo experienced the strangest sensation of absolute clarity. She lifted her gloved hand into the air and threw a gentle beam up against Adrianna, halting her mid-stride.

Adrianna looked surprised but didn't resist. "Yes?"

Lo shook her head sadly. "I'm sorry, Adrianna, I'm really, really sorry."

Adrianna nodded. She thought Lo was apologizing for how she'd treated her.

Lo turned to Bob, now standing on the gang plank. "She's not going with you."

Adrianna shouted, "What?"

Bob said, "What now?"

"No, Lo," said Lurch. "Someone has to go. We all agreed."

Lo replied, "I know someone has to go. But not Adrianna. Me."

"What did you just say?" asked Adrianna.

"Me," said Lo. "I'm the one who has to go to the Orbitals."

44

The crowd went wild. Most of the voices were shouting some variation on "What?" Lo raised her hand to silence them, trying to catch as many eyes as possible as she did so. Only some stopped shouting. Scanning the thirty or forty people now gathered, Lo realized that some very important people were missing. There was no sign of Reid. Only half her crew were present.

That was too bad. Bob was definitely in the process of leaving, and he really didn't care if he went alone. Lo knew she had minutes, if not seconds. She lifted two fingers to her lips and whistled loud and sharp for silence.

"It has to be me—the leader of Saugatuck—who goes. I think I've known this ever since we decided to send one of us, but I couldn't face the thought, so I let Adrianna volunteer. But Adrianna is not enough. Only an official Earth leader will have the impact we need. And you know I will fight for Saugatuck like no other. *I will stop the boxes!*"

A couple of women cheered. Lo saw many others nodding—most important among them Pat, Helena, and Yaz—but also many other familiar faces. The women of Saugatuck. Her family these past thirty years. Yaz and Pat beamed her simultaneously:

support—decision—understand

it will be good for you and good for us

Others beamed too, too many words to process at once. Lo shut the line for a moment. She could still hear shouting, though—many conflicting points of view.

"It's not like it's forever."

"You're just running away from your problems."

"Go for it, Lo."

"You can't just leave us."

Lo shouted over the top of them, shaking the trees for extra effect as she did so. "I'll be back within two years. You'll all be fine. You're so strong. You don't need me here telling you how to do everything anymore."

She looked across at Helena, who raised her hands to her face, kissed them deeply, then held them back out to Lo. Lo blinked away the sudden pricks of moisture at the back of her eyes. She held her hand up, as if pressing against a departing train window. Oh, Helena. How badly she had treated her. Before she had time to say the right words though, she felt a sudden gust of wind rock her body. The force field around the orbicraft was pulsating now, casting out small bursts of air that blew the women about, not off their feet, but close. The crowd shouted a communal "Hey," but they all turned their attention to Bob.

"I don't have time for this," he yelled. "One of you women needs to come through the force-field. It makes no difference to me which one. You're both the same to me."

"I'm coming," said Lo. She went to move, but found that Adrianna was now holding her tight in their strange air-embrace. "Let me go, Adrianna. That's an order."

"Fuck your orders. How dare you try to steal my opportunity?"

"There will be other opportunities for you, here in Saugatuck."

"Fuck you and your bullshit. You're a worse traitor than Janine."

Lo tried to pull herself free, but Adrianna held her firm. She was afraid to tussle with her, standing so close to that pile of Vroom. Lurch was standing there too, but he was powerless to help. Lo tried to beam Pat for backup, but she was too late.

There was a great whoosh of air as Adrianna drew back both her arms and threw a wicked energy beam at Lo. Lo threw up her own arms and deflected the energy in time, but she lost her balance. She took a step or two backwards, landing on Will's foot as she did so. Slipping on the slick bodcoz fabric, she wobbled and began to fall asswards. Will bent deep to catch her and was pulled down by her falling force. They landed on the ground together in an awkward embrace. In those few moments of confusion, before anyone had time to act, Adrianna moved again.

She pulled some of the Vroom balls out of a bag and sent them hurtling at high speed at Lo. Frozen in an awkward free-fall, Lo couldn't raise her hand or bristle the air. Instead she ducked instinctively. The three small missiles slammed into Will's upper body and face. They smashed upon impact, leaving two patches of squirming brown sludge all over Will's grey bodcoz and one on his dirty, surprised face. There was no splatter. The Vroom held together, like the inside of a snail. The globs on his costume immediately began wiggling toward the smear that was slowly dissolving into Will's face where a hint of rapture had already appeared. Seventy-two beautiful hours; death a near certainty. She saw Pat rushing to her injured brother. She saw Lurch backing away. She saw Adrianna standing frozen as she realized what she had just done. She saw fifty people all waiting for someone to tell them what to do next...

"Get in here now!" shouted Bob at the top of his lungs, gesturing to a small glowing yellow line that cut the air like a laser projection.

Lo didn't hesitate. She pushed her hands into the ground, kicked herself off Will's slumped body and projected her own balled-up body through the slash. She crashed straight into Bob, bounced, and fell down onto the jetty. She shouted out while still trying to get up.

"What about Will? Can you help him?"

"Nobody can help him now," said Bob.

"There must be—"

"There is absolutely nothing we can do," said Bob firmly. "Not now the Vroom has touched his skin. I don't understand how that happened. Those vials don't usually just open like that. Adrianna must have overheated them with her hands. You women need to be careful how you handle the stuff." Not a word of regret for his fallen colleague.

"Tell the High Council what happened here," shouted Lurch from outside. "Make Wl-Wrrn's death count for something. Make them see..." His voice was choked.

Lo pointed to the Vroom. Five crew had gathered around it. Three others were holding a struggling Adrianna. "Burn it," she shouted. "It's not a weapon, it's a virus."

Bob yelled out. "It's all about handling. Nobody should go near Will until the Vroom has deactivated—72 hours plus another 24 to be sure. And cremate the body."

He was pointing at Will, still lying on the ground. Pat was cradling his head in her lap. The Vroom was still wriggling on his bodcoz, slowly moving upwards.

"Get away from him, Pat," shouted Lo. "It's too dangerous."

Pat lifted Will's hand and held it to her face.

"Somebody move her," screeched Lo, "do it for her own protection."

Somebody with wires began dragging Pat's body through the air and away from Will. Pat's arm wrenched awkwardly as she finally let Will's hand go. Yaz pulled her into her arms. Lo tried to tell Yaz that she and Pat were in charge of Saugatuck now, but Bob grabbed her by the arm and pulled her to the door of the orbicraft.

"I'm sorry. Time really is up."

"What the fuck?"

"Don't waste your last words," said Bob. "Say your goodbyes, Lo."

He was right. Lo began shouting behind her as she let Bob pull her along.

"Goodbye Will, Rest in Peace. Goodbye, Helena, I'm sorry, Goodbye, Reid, wherever you are, I love you. Goodbye, Yaz, take care of everyone. Goodbye, dear Pat, my rock, Goodbye Ruby, Leslie..." She kept shouting out names even as Bob pulled her into the orbicraft and shut the door behind her. She even called out to Adrianna. "I understand. I hope you understand."

And then they were gone. Inside the orbicraft she could hear nothing but a muffled version of her own shouts. She stopped shouting and began beaming. It was futile. The lines were all dead. She kept beaming anyway. It was like being entombed inside the velvety dark cabin of the orbicraft, not a console or wire or even a light in sight. Where you might expect to see windows was a series of computer screens, all but one dim and overwritten with text. Lo saw the figure of Bob seated in front of the one bright screen, a large corner wrap-around panel that offered a wide-angled view of the scene on the lawn. Lo could see women anxiously staring at the orbicraft, mouths moving animatedly in discussion, some waving and shouting. Will remained slumped on the ground, beatific in his slumber. Everybody was giving his body a wide berth. He was truly abandoned to his fate, now, her brother. Something in her body literally sank at the thought, her heart, something metal, or perhaps simply her posture.

"Sorry about the lighting," said Bob, pointing Lo in the murky direction of an overstuffed chair to the right of his own. "My retinas are enhanced for this environment. It will be very dark for you for a while, but eventually your eyes will adapt. Maybe your wiring will help…"

Lo edged step by step to the chair, which looked like a transparent bean-bag on a stem. The minute she sat down, a spongy feather-light cocoon shaped itself around her body. Screens all around her showed various views of the river, but they were all very dim. They cast no light into the dark space. Lo looked across at Bob's screen. The colors of the summer day dazzled, as did the brightly dressed people. Were some of them beginning to walk away? She hadn't left yet!

"Is there any way I can communicate with the outside?" asked Lo.

"No. We could try the radio room, but none of our attempts at communication worked when we arrived. Besides, what more is there to say? They'll work it out for themselves."

"There are still things I need to explain."

"I don't think explanations are necessary, Lo. I think your leaving says it all."

"Is there any chance of communication once we get to the Orbitals?"

"None at all," replied Bob. "We ambassadors *are* the communications system between the Orbitals and Earth. Why else would we make these horrocious trips?"

"Please don't talk like old Bob. I didn't like him anymore than I like you."

"Fair enough," replied Bob. "Just trying to keep things light. You seem nervous. I guess you're starting to realize that your powers don't work in here. They won't work on the explorer either. On Crn there will be also be limits to what you can do—although there'll be plenty of opportunity to perform tricks. I'll bet you didn't think about how a trip to the Orbitals would impact your wiring when you rushed to join me, did you? You don't do two steps ahead."

"It doesn't make any difference," said Lo, shivering inside, her wires suddenly too cool for comfort. "I can handle myself with or without my powers. Don't you worry about me."

"Believe me, I'm not worrying about you," replied Bob, "Courtesy is just an Orbital habit. I'm going to turn on my illuminated air-charts now. Without any retinal enhancement you will probably only see fuzzy outlines. Don't worry if they dance around you. That's normal."

"Is it going to be this dark the whole way to the Orbitals?"

"No. The environment in the explorer is different. You'll see soon enough. Now silence while I get us out of here." Bob nestled back comfortably in his cocoon-chair and concentrated on flying his ship, his hands playing unreadable symbols that hung luminous in the air above.

Lo could hardly bear to watch his screen. How could she be here inside a departing orbicraft while her brother lay dying on the ground below? It came almost as a relief to feel the ship take off and see all the people on the lawn shrink from sight. That feeling didn't last long. A physical rush of emotion hit her as her world became little more than a disappearing satellite view — great pulses of despair flung her back and forth. Silent, violent, keening. Struggling to control her physical distress, Lo rolled onto her side so that she was facing away from Bob. On that side of the orbicraft a small view of space was now visible. It was just like in old footage, making it feel more like she was watching television than traveling through space.

As she lay there on her side, gazing at Earth's dwindling curvature, she finally allowed herself to cry — a great river of tears, built up over so many years, never allowed to run free. Lo pressed her face into the chair so hard she should not have been able to breathe. The chair allowed her, gave her air, took her tears, muffled her sobs. If Bob heard her, he said nothing. Indeed for the next six hours he left her alone in her sorrow. Perhaps he thought she was asleep. She was not asleep. She was destroyed. If he'd tried to kill her, she would have let him.

Then suddenly in the dark she heard something — at first just light crackling, then a series of static farts. Looking across at Bob's screen she saw the outline of a ship. It was made from the same metallic red Lego blocks as the orbicraft but shaped more like an enormous dragon-boat. She heard Bob begin speaking in the strange vowel-less Orbitaal of Lurch's people. Were they speaking back into his head? Lo had no real idea what those Orbital cruxes could do. From out of the depths of her dark lethargy came a familiar twinge of alertness. Her wires fizzed with nervous tension. Adrenaline surged. All her survival instincts began to kick in.

"Here we are," said Bob. "Impressive isn't it."

"I've seen bigger," said Lo.

She was ready.

Author Biography

Jackie Hatton was born in Australia. She spent a glorious girlhood in Tasmania, came of age in the suburbs of Melbourne, became her own person at Melbourne University, then jumped at the opportunity to move to the US for graduate school. She was taught by a long series of strong-minded women who encouraged her in many different ways and to whom she is permanently indebted.

Since completing her PhD in American Women's History at Cornell University she has done many different things, most of which fall under the rubric of "pen-for-hire." She has also lived in many different places, including Westport, Connecticut, New York City, and, for the last ten years, Amsterdam. She is married without children, and her favorite thing to do is swim in warm seas.